Also by James Whitehead

DOMAINS (poems)

JOINER

JOINER

James Whitehead

Alfred A. Knopf
New York
1971

THIS IS A BORZOI BOOK
PUBLISHED BY ALFRED A. KNOPF, INC.

ISBN: 0-394-43143-x
Library of Congress Catalog Card Number: 69-10687

Manufactured in the United States of America
First Edition

For Bob Padgett
and Mark Doyle

Hit, hit, hit!

—FINNEGANS WAKE

One must undertake [work]
with confidence, with a certain assurance
that one is doing the reasonable
thing, like the farmer who drives his plow,
or like our friend in the scratch
below, who is harrowing, and even drags
the harrow himself. If one
hasn't a horse, one is one's own horse.

—Van Gogh, in an illustrated
letter to Theo

JOINER

1

IT STAGGERS THE WEARY MIND and stuns the size-eight head like a perfectly misaimed forearm shiver would, but the truth is that sweet April, my silkyblond and close-pored ex-wife, is marrying a Jackson lawyer in a couple of days—and Jackson's not Dallas or Atlanta, places that already have pro clubs, but it is one helluva lot better than Bryan, where I come from—where Miss April and all our other friends come from. Royal Carle Boykin, who's really from Bryan too, is the lawyer's name and the hell of it is I've done much violence to protect that man, both on and off the field. Murder is what some people would say I've done for Mr. R. C. "Moon Pie" Boykin.

I'm out here in Texas—knotty little trees and no rain except when it comes in floods, and a sky like a cheap birthstone—I'm out here in Texas and I've got my booze and my ben (to diet on) and I've got me a fine modern girl for a mistress, Mary Ann, who last month wrote a paper entitled "An Imagined Dialogue Between Gerrard Winstanley and the Editors of the *New York Review*." Swarthy Mary tells the world that we're not about to get us a proper sort of neopopulist-democratic-socialist order (with tendencies toward pacifistic syndicalism) so long as our reform organs are scatological in format. Mary Ann is raunchy and she is learning to sweeten her body. She's learning to enjoy her own female body.

And I've finally got the right kind of work out here at the Unitarian Progressive School. Amen, brothers, for all the lords of heaven and earth have been kind to Big Son. I ought to have been hanged, or jailed a little short of forever, but here I am in

Fort Worth, Texas, and I'm doing fine, fine and mostly angry as hell, with that excellent coppery taste of blood up in the back of my throat again from time to time. Spit pennies, man, but you'll never get rich!

Kill Kill Kill—as the bard says. Boykin! Notes from the plains, notes and stories and journals from the fastnesses of Texas, the traditional exile for runoff Mississippians.

Sticky nigger pop and supersized gooey nigger cookies— Royal'd always go right on ahead and eat that stuff in the afternoon before every game, and I'd always take up for him when our other friends would want to tease his ass off for socking down all that niggerfood. Sometimes he'd even include sardines and crackers in that crazy feast of his. Somitch was always asking for it.

We'd see the chosen Boykin boy (legally adopted, carefully picked from the Home in Meridian)—we'd see him off down the street, and we'd know exactly that he was doing it all on purpose. He's standing in weenie jeans out in the sunshine by the gas pumps at Magee's Gulf station and he's by God getting vanilla and chocolate and cola juice all over his plumpish hands and face. He's exposing himself to every possible common kind of ridicule: "Super Moon! Super Moon! Nigger Pie! Yaaaa Yaaa Yaaaa." He was like one of Brother Dave Gardner's bad jokes.

And you'd think they'd of been done with that manner of cruelty by their age, and by that year. Hell, the Supreme Court had already said that niggers was people.

Anachronisms are sins. No chance in the world for sympathy, good government, and ecstasy so long as we've got all these greasy anachronisms galumphing all over the towns, and you wouldn't think they'd pick on a relatively competent athlete like Royal Carle Boykin. He was the goddamned co-captain along with me. They'd *elected* us. That boy was really good. You could trust the plays he called from under the helmet that never entirely covered his red curls in the huddle. He was always loosening his chin strap and pushing his hat back for comfort's sake, and you could always tell he was thinking way ahead and up short at the same time. He was a worrier all the time, but especially for four quarters on Friday nights.

He was a good lad, but also he was seriously flawed, for when he was smoking and drinking beer, generally fucking around with the rest of us, there wasn't a great deal of gusto to it. He'd suck down his Camel and Picayune smoke, or maybe a Big Red, but even when he was young, with good taste buds and a ripe throat and a tender mouth, like the Pardoner says, he never grinned with solid pleasure the way he should have. Hell, smoking good cigarettes the first year or so is like eating sweet wood (a truly natural desire), fresh and warm wood, straight from the kiln—it's like sappy pine bark the sunshine's on—it's a genuine privilege for a few years, and Royal never appreciated it. Good smoke that tasted the way wood smells. And the sunnavabitch never celebrated the first beer he'd get at the Red Cat or the Second Stand on a hot summer's night, after a hard day at the lumber mill—which sensations were entirely lovely—like the inside of your entire mouth, throat, and gullet was putting out a new growth of pink skin that's blooming and panting in the sudsy dark. (The fermentation of the hops was the beginning of civilization. Screw the wedge and lever and wheel!) He lacked proper gusto for his vices and he seemed ashamed of his virtues. Christ, he acted like an Eastern Intellectual when he was no more than a Southern Adolescent.

What pissed off the others was they knew he wasn't on comfortable terms with the very best things a man can do while breathing air, and a young man ought to enjoy all the ways of breathing air.

Bobo and Stream (even Stream, the gentle and saccharine Preacher's Kid) and Doyle Phillips, they'd be ready to snicker-snack the hell out of him. "Soooooopurr PIE! Soooooopurr rah . . . rah . . . PIIIIE!" They'd yell that at the Good Gulf Station with the big tall stately old-fashioned simple orange circle that was like a swollen and dying sun marked with the name of an almighty and mercantile maker—they'd yell at about the time Royal is hunkered down at the water spigot to clean up. Vulnerable, and before they could start up that mean cheer again, I'd say, "By Gord, here's ole Captain Moon Pie and he's done taken on his high octane powers. He's got on his vanilla pants and his chocolate cape. He's *ready*." And then I'd gently bump his ass with my bargelike loafers. Royal, he grins up at me like the ancient and perdurable possum eatin' his famous tasty and perdurable grapes. He grins up at all of us like a cat chewin' screenwire; which nervous grinning—no matter how hard he tried—didn't please the other troops at all, for Boykin did not qualify for sainthood. (It must be said that Bobo and Doyle would have loved him had he been a proper saint.)

After his postprandial cleansing, he'd rise up from that true inside hunker, his face straight and passionless, eyes like a stropped steel blade poised on a raisin. He'd rise with clean hands and smudged heart to say, "Let's win another one." He'd say that hard and straight the way a mancub should, and everything would be all right for a while. Then we'd bop off down the street like good buddies should: Our Gang and the Great Penrod.

Violence and bad habits have got to go.

There's nothing worse than a pregame meal: dry toast, roast beast as thin and dry as parchment, a tiny trough of honey for the plaster roll, a pile of mashed potatoes, and dull slaw—bad food and all the meager obligations of neophytish hardrollers. We had to act like that tasteless and Spartan plate was just the ambrosia to make fierce ichor rush in our veins—opaque and grainy goddamned meat being just the thing to get us ready for battle.

In we'd swing through the door of Nancy's Cafe, me and Boykin and Stream and Lurch Bobo and Doyle, the offensive center and the entire offensive backfield, all seniors, all already approached by the college scouts (hell, they'd been camping dismally at my house for two years already, making peaceful R. S. Joiner, my good daddy, miserable), and we, believe it, did have obligations in that cafe. We had to set the tone for the evening.

It was awful. The low sun streamed through the yellow plastic membrane that was always dropped over the Cafe's big window in the evening—and that low and filtered sunshine mixed with the flickering fluorescent lamplight, creating a diffuse, nervous, and banally sacral glow for us to eat inside of.

We always showed just a little late, which lateness was expected and required of us. We appeared late, but once in the room one could tell by the glints in all ten of our eyes that we knew it was up to us to officially begin game day. It was the expected thing. The other players, and coaches Morgan and Topp, had already begun to fork around in their grim plates, but countdown wasn't under way until we seniors, the chiefs, entered.

Royal and I did a vain sort of camel walk once inside. We did our little skip and step and then we'd bash right fist to left palm in rhythm: whomp—whomp—whompwhompwhomp. Black Lurch, he always stopped at the door and spat back outside onto the street, suggesting disdain of fear, and pleasurable expectation of combat. Finally, in strode Doyle and Stream, the impassive sullen ones—Stream's right eye squinting above his chinlessness like he was finding the bead down at the end of a .410 barrel. And as we all slipped into our own half-circle booth up front by the yellow light, the room grinned to see us settled in. We gave all Bryan a lot of peace of mind by confidently entering that way.

Linecoach Topp grinned and pulled on his long, pitted nose, pulled that whiskey schnoz and gave us a grave wink from the far end of the room, down where the wallpaper was pink flamingos dipping their beaks in gray water. Ole Topper knew it was an act, and he knew we knew it. Fuck it. We sat and ate and talked about the night's game. We talked about the game plan and how it was we'd get some pussy afterwards, all of it in low tones, and fiercely. We crafted that hour right—but still it was the great crime Dullness, and I always felt like our booth was some kind of Redneck Iron Maiden about to close her terrible spikes on me.

Goddamn you, sweet April.

It was indeed very damned grumpy and I'm positive that Royal was the only man on that team who ate correctly before a game.

Some of us might have sneaked some Nabs and a Coke back at the house—but not one of us ever blatantly tried to enjoy the R.C. Cola, the Moon Pie, and the Seafest Sardines on Woodrow Wilson Street in front of God and everybody at the Gulf station. He knew how to do the right thing but he never once tried to convince the rest of us to do right. He lacked real authority in his convictions.

Recently I've come from 310 pounds down to 290 pounds on a goddamned diet that George Gordon, Lord Byron, would admire, and when I'm trim, sleek as a fracking mink, I'm going home and kill both their asses.

And the meal after the game was even worse, a meal intended to be a genuine celebration for our regular victory. Bryan being an essentially tolerant town and county about some things, there was a tradition for the grown men, after the game, excepting coaches, to drink beer right there in Nancy's while the team was eating the victory meal—they wandered up and down the aisles smoking cigars and spreading plenteous bullshit.

Most did just that, but not my daddy, or Royal's, or Stream's, for what it's worth.

The good part was that Nancy always turned up the juke— "Cheatin' Heart" and "Don't Take Your Guns to Town" being the favorites. That was good, and good also were the young and middle women coming in to really pleasure and jazz that stale room a little. They'd drift around and sweet-talk the players. They'd hang around the wall and move in rhythm with the music. Shit, they were all hot as forge coal watching us go at those steaks. Women. Women moving in the shadows at the mouth of the cave.

And Lordy those were beautiful steaks. K.C. all the way. And there were steaming potatoes in their skins (the skins being the best part, with the real butter we got for winning) waiting for heaps of cool sour cream and green chives, and there was always an excellent refrigerator-fresh, tossed salad with blue cheese dressing. Abundant! BUT, but, mallafatchie, if you'd played good and hard for forty-eight minutes you were too beat down, sick, and exhausted to really enjoy it. What the bravest roothogs usually settled for after the game was 7-Ups and maybe a taste or two of the fine meat. Drink a 7-Up or a Squirt, talk up the game with the fans—but, friend, you better avoid the whole meal if you want any vigor left for the dance and your date later on. Eat all that good food and you'd chuck your cookies.

Postgame meal was something to tolerate, except for the music and all those women in their trances.

It was a version of misery, but I always went in there and did my duty after the game. Hell, I'd even managed to tolerate the hugs from all those middle-aged women, the ones who always slapped their taffeta-covered snatches against you in the process of the squeeze and the wet cheek smack. Wild payment for blocks and tackles. Then I'd take April to the dance. I'd scratch off from the Cafe in the family Pontiac, which I always got after the game (my people going home with the Boykins), and April'd start going at my head and face like it was ice cream in July. I'd drive for the gym, where some more good music was. All in the world I wanted for my work was slowdancing and loving, slowdancing and loving, and a quiet stomach.

My God, she was perfection. She was slim and moist, and in the car she'd kneel beside me, showing milky white thighs with only now and then a little sprig of white hair up high. Mary Ann, my mistress at present, says April was the Great American Wet Dream. But that, friend, is incorrect. She was and is very real, and she was mine for six years. Mary Ann says April was a *stage* I was going through. Fucking-A—she was a stage called life. But I'm being too tough on my dark lady, kind and beautiful Mary, whom I love.

Truth be told, there was very little that was very good about game day until we got down to the locker room for brute meditation. Nothing very good at all except for when I was walking in space without even the least thought that *there's Royal with his Moon Pie beneath the Good Gulf sign and now Bo'll want to hack at our friend for no reason.* Before there were any troubles with the game, there was simply the pleasure of drifting in the light of the afternoon with its secure nameless forms and dimensions. There was simply breathing air as I walked the two miles from our house to the Cafe, and the only words anywhere in my head were *air* and *light*. At first those were the only words. Then *shadows*, the strict shadows of September. Light. Air. *You love this because your father loves the shapes that wood can be skillfully cut into at the mill, and because your mother loves Hopper and Vermeer.*

I'd drift that way in my own trance for forty-five minutes, and people never offered me a ride because they knew it was Big Son pondering his game. But what they never knew was how sweet my abstract pleasure was as I walked along the road there, or how far away my mind was from any goddamned football game. My reverie was absolutely without narrative (which is the best way to understand Vermeer and Hopper)—it didn't have any story at all until I met the others at about the city limits, and then there was Royal and history, game day, Royal with his Moon Pie and R.C., Royal taking on his powers.

That walk, before I met the others, was the joy of the good creatures, and let's hear it for the simple joy of the good creatures. Let's hear it for the simple joy that is given to a few children by their good human parents.

That ability of just being able to walk along in pleasure may seem corny to some people, and I'll grant that it is possible for such good exercise to give way to dumb meandering and maundering, but, considering the tribulation of most of our hours, I still appreciate my parents' examples in wise passivity.

For to watch my mother working at her easel out in our long front yard by the ditch and the road was something wonderful to behold. She's a big rawboned woman with knobby knees and skeins of yellow hair. She's not at all the delicate painter lady you find in a lot of small towns, and she can draw damned well. She can draw most of what she looks at in real life, and she can imitate other people's pictures and photographs, all that; but she has never had much sense of color. It's almost as if she's blind to it in a curious way. Her skies are always white, unless she goes to clouds of gray and black. Every other color she gets well enough, though she tends toward the primaries of red and blue and yellow, which makes for a certain redundancy in her work.

I've said that Mother liked Hopper and Vermeer. True enough. She collected their prints in expensive portfolios and art books—she loved their light, but finally they frustrated her terribly because of their human figures.

Mother could do the most delicate drawings of a tree or a bush, almost in the tradition of Dürer's fronds—she could picture just about anything from a live oak to a mimosa, or even one of our Plymouth Rock hens, but human muscles and limbs were finally beyond my mother. And this weakness had not a damn thing to do with priggishness. She drove the fifty miles over to Southern every weekday for an entire summer semester to take Life Drawing, and in no way was she ever embarrassed by the naked people. She never mentioned it. And she made her A. She took that class in human bodies so seriously Daddy and I were afraid she'd want to go up to Jackson to the medical school for a straight-out course in anatomy.

Her efforts to get human figures on canvas went to great lengths. Great lengths indeed, for she actually got my own publicly shy and almost pathologically taciturn father to pose for her in the nude in her studio.

Since I was finally an only child we had an extra bedroom, which got used for her studio—and on one particular Sunday morning I got my tail pulled up short and fast at the back window. (It was about 8:00 a.m. when I'd been out all night with April.) But what a lovely sight it was. There my parents were, both naked as jays, and Momma painting away. I'd always known they were pretty natural with each other, but truly I'd never seen the likes of this: good old leathery R. S. Joiner right there, buck nekked and reading the *Times Picayune* in Momma's overstuffed chair she used for studying her art books, and he's got his hard legs thrust out so Momma can work on foreshortening.

I stood there and gawked at them, but finally it fell over me that there wasn't anything all that peculiar about their nakedness, Momma probably having stripped for no other reason than to encourage Daddy. Momma had her lean face screwed up intently, and Daddy was toughly passive while studying the paper. What the hell?—so I slipped in and quietly went to bed without disturbing them.

And I don't mean to suggest that my people are noble savages, because they aren't. They both had a lot of fear in them. They gave me a lot but finally they lost control of my life because of forces in the world they couldn't possibly control.

Damn right—it wasn't R.S. and Maisie's fault—and I absolutely believe that I could convince Freud and Jung—the entire sullen and reactionary Austrian mulch pile—I could convince every one of those stupid turd tappers that it wasn't *my* people that bent me wrong. I grew up with room to run in, an acre of well-kept yard, and in any other direction I wanted to go there were fields and woods and swamps—and though he hardly ever talked to anyone else, my old man did talk to me and my mother, and I was always lovingly disciplined. I had what has got to be called a wholesome childhood. God damn it, they were and are beautiful humans, prime yeoman stock like you see in *Let Us Now Praise Famous Men*, except we weren't ever poor, dirt poor, or anything like it. We weren't the kind of folks they built the Roosevelt toilets for. We never had any old autos set on blocks in our front yard. In fact, my people had both gone to one of Bilbo's junior colleges, Daddy in mechanics and Momma in home economics. (They had to bury Bilbo face down, but he wasn't deeply evil by any means. He was a better man than any goddamned Delta governor of that day and time—Delta men who only built the roads up to the steps of the Big House, and down to the levee, but no place else.) My people were sanitary without being neurotic, sexual without being obsessive, and they were Methodists, Wordsworthian Neopopulist Methodists, and they were even tolerant of niggers, which was entirely unusual but not absolutely unheard of in Mississippi in the thirties, forties, and fifties.

It wasn't Momma couldn't draw a body, it was simply she couldn't get a body drawn against a background from nature. Against monochrome backgrounds she could do the portrait of any man—but she never got man and greensward on good terms—Momma never got her angel set against her *sfumato* right. It's strictly one or the other with Momma. Man or nature, take your choice.

And R.S. and I asked her once why she didn't just leave the sky part blank, and she was angry and enigmatic and practical when she said it was because you had to cover the whole canvas with primer, but primer wasn't true white. She warmly glared at us like we were surely the world's first dumbheads—so we simply shuffled back across the yard, where we were sprigging grass next to the azalea beds. Daddy stuck in a couple of sprigs and said we had no business teasing the good woman.

State the obvious.

It was the *others* that caused the trouble.

They and their parents are the reason I'm out here in Texas serving God's own Reason and God's own Revolution, and not back in Bryan, where I ought to be.

They and theirs, you and yours—and not even reasonable Mary Ann believes me. She is far better than anybody else inside my past, but still she's bound and determined to bring me and my people down at some psychological gap or another. She's a nice girl with all the contemporary problems and she thinks she has got my parents upon the subject of death. She is satisfied the problem is that most common of themes, the death of a child by fire, my sister's death—The Death of Lucy Patricia Joiner.

II

Lucy died before I ever saw Bryan at an age old enough to remember it well. Daddy went to work at Hercules, the dynamite company in Hattiesburg, for the duration of the war, which war he missed because he lacks his thumb and first finger on his left hand, the result of another accident.

His first year or so at the old Chalmers' Mill in Bryan he was fitting a link belt back on the cogs, when an old one-eyed nigger switched the damn thing on and slowly ground them off, took off that finger and thumb, and caused him to crash and break his front teeth an instant before he let go of a scream I'm told you could hear over the entire terrible noise of the Mill going full blast. But Daddy never blamed anybody. He never blamed that blind nigger for making his left hand look like the terrible paw of some obscure animal.

What I remember first in my life is a dogtrot house at Rawles Springs, out from Hattiesburg, and it was there that Lucy got hers. My sister was a corposant . . . foxfire . . .

For I've got a memory that goes back to three—and this thing was at five, and it's pretty goddamned vivid, praise God—it's enough to keep that good child, Lucy Patricia Joiner, and all other good children fast in my heart forever, including my own son Aubrey, whom Royal's getting.

Lucy was gawky like Momma, an energetic pale child with huge feet and the largest toes I ever saw. She was always rushing around on weekends and evenings, helping tend to me and the washing. She hustled around with wide blue eyes and short lashes, and she could be trusted with the wringer-type Maytag on the screen porch at an early age—and what I remember first about her is how she moved along the clothesline like it was an event in a girls' track meet. She had a step she did there in the hardyard in the sunshine—she pushed the wicker basket with her left foot, crimping those long toes over the rim, shoving. She could pluck the wooden pins from her mouth at an amazing rate. Pushing and bending, securing our clothes, white underthings, prints, and jeans and khakis, on the blue wire of the line.

Lucy was a dancer and I knew that never in the world could I do anything so worthwhile and graceful if I lived to be a hundred years old.

I loved my sister very much, and when she was prettied up in a dotted swiss dress at twelve, I guess you'd have to say there was something carnal about my feelings for her. (Mary, I grant you that.) So now I'm ready to offer the tragic event, *tragic* or *awful* or *terrible*, and probably I can be such a bastard about it because Mary Ann demands making an issue of it. There have been three big fires in my life and Mary Ann believes they constitute a psychic trinity, but they don't. It wasn't merely fire that got me out here in this house with her in exile. People react to different things in different ways.

It was an accident when Lucy backed too near the space heater and blazed up and ran past us all and out the screen door almost before the yelling started, and then the screaming. I finally knew it was an accident because Daddy's favorite saying has to do with trying to change what is in your power to change—*change what you're free to change, and try to forget the rest:* or did he say *forgive?* Hell, she even set the field on fire.

I was standing off across the room by the cypress dining table Daddy'd made (a magnificent gray thing with no nails in it)—I was watching Momma fuss around Lucy's 4-H party dress. And I think I remember drinking wonderfully lumpy and yellow-flecked and cold buttermilk straight out of the pitcher from the icebox, and in my memory's present eye R.S. and Momma are like wax figures from Madame Tussaud's (a rear view), for when the first smoke curled up, they were stiff and unnatural across the back and shoulders—Momma's blades like they'd split clean through her gilliflower cotton print.

Lucy Patricia broke from around them like they were a basket-ball screen and she was a small guard moving in for a quick lay-up. Out the kitchen door into the breezeway she ran on fire, out the front door of the house and into the hardyard on fire, and all the wax figures were alive and yelling and running after. Lucy's hair had been combed out and brushed, a yellow ribbon pulled tight at her crown—and just before I joined in the running I was thinking it didn't make any sense for her to be so dressed up and then catch fire.

We all followed after as she ran a zigzag course through the fallow field to the west of the house, and when we finally got to where she'd fallen over a worndown ancient cornrow, she was out cold and badly burned, but at least that terrible single syllable she'd been crying had gone away. R.S. said, "She's burned bad, but she'll make it." Her new dress was almost entirely gone, with only little patches of scorched slip stuck to her skin. And in the moon-light her face looked flushed and her body was reddish, but she didn't look entirely ruined. And there *was* a little fire around her in the brush and dock. It was sputtering and lapping slightly the way it does when farmers have their burn-offs under control. Daddy kept saying, "She's hurt O.K. but she'll be all right," as he knelt to lift her up—ole bearlike R.S. lifted her easily and gently into his arms and then ran a strange stiff jog across the field to the truck, leaving Momma and me alone. The motor caught the second time, but only one headlight went on in that instant before he turned out onto the road toward the hospital in Hattiesburg.

Momma didn't say very much the whole time they were gone, and neither did I. What she did was go back to the house and wet down some gunnysacks to beat the fire out with. Correct. She wet down two at the pump behind the house, then we walked back to where Lucy'd been, and she beat out the little fires that were left. She was strong against the fires, but she never went crazy and acted like they were to blame. Momma never lost her mind over it.

We did those things and then went inside to sit at the table and drink coffee until we heard from Daddy. Momma said a couple of times that Lucy'd be O.K., but when Daddy got back home it was to say that Lucy was dead. It was a cold December night in a drought and Lucy Patricia died of shock that night as much as anything else.

So there. Now we have it—Eugene "Sonny" Joiner did see his sister running and dying and crying out, like ambulant foxfire, across a dockfield some time near the end of World War II. And he remembers how the hair around her narrow face was singed—but her inexpensive casket was never opened—and *my* mother never got up from *her* pew to try and climb in with the dead child the way Billy Weatherford's mother did, after I'd killed him. And our good Methodist preacher didn't tell us she died to teach us all a great goddamned *im*portant lesson about the meaning of LAF, which is exactly what that foot-washing, ignorant sonofabitch did at Billy's.

Daddy said close it, at the hospital, for we wanted to remember her the way she was in the time of her life with us and not the way some mortician imagined her; and at the Rawles Springs Methodist Missionary Chapel there was a quiet and decent celebration of the life of that energetic and good-natured and helpful young lady, attended by friends and family, including the Boykins (later to die by fire themselves), and Henry Smith, April's father (also to be burned)—all of them old friends from Bryan.

The preacher said the Lord Himself probably didn't have anything to do with Lucy's death. He was a fellow of about forty with blotchy skin and a B.D. from Emory Seminary named Taggart, Stream's daddy, and I can see now that what he said was absolutely miraculous for that time and place. He told the assembled congregation that though God created the world and loves His creation, loving man most of all, He requires man to *complete* His creation. I sat like a flat rock in a dry bed and listened the way a small child does in Mississippi when God is the subject—and Reverend Taggart was nervous about what he'd said. He was afraid that he'd suggested that maybe it was the parents' fault. Maybe the bereaved were blaming themselves for letting the girl get too close to the heater. He rolled his eyes up to the exposed ceiling beams, with what I now know was a God-get-me-through-this-hour look —he trembled there in his place, fluttering his long fingers on the front edge of the pulpit, and then he went cautiously on to say that sometimes things happen in this life that are *not* God's will— sometimes things happen not because of God's will and not because of human mistakes either—sometimes we suffer accidents . . . sometimes the good . . . sometimes the bad, and when the bad, even the entirely terrible, happen on us, God Himself grieves.

The preacher had struck vision he didn't expect.

His eyes shone with a look akin to joy. He pulled himself to his full strict height and spread his arms wide. He said: "Dear friends, the Lord God in Heaven Himself . . . *grieves* this child's death. The Great High God is . . . *confused* to see her here, and us in all our misery today. How *could* we love a God who never suffered our confusions?"

And he got away with it.

Nobody in the house knew or at that moment gave a rip about theology, so he got away with it. Damn near the whole small church broke out crying when Preacher Taggart said that. They did exactly what they had to do. Man, it was the kind of scene that broke Big Jim Agee's heart, and if Walker Evans had been there later at the graveside with us, his camera would have wept from its one keen eye.

All those fine adult people stood there under the loblollies and around Lucy's gravesite—the goddamned lonesome pines—and the cheap vault being lowered—and sometimes it happens exactly that way—the resin all beaded out like jewels on the coarse bark, and the air with a terribly beautiful hungry taste when you breathe it in, and the only hymn we sang was "Farther Along." *Farther along we'll know more about it, farther along we'll understand why!*

How does *that* grab you, Mary, me dear, me dear? Kinda makes you harelip, don't it? Kinda goes against the grain of all your foolish de-fense mechanisms, don't it? Decency. Decency. De-cency. Decency. Decency. It was a decent afternoon with a lot of fellow feeling in the air. Pine needles and gumbo clay, pine barrens, and sweet songs—it was the goddamned animal at his best, and almost everybody came to the house for supper, Mrs. Boykin having brought it over from Bryan—she brought us black-eyed peas and ham, like it was New Year's Day. Tiny Mrs. Boykin had herself some proper traditions and a good deal of imagination to boot.

It was, in fact, a strangely good day and the first time I met and played with Royal and Stream and April. Reverend Taggart lived in Petal and didn't preach for us but every third Sunday, and of course I hadn't seen the children of my people's old friends yet—or didn't remember if I had. It was the day of the funeral and the day I met my lifelong friends, and also it was moving day, which is curious in a way, and something I never entirely understood about my parents. I can understand them wanting out of the house we were in then, and I can even understand how, in a troubled time, they'd want to be in the town they knew best, which was Bryan, but why did they bury Lucy in Rawles Springs?

Years later I asked Daddy why, and he said it's only forty miles from Rawles to Bryan. And Momma thought I was accusing her of something evil when I asked her the same question. "We get over there plenty often an' keep Lucy's the best in the world . . . Eugene?" My question moved and spooked her. And the nearest I can come is to say they're superstitious. They believed their luck was down.

"Daddy, you moved to change your luck didn't you?"

"I moved because I had to move," he said. And then he walked away. He had the Big Wheel Yazoo mower to oil.

The day of Lucy's funeral we all played outside after the early supper, while the adults were talking, packing and talking, and loading all our things into the pickups. We fell in with each other very comfortably, and it wasn't long before I took them out into the field to where the patch of burned grass was, which wasn't really a ghoulish thing for a small boy to do. We gathered in the burned place and waited in solemn anticipation for something that never quite happened. I remember them clearly. Royal was fat and active, and even when he was trying to be still he bounced like a redrubber ball that peels—and he made a kind of rolling motion when he ran, like there wasn't really any flat ground anywhere in the world. He featured himself as Lash LaRue and had a twenty-cent McCrory's whip to prove it with. And Stream was Stream—named Coldstream Taggart because his momma loved the Cold-stream Guards she'd seen in a movie travelogue once—Stream's a turkey always jabbing with his head and pecking around—and when he plays anything he's a chicken with its head off, a thrasher and a flopper, not a roller or a strider. The nicest thing you can call him is *loose*.

The day of Lucy's funeral we ended up by playing soldiers and grenades with pine cones.

What the hell? And, yes, there she was, little April. I remember she had some kind of plaid wool coat on, and that she was entirely white-headed, what my momma called a "perfect blond." She was frisky and agile and played what we boys wanted her to. We stood there in the burned grass and she picked up a little piece of scorched net, and she asked me if I wanted it. Royal bobs and bounces silently, and Stream groans, "OOOooo," then runs off to the trees and the gloaming.

She asks, "Would you want this?"

I said I didn't, and she looked embarrassed. She dropped it back on top of the old cornrow.

And nothing happened, absolutely nothing happened until Royal clicked his little whip. He tossed his red head from side to

side, like he was working a crick out of his short, thick neck. Then
he made as if he were boarding his trusty horse. "Giddyup, hoss,"
says Royal. We agreed we all had horses—we agreed that we were
cavalry in World War II—so April and Royal and I galloped away
toward the woods where Stream had gone, toward the woods
where, in fact, the sun was going down.

III

Swart Mary crosses her skinny legs. Uncrosses. She fixes me with
a cautiously withering gaze from beneath her black bangs. The air
is out of me. I'm de-mythologized for the moment. I'm an essentially honest fat giant who, God curse the same, enjoys histories,
and how they get told. Mostly how they get told.

I have accounted for, reckoned with, analyzed, and celebrated
the past, and I'll continue to do so. I'll do anything but submit to
the Burn Theory of Personal History. I've got *good* scars. That's
where the longest hairs grow. All I said was that Boykin is somewhat disloyal, plain old disloyal. But Mary flips the pages of Keats
and says that's a crock. She says I'm evading the real issue and
problem between us—between me and Mary—which is the fact
that I'd planned to go home and remarry that bitch April again.
She says I *still* want to go remarry sweet ole Beulah Land.

Ah, women, the shrewd bewrayers. Keerect, my dear, for so I
did intend, though I'll never admit it to you. I'd meant to love you
well and leave you shortly. But Royal has fixed all that.

So, Mary, pivot me no pivots, and twist me no twists, in your
orange chair from Sears that looks like a huge diaphragm on a
tripod—the ultimate joke by Duchamp. And, Mary, don't tell me
it was Lucy's fire or Royal's fire or even the Klan fires that got me
here. It was the game and all the game entails. (A man ought to try
for the *entente cordiale* with every lady he knows.)

Mary has the idea I should be more than slightly revolted by
my memories of the locker rooms. She gets her little twat quite

exercised about how perverted the *en*tire locker room scene is. My, my . . . but, honey, wouldn't you like to be invisible in such a place? It might just change your mind about purr-version, for a locker room isn't a steam bath full of fat dirty old men; it's packed with clean and oftentimes virginal *young* men . . .

It is a pleasure to lead a smart woman on.

"Certainly I'd like it," she says, looking at me with condescending understanding. "The question is did *you* like it . . . wouldn't it be better to have boys and girls in the room *together?*" Saying such things while offering me a good squirrel shot from her contraceptive chair.

"Well sure, honey, that's a nice ideal to work for. Capital. Let's have all the cheerleaders and majorettes treading around in their panties and padded bras. Sure thing. All them lovelies swabbing down with isopropyl alcohol and stepping into their official and morally viewable shorties. Dandy idee. Though it might just confuse the chalk talk a little, complicating concentration on the offensive O's and defensive X's. Might heat things up a little too soon, ya know—hell, it might disturb the pacing and the drift of the evening. It *could* fuck up the game plan. But the answer to the question is *yes* I did enjoy it. . . ."

"Why?" she cries in mock horror.

"Because it's nakedness with a purpose."

"_____"

"Woman, it's a form of sublimation—but it's not queer or really any goddamned Spartan military camp. Only the brave deserve . . ."

"An' you gotta be a football hero . . ."

"Almost. Damn right. It's only your faggot artists who want to make it nasty." And that's the bleeding truth. Sports . . . athletics . . . are good for growing boys.

But I should not be so cruel as my lady. She grew up in some kind of convent academy for biddy Catholics in El Paso, run by Irish nuns and priests, and she's still in that sex-freedom-and-reform-is-holy stage—which stage, with her, is very handsome, because she isn't faking it. She really loves to love. In fact, friends, she, this Midcentury Southern Ex-Roman Catholic Graduate Student, knows how to make imaginative love almost as well as my

timeless ex-wife did. Mary has got black straight hair all the way
down to her lean butt, and she can make it high and wholesome and
tender—she can make it on the wall and in the hall, like the old song
goes, and as lowly as any animal—even though she does need some
help in history, art, literature, and dynamic sociology. And she
loves to dance. All kinds: waltz, minuet, and standard raunchies.
When she was doing her paper on Pope, she had an actual minuet
party for her professors and some of our boho friends. She dances
very well, and April never did.

When we got out of Nancy's we always headed for the locker
room to further prepare ourselves for the game. We walked *en
masse* down Woodrow Wilson St., at about 6:00 p.m., a good stroll,
a ritual movement toward the stadium, where, already, the Lions
Club vendors were icing down the Cokes and fixing the popcorn.
I'm big on walking—alone or in a crowd. I loved to walk in that
crowd and I was unobtrusively in control of the crowd—we
strode and took the waves from the people on the street—camel-
walk, bop step, stepping out—we moved five blocks through our
town to where the gym stood above the gulch and the stadium and
the playing field. We never had a parade with the band except at
Homecoming—but that weekly procession was the same thing, and
better. Bryan had a sense of priorities. Bands are fine for half times
and special occasions—but for your week-to-week combats let the
long march of the players themselves suffice. Yes, indeed, it was a
fine high pride we wore as we walked through our own warm
streets, and we walked that way about the time the mercury vapor
streetlights were flickering and turning on, casting a mysterious
purple glow over everything—and all the traffic moved aside and
barked and yelled encouragement as we passed by, all those
cheering clerks and bankers and niggers and necks, which was
pretty heady stuff for a bunch of boys. We were Bryan's finest
thirty-nine or so young men, and that's the truth, with very few
exceptions. By any national standards we had us a good wholesome
bunch of boys, with a few exceptions.

Filing through the high storm fence and gate down at the
stadium was the beginning of the evening's drift—drift, creative

and cool and private drift—like when you put Segovia or Vivaldi or Wagner or the one late and great Jimmie Rodgers on the stereo at 3:00 a.m.—after mixing up a full quart of Gibsons in the Mason jar. More often than not I had that kind of drift while we were preparing our minds for the game—and during the game itself, sometimes.

Stream and Lurch would always poke at the bats up in the corner of the stadium pilings, for luck, they said—they'd make those ugly creatures scream and cry, before they followed me down the runway into the locker room. Shit, Dr. Peale, *that* was peace of mind out of mind. Peace and the womb maybe, but it wasn't finally a belly you wanted to stay in forever; you didn't fear the reality of the game to come. The belly was good, but being born onto the green field was even better.

The locker room itself was spacious and white all over, ceiling, walls, and floor—strictly antiseptic—none of your foul appointments like you find in crude places like Hatcher, Alabama (ropy turds in the showers)—three of the high walls had little slit and wired windows at the top—the room was cool and spacious and always smelled of Pine Sol, and the lockers were built of raw twobys, our names in red marking ink on the tape stretched across the top board of each—and the benches were sanded and clearvarnished to keep the splinters out of our asses.

For the better part of two hours it was mostly a hushed place.

We stretched out on gray mats and thought of our responsibilities to the team's tradition—a goddamned three-year winning streak, slightly more than three years—thirty-five games at an average of twenty-five per. Win this one and we'd be on our way to our fourth straight championship season.

"That was a crock," says Mary, after recklessly throwing her Ben Jonson across the room, bouncing it off Modigliani's *Seated Nude*. Mary—tilting her head the way that splendid painter loved.

It *was* a crock, agrees the little piss ant inside of me: that part of me which desires to forget and reject the entire past—father, mother, friends, the game, the revolution—the part that says all of it was shit.

But my answer to the piss ant is orderly and true: I say a man's a fool to reject his drifts, past drifts that flow richly into the present ones; meaning that the smell of pine oil and Tuff-Skin and freshly stripped tape are good things, and not to be jettisoned with impunity. Things like two pair of clean socks and the clean Bike jock, everything with the Clorox smell of come—and the precious, oiled game shoes with unfrayed laces—and the curiously waxy smell of the entirely red uniform except for black numerals.

I walk on my knees across this Fort Worth room. I kneel before my lover. I say, "Sweet baby, sweetheart, hear ole Son. For Christ's sake listen: if I cast out the living past, my moral prick is dead for sure."

Creates Pride! Creates Vanity even! Locker rooms are the larders of violence and the murders that continue, says Mary.

Says, "You, boy, were a trained killer. That and the fires." Gets up for a handful of cashews, rejecting my loving arms about her legs, does sit-ups and squats, a jumping jack or two, to taunt me, and for some reason I've never beat the hell out of her, the way I did April.

What she says is not the truth, not the whole truth.

Because . . . while we were in that sweet, rank room, while we were fitting on our chain mail and greaves and our black helmets, assessing our reflections in the mirrors above the lavatories, others, the Billy Weatherfords and the Andres of the world, were already going down in the county tonks. The hoods were sinking toward the really dangerous miseries.

That damned Weatherford came out for spring training the spring before our senior year, and he was great. He's six feet tall and hard as bolts, and, in spite of a vicious family and smoking since ten, he can run—he can move out with hands covered with Elmer's glue—he picks up on the game very fast, and he's touted for All-Conference even before he's ever set foot in a real game.

He was so good in the spring he took the position of Catfish Fletcher, a kid who's already a starter, and who now drives a Blue Bird bus for the D'Lo Consolidated Schools. Hell, even I had trouble with Billy, he's so quick. On defense against him in the spring I had to resort to tossing a little dirt in his eyes as he blasted past me. I'd whack him with my forearm and leave dust in the air for him to run through on his way downfield to catch the pass anyway.

Billy was definitely tough shit and could have been a great athlete had he not already been ruined by his environment, which mostly was a sublime love for tonk life and tonk women—he could have survived if it had not been for his rancor for normal behavior. He racked us up in the spring—he was a little clumsy, but his blocks were smashing—he simply charged at his man, charged at the eyes, like a pro, screaming as he came at you. And as far as I remember, he never dropped a pass.

Royal and Lurch and I weren't in the tonks. We weren't pussywhipped by tonk women at eighteen.

Weatherford never showed up for practice on August 15th, and when Coach Topp called him at the house soon after, Billy said he wasn't coming out. "How come?"

"Because the equipment is uncomfortable."

"What's that?"

"Because I ain't no mule," and Billy hung up, leaving me that last high school season with Catfish, who was so depressed by what Billy'd done to him in the spring he never regained his form. As a linebacker on defense, I sweat blood all season about the left side, where Catfish was. With Billy it wouldn't have been that way. With Billy around, things would of been fine.

Pussywhipped, Billy was in luv—got his rubyred married to Polly Roberts, an important girl that even I had drilled. Billy got her knocked up and locked himself into a job driving produce semis and solidbodies, flat-faced Kenworths and Internationals. While we're getting ready to play a football game against Mendenhall, Bill is up on bennies, dropped out, and balling toward Mobile through the ripe dusk. He could have been a great end, but he's hustling trash in Bay St. Louis, while Polly's home with swollen tits and a baby that won't do his part. Bring on the breast pump!

Lurch got sick that night, the mullygrubs, the galloping intestinal flu, right there in the locker room. He tossed Nancy's worst in the pisser, then shit till he couldn't walk much better than a year-old child, which didn't do our preparations and meditations much good. He was sitting on the bench across from me, and when I saw him start scouring his black ducks with his knuckles, I knew the dumb bastard was hurting. He got very pale quickly—and you might not think that a truly stupid sunnavabitch like Lurch could ever get so important—but Belafonte Bobo of the pigeon toes and the essential redneck saunter (a sort of spread-legged and addled gait) was our single natural star. Puke pale Caldwell Bobo, on a good night, could do it all with ominous power at 175 pounds. He played tailback on our old-fashioned Tennessee System Single Wing. He was tall and, as I said, he didn't stand the usual way. He lined up in three points, feet close together like a sprinter, making my already difficult snap a real chore, because I had to fire so low and hard. He was witlessly and wonderfully swift of foot and he made it to scrimmage as fast as any split-T halfback, praise God.

How'd he throw passes?

By throwing the short ones up near scrimmage, which gave him the quick dash for an option, through the 3-, 4-, or 5-hole. And when he went to throw the bomb he wheeled around after the first great stride, wandering freely as long as he wanted to before he let go of the ball in the long true spiral. That boy was so bony without hip pads a fellow could slice off a finger trying to bring him down. All by way of saying that no matter how well Royal knew the plays for the whole team, and no matter that he was better than the sophomore second-string tailback, still, Royal wasn't Bobo no matter how you looked at it. It was going to be a tough evening. It was one helluva way to open the season.

.   .   .

Again, a crock, a crock, a crock, and I'm about to agree, having gone on so long about a mere game. I'm about to—but not quite.

Youthful Mary says such exercise as football is not *planting, digging, dunging, liming, burning, grubbing, and right ordering of land to make it fit to receive seed, that it may bring forth a plentiful crop.* She says it is *useless* labor and bestial play. She attacks me with Winstanley's wisdom, gets all her clothes off and strides around the room, making motions over our fake Persian rug like she is hoeing—then she gets down on her knees over the intricate design and begins to play like she's setting out tomato plants. She cups her hands and gathers the soil in mounds around her plantings, and she's swinging her free titties gently above all her agriculture. Strange rhetoric, that.

But finally I say to hell with her: I was and am a Populist, in spite of the game. By any lights in those days the game *was* proper labor. It damned well *was* digging and grubbing. Anybody who ever spent an afternoon doing two-on-one drill when it's 101 degrees knows goddamned well about digging and grubbing. Except for my own people, the whole world (except also for Davis Benton, the Sheriff)—the whole world said it was the natural thing to do and a better art than the cornet. Cup them hands and swing them titties, Mary, but in no wise will you ever change my sense of history. The great Vico knows: there is no true wisdom except for the sweet patterns you yourself have made. Understand the configurations of your own dear, meaty life and times, and you've got the bitch by the bush. Blake said that.

Royal Carle Boykin against Mendenhall. Though he was a blocking back most of the time at Bryan, he could indeed throw well enough to play the tailback position (in the traditional upright stance), presaging his amazing career as quarterback for Tulane.

It's amazing he ever survived the Southeastern Conference.

In fact, he was so small, thinning by then, they put number O on his back, which gave him a lot of publicity: he got called "The Most Valuable Ripple on the Green Wave" by all the Southern papers. And he was a sight to see. He'd fade back in those glossy and neats'-footed high-topped shoes he always wore, he'd fade, stumble clumsily, and nearly fall down while getting set to throw—but he was plenty accurate enough in that vasty and half-empty steel stadium in New Orleans, the Sugar Bowl, by God. He threw soft passes and he couldn't ever really throw the bomb unless he absolutely had to, none of the long, true spirals like schoolboy Lurch's or the great professional Baugh's. Royal was more in the Van Brocklin tradition, with the ball sometimes going damn near end over end. He was sometimes messy in his style and detail work, but R.C. did get the ball exactly where it had to go, and he was flawless on handoffs. Yes, sir, all things considered, his was something of an achievement, going, as he did, from blocking back on a Tennessee System Single Wing to quarterback on a major college split-T. Hell, at one point during his junior year, he was leading all the passers in the nation. After seven games he'd completed 60 percent of his passes. He could do some good things on the field, but he never had much class to him. He's even fool enough to pass up his senior year of eligibility so he can go to law school a year early.

Painful. He never *had* to play, and I'm sure he never really enjoyed it. He did it because it was required by the town, and to please his foolish father, and often Royal himself looked plain silly sometimes (for all his having been adopted and chosen with care) with his awkward moves and his dwarfish torso and stubby legs. Christ! in those high-tops he looked like my Aubrey does right now in his childish shoes . . . You take Royal all around and he's ugly, with his eyes up close to his nose like a crawfish's—what nose he's got—no Vico or Sonny he—and that stupid-looking lantern jaw sticking out from his tiny face, and all that red kinky hair almost as sad as a pink nigger's. We called him "Face" for a while sometimes in high school, to go along with the other names, and it's a shame it didn't stick. And pardon all the flat talk about Boykin, but he does deserve his due, while I'm deciding whether I should murder the bastard.

.   .   .

The thing about Boykin is he can get the job done—a regular Alfred Thayer Mahan, a captain who makes precedent out of chaos, "crossing the T" and such like.

Royal gets it done by himself or he gets somebody to do it for him, and he's happy enough when his help gets the credit for his ideas—like when the Mendenhall quarterback is a flashy kid named Prentiss, who later goes on to fame at Ole Miss, leading some truly great teams, and Mr. Prentiss has got us all tied up at the half, by throwing a lot of jump passes: 21–21. Billy Dwayne Prentiss is leaping in the Gilmer tradition—he's up in the air, arched, and exposing a lot of rib cage—and without a doubt he is showing a trickier product than Royal, in his unnatural position, can offer. At half time, while the majorettes are prancing and dancing to the tunes of the band, and while Coach Morgan is calmly showing the defensive backs how to handle a flooded zone, Royal drops in beside me on the back bench—the fucking mourners' bench, since we're in bad trouble—and he says in a small, almost delicate voice, "Why don't you pace your rush and really hurt that son of a bitch when he's doing that jumpin' shit?"

Excellent advice, for I'd hit ole Billy P. a couple of times before he got it off, but I hadn't nailed him on the leap. Fine idea. And I did it. I sloshed my half-time Coke in the trusty Lily Cup and then went out and did a proper job of work for Royal and the team. I lay for that tricky bastard passer from Mendenhall, timing my charge and checking the moves of the halfback who's in the way, and I developed just the right swat to give the ridiculous guard who's trying to impede me on the red dogs—and midway through the third quarter I got my clear shot.

WHAT TRADE should mankind be brought up in?

Now, Mary, you put yourself right back into those net stockings—you flash Joiner a beaver, as Yankees say, and listen to *my* favorite quotation from Winstanley, the truest Leveller.

What trades indeed?—*In every trade, art and science whereby they may find out the secrets of the Creation, and that they may know how to govern the earth in right order.*

They'll teach your bumpy head the *Areopagitica* and tight-assed essays of Christian devotion by the late Jack Donne, but never do they offer Gerrard's great prose: *There are five fountains from whence all arts and sciences have their influences. He that is an actor in any or all the five parts is a profitable son of mankind. He that only contemplates and talks about what he reads and hears, and doth not employ his talent in some bodily action for the increase of fruitfulness, freedom and peace on earth is an unprofitable son.*

But what I did was not unprofitable. In fact, call me Profitable Son Joiner. I racked his ass—I piked that courtier when he's jumped up like Gilmer used to, way up precariously in the stadium lights and arched backwards, his arm cocked to throw. I hit him with all the 230 pounds I had on me then, and I'm sure it looked a lot like Pollaiuolo's *Hercules and Antaeus*. The good shock of that initial lick ripped through every cell in my body, and as I charged I had an eye on the scoreboard (21–21) at the end of the field, that goddamned smug black sign with its white bulbs glaring. I saw what Prentiss had done to us, and as I crashed toward him I thought of Pride and April, the County and the Team. I carried him about five good strides before driving him down into the grass and the ground as hard as I could, by God, planting, dunging, liming, burning, smashing, and grubbing the mother. Billy Dwayne fumbled the ball in flight, right into Doyle Phillips' hands, and Doyle sprinted in easily for the score, 28–21, after my snap and R.C.'s point. It was an elegant picture-book tackle, and he didn't quiver when I got up from him.

Prentiss was out of the game for sure.

All Bryan was whole again.

The Comanche Band struck up the fight song . . . and, yup, it was a vicious thing to do, in a way, however profitable—however much it served the vitality of the community, but a man's a damn fool to deny the pleasure of such moments. I was decked from head to foot in laurel and it *was* short of killing. I never killed Prentiss. In fact, I felt a certain affection for him as his coach and manager pulled him up and down gently by his belt, letting breath back in—

and I was genuinely upset when, after he is breathing and whining, they folded his jersey up and showed a bulge on his right side. I'd popped his gut wall into a hernia. They brought the stretcher and hauled him away with great cheers from both stands. He got a perfectly honorable exit—and it was the *others* on our bench who'd screamed in glee about me tearing him a new one—Joiner'd damn well acted properly—but the Mendenhall coach wasn't particularly of that mind.

This young coach named Revis, fresh from being a fine defensive end for the Chinese Bandits at LSU, he walks up to me where I'm standing glibly by Coach Topp, Revis trots up and says, "Joiner, that's a beautiful tackle. You did it ezakly perfect, and it's real cheap shit."

He spoke briskly and with more venom than I'd ever faced from anybody in my whole life. My mouth is drooping, but Topp doesn't even blush when he tells that man to get on across the field and tend to his own boys, and he tells our bench to shut the hell up when they start grumbling and stirring over the event . . .

The fifth fountain, from whence reason is exercised to find out the secrets of nature, is to observe the rising and setting of the sun, moon, and the powers of the heavens above; and the motions of the tides and seas, and their several effects, powers and operations upon the bodies of man and beast. And here may be learned astrology, astronomy, and navigation, and the motion of the winds, and the causes of several appearances of the face of heaven, either in storms, or in fairness. But I had me no fountain then. All I had was Confusion. The great god Confusion and his next of kin, Shame, struck me a momentary blow. I felt like a bed wetter and the jackoff champ of the world until the Topper swung back to me and said Revis was no more than upset, and that the man knew better than pull a stunt like that, and anyway, if I'm feeling bad about it, don't: "You'll get yours someday, if you're really good." Topp was a miracle for that league. He slapped me across the back and suggested I get off a good snap on the extra point, which I did.

I stood there over Billy Dwayne's body in all my pride, amid the yelling and the music. Somebody got hurt to get me the ears and the tail—to give me that fine memory, and that's just the way it has got to be, said hairy Topp, who was right all the way down the line. Damn right. Because I can't really say that I now resent the guys who tore my ass off to get their place in the sun. Like the time St. Claire Granville of the Colts picked me up and flung me, in an N.F.L. game, about five yards. Flung me, who isn't small. St. Claire was 310 pounds and quicker and stronger, and it was terribly embarrassing to find myself flying through the air of Dallas, Texas. He didn't get to our passer with all that attention he paid me on that play, but that didn't do me a whole helluva lot of good when I had to look at the game films. St. Claire Granville, he's still in The League, and I guess it's people like me who keep him making All-Pro year after year.

I don't want to give the impression that I was some kind of profoundly sage youth and child. I was surely blessed with size and the security of a good home, and I almost always enjoyed a powerful ease with my mates—and, yes, the drifts before and during games were graceful patterns of violence that freed me from most frustrations in the mind—but an experience like the Mendenhall game was capable of bringing on all manner of sinking feelings and disjunctive emotions. Caught between the truth of Revis and the truth of Topper, I suffered alternating shames and elations sufficient to make me feel sloppy in the muscles and queasy in the stomach as I headed back into the game.

How much right is too right?

The rules are the rules, aren't they?

Preparing to snap the pass for the conversion, and looking at the world upside down, a really sage youth wouldn't have been bothered with such questions.

It was guys like Revis and Weatherford, and later the niggers, that taught me shame—it wasn't any root and bole sickness built in by mommas and preachers put the hurt in me.

Fuck it—I cleared away the painful nervousness late in the fourth quarter, after they'd scored again, and tied us again, on a goddamned draw play that sucked me in and passed me by entirely.

We did it on 21, the tailback sweep with unswift Boykin hauling his randy ass. Twenty-one is the play where I break free of scrimmage after a jab at the middle guard in the commonplace seven diamond defense and then blast scrawny defensive backs clean off the field and into the middle of the cinder track.

.   .   .

Coaches with their white sheer socks rolled down over their ankle bones, cheerleaders with those glossy green tights that have the red stripes on both sides, photographers, official timers, and the whole enemy bunch—including pious Revis—went scattering like leaves before a hurricane when I released myself into a signal flying body block at about the 50. I made it easy for R.C. to pick up the first 30 yards. And during this particular action of which I speak, I picked myself up from the cinders—bit black rocks out of my bleeding hands on the leap and run—and then I dodged through all that confused and frightened crowd on the sidelines and pounded on down the field, a total of 80 yards at a lean 6 feet 7 inches and 230 pounds, to throw a final flawless block for Royal. Being so much faster because of my big feet and overall immense energy, sweeping over the green grass like a surface-piercing hydrofoil-type speedboat, gliding along like the clippership *Nightingale*, I moved up along beside Royal—I came along beside and shouted: "Have no fear—Big Son is here!"

Mary, that was joy—

Catching a quick vision of the safety man closing in at a swift angle, I again gently tossed my full self into the air, looking rather like a free-style swimmer does when he lunges out across the water as the sprint begins—

I cut him down and rolled sweetly over in the Bermuda to see Royal crossing the goal line. Man, he was running like a little child who has seen a bad shape in the trees. He looked silly as hell no matter how far I'd helped him go.

Royal and I, we celebrated with a whirling dance together beneath the crepe-strung goal post. Hell, he even had the sense back then to throw the ball up into the nigger stands just like a pro, and then with a fresh ball we put the signature and hair and seal on that fine ramble with a very smart extra point, which won the game, as you might have guessed.

That was our last full year together and we took the measure of the best teams around. We took it all. We wiped out Beulah,

Pinola, and Mendenhall. We even beat big Columbia in the Tung
Bowl. And they were all there all season long. Daddy and Momma
were always perched nervously up in the corner of our new cement
stands, up there where the crimson pennants fluttered—the shy
Joiners were always there, and Daddy always shuddered in his
seat when my name was called out on the P.A. That man *suffered*
when our name was belted out in public. TACKLE BY JOINER.

My daddy finally could not understand what the hell all that
yelling was about in the keen autumn air (though he did not finally
resist his boy's fate)—and he certainly couldn't figure why the
Boykins wanted to sit right next to all those glinting sousaphones
and slide trombones—garrulous Roy and delicate Merle Boykin
bawling their lungs out and down low.

And Preacher Taggart, when it was his week to pray over the
contest, always liberally suggested that Godalmighty bless both
sides equally (a world of ties).

And after every victory there was Sheriff Davis Benton overseeing traffic control for a game he considered *in*sane and mostly
unmanly, a total rejection of the peace and tranquillity he desired
for our county. D. Benton and Robert Simpson Joiner were surely
the only men in a hundred miles of that stadium who were completely apostate. Had he known the word, Benton would have said
the festivals and dramas of Bryan County were lacking in *ataraxia*.
Our new stadium beyond the eroded declivity behind the courthouse was cockpit, amphitheater, and bawdy house to all the citizens of Bryan, and on Friday nights I was Saint Henry Suso drinking Christ's blood from all five wounds. I was squire and ogre and
I was doing exactly what I had to do—I was a young man well
trained to seek the deeds and exploits of war, which are claims to
glory. The whole tapestry of life at home is something out of *The
Waning of the Middle Ages*. Let's hear it for J. Huizinga, great
scholar.

And when the Moon Pie was puffing along, still swaddled in
baby fat at blocking back, larding the carpet grass of our scientifically graded turf, I punched big holes for him, making it very,
very easy for him to get beyond scrimmage for one of his desperate
and clumsy blocks. He *flung* himself at people. He successfully
managed to get in the way with no style at all.

Cease and bring Reason to the Heart.

For there's not a damn thing wrong with what Royal Carle Boykin is doing. He's taking a wife, that's all. My ex-wife. And he has had his problems—both parents dead of fire—and now he desires the security of home and family—hearth and home and some politically unassailable cunt, and my one true woman is entirely suited to fill that need. She's 5 feet 4 inches, thin and pleasantly proportioned, with high tight breasts that were almost nippleless until Aubrey came along—breasts like Verrocchio's *Lady with Primroses*. She has a face disturbingly similar to Cecilia Gallerani's, Leonardo's *Lady with an Ermine*, and she has Cecilia's delicate long insensitive fingers too.

Royal, friend, that woman knows ezakly how to hold a mean voracious little animal. That small woman, moist Norman skin and hairless body, is going to take you in hand like you never got taken in hand before.

O.K.

But Royal never to my knowing ever had anything to do with her sexually until recently, and I know for a fact he never rested a lustful hand on her or ever came around our house at any time while we were busting up last year, at least not until I started my revolution and pissed in the grits for sure. I was gone across the Sabine and divorced from all that Bryan shit before they got together profoundly. I'd flicked that golden ring from the station wagon window before he made his move. Had Royal moved in on me before a proper time, had he given me some kind of absolutely disloyal *offense*, I'd have had to kill his ass the way I had to kill Billy Weatherford's.

For I did break Billy's pretty head and watch him fall in that heap of burst watermelons for nothing more than pulling a squatty target pistol out of his boot—nothing more than that. However good Billy was during his brief trial with football, he was essentially a cruel, depraved somitch—he was a threat to my life, a threat to Stream and Bobo and Royal . . . my friends . . . God bless the same.

Had Royal made his carnal move too soon he'd have been worse than a physical threat. For that he'd of been a disloyal friend and some kind of rat raper.

I've got a clean eye for Man's Weakness, but it gets often cluttered with love—and Billy Weatherford died on the white line of Highway 49, as the old song goes, and it was all brought on by a full summer moon, cheap wine, and a single winsome prank—good clean down-home bucolic fun.

It's not a pleasant thing to consider, or reconsider, ever! Yessir, winsome as four dinosaurs straight out of *Huck Finn: Brontosaurus, Tyrannosaurus rex, Triceratops,* and *Iguanodon,* all of us having some simple ole vacation and pre-college fun in my aged but nevertheless lively DeSoto convertible. It was a graduation present from my people.

God, in chastising a people, is accustomed to burn his rod. The empires of these oligarchies were not so violent as short, nor did they fall upon the people, but in their own immediate ruin. Keep that in mind.

Obviously enough, I was not unfamiliar with violence and other curious forms of behavior at the age of eighteen. I knew something about the high blood and responsibility for physical power, and I'd lived with a dramatic critique of the entire experience: my parents, the craftsman and craftswoman.

Therefore, he said vigorously, I continue to be unhappy with ex-wife and mistress when they see my first killing as the inevitable result of all my days. The women believe that that bleak and exaggerated roundhouse right simply had to happen. The very next day after the murder, nubile April said that Billy *naturally* came to a bad end, suggesting that wretched Sonny was no more than a pure instrument of poetic justice. BUT—but five years after Billy's in the ground, and after I've whipped up on *her* a couple of times, she says I'm a man who seeks and finds his victims. And nowadays, out here in Texas (coldest land of heartless political crime and bullshit), Mary shifts the blame to the *state* I was born in. Goddamned women tend to detest both a simple mystery and an obvious truth. I crushed Billy's parietal, sphenoid, and temporal bones because he was about to shoot bullets into me and my friends. Any reasonable man, eighteen or sixty, would have reckoned with it in the same blessed way—and that should satisfy the curiosity of the world, including women.

And let their randy snatches ponder more carefully Billy's mother at the funeral. Why did *she* do the things she did? Let them be filled with wonder at this phenomenon—a fortyish country slut who does an almost effortless western roll into her eldest son's casket. She truly high-jumped—she sprang on spiked green and transparent heels from the threadbare purple carpet of the Christ's Gospel Church, exposing pink garter belts, silverish clasps, and gray flesh—she high-jumped right up and into where her dead boy lay.

Only the goddamned footwashers are vile enough to show a corpse for the duration of an entire evangelical funeral sermon. That miserable chickenfat preacher (I speak truth)—that crewcut, ex-athlete, ex-schoolbus driver, ex-unemployed garage mechanic—he used poor Billy as a vivid example of how our LAF on earth is BREE-UFF. All that tender and greasy pleading for our souls, but he never once suggested there might be some malice directed at me and the others who set forth on the night wind and got Billy dead. Shit no. He was obviously delighted that that sourceless and monstrous event had happened. Hell, didn't it get some of the finest people in Bryan down into that hole of a church? Literally a hole.

Ladies, why not concentrate on all that pain and confusion? Just sense it and let it be.

Dear reader, it was a subterranean episode—literally underground—meaning it was all basement, rising no more than a foot or two above the surface of the raw gumbo. It was built that way to economize on walls and roofs and taxes, or maybe in some ghastly and unconscious imitation of the primitive Christians, even though it was air-conditioned. It was a long tomb with red walls and a blond pulpit up front and center where the dead youth was, and where that porcine shithead, Morris, was. He shed womanish tears amid his cries of "Brief, Brief, Brief . . . Brief and Cruel," and he was *not* displeased to see Mrs. Weatherford carry on so; he only shuddered his blubber faster, and sputtered more; he was *moved* when she jumped in the casket, "moved-*uh* to say-*uh* that real

GREE-UFF-*uh* is on us-*uh* and-*uh* the spurt of the Lord-*uh* is moving-*uh*." Or something like that—those lascivious gut and throat grunts of Holiness types . . .

The casket and vault almost fell off the low table when she began to flail around on her child, flinging her patent leather shoes as far as the wall and the Sallman picture of Jee-sus. It was then that Morris finally waddled fast to comfort the ruined Mother. She was *alive* with some curious grief. It covered her body like lice. She was radiant, with an actual flickering rash about her cheeks and neck, but ole Billy's face was strictly changeless. It was the triple horrors—and when Billy's wife, nee Polly Roberts, rose to assist, the older woman attacked. She climbed down, pushing the loving preacher aside, and attacked her son's wife. She let loose a bawl and swarmed out of the vault and onto Polly with such language as I actually blushed to hear—but never once during the whole thing was there any hostility directed toward me, the killer.

Billy's mother and Billy's estranged father and Billy's semi-estranged wife did *not* hold me responsible for his death. In fact, as I worried myself at the Parlor (the day before the funeral), they all stood with odd smiles of compassion on their several faces. Billy's daddy—a pulpwood hauler located in Monroeville, Alabama, a tall individual with a Jack Palance-type face and mean smile—he even put his arm around me—to console *me*. And Polly (for all grief is passing strange) reacted to my sorrow among the potted ferns as if it were a splendid compliment to her.

The fight. It didn't last but a moment. Morris and Mr. Weatherford calmed the woman and got everybody arranged again on the front pew. Groans, lamentations—even a few people breaking into some bars of "Almost Persuaded" as preacher and father tidied the disfurnished and disheveled corpse.

Then Morris went back to the pulpit to preach some more. And air conditioning or no air conditioning you can imagine my parents' suffering and embarrassment at that funeral (in some ways it was worse than Lucy's for them), which embarrassment is the living pain of that recollection, for me. For they felt *obliged* to go down into that crazy catacomb with me. While all the initial shout-

ing and fussing and preaching was going on, they sat stiffly with
me and made small ummmmmm sounds—my dear people and the
Taggarts—gentle Reverend Taggart appalled by Morris's cruel
vision of judgment. And my poor father's maimed hand was
clenched and white as a flounder's belly.

April came along, too, which was probably in bad taste by some
standards—and it certainly was discombobulating when *I* began to
weep a little, out of confusion. She said, "Hush, Son." She considered my tears unreasonable, and no doubt she considered
Royal's tears unreasonable too, but he wasn't her responsibility so
much as I was. He was beside me and he wept as much as I did.

Lurch, he never showed for the funeral, and Stream was sick in
bed for weeks immediately after the killing and Sheriff Benton's
investigation . . . Royal and I were in that lonesome valley all by
ourselves, and it was the longest day of our youth together—it was
what my nigger buddy Slater Jackson calls *a kneeway journey
home.* A great line.

And: *Is it not an error to consider some actions less worthy
because they are necessary? No, they will not knock it out of my
head that the marriage of pleasure with necessity, with whom, says
an ancient, the Gods always conspire, is a very suitable one.*—
Montaigne (I think). Why the hell didn't I attack that pulpit the
way I did Billy Graham's the summer before?

Royal's parents and my parents and the Taggarts, sans Stream,
sat together at Billy's funeral. We all sat together in a cool air-
conditioned mortal sweat while Morris preached an hour and a half
to save our souls (I checked it by the trusty Swiss watch I got for
making All-State). But finally it ended—with Billy's mother and
father rededicated and reunited to Christ and each other for a
while. Little children came to be saved, cousins of the families, and
there was considerable shouting and crying and jubilation when
the casket was finally closed and carried out the back brick steps
and up the clay bank to the hearse. Bedlams of voices that day—but
not from R. S. Joiner.

R.S. had been almost speechless since it happened on Saturday
night, and this was Tuesday. The killing and that funeral racked

my daddy up. Something he'd meant to avoid had, again, *not* been avoided, and he and Momma were moved and gone to Memphis before the summer was over. He has said very little to me at any time since Billy's death. And I goddamned well blame him for acting that way! He never even went to any of my college games. He never gave a damn I went pro.

Damn it, Royal, you and I knew what we were releasing wee tears about. We were simply very unhappy that a young man had done something to get himself dead. To an athlete dying young— good stuff like that—and we knew that Billy's sentimental and drunken parents would go home and wail it up with their equally sentimental and drunken friends and relatives—and then at some time during false dawn they'd awaken for a terrible, sodden, and Godblessed fuck the likes of which they'd never had before together. "Hush, Son."

We sensed this reconciliation—but we weren't satisfied, for it was selfish. It was selfish and ignorant. We knew they'd missed the point.

"Hush, Son. Be a man, Son." April hissed it through her teeth.

Mary Ann says the real tragedy was those slicked-up children dressed in their little-man and little-woman clothes from Sears, Billy's distant cousins and a half brother, who got converted (to something) under such morbid circumstances. Which isn't exactly a bull's-eye either, Mary, though it is certainly true that such an experience can hurt a child's head.

But maybe Royal had more reason to cry than I did. Maybe my big fist was less guilty than his idea about a last celebration together, his idea that grew out of a conversation at the Methodist Youth Fellowship the Sunday before it happened. Maybe it was Royal who had been most petty about Taggart's banquet (and all things petty kill)—which "banquet" was Reverend Taggart's annual attempt, however wrongheaded, to offer a proper rite of passage for each generation of decent Protestant youths in Bryan. But unfortunately the tone and fare were very similar to the pregame meals I've already mentioned.

Ah MYF!—those grab-ass hayrides and possum hunts and swimming parties and picnics. Also the fact that a little piety was understood to be enjoyable, even incumbent upon, healthy young people in a place like Bryan. Yes, piety, and also the pleasurable knowledge that we were being hypocritical—that profoundly civilized enjoyment of faking off the authorities. We were (we knew in our hearts) fornicators and violent boys and girls, but Taggart—and most of our parents who were his lay leaders—did not fully understand these things.

Yet it wasn't these sins that brought us back Sunday after Sunday. No, sir. It wasn't the promise of carnal pleasure and hypocrisy that brought us back week after week to a frequently dull place.

Mainly we came because MYF was the most intellectual organization in town.

The pity, the pity, the more's the pity, that a desperate, soft, and doubting man like Taggart, a man who never got beyond the terror he found on first reading Hume, should be our mental leader. But he, this merely kind human, was the seminal thinker for seven counties around. And he knew it.

His sermons sounded to us a lot like the things we were reading in *Motive, Life,* and *Look.* He was up to date in our eyes, and some of us did like the idea that we knew somebody far enough out and generally tolerant enough to have the Citizens' Council and the Klan down on them. In fact, finally, Taggart was too big for Bryan, lasting only three years before the bishop in Jackson sent him to Tupelo, where his brand of sophistication would be appreciated by the young and progressive element in the business community.

The point is how very important it was to have him around for my three years of high school, however much of a fool he was.

What I'm trying to say is that Royal, and the rest of us, would not have gotten in deep trouble had we respected Reverend Taggart, even though he did think Norman Thomas was damn near the equal of Jesus.

He'd read things like *The Modern Temper* by Joseph Wood Krutch, and when he looked at his youth choir on Sunday nights, he saw our young faces waiting—and so he preached *for* dancing, saying joy in the physical body is the Lord's will indeed—and he preached *for* integration, saying that the Kingdom of Heaven is not exclusive like a country club.

We didn't have a country club in Bryan then, and he knew that the crudest racist in the country hated Delta men and their clubs almost as much as niggers.

He never did, but he should have been quoting the Leveller Coppe from time to time.

A line I love: *Give over, give over thy midnight mischief.*

And: *Be no longer so horribly, hellishly, impudently, arrogantly wicked, as to judge what is sinne, what not, what will and what not, what blasphemy, and what not.* Which lines might of saved Billy. It's midnight mischief that hurts us all.

Royal was too damned hard on the preacher. Even though Taggart finally wasn't naturally strong the way youths require, Royal should have been kinder.

The bleak fact was that the best the preacher's passion could raise was plain style and occasionally a bitter hoarseness when such things as the burnings and killings were going on. Exacerbated, enervated, hunted and driven, beak-nosed and chinless, Taggart gripped that walnut pulpit three years in Bryan and preached a long confession on how he didn't know where the world was going. He knew damned well he wasn't your proper visionary. But, come what may, he wished the world well. Which shit is not going to satisfy even a *young* Royal Carle Boykin.

And on the night of the banquet Preacher spoke to us about how the life ahead of us was a rose. A rose!

He said we could pluck it and devour it, thorns and all, like a madman, or we could pick it and many others to make a weak bouquet in a sterile room—or we could be gardeners and grafters, creators of a new strain. It was a far cry from the insight he'd struck at Lucy's funeral not all that many years before, and it gave me a very uneasy feeling to see him soften up so much.

We wanted him to tell us something about how to live with the murders and the burnings that were going on by then: What *about* the NAACP and CORE and Dr. King? He'd pushed us toward sympathy with our fellow man, and on that Saturday evening in the Fellowship Hall of our church we desired a summing up of some sort.

But instead we got botany and bad poetry. "Don't merely *pluck*," he kept saying. "Do *not* merely *pluck* the rose of life."

And the misery caused by that kind of vagueness is almost too obvious to mention.

When Adam delved and Eve span, who was then the gentleman?—Preacher didn't even rise to that at our summer banquet. "Beauty is the only thing that counts, beauty and the hope of this great land of ours . . . American Beauty." He shuffled on the asphalt tiles where he stood. He thrust out his weathered neck and ran his long fingers down to the starched collar of his sports shirt.

Royal whispered in my ear, "He's a beaten man."

It shocked me for some reason—to hear Royal say something so harsh and true at that point in the evening, though I did know R.C. could be plenty tough.

"Shush," said April who was on the other side of me.

"Shush, yourself," I answered, as the Tag finally gave out of gas and pollen and wished us well in all the hours and days and years ahead of us in coming maturity.

Poor bootless Taggart wished us well, but Royal, *enfant terrible*, knew better than any of us that none of Wesley's hymns washed, and that, unfortunately, Reverend's social gospel couldn't cut it either.

Knock some biddy up and the preacher'd send her off to Texas or Louisiana for an abortion. He damn well did understand the virtue of a treasured secret. He'd marry you and he'd bury you, but he never proved to us by act deed or word he knew how scared we were.

"He's too busy being scared himself," says Mary Ann. "He's been scared all his life of the high cheekbones and razor noses of Snopes—he knows that goddamn Faulkner never exaggerated— he's scared of Royal's hard little pink eyes and he's also threatened by your size, Son." (Funny how Mary has got all the straight skinny on people she has never met.) "He believed Roosevelt was going to drive cottonmouths and corals and timber rattlers out of the state. Goddamn it, Sonny, he is a man of your parents' world, and if you put him down, you put down *Momma* and *Daddy*." Oof! Gut shot again.

She glares at me, accusing me of rejecting the honest, scalloped paper plates of the Fellowship Hall—accusing me of rejecting all the beautiful beds of thrift and driveways bordered by tire halves painted white—she begins to cry while gulping vodka from the Mason jar, and she accuses me of preferring the Weatherfords and Morris and Lurch to Taggart and my own sweet family in Memphis: "You stinking redneck, you pitiful throwback, what you want is busting heads and dicking around in greasy tonks, and you never once really gave a flying fuck about the first Negro . . . no matter what you've said you did . . . you pussy . . . you want her back and Royal and all those fucked-up people. Sonny, you poor sonofabitch, don't you know the sun never shines where you came from?" She goes off to the shower to steam herself flabby. And she's wrong because I do have some sense about priorities.

I killed him, Billy, in a fair fight. Billy was the first I killed, and I killed Foots Magee in a fair fight. He was the second man I killed. I didn't never kill no women, and don't intend to.

Understand. Tomato aspic at the Bryan Methodist Church will give you a skin disease, and Royal had us out on the road a week later—his idea being to get at the *real* meaning of our years together —he's making this last-ditch attempt to prove he's *sensual*—he has got us out driving from tonk to tonk. We're drinking Mogen David and Jax and brooding over Sex, Death, Ambition, and Eternity— we're singing "Rabbit Ain't Got No Tail At All" like ten-year-old boys in that DeSoto when we see ole Billy's truck pull into the stop at D'Lo: "Goddamn ole Bill's truck, an' look at them melons."

Melons, for Christ's sake. And it ain't nothin' but obvious what's in order. When you got yourself a raggled-assed DeSoto convertible and you getting toward drunk you by God decide to fill the mother up with stolen melons. Good clean fun, like digging up Jew and nigger graves—stealing tombstones. There's ole Billy W. who made us have a hard season because he don't like the feel of a jock and shoulder pads—Billy, who is *married* to a woman almost all of us have fucked. "Let's get that cocksucker," says Lurch. And we do. We do indeed in fact. We do get Mr. Billy Weatherford. While he's gone in the stop to have a beer with his wife, we pull up behind his solidbody and start loading up. All of us. Lurch is pulling them out of the straw and handing them to Royal, who tosses them to me in the front seat, and Stream in the back, with a lot of them stripers busting and crashing on the hood and windshield and seat. Man, we were eating hot watermelon and throwing them around. It was a frenzy of seeds and meat and *Rabbit ain't got no tail at all, He's just got a powder puff*. And all the time there's a queer little voice back behind the fog in my head, and it's saying how it is that this shit is bad news, a small voice crying, "Trouble, trouble, trouble," and Royal's eyes are *closed* throughout most of it. He's dropping half the melons and wailing like a banshee, which is a sad sound connoting failure to *en*joy—but also connoting a rejection of Boykinian Reason—connoting the same damned sense of doom I was feeling. *Give over, give over thy midnight mischief* was running through our minds—some version of it was . . .

Then Billy and Polly appeared. It brought me around to near sober, for they were a sight to see. I could even tell, through the half sick and drunk buzz I was in, that Mr. and Mrs. Weatherford had partly made up, from some constant misery or another. They came striding out the screen door with arms a-swing and big smiles. *Now ain't that fine* cut through my mind.

Oh Lord—Oh April—Oh Royal—we were caught red-handed. We were caught and we looked like fools in all that mess we'd made. It's 3:00 a.m. and we're playing off in the shadows of the big gravel lot. But still a little crowd gathers, a couple of drivers and the manager of the D'Lo stop, buddies of Billy. And my boys were backed up against front fender and tailgate, but it wasn't about to develop into an old-timey fist fight. (Christ! that it had.) He saunters up with his wife, and *saunter* is the right word, because Bill is in control at first. He's pissed, but he and Polly are making it just fine for a while and here's his chance to show out in front of all these boys he don't like. He's satisfied to put up a fire of curses and threats. We were a bunch of worthless bastards and we gonna pay for ever damn melon an' rat now . . . an entirely reasonable solution

and me and Royal start handing over money as fast as we can, about
$30.00 for openers, while Stream is promising a check—payment
in full—by noon the next day. We were contrite and the other
drivers and the manager are enjoying the hell out of Billy's victory.
But the dooms were still coming—the goddamned dooms were
making my molars ache. We're paying double the retail price and
it would have solved itself if dumb Lurch hadn't been drunkest and
generally dissatisfied with the scene. He starts squeezing off slick
seeds in the general direction of the enemy, and finally he says that
he's not about to pay—nothing—and he plainly states how Billy
is chickenshit and Polly's a punchboard. He's drunk and sour as hell,
but what he's saying is coming through loud and clear, and I could
not believe my ears, nor could Royal—and Stream begins to moan.

"Cut that shit," says Royal. "Billy's got his reasons..."

"*You* cut it," says Lurch. "How come I got to listen to this..."

So I gave Bobo a good shove away from Billy, intending to
show good faith. I pushed Lurch away and he fell backwards into
the slime and rocks, which was *the* mistake that caused it all. Childishness. Childishness, evil *machismo*, says Mary, and so it was; for
when Lurch got back up and lobbed a chunk and struck Bill in the
face, I smiled a slight smile. I smiled because the black train was
passing through the yard and was nearly to the station—and, for all
the terror, it was some kind of relief to hear it coming.

"The big one thinks that's funny, Billy," says the manager of
the D'Lo stop.

"No I don't; not really," but it was all up by then. He is bent
over and going for his engineer boot—he's rising and showing some
kind of black pistol—and I'm in the process of swinging my combination of roundhouse and bolo punch. It was perfect drift—it
was that feeling of working in perfectly articulate slow motion. I
was doing it and looking at it at the same time. I could even see myself with X-ray vision and feel the abstract physics and miserable
calculus of the muscles and bones that were doing it—pectoralis
major, sternum, trapezius, clavicle, triceps brachii, and humerus—
my body was wise—my goddamned pile-driving blood was wise—
my commander mind was wise—we were doing what we had to do
—and all of it was JUSTIFIED. It was a terrible blow that caught
him on the side of the head while he's still bent somewhat at the

waist. I felt and heard things break at the moment of impact. Hit him just in front of the ear, on the temple, to make him lift clean off the ground and turn a strange and awkward pirouette in the air before he came down in an obsequious heap on the rocks. Bill puked, shook, and stretched out on his belly, and he was bleeding from the nose and mouth. I'd bent a little to hit him with all I had, and I did, indeed I did.

Whad you feel like, Son? Whad you feel like? Howzit feel to know you killed that man? Man pull a gun on you . . . and it don't even break your hand.

I'm protecting my friends. It was JUSTIFIED.

It was funny how we all gathered around the hurt boy— pulled in a little closer—but he was of course, among other things, out cold—and it was in all our minds that Billy was dying. The D'Lo manager called the Clinic ambulance, but he might of well have called the Parlor right then. Dying, yes: a realization that creates a variety of effects. Billy's friend, Ernest Toess, commented how I'd hit him very hard and then went on to say he knew the gun did make a difference.

"He pull a gun," rumbled Lurch who was scared shitless and acting drunk again. "Whad'll Benton do?"

"Benton won't do a damn thing," said Royal kneeling beside Billy and checking his breathing. "You realize that guy went for the ambulance without even checking this man," and his voice was sullen but respectful. It was sullen and respectful of what he knew I'd done. "Went straight to the phone, yessir," says Royal Carle Boykin.

Mary's out of the shower and repeats the question: "How did you feel, Son?" She's tranquil and rotating in her chair. She has got a flowered towel around her head, which towel she got from a box of detergent. "Weren't you pleased, sweet Son?" And she is talking like in a dream. "He was a handsome feller and a wonderful ath-a-lete, right—you must have had some complex emotions— right?"

Wrong, wrong, baby, wrong, unless embarrassment is complex in the way you mean. I noticed how his sideburns had some blood in them, and I was sincerely afraid that he would die, because I knew I could kill a man with my hands (I'd dreamed it the way that every boy dreams of such a thing), but mostly I feared what Benton would say, I shared Lurch's fear. And I was sick to think of how my parents would respond.

I waited until I saw Billy in the box before I grieved for him. It wasn't until the Parlor and the funeral that I felt strongly enough to cry and to understand how sad a thing it was.

She spins and she spins and wants to know why I didn't speak to him and reason with him, and I allow you don't reason with a glintless pistol, even when, in an instant, you figure it's only a .22.

But Sheriff Davis Benton knew. He didn't confuse the issues. Hell no. He hardly bothered with the death, though he grieved it. He knew better than to try to have charges filed. Legally he knew we were clean as far as the murder went. Benton sent Polly off with the ambulance though it was clear she'd rather have stayed with the boys that did it. She couldn't say enough about how "Billy'd pulled a gun on those boys . . . and Son just hit him to protect . . ." Davis sent her off in the ambulance to the Bryan County Clinic and Hospital and then he turned his attention to the thieves.

Thieves!

He drove us to his home—got his wife up to make coffee, seated us all in his tasteless living room—

"Hijacking! Disturbing intrastate commerce! Thieves—all you guys are *thieves*—and worse—damnit . . . you people just had to provoke that poor sonofabitch, didn't ya?—had to *steal* something —and him all in a stew about his wife messin' around on him with a Cajun guitar player." He knew things we didn't. "Got to steal from a poor worthless bugger who had never had any *opportunity* at all." (Which wasn't entirely accurate.) Benton's a veteran of the Korean and Second War but still he's teary while lecturing us. He means to make us feel bad, and he does just that: "Got damn it, Billy never will get himself another chance. Shit!" And Stream was slumped double so much his nose was against his knees, and he was well on his way to his own crying and the collapse that lasted the rest of the summer, if not for the rest of his life.

Lurch, the efficient cause, merely slumped, while Boykin was stiff—strict sitting attention—with his eyes popped wide, watching the law pace frantically on his oval, hooked rug of many colors— watching the goddamned amazing liberal law pat his mustache.

Benton: "I could send all you guys to Parchman for twenty years! How'd you like that?" Then he pivots on his boots, with hands on hip and holster.

"We wouldn't," says Royal, sincerely.

"An' I guess, by *God*, you wouldn't—what with the *future* lying before you so slick and clear. I'd guess, by Christ, *you wouldn't*—but you boys are gonna go to that hospital tonight— and you're going to the Parlor, and you're going to the funeral— because if he wasn't dead when we put him in the meat wagon, he's dead now."

Mary, how'd he know that?

Davis was doing his best—he'd read upon justice and mercy— and from taking all those popular magazines, including (wonder of wonders) *Harper's*, he'd got himself a proper sense of moral *ambiguity*—but we knew that he was, to a significant extent, faking it. We knew he knew our world forgives Tom and Huck, especially after they've made the Wigwam Wiseman High School All-American team. We knew all that striding and bitching was by way of saying we were all in for a tough week, and let's try to get through it together as best we can, which includes the sermon. And then Bessie, Benton's wife, served us all black coffee, without the least suggestion that anybody might want cream and/or sugar. Black coffee and lemon snaps on a Melmac peagreen platter. But nevertheless she was courteous and huge and beautiful at 4:00 a.m. in her cuffed white short shorts, bare feet, and State College T-shirt that lay over the most incredible six-hooker I ever saw.

We all settled in for our coffee, and, while Benton was staring at his reflection in the picture window, Royal lit a Pall Mall cigarette. He puffed a couple of times, then he observed, rather vacantly, "We hurt his feelings. We sure hurt ole Billy's feelings."

2

Here's her fatal letter, her deathless prose, her withering logic.

Dearest Sonny,

Royal and I are getting married on the last day of August and I want you to know it because I think, though I may be wrong (as I so often have been) that you will be pleased, that is, more pleased than not, knowing an old friend will be taking care of Aubrey along with me, and because I know you know how it plain turned out to be no damned good for us after all the trouble you had in The League. You "Must" agree with me, because any wife that drives her husband to what I drove you to do to me and to your own home town isn't going to be happy in any way. Right? We never really talked about these things enough before you left, did we? Sonny, sweetheart, that visit and fight of Royal's with Daddy turned out better than I could have ever planned or even imagined it!

So if you want to come to it you can (both Davis and Royal say it's O.K.) and we'd all love to see you, except for Aubrey, who though he wouldn't exactly know who you are, shouldn't probably see you yet, and for that matter maybe never!!

I mean it, Son, now you come on over if you want to and bring your girlfriend, because I'm sure you've got one by now, and a good-looker I bet.

Well, we're all fine, even Daddy, who's in New Orleans for the summer—and maybe forever now he's semi-retired—not liking Royal (in spite of all the respect he has for him). Daddy's down there, and he's pretty sick, but he's with "his" woman.

*Sonny, I regret nothing, not even the wounds, and best to you
in all you desire. How are you doing?*

*Love
April*

The whole of it in flawless Spencerian script learned from her
converted Catholic Aunt Helen, who didn't like the ugly style
that April was learning in public school, mere printing and simple-
looking, and so took her aside at home in the evenings and taught
her how to do it right. Yes. I agree with Horace Mann and Mr.
D. F. Sarmiento, the famous historian of Argentina: education is
the most important thing: *On ne tue pas les idées!*

It's a perfect letter. It is absolutely sincere and every nuance of
her love and outrage is there, except for something about the niggers. She can't deal with them even now, but what the hell? It's
all a matter of getting her ideas across to me—keeping everything
complex and clear—and damn well getting what she wants! Which
isn't me at her second wedding, though she'd like it, because she *is*
sentimental about her friends and all. She gets me cheap and I
shrink up—then she gets Boykin who's Sanforized. I was the best,
whatever—Harris Tweed from the bleeding Outer Hebrides,
until she dropped me in the well like a character in Mark Twain.

Christ! That I could just shrink.

But I've said goodby to all that, and now I'm finally suffering
my way back to sanity in a sixth-grade classroom. I'm teaching my
little ladies and gentlemen to love details, like where Butte is, and
why a tomcat's balls look like pussy willow buds set side by side.
Half the day we spend on retained objects (very progressive) and
math, and then I attempt to teach them World History.

Oh God, the terrible responsibility of teaching the history of
the world.

Then I have to listen to Mary Ann, my mistress, say that all
that makes them learn is the fact that I'm bigger and uglier than
Puff the Magic Dragon. Six feet seven inches and recently down

from 310 pounds. But they do learn. I say, "Mary Ann, they do learn," and then I get some ice from the fridge, and scoff down another Olde Bourbon. They do learn and I am a happy man, and Mary's not serious in what she says—she is proud I've done so well at the schoolhouse. I keep good school. Son's done a fine job in an experimental school, teaching Spades and Wetbacks and all kinds of spooky little Wasps and she is proud of me. Mary realizes that the people at the U.P.S. showed great courage in letting me join their staff, and she knows that I have never let them down.

There's no justice. A narcissistic person and double killer like me ought to suffer the miseries of the damned, something worse than the *Disasters of War* by Mr. Goya. Eugene Joiner with a tree limb stuck up through his ass, and sticking out his back a little bit, but with my mistress Mary Ann snuggled up against me I sleep like a baby, and every morning I get up and stare at the world as wide-eyed as the Duke of Wellington.

Miss April and R. C. "Moon Pie" Boykin—who'd of thought it? Bound in adamantine chains, they'll clank off up the road to Jackson. They'll become quasi-liberal Presbyterians (a contradiction in terms) and work like hell for the Lung Association, all the while (both of them) casting greedy eyes on the Capitol and the Governor's Mansion. They're greedy for the world's stew. Never trust a Bryan neck. We're all the same.

I grieve to think of it, for Jackson's a clean and brutal town. It'll break Royal's heart.

She tired of ecstasy. But who gives a damn if she did look like Saint Theresa when she was thrashing and coming—me riding high on my elbows to get a good look at what I'm doing for her, riding like a carrack or cog that is giving her pitch, surge, and heave all at once? I gave her some fine times and took her a long way, but now I've lost her perfect skin forever, which skin is the texture of almost greaseless peanut butter. Ah, Smyrna, the earthquake has come, and Petra is mostly gone as well, all facades in ruin.

But if I do teach well, if it does turn out that the Magic Dragon can convince the nation that mature men should be in the lower grades, as so many significant articles in *Saturday Review* suggest, then quite possibly I'll die with a school named after me. P.S. Joiner, something lasting and pure. And yes, I'd like for somebody to carve my likeness in fine stone, which, by God, would do a great deal to make my fat forgot by all the locals back home in Bryan, Miss.—this terrible damage the gooey Jiff has done me—a piece of pink marble worked over with a loving fury the way that Andreas Schlüter used to do—a cool stone that will show my face in a thin agony, a goddamned image that would never let anybody recollect the flabby and massive death I'll likely die out here. My long lashes will be bent down to participate in a fierce grimace, and the long hair will be delicately amok behind the shroud that's wrapped around my fevered brow. Those sprigs of manly beard will be set in order forever. My bitty ears slap up against my head—my small yet hellish pit of a mouth, that Carlsbad of gluttony, miraculously full of teeth in spite of all my years under the helmet. Let's hear it for the warrior mask of Eugene "Sonny" Joiner. And let's hear it for Bernini's little David Carle, whose lips are sucked in like a toothless old man's—his sleek body taut, prepared to cast the lethal rock against the giant. And let's hear it for Saint Athanasias lost in reverie, bold, but with whiskers whipped to rage by the cruel maenads of all his pussy dreams, coils and roils of Eugene's black hair struck forever in stone beneath the sad Texas sun.

(Mary Ann, who is my mistress now, thinks the best thing that ever happened to me was being driven west and away from those lunatic Mississippians, especially April Smith Joiner Boykin, which means she doesn't understand. I'd intended to be a credit to my race.)

And no doubt is about it, April's gone a long way since falling in love with me at the World Champion Tobacco Spit at Salem, which is out from Hot Coffee, which is out from Bryan, which is out from Jackson, which is out from Dallas, which is out from N.Y.C., which is out from the world. . . .

But now a brief word from a favorite historical writing of mine, "A Declaration from the Poor Oppressed People of England 1649": *Shall not worthy Royal Carle, the soggy cookie, have her*

*rightfully, be, in fact, the most worthy inheritor of all her mag-
nificent and sparse short hairs?*

Hell yes, and let the Commies have France. It'll ruin the Party.
Let the vagrant floods of history roll on relentlessly and foolishly,
while I teach my little scholars to divide and multiply with master-
ful precision. I will teach them to write with a quiet and classical
grace. They'll learn the value of fable, chreia, proverb, refutation,
confirmation, commonplace, encomium, comparsion, description,
thesis, legislation, and conclusion, to name a few. I'll get Leroy and
Roosevelt and Chico and Paco and L.C. to spell, goddamn it, each
word so correctly no man will ever embarrass them again for being
rednecks and niggers and greasers—I'll teach them the rituals of
science and mechanics, especially electrical motors, which are so
very important in our modern world of today, and a lot about the
science of total health and longevity, blessed Hygeia, daughter of
April and Asclepius. But I am about to reconsider this business of
history, for the mysteries of my discipline are probably too terrible
to continue. Strike it down. Bring on the halberds and the napalm.
I'll educate according to the *De Partitione Oratoria* and by way
of the best computer science. I'll try to give them what they never
had: *Sprezzatura.*

II

Waiting my turn to spit, I saw April at a distance off through
the pines. (I hadn't paid any attention to her for years, since we
hadn't been at the same school). But now, friend, she moved like
honey pouring from the comb, slowly, for she is essentially lazy.
Even at a distance of twenty yards I could tell that she, in a
country-tight cotton print, had no panties on—but this condition
was clearly not the result of any lust she would have recognized,
and certainly it was not out of the desire for mere ease. She'd just
forgot! Thoughtlessness! Got Damn! The beauty of molasses on
a mockingbird's wing. So let every soul within the hearing of these
words take off his track shoes and flex his toes. Let each seat himself

on an ancient cypress stump in the dark swamp and listen to me
while I limn her going through the odors of those cones. I'm half-
educated, but I knew her immediately for a beauty when she
walked that way beneath the brave loblollies of Bryan County, and
it cost me victory.

Dear friends, the Bryan County Fair and World Champion
Tobacco Spit is probably ground zero for the coming apocalypse—
the Bryan County Fair and World Champion Tobacco Spit *is* the
perfect spot for our civilization to come to an end. There at Salem
on those ridges and in those barrens and draws amid the kudzu
and near the mossy banks of St. John's Creek (for so it is called),
tread all the creatures of this earth. Dear bucolic bodies of the
White Race, like April, glide and drift from contest to contest
(coon on the log, field trials, and, of course, the Spit), from display to display, bowls of vegetables in great aesthetic piles (gourds
and apples, cucumbers and squash) and then on down through the
gate to the race track—the trotters—the swells and rolls of ground
beneath them being a Mediterranean for them to sail upon, those
Byzantine lateeners of my youth. Ah, Christ! and here and there
are the nigras tacking back and forth against the wrong winds of
Bryan. And here and there are Syrian merchants from Vicksburg,
Chinese merchants from Greenville, Jewish merchants from Yazoo
City, and patriotic Greek merchants from Jackson. And year after
year the pavilion fills with politicians who cry out for the preserva-
tion of the old order and the one true Anglo-Saxon race (and they
get away with it), while fat Indians hunker near the brush.

The law can forbid only that which is injurious to society; it
can order only that which is useful: give 'em hell, Robespierre—
I've seen you up high on the limb of a primeval water oak, just
beyond the grand pavilion, you with that silly Phyrgian cap on
up in the trees. But remember, good buddy, old cock, there wasn't
any way for Bryan to know that Eugene Joiner was going to grow
up and be a threat to liberty and democratic society—there was no
way in the world for the good people at the Spit to know I wasn't
ever going to be what is called useful, to them.

.   .   .

Off she padded on her thongs across the pine needles and then disappeared behind the shaggy trunk of a turpentine tree. I was done for—no World Championship for me on that day. The subtle balance of force and high seriousness had been destroyed in me, and my seconds knew it.

"Get your mind off that split-tail," says Bobo, who has got twenty bet on my final spit. And Coldstream is angry as hell to see vagueness show in my eyes at the very moment of truth.

Stream wants me to defeat this known member of the Klan—he wants a brilliant gob and quid that will strike down the reputation of this unreconstructed demon from the cuts and draws of Buster's Hollow, this heir of folk who seceded from both the Union *and* the Confederacy—and as much as I detest Stream I must admit that even back then he was wise enough to understand how awful my predicament was.

A group of relatively sensitive young men who wander around in a two-hundred-year-old oak grove and pine stand can sense many things while watching a Chinese mortician laughing his big Charlie Chan-type laughs with a Greek bootlegger who has just made a deal with a Catholic politician from the Gulf Coast. Good boys learn fast what's serious business. How the hell can I concentrate on being World Champion Spitter when the Supreme Court of the United States is up in Washington passing just laws, goddamned *justice* being the very thing that will blast the lid right off the great gazebo of the Bryan County Fair and World Champion Tobacco Spit?

I realize that some of this is piercing hindsight, but Stream and I did feel the dangers back then, and when I saw this fluid pussy marching mindlessly amid the potentialities of history, I was relieved to try and shift the action from my heart and soul right on down to my joyously crimping balls. I wanted to but couldn't.

Standing there about to make my epic spit, I knew I should try to beat the Imperial Wizard, the Chief Druid, right here in his home oak grove—I knew there were killers of all races, creeds, and colors around, and somewhere in the narrows of my veins I feared this scene would make me a killer too (and this a year before the incident with Billy W.): I feared I'd have to see those trees adorned with hanged men at some time in the future: a night in the future when the pavilion itself would be packed with bodies and be set fire to, a rich pagan sacrifice to all the gods of violence we love. I sensed how this dear fair I loved would be destroyed in the firestorms of *justice*. And this black picture is entirely natural to the place—because on the infield of the track there's a fifty-foot metal pole that trapeze artists perform on every year. They do in fact come from the four corners of the earth to whirl around on that pole. They hang by their teeth and make great circles in their glittering tights, and always there is some muscular fellow with a lady on his shoulders, and he finally stands on the red ball on the very top of the pole.

And one year the master of ceremonies, Davis Benton himself, announced that he was sorry to report that "The Supreme Morganta fell to his death in Macon, Georgia, last week and so cannot be with us." Jesus! Davis popped right on along and said that the show would however be able to go on because the Flying Swedes from Stockholm were here and ready to step in.

Out from behind the stage run a fair couple in blue tights, and up the pole they go. And I'm positive they were from Sweden, and I'm positive they had been on the Ed Sullivan Show, just as Davis said. They hung from ropes, they hung from chains and straps. By their teeth they whirled so fast they were blurs before our eyes. Lord God, it isn't gothic—you can't possibly exaggerate it—and it isn't quaint. There has somehow got to be a way to get beyond the myth and fiction of those Scandinavians rotating up there in the blinding Mississippi sun, and somehow your natty journalists with their satire can't get their minds around it either— those pearly Swedish teeth smiling down at us—because it's history, and history is not just metaphor. EVERYTHING IS HAPPENING. And the Supreme Morganta actually did fall to his death in Macon, Georgia. Apostates! Gentiles!

Now. Back to the Spit.

Royal, the young Boykin, is about to bust a gut laughing at the misery so obvious upon my face: "Spit, Son, spit. Let 'er fly. Lay it out there, Big Son. PUCKER, pucker, pucker, pucker," and all the while he's reaching up and rubbing my shoulders like a fight manager. Ass hole Boykin! Says: "The famous two-finger spit, give 'em the famous two-finger spit."

Three thousand people packed in the bleachers and packed in
against the ropes to see the Spit, and somebody is saying in an
official voice that no hacking or blowing is allowed—just the pressure and release of the long squirt. And I was pitted against old
Morgan Turner, holder of the world's record of twenty-five feet
and three inches, a record I'd tied with my first spit, a record he'd
immediately broken with *his* first spit of twenty-five feet and six
inches.

And I genuinely regret being diverted from the full grandeur
of that afternoon. I wish April had been coming *toward* the Spit,
like any normal person would have been, rather than wandering
away from it. Then we could have shared the excitement of three
thousand people watching Floyd Hamer unroll the white wrapping
paper over the boards for each contestant—which lets you observe
the distance of the drops and droplets better than if you spit in
sawdust, or real dust, or adust dust, or dirt—obscene spatters in
the loess.

The goddamned T.V. from Jackson didn't come, thus rejecting
an essence of the State's heritage, but a crew from New Orleans was
on hand, flown in by Lear. And the editor of *Folkways Magazine*
was within a few feet of me, and (I hear later) there was even one
foreign Norwegian named Bruun high in the stands, a reactionary
defender of the Old Language who'd come to see how the verities
were holding out in other parts of the world. And a year's supply
of Red Man Tobacco was first prize, along with the trophy. All
that! And yet my vision, my lovely soft-leg, wasn't having any.

I hauled back my shoulders till I thought my T-shirt would
rip in two across my chest. I threw my head back and peered up
at a high and stationary cirrus. I flung my face forward with terrible energy, and spat. Cheers—encouragement—especially from
the youths present as they spooled out the tape measure toward
where my Red Man drops had come to rest after my grim and
viscid parabola, and I had bested Turner by a good two inches. The
entire congregation was laved in a nervous sweat. Their very souls

were concentrated on the lips of the giant boy and the gnarled old man—the souls of the fans had become the very vulgar juices these adversaries launched. And what a pleasure it was for each of them to be cast through the motes and prismed light of that glorious afternoon.

Strophe: Turner, TURNER, Turner, TURNER.

Antistrophe: JOINER, Joiner, JOINER, Joiner.

And then all of it ran together.

I had done well indeed, but had she not moved away from me like whiskey smoke above that light breeze of a summer's evening, grays and blues at the pale horizon, I'd of won. A woman's feet in thongs, a woman with no panties on, can drive a good man wild inside the odors of thick resin.

And Turner's last spit was a magnificent thing to behold, for he'd gotten entirely serious.

His bitter soul was on the line. He realized that unless he beat me he wouldn't amount to a hill of beans at any courthouse or tonk in South Mississippi. Bootlegger, Free Will Baptist preacher, and once or twice, at least, an idealistic killer, a man adept at wrapping chains around a nigger's heels, a man who, one bleak story goes, had shot a Jew once in the twenties. Turner was an honest to God folk hero to some citizens of Bryan. That last spit by Turner was his agony—and I pitied him as much as a boy could who has got some lyric snatch on his mind.

Morgan rolled his quid in humorless silence for a good sixty-seven seconds, then suddenly, fast as a lizard's tongue, he zipped his head forth and back with such a quickness that it should of torn every tendon in his neck loose. From that terrible effort of will and flesh and bone and sinew, he should have been a physically maimed man at the very moment his juices rose in a high arch—and certainly by the time they fell at the incredible distance of nearly twenty-six feet.

What a spit that was!

And the crowd was stricken with a true delirium of humane howling.

That foul old man was somehow for the moment forgiven all his sins by even the most liberal Jackson professors up there in the stands. I roared and cheered right along with Stream and Moon

Pie and Bobo. Even the cruelest Bobo, bald at eighteen, felt joy
with an old killer on that day in Bryan County at the World
Champion Spit. Old Morgan made the day for all of us, all us
breathing and ripe human bodies there in the close dust of August.
Lord God, how he laughed.

*We blessed God that he hath given us time and hearts to bring
it to issue, what further he hath for us to do is yet only known to
his wisdome, to whose will and pleasure we shall willingly submit.*

With a child's delight Morgan cried out, "By God, I done done
it! I'm still the World's Champeen!"

At that the crowd cheered once more and then began to settle
itself, and as the newspapers, AP and UP from coast to coast, noted
the next morning: *There were smiles to be seen everywhere, upon
the Old Man's victory.*

And the record that he set that day still stands. It is, in fact,
honored by a goddamned shrine, and it was my defeat that helped
to build it. The citizens of Bryan County and the trustees of the
Spit have paid out good money to raise perpetual monument to the
achievement of Morgan Turner. Out at the fairgrounds, on the
dusty little plain just east of the pond there's a big pine stump with
the following words cut into it: HERE MORGAN TURNER SET THE
STILL STANDING WORLD'S TOBACCO SPIT RECORD OF TWENTY-SIX FEET
[a slight exaggeration] IN 1958. And that field and grove just east
of Hampton's Pond is not the Windy Plains of Troy, and the Gulf
of Mexico, still farther south, is not the wine-dark sea, but, given
the madnesses men celebrate, I'll take Turner's monument as equal
to any erected to honor Roland, or John Reed, or Vardaman, or
Jesse Owens, or maybe even Bill Wallick. Why the hell not?

So Bobo lost his twenty, and the Klan was vindicated for a
while, and Royal Carle had himself more proof than ever that the
human race is deeply to be feared—but I myself just shook the
winner's hand while photos were taken and the T.V. camera
ground on—I shook that gnarled hand and offered a classical and
lying Joiner smile before I trooped off into the gloom, looking for
my lady of the unchaste feet.

.   .   .

April Smith was sitting on the steps of the pavilion, and she, to even more strip my already badly meshing gears, was double-clutching on a Chesterfield cigarette. Long size. One of the dozen or so she's smoked a year since she was fifteen. And the curious thing is that every time she does it it looks quite comfortable on her. I moved right up on her, huge and quietly, and with the most reasonable sort of dignity a recent loser can muster.

Sitting there so nobly on the wooden steps, the unfiltered smoke moving up around her more or less blond head in a wreath, she was somehow even more lovely than when I'd seen her moving away at a distance. She's got this perfect posture to hold up prop-erly what is surely the most flawless flesh I ever saw and wanted into—except for maybe the line of white down above her upper lip—but that fuzz is, of course, the proudest signature of complete beauty, the necessary imperfection. Yessir—I took her from the World Champion Tobacco Spit up into The National Football League, and there'll be little surprise to me when she gets herself inside the gaudy halls of Congress in Washington, D.C., by way of Royal Carle. She wears so goddamned well it's hard to see any-thing at all that time's done to her. She is like that, while the rest of us go down to fat and ash and pure suet.

I said Howdy, and well, April, it has been a long time, and what's this about you coming into Bryan for the senior year? And how comes it you're not at the Spit part of the Fair, especially since I notice you smoke so young? She touched the tip of her tongue to her upper lip and blew smoke from both sides of her mouth, but she wasn't in the least flustered. She says that at such a hard-rolling and crazy place as this fair it seemed right that she sit and smoke her rare cigarette in peace, and when she says *rare* she puffs out one corner of her mouth and then the other: "Son, you're a lar-idge chile, how is it you didn't *win* the Spit?"

"Because the Holy Ghost set down on his shoulder that last cast he made."

"Well that is too bad, but next year you'll be the saved one," and finally she smiles that easy forceless smile I still love. She smiled at me like she was looking at a great deal of cash money she knew was hers for the reaching—which should have been my cue to get the hell out—but how does an eighteen-year-old meathead know how to fear a woman's encouragement? No way at all. And so we toddled us off to get a Snow Cone. Yeah, I felt like I'd been crowned with a golden crown. I figured, as it were, that she'd laid hands on me already and that I was about to fly on to glory on the bare back of The Great Speckled Bird. April Smith from Stone Creek Community, rediscovered old friend of the family had flown down on my broad shoulders like a pure white dove, and by the living spirit of Jimmie Rodgers I took an oath that night to make Miss April a very happy woman. In short, I was in love and still am. Goddamn her eyes.

And certainly I'm obliged to suggest clearly what it was she had. Has.

What I've said is she was lean and blond, with a good complexion, and I've said she was tough-minded.

But—and woe to him who must state the obvious—but I *haven't* said she is the lost girl in the Spun-Lo panty ads and a gatefold in the flesh.

I flounder and feel the fool; for she deserves description by an IWW Solomon. Think of one of those blonds in a Breck ad, and then let enter the slight olfactory image of outhouse lime. Once again: she is a white woman, the long strands of honey hair over the shoulders, that natural action of Scandinavian movie queens, and she also offers an Asian influence—*her nipples at eye level look like pink coolie hats seen from directly above.*

And her belly button was a marvelous go-inner, and slightly puckered. It is a little trap where one always expects to find a cleanly dingleberry, but doesn't. It's merely empty and merely clean.

Aroused she looks like the girlie on the plastic card beneath the plate glass at the auto parts store.

Love, says Mary Ann, is always *curiously* grotesque. April and I with our springy youthful strides, as we headed for refreshment, were curiously grotesque, and an hour later, as I wandered with her the dark forest and near into the creek, illuminating frond and stone with my trusty Ray-O-Vac, that, too, was curiously grotesque. And when we settled ourselves on a mossy bank to embrace

and to pledge our love to one another in the velvet and scented
darkness, *that*, in the sprung, jealous mind of Mary Ann, was
curiously, curiously *grotesque*.

No bugs dared to bite on me and my April, and not one snake
intruded as she rolled on top of me and said she craved my size and
gentleness.

Mary Ann, whose soul is blackest and most bracing coffee, sits
cross-legged on our mats, dressed in a cotton sari, scoffs down
another bennie and says (she's not bothering to study tonight):
"Sonny, it was that one bucolic night that set you on the course
to me. Ain't that grotesque enough for anybody, Fat Man?"

> *Ere the wholesome flesh decay,*
> *And the willing nerve be dumb,*
> *And the lips lack breath to say,*
> *No, my lad, I cannot come.*

But do please understand that Mary Ann is not truly a vicious or cruel person. In fact, intellectually she is my equal—
brighter than April, at the outside (if not the inside)—and Mary
will, with my help, write a brilliant thesis for those people at
T.C.U. She will make it clear that "The Honest Man Is the Essential Mythical Character in American Literature." Mary believes
the nation is dying of honesty—she says all our heroes have innocent eyeballs (which ain't Greek, baby) and thereby create an
irrelevant Ideal, since an innocent man won't ever be able to *actualize* a *possibility*. Reason, she says, is a clear vision of what is
needed to *actualize freedom*, but clarity of vision without sufficient
will to act is all dross . . . no shit . . .

Mary and me, we live at war, because she sees me as some kind
of freaking archetype and revolutionary. She sees me as a man
who must finally be a Phoenix and rise from the brutal ashes of my
Mississippi youth. She sees me moving on up the line from teaching
grammar school into Areas of Greater Responsibility. After I've
proven that grown men are best for teaching children (an essentially conservative idea), I'm supposed to finish my Ph.D. in
Radical History. I'm supposed to thin down to a skinny two-
twenty, and then I'm supposed to SEIZE POWER.

Yup. Seize power for *her*. Believe it, Mother, for that is what they goddamned well want. I'm supposed to find my Finland Station, says Mary—but what *I* want to go on about is that it must be understood how unusual that first grown day and night with April was. For whatever the history of Robert Simpson Joiner's son was to be, and however much he was to be blamed for destruction of life and property in the future—he was, my friends, that day at the Spit, neither violent nor obviously grand. If examined closely on that day, he would have proved himself to be as gentle as his father, the Inventor. He was a normal horny boy who flogged the log with the best of them. And, yes, once, before her, he'd had what is maybe called a piece of ass, which piece previous to April was in fact also a wholesome encounter, for the most part, name of Polly Roberts.

The new girl from Stone Creek Community—who'd be in Bryan for her senior year in the fall—was a wonder of competent movements and magnificent silences. She was a clean young woman who moved over the ground like a graceful skater, and she touched the night air and fondled berries with little hands whose fingernails were cut short. She raised not one rose hip of blood when finally there on the banks of St. John's Creek we clung together. We sogged there on the mossy bank that eased on down the ridge to St. John's Creek. We touched each other through our clothes at first, and she even put a quiet hand, for a moment, on the happy bone beneath my jeans—and then, with the dance music from the pavilion floating out especially for us (rather like something romantic by Hank Williams, but in a Meredith Willson setting)— we did indeed, *grotesquely*, pledge our love. Mary's a damned fool, because all the perfect blocks and tackles I've ever made, and all the tracts and speeches I've memorized, and all the profound books I've read, all are less than how love was the night I lost the Spit.

You couldn't say that what happened was any kind of big-time sex. For it wasn't more than three, four strokes. It was a night of gentlest and brief wickdipping, but, Mary, getting wet that way was jet-stream action at forty thousand. It was Clear Air Turbulence, even though in the physiological sense I didn't make it. I was in love and I was being responsible. It didn't make any difference that I might show some moss stain when we returned from trysting, but it was entirely important that the lady not be too rumpled. So with her on top, I simply folded up her dress in front, and then unbuttoned myself just enough.

"Honey Love" was being sung badly off through the growth and sweet odors, but that didn't hurt at all. Love, Love, Love, Careless and Romantic Love—and the courts of Southern France never knew such hankering as was known in Bryan County on that night. And afterwards, when we waded in the creek, I shined my flashlight down into the running water and batted her some minnows up onto the smooth stones, like a bear, April said, and then she laughed a laugh that put ole Turner's to shame. As shy as we were, and as fine as it had been there in the dark with watersounds, I was still amazed at that laugh she pumped the air with, and a little fearful that everybody up on the grounds would hear it and understand. She lifted her dress damn near up to her sweet snatch and kicked her feet in the moving water—she threw back her lovely head and laughed a round, high woman's laugh that made the weather turn around in all the states of the Lower Valley.

And now let's hear it from a man who understands how vanity so easily dissipates on the night wind: *Since it is a question of management and intrigue, it is necessary to employ those means to maintain yourself as to regain, from the depths of misery, the mean of re-ascending to your former estate. If you cultivate the arts whose success depends upon the reputation of the artist, if you turn your attention to those employments which are obtained only by favor, of what use will it be to you, when rightly disgusted with the world, you disdain the means without which you cannot hope to succeed?* Let's hear it for Emile and his friend, that lost soul Rousseau...

Royal and Stream and Bo, they never expected it, when I disappeared from their company after losing the contest—they never expected that Brute Joiner was about to wander into Eden after his defeat. That True Romance might be within the grasp of a mere lineman didn't enter their minds until we reappeared, me and

April, at the pavilion, hand in hand, to hear the governor's annual rant about the "Sovereign State of Mississippi," and about how said Sovereign State would endure against the most miserable and womanish politics of the East. ("Softness is Northern," as the poet says.) Right away, on walking back into the public light of the fair, I could see that Bobo was checking my britches for pecker tracks, and damned if Royal wasn't entertaining some signs of a lewd grin. Stream was, however, the truly stunned one, thinking, as he always has, that Eugene can't possibly score at anything worth having.

God love her, she did it right—eloquent and austere lady gestures mostly, curling her toes now and then—and every one of her blond hairs was patted into place before we walked back into the public area, and her dress was not unduly mussed.

It was a fine little scene for me and April to behold, the three of them standing there in the loose crowd below the band, which is kicking the living shit out of "Cheatin' Heart"—the lyrics being murdered by some Modene Grunch from Rankin County. April is holding my hand, my right hand in her left, and stays in close by my side, suggesting affection. But that's the least of it, the very least of it. What she most brilliantly does is to rub and pat me gently on the stomach. "How y'all doing. How you, Little Roy," and rubbing me vaguely on the tummy. It was a triumph. It tore the three of them a new one.

"An' April here will be at Bryan this fall, an' won't she be a fine cheerleader," says I, offering the beginnings of a Sally League conspiracy that the four of us studbuddies could pull off with ease. We could have rigged the election with no trouble at all by just getting out the word that we wanted the new girl to have the job.

But April wasn't having any. She squeezed down on my hand and then popped me lightly in the solar plexus: "No, Son," she says. "That's not a thing I like." (Fine! yes, modesty, the rarest virtue.) "But I'll celebrate every victory better than anybody," and she smiles up at me with loving obviously in her eyes, and on her mind. "After the game . . . I'll win the party." And that with a Clara Serena smile (Clara's and also something of Marie de Médicis'). I was put down, but not harshly, not yet.

Amore Cortese, Amour Courtoise—amour propre. And that Rankin woman up in the pavilion had finally hit the vein and was singing pretty freaking well—*You'll cry and cry and try to sleep and pray the love you threw away.* That shot-down woman, sallow skin and wore-out in the sex, almost seemed to understand a little something about the scene that was going on down on the ground below her. She wrapped us around in her song, environed us, and made of the evening all I'd ever dreamed. For April *was* chaste, virtual virgin or not. She was pure and sensible and she wouldn't let us buy her off with that cheerleader foolishness. By God, the only thing that she had on her mind was me, me and the water of the creek we'd just trudged up from, and the kudzu cut, and the rabbit warren, and the vines and weeds where no snakes were: no Eastern Diamondback, no Pigmy Rattler, no Coral snakes, no Cottonmouth, no Canebrake Rattler (4 to 6 feet)—and not one of the harmless snakes either: no Pine Snakes, no Southern Black Racer (that mythic beast), no Rough Green Snake, no Mud Snake, no Indigo Snake, no Rainbow Snake (rare, so rare), and, no there was never an Eastern Coachwhip Snake down there. April was remembering where we'd just come from.

My lips on hers were fresh within her mind.

She was remembering how I wasn't rough with my big hands. She *was* concentrating on touching me in front of our friends, and she never did give a significant damn for the raunchy music that was moving in my body (she never liked music much), or for the political speakings about to begin. Ah, Christ, she'd of rather been down at the stock stalls slapping the rump of a blue-ribbon Santa Gertrudis than be there hashing over trivialities with me and my butthole buddies. She'd of rather been alone with me somewhere where I could have proved something important to her—like why it is a cow has got a name as curious as Santa Gertrudis.

But mostly my emotions were wrong by then. I was feeling giddy and prideful—no dignity at all. My own friends were making me feel vain and shameful. How could I tell them I was simply pleased and happy and full of sudden love for this girl? It's not done. And they were giving me terrible sensations, a very athlete's foot of the soul.

I could not speak my mind to my friends, while patting my Acme boot in time with the drum. I could not say, "Friends! I just knocked off a little. A very little. And I didn't even have to ask. And she's *still* the nice girl we all think of her as . . . she doesn't go down for gum wrappers . . . Puff . . . Puff . . . I love her and I'm gonna marry her and be a father and grow up and live in a white house by the side of the road with April, April here, our long lost friend. See her. Look goddammit at this beautiful thing that's patting me."

I couldn't come out with that, and so I just itched in frustration and acted like a horse's ass. I told my friends they'd have to get another ride home, because April and I were taking *my* car. "I think me an' April'll just go on now."

I was saying that sort of childishness out loud—it was my own voice and I couldn't believe it. I sounded the fool, and they knew it: "O.K. Big Son," they said almost in unison, in mock meekness, all of them looking at April. All of them wondering how she could stand touching such a lout.

She lets me have it again. "Sonny, I can't," she says sweetly, for, of course, I'd forgotten to ask her. "I've got to go home with Daddy and Aunt Helen." She points at a couple standing not more than fifty feet away, the skinny gray woman whose hair is up in a furious bun and an equally thin man with curly white hair—Henry Smith, the tough ole foreman at the Bryan Mill.

"Come on and let's talk to the man," says Royal, and the truth was that he knew I was suffering. He saw how I was already racked up and toeing around in the dirt and sawdust, and he was trying to get me unhooked. Good R.C. was doing right by me. He was sometimes sympathetic with ignorance (including his own), which is a great trait of character. Royal helped things improve in a great hurry, for it wasn't a minute before Roy and Merle Boykin had wandered up to join the claque, and then the Taggarts and my own people. We all shook hands and hugged and chatted, and it was pretty nice to be there, because, without anything being brash or obtrusive, everyone could tell that probably April and I had been out walking together and how we were more than a little friendly. All of it was social and completely acceptable on a summer's evening at the fair. All the adults were comfortable and affectionate, and for a second I was so ridiculously happy I thought I'd start crying. It was Community and Unity of Being—it was the Agrarian myth come alive for a moment—and nobody is going to make me deny it. It was partly Bosch of the devils and terrible eggs, but it was also something of the happier Breughel—the kermess and the peasant wedding. Although even that is a good deal more morbid than how we were.

We chatted and then turned up to the pavilion to hear the speakings.

And cruel was the turn when we put our attention on the larger domain of politics, cruel but natural. (For the speakings are as much a part of the Fair and the Spit as harness racing and field trials, and acrobatics and pie judgings.) Just when Modene is getting good, the politicians move her off the stage.

With most preachers sending your soul off to torment, and with most women in the world unable to make up their minds whether they want you up or down, spotted or with purple streaks —and with other forces of nature tearing at all your holdings with fire, flood, hail, and rain—with plenty of normal built-in daily misery, you wouldn't think that people would want their leaders, their public servants, to be gouging at all the psychological demons in their bodies—you wouldn't think it, but that is exactly what happens at night as the final event of the Bryan County Fair and World Champion Tobacco Spit.

Why wouldn't I think of it? Asks Mary and her kind. People who will shake a coon twenty feet out of a tree onto the hard ground, and then wrestle it into a sack, will do anything. Twenty times the coon falls twenty feet through the branches and thuds against the ground to face a man or boy who's holding a burlap sack. The coon fights like hell. It bites clean through one fingernail, hangs, is swung around and around by the wounded contestant.

It is called "Sacking a Live Coon." Expect anything from men who'll sack a live coon.

And then there is the coon in the cage on the inner tube. That is terrible too, says allegorical mistress Mary, and the others. A coon should *not* be put in a cage as bait—caged and tied on the inner tube to be pulled across the pond ahead of the swimming hounds in an event called "Swimming Races." The beautiful blues and reds strain to get in the water, but most powerful of all is the straining of a Plott hound, a brindled creature who actually requires two grown men to hold him back until the coon on the tube is far enough out. Heat after heat they swim, baying as they struggle in the muddy water—fifty yards a race—and I for one think it's a great thing to see and hear.

> *The coon that fell from the tree survived . . .*
> *The coon in the cage survived . . .*
> *Nothing is killed at the Spit . . .*
> *Everything is short of killing . . .*
> *No it ain't, says Mary.*

There is nothing wrong with the events of the day. I swear it. But something *is* wrong with the politicians, which isn't exactly a novel insight.

Here's a family gathering of sorts, with all of us there together, our destinies shrouded in mystery, a gathering of old and new friends happily munching on hot dogs and hamburgers, a lot of genuinely pleasant social intercourse set in motion by everybody involved, and then we have to listen to a stupid man who's running for Land Commissioner tell us he'll fight Communists with his whole heart and soul because our state has got more reds than roaches. And niggerlovers: Why it seems the entire region is flooded with niggerlovers whose only intention is to get a nekked black buck in bed (patriotic Land Commissioners alliterate a lot) with every pure blond Saxon woman in America.

Now if I'd told Mr. Smith I'd made love to his daughter, he'd of killed me more for speaking of it in public than for doing it in private. But he'll stand there and listen to the vilest filth come spewing out of a politician's mouth without doing anything more than blink his bucolic eyelids. Hell, truth is it gets the old bastard's juices running, and April's Aunt Helen is so turned on by Dalton "Slick" Fletcher I think she's going to spasm before he puts us at ease, saying there's no such bad men in this race for Land Commissioner—it's just he can fight Communists better than anybody, being an ex-F.B.I. agent and a Marine Veteran. At which time he yanks up his trousers to show us how he's got a false foot on, which foot was of course lost while fighting in a distant, far-off land where there are damned few patriotic Land Commissioners. "Slick" finally is helped away amid mild, sympathetic applause. Note that I say *mild*, not *wild*, for therein lies part of the tale.

He stirs them inside, but no longer do they demonstrate their passions outwardly very much, and he also of late has gotten the reputation of a bad drunk. They say, yessir, you're right, and yeah, yeah, under their breath—but there isn't any yelling and stamping and screaming the way it used to be.

But that speech did put a stain on the beginning of my love for April. I was shocked to see her father and aunt so involved with Fletcher. I could see it in their eyes. I could see their lips moving. In spite of their other virtues they were easily seduced by rant and rhetoric. But they were the only ones who were so moved. For the other adults were not rich ground for those seeds of bitterness, cruelty, and violence.

As I've said, my own shy father never indulged in the worst forms of prejudice. My daddy is what you might call strong against killing. He is foursquare against trace chains being wrapped around a nigger's ankles before he's dropped in the river. He has taught me all my life never to be tolerant of anybody who will stand up in public and go into great detail about how some Mexican scientist claims to have mated a nigger woman to an ape with the result being a female creature named Julia Pastrana. Daddy taught me not to trust people who'd dress up that Julia in a brocade dress and have her picture taken for the Anthropological Institute in London. Ole Slick had gone into all that stuff about Julia a couple of years before, when he was running and losing for the first time.

Yes, sir, since the Korean War Momma says Fletcher has been

"off" (and he never was, she says, in the F.B.I.), and she says she'd rather I married some kind of ape and Pastrana than any daughter a Fletcher might have. The most extreme public racism is definitely out of date in Bryan, except for a killing now and then.

I mean a lot of people may believe that the frontal lobes in the brain of a high-browed White are developed to a greater extent than in the Negro Race, and they probably do believe that the Negro ear is smaller in proportion than the White ear, with tips that turn in like those of a rabbits and horses, but it's strictly out of date to talk about it in *public*, and it is very, very crude to make a verselike chant out of it the way "Slick" used to do.

People in Bryan are getting to be exactly like the Yankees I met in the cities around The League. Damn right.

It's more or less O.K. to sit out in the back yard with the rotating yard sprinkler popping away off down the greensward—O.K. to sit there chewing up the onion you just fished out of your Gibson—it's damn near proper then and there to get a little serious discourse going about how the auditory canal just *might* be straighter in a Negro's ear, which probably *does* account, in some degree, for the Negro being unable to appreciate the melody of White Music—all that—but do not publish it in the streets or in any type of public speaking.

Better days are here.

Nobody much would really be comfortable with Dalton's famous lecture of the early fifties, the one he punctuated by pounding on the boards with his wooden foot. No longer would the citizens of Bryan belly laugh at his Barnum's gorilla act—Slick stomping around the stage while he yelled much like the preacher Morris: *The Nigger's Arm IS long compared to his leg/ the Nigger's forearm is larger in comparison with a White Man's/ his thigh IS shorter in proportion to his lower leg/ and/ and/ and/ the Nigger's hands and feet are larger narrower in proportion to white hands and feet/ and/ Dear Friends/ the Great Bone of the Negro heel IS larger and projects BACKWARDS . . . godhelpus . . . God help your sons and beautiful little daughters—a-mong APES (and monkeys) the heel bone projects in that very manner . . .*

.   .   .

In Bryan where the races have suffered together for a long time it's no longer right to be too public about anything quite so specific.

Even Slick knew it was out of date to carry on like that, but just for a moment, on the evening I first loved April, and not entirely consistent with all his talk about Communists, Slick did break off and tell us how the Great White Race is responsible for the Civilizations we have today, under the blessing of the Lord Jesus Christ. Slick did break off and clomp and then begin to cry as he said the White Race is being destroyed, and White Women with it . . .

It was sad and especially sad when Sheriff Benton had to go onto the podium and comfort Slick, and help the poor fellow back to his chair, which duty was revolting in the extreme to Benton, though he never let it show.

Other speakers, including the governor, came and went in the same vein, and the recollection of it hurts my mind—but it especially unmans me to think about that gathering because of what was to happen within the next eighteen months: Bobo off to the Asian wars, and Roy and Merle Boykin dead in the same auto accident that scarred and maimed, outside and in, that good man Henry Smith, and my own Momma and Daddy gone to Memphis because of what I did to Billy.

No, sir, Royal took nothing away from me that night, and him the one who did suspect the true nature of what had gone on between me and April. Royal loved and loves me. And cruel Bobo wanders off into the crowd—he's looking for a cock fight maybe— and Stream cuts out with a lipstickless and nondancing religious girl, name of Edna Motor, going, I'm sure, to argue the relative merits of pre- and postmillennialism. (Edna was a slight young woman whose nipples were reputed to extend out a full inch from the pink meat of her titties, and who finally, to make screwing sacrosanct, married a Baptist preacher from Chattanooga—and later on there'll be more about this same Taggart, who I wish I had killed that time I caught him in the cold room of the icehouse.)

.   .   .

And now with Royal engaging the mortal elders in easy conversation about how this year's Spit was the best ever, I take April up into the pavilion to dance, the speakings being over. And she's no Julia Pastrana with a beard and hairy arms. April's got on no Mexican brocade—just absorbent Delta cotton. She's a young girl who's light on her feet in any man's arms, but especially within the arms of a large man like me.

"Be good to me, Sonny. Be good to me an' I'll love you forever. I will." And she would have. If I had been.

"How come? How come you'll do all that?" asks I, who's being a little of the hardroller to make her love me more. "How come, white woman?"

"Because you're the biggest thing I ever saw, and because you've had me." Dance, dance, dance.

"You call that having?"

"Sonny!" she squeaks it, she pulls up close.

April kicked her thongs over under a bench and moved like gossamer along the surface of the linoleum.

> *It's the cause, it is the cause, my soul.*
> *Let me not name it to you, you chaste stars!*

And chaste she was, and delicate, and chaste she is. . .
Royal, you dumb turkey, she will always be chaste no matter how much you peck at it.

> *It is the cause. Yet I'll not shed her blood,*
> *Nor scar that whiter skin of hers than snow*
> *And smooth as monumental alabaster.*

Royal, she never means to do harm. In fact, she never means to do a thing to anybody else. She's doing it *to* herself. Come black frost or smokestack lightning, come supernova and apocalypse, April is doing it to her own self. Royal, she is a terrible woman.

3

IT's JULY. School's out. More time to bitch and eat—and Royal
Carle, he'll get along anywhere. Dear Diary and massive auto-
biography, he's what you hear called a promising young man, the
kind that says with Marlborough: *I am now at an age when I find
no heat in my blood that gives me temptation to expose myself to
vanity; but as I would deserve and keep the kindness of this army,
I must let them see that when I expose them, I would not exempt
myself.*

At least that's what Royal'd say if he had a memory like mine.
How the hell he got through law school I don't know, because I'm
the one who has the total recall—Eugene of Savoy to his right and
Lord Cutts on his left, hot damn, and seven miles from Tapeheim
to Höchstadt, at the battle of Blenheim—Christ!—to murder fifteen thousand he'd never bat an eye to lose twelve thousand of his
own. Sunnavabitch drives his main force right in between the
French and Bavarians. He scooped them out, horsemen battering
some of them down into the ground, all those handsome uniforms
reduced to gore. He drove thousands of those pitiful souls right
into the Blue Danube River. Royal Carle'd have made the Grand
Monarch miserable on *that* day. The Sun King got put down by
the cruel Englishman. That brute who's quick and forceful on his
tiny feet. Quick, quick, though slow, Jesus, slow as a clubfooted
crusader on a forced march along the salty tip of the Dead Sea.

Quick's not fast, and fast is certainly not quick.

My God, the glory of men moving in well-protected columns:
*March always in the order in which you encamp, or purpose to
encamp, or fight.* It would be beautiful to be marching under the
leadership of Marlborough or Eugene or Cutts, or, best of all,

moving toward Fleurus under that Faustian, hunchbacked poisoner named Luxembourg. Christalmighty, what a leader—at sixty-two he's able to sit on his horse an entire day and night if that's what's necessary to bring his genius for murder to fruition. Foul-smelling and crippled—in fact, a dead man had it not been for a few friends in court, and because, baby, he never lost a battle, that little military pimple launched a frontal attack against the Prince of Waldeck at Fleurus. Luxembourg smashed the Prince with cavalry swinging to the left into the woods, and then, with himself all plumed and jaunty as a mere knot of human muscle can be, he attacked on the right, and it worked. And for that kind of genius Louis told him to get back in line with the rest of the generals. Quick, quick, quick, and it was the Luxembourgs of The NFL that destroyed me . . .

Vauban says: *Thus our attacks reach their end by the shortest, the most reasonable, and the least bloody methods that can be used.* Which attitude is finally the cruelest imaginable, or at least the least satisfactory to the human spirit. Mary storms out of here this morning because I'm brooding and scratching away here at my cypress table—says Joiner will never learn gentleness of mind—says the man's memory is all raw meat.

Sobeit.

Piss on her. I never claimed to be no goddamned vegetarian. Let the field be strewn with bloody jocks, let the jerseys be shredded, let arms, legs, and all manner of viscera be a-droop from every bush, tree, and shrub (even azaleas, camellias, and magnolias)— that has finally got to be better than a defeat suffered in a lace war. Give me the battle of Malplaquet any day.

Ah, what a way to spend an afternoon. I've got a case of Busch and a quart of Dant and I'm studying Montross's *War Through the Ages*—and the little woman has left the house. She's never been able to grasp my vocation. Boilermakers!

Now here's some great writing: *Still, France had one son who could strut and boast. Marshal Villars, a Gascon by birth, shared the miserable rations of his soldiers and bragged so loudly that the whole kingdom heard. His quips and vaunts were repeated every-*

where by haggard countrymen who alternately laughed, wept and believed.

Shit fire and save matches! That's just the way it was with me and my niggers—that's ezakly how it was when I was getting them set to fight the real killers—me and ole Slater Jackson getting them armed and proud and ready to resist the fires and bombs, and the rifle fire in the night. Let's hear it for Medgar Evers.

Never, in truth, since Joan of Arc had Frenchmen given their trust so devoutly as to this greathearted Falstaff. Genuine volunteers joined the ranks, and it was not altogether a gesture when the Grand Monarch himself offered to serve if the need arose.

Louis stripped the palace of jewels and gold to raise funds. He taxed the nobles and debased the currency.

FINE FINE

And *Meanwhile he kept up a modern propaganda campaign with circulars explaining his rejected peace offers; and angry country folk armed themselves with forks and flails as the allied tide swept on toward Paris.*

Lille had fallen that winter, despite the heroic resistance of the aged Marshal Boufflers. During his whole career Marlborough did not incur a failure in siegecraft, and Tournay capitulated in the spring after a costly attack, which is more than can be said for our assault on the Bryan County Courthouse, for we were, for all reconnoitering and superior firepower, finally beaten off.

But on: *The victors moved on Mons in August . . .*

Moved on Mons—moved on Mons, moved . . . on . . . Mons . . . in August: excellent style.

But this time Villars was willing even if not prepared to fight. With an army of 90,000 including a large proportion of raw and ill-equipped recruits, he stood squarely in the path of the 100,000 allies led by Marlborough and Eugene. There were two taut days of hesitation, then the final test came in the greatest struggle ever waged so far by armies of the modern world.

The Battle of Malplaquet—

． ． ．

On this decisive day Villars' generalship proved worthy of his own high estimate [of himself]. *Far from being beguiled by the containing attack on his right, he managed without weakening the other wing to involve Eugene's troops in grave difficulties. The French fought like demons, recruits as well as veterans, hurling back the Dutch infantry time after time with fearful slaughter.*

Marlborough launched his main attack against resistance such as he had never met before. In the crisis Villars took personal command of men who sold every trench and palisade at a terrible cost.

Nota: *When the valiant braggart suffered a bad wound, he continued to command from a chair until falling over insensible. Next, Eugene was wounded in the head, and Marlborough nearly collapsed in the saddle from exhaustion*—which is strictly tough tiddy about them generals, ain't it?

But, *By this time the bloody affair had turned into a "soldiers' battle" in which the opposing lines surged back and forth with more fury than direction. After seven hours of fighting the allied centre, until then but little engaged, advanced across the open with serious losses to push back the weary defenders. Old Marshal Boufflers, who had succeeded to the French command, wisely decided to withdraw in good order.*

The allies laid claim to a victory on the usual grounds of possessing the field, but all the other benefits of Malplaquet went to the French. Their losses were 10,000, while no less than 24,000 Dutch, Austrians, English and Prussians lay dead or wounded after a battle that was not matched in bloodshed until the year 1812.

At first the slaughter seemed barren of results. It did not even save Mons, which the duke took before going into winter quarters. But as time went on, the far-reaching effects justified Villars' boast to the king, "If it please God to give your majesty's enemies another such victory, they are ruined." And, in fact Marlborough was disgraced, cast down, toppled from the pinnacle.

Yes, give me the battle of Malplaquet any day. Let Royal move his squares of neat troops around the field in unromantic ritual.

Hell, he's no Marlborough *or* Villars, he's a mere Berwick, which is pretty goddamned great.

Royal's slick as owl shit, but he won't fool everybody, because Henry Smith, who was my father-in-law, doesn't like him. Henry, who's foreman of the Bryan Mill, is not about to take any foolishness, especially from Royal, who's like a bad son to him. Henry spots a field rat from a thousand feet up. He's a fracking hawk the likes of which Hopkins never imagined—he's a blue darter.

April writes me a long letter two weeks before the one with the goddamned wedding news and says she's had one helluva big time because her daddy, Henry, has damn near shot the balls off of Royal Carle Boykin, and would have except that M.P. moved in fast between the Luzianne coffee and the Picayunes and talked him out of it. My, my, it must have been a great satisfaction to her when Henry got down the Three-in-One Oil and cleaned his twelve gauge. She could tell there was conflict in the wind, and she must have gone into every corner of the house with the old toothbrush she uses for close work against dirt, especially when important company is coming.

The Kirby vacuum cleaner must of set up a terrible roar as she drove it from room to room sucking all the dirt from the floor and all the body ash out of each and every mattress. Certainly those rugs and beds were finally clean and frayed from the vigorous care she set on them, and not a ring to be seen in any tub or stool. For the King with the Ax, she got very, very tidy. I'm positive she scrubbed down sweet Aubrey and washed her own blond hairs and waited joyously for Royal to come into town to take his chances against Henry.

Back in the days when I first loved on her she wouldn't have reacted with such pleasure to the prospect of violence, but over the years she has developed something of a taste for watching men go at it. But that's probably not quite right either—because even at the beginning there's a look she got in her eyes when boys got in an argument or a tonk fight, the kind of look a child gets at the zoo when you know he's thinking that those tigers and lions are a helluva lot more interesting than people. She never cared much for the Spit, but if her horse did well in a harness race she'd pound your shoulders black and blue as the creature went flying across the finish line.

"Royal Carle graces a place" is what April used to say long before she ever thought about shifting from me to him, and you've got to give him credit because he's not just relying on madras jackets and dull ties, even though he does wear Florsheims and Big Macs for his high arches. She said he was elegant without being showy and that he'd be a success wherever he wanted to. New York or Philadelphia or Dallas or anywhere. You couldn't say he was in the class with players like Hinkle and Herber and John Blood—but you got to agree he's got this presence about him. (Call it fear.)

He sets up across the street from the competition the way you're supposed to. He gets out in front of the store and waves at everybody from the ladder where he's just finished putting up the Day-Glo streamers, and then he climbs down, all the time still giving the V-sign to his wonderful friends and neighbors who simply can't wait to start throwing good money into his cash box. He's waving from inside the sparkling Windex-clean window now, as he puts up very imaginative displays—especially the mechanical device that bounces Ping-Pong balls on a stream of air. And later on he'll be ordering a genuine water fountain with colored lights that play on it at night. He stays open late. He steals the people right off your lot. By God, you'd still be asking the man who owns one if that little sunnavabitch had been selling Packard cars.

He could sell old-fashioned wringer-type washers to ladies who could afford an entire home laundry. He'd tell those ladies they wouldn't want to take all the excitement out of their lives— he tells those women there's something wrong with a person who won't take a chance on their nigger maid's hand getting caught in the wringer—and believe me when I say that not one of those pale ladies with the flaccid tummy pooches will ever notice for a minute that Royal's boots are full of Dutch blood.

But I'm not bitter.

It was all my fault anyway, even him taking Aubrey, because I never gave my chap the attention he needs. That boy of mine and April's needs somebody to punch him on the arm and grin at him, somebody to frog him and be funny, not a mean-eyed ape like me. He needs somebody who'll teach him how to shoot birds right, the right shot and gauge and gun for a frosty Delta morning. Only thing *I* point is my goddamned finger. Up until my revolution (and then it was too late), I couldn't concentrate on either April *or* Aubrey enough, but focused Royal Carle will.

Moon Pie'll do things on schedule. He's a Khan Timur the Lame. He's a builder and planner like the great Vespasian. He's paid the price and now he turns his hand to re-creating order: *Ravishing was mixed up with slaughter, and slaughter followed upon outrage. Old men and women, well stricken in years and of no value for plunder, were maltreated by way of sport. Grown-up maidens and comely youths that came in the way were violently torn to pieces by ravishers, who ended by falling in murderous conflict with each other. Men carrying off for themselves money or offerings or solid gold from the temples, were hewn down by other strangers than themselves.* Or so said Tacitus.

Royal's ready to settle in now, Pax Romana and all that good stuff, buildings, roads, and plenty of bone-breaking labor for the poor to earn their money under, while R.C. goes home on Monday night and reads *The Three Bears* to Aubrey. And Tuesday there'll be *Little Black Sambo*. Aubrey'll know how to interpret the Constitution strictly by the time he's five—he'll understand the necessity for a good relationship between princeps and Senate, and he'll be writing essays on the Federalist papers by the time he's nine—eleven, he'll know the ins and outs of functional finance and how it is there aren't any canons of fiscal propriety anymore. Royal and Aubrey, they'll snuggle up on a handsomely constructed oak bed in a fine boy-type room, with little historical model airplanes, Lancasters and Corsairs and 38's dripping from the ceiling on strings, and boats too—whole goddamned fleets (*Mauretania, Monitor,* and *Dreadnought*) set neatly on the top of the bookshelves. Snug as a bug in a rug, father and son, discussing Crosland's *Future of Socialism.*

Royal will get him a big house with low ceilings in Jackson, never realizing that within a few years his son will be so tall the lack of total volume will begin to create claustrophobia in the lad. Royal has got the frenetic mind of a short man.

And Henry won't finally ever like Royal. The best the old man can do is accept the fact that Royal's on the scene.

Bless her heart, Miss April *is* civilized—she keeps in touch just like I was her brother in the Foreign Legion. Up until the wedding letter, she writes me about once a month (which'll now no doubt begin to peter out), and I'd have to be some kind of monster to want Henry to have won that argument, especially when it's clear how good Boykin'll be for Aubrey.

II

Dear Sonny,

It would certainly break your heart in a way to have seen Daddy so upset the last couple of weeks, but thank the good Lord for small favors because now it seems O.K. and I'm positive it is somehow the results of the burns and that terrible grief he stills has over the death of the Boykins. Which was part of the pain that came with that evening at the Fair. It actually wasn't eighteen months later the Boykins and Henry were taking a drive after night church, and crashed. It killed Royal's people and burned Henry completely about the head and the upper body, leaving him a grotesque creature if you ever saw one. He's purple and glossy. He has no eyelashes or brows, and it's a miracle he's not stone blind. The Jackson doctors did their best, but still the grafts pull down the corners of his mouth and show his broken teeth, and hold his chin tucked in like a man who's commanded to stand at strict attention. Two of that little crowd who stood there listening to Slick go down on the Commies were dead before two more fairs had come and gone. Which is the sort of curious vision of mortality that hurts a young man. *It is like all the romance went out of his life when Roy and Merle were gone, you know, and I guess that woman in New Orleans is the only thing that's kept him going.* Which woman craves him as man and subject for her pictures—says she means to capture the texture of his skin before he dies/she dies. *But remember how the doctor did tell us that such burns are often never got over.*

I mean it's like he's two people. The New Orleans Daddy that you say is so happy in both the art part and the life part, and the Daddy we all love so much. Except that Daddy is entirely intolerant and getting much worse when he's not in New Orleans. I guess it has got to be kind of Liberal with him down there since he does live with a painter (you say) and keeps on getting himself painted and sold in the streets.

In New Orleans he's tolerant enough I guess, but home he's got almost crazy over the subjects of politics and religion in the wrong way.

Sonny, you just wouldn't believe the way his room looks these days, the room I had built on especially for him. He's too ill to stay at his house, though he doesn't believe it. Such a clutter of foolish things compared to how neat and clean he used to be. He put up a full size American Flag on one wall, and a Confederate one on another, and the Bonnie Blue Flag on the other. And, Sonny, he uses those flags for places to stick on pictures and stuff. I told him that putting a picture of Jesus on the Bonnie Blue Flag wasn't evil, but I also said it wasn't at all in the best interest of true historical patriotism either. It's fine, it's fine, he says, and stares at me with those watery blue eyes that just destroy my control over myself. And Sonny! he has got this horrible, horrible picture of Julia Pastrana over the stars of the American Flag. I can't even let Aubrey get near the room. Because the one time he did get in there and saw that poor, pitiful Julia, he asked Daddy if he could have a doll like that. It would be funny except that Daddy spanked him so hard and then told me that Aubrey was already a homosexual before he drove off in a towering rage to New Orleans. It's terrible to face my daddy who's almost naked in his shorts, him screaming at my child, and Aubrey crying because all he asked for was a play-pretty, even though it was a Julia.

Sonny, without you here it had gotten to be a very dark and lonely time for me. He is always down the hall with the radio on full blast to some patriotic program or another from Texas or Oklahoma. God I hate the politics. Or if not that he's playing that hillbilly music I hate so much on the radio or his old victrola—those terrible scratchy Jimmie Rodgers records being the worst especially with the yodels. And that Picayune smoke boiling out under the door and stinking up the whole house I work so hard to keep clean and fresh for us. And all the time this trouble is going on she's thinking that maybe she'll go see Benton and talk him into letting me return, because she's positive I'll come if given half a chance, and then she decides I'm probably not punished enough yet—and though Daddy is crazy as hell he won't hurt her physically, and Sonny might, again. She concentrates on washing windows and sucking up lint and dirts and cobwebs and body ash with her trusty vacuum—*Sonny, with nothing but hate mail and tracts pouring into our house, I hope you can understand why I finally wrote Royal up in Jackson and asked him down for a visit. For old time's sake.*

I mean it got to be so ridiculous that Daddy went out and actually found himself an auction in Bay Springs and bought one of those cigar-store Indians and carried it right on down the hall into his room and then he sticks a tract he got from Oklahoma City called the "Last American" on the goddamned Indian's forehead. And then he turns up "Kaw-Liga" so loud on the victrola that I have to take Aubrey outside in the yard. You never did ever believe how much I hated that goddamned Hank Williams. Pardon my French. But even so I can see a little of the good side of things. Because Coldstream would be right if he said that Daddy was to a significant extent getting poetic in his old age. But if that's poems I don't need any. Just look how much you loved football and history, and what happened to you? Well I won't go into that because I realize how much I was to blame.

But understand how hard it is on me to be alone and to know it's over with us—and it is! God knows I wouldn't want you to come back in spite of all my caring.

I called Royal because I thought it might soothe Daddy down [a lie!] *but let me tell you for a fact that I've never been so wrong about anything.* And she'd done exactly what was best for her, and she knew it. *It's like I cleaned out a rotten tooth with an ice pick for him. All I did was mention the name of Royal Carle after I'd called him unbeknownst to Daddy, and he went off like a goddamned burlap bag full of cherry bombs, as you'd say.*

I never did realize how much he holds a grudge and then adds to it. Which is another outright stupid thing to say, for she knows her old man is full of bitterness and guilt and love for his old friend Roy Boykin and that poor Royal managed to earn the privilege of being the scapegoat for all that pain. April never cared much for sentimental Roy and Merle Boykin—which makes it impossible for her to understand her daddy. April's insight is sometimes limited.

Royal's father, who wasn't his natural father, was a pretty good mechanic at the Mill if you gave him extra time to fiddle his own way, but mostly he was dreamy and sick with legends and vague religious feelings—Roy Boykin was a talker, a pathologically garrulous man who collected lore and planned for twenty years to write a history of the county. But he wasn't weak. Nevah! For the simple reason he didn't collect romantic lies. He delighted in the fact that Bryan County (in those days called Hamilton County) had the highest desertion rate from the Confederate Army—and he thoroughly enjoyed telling how the Indians of our region (the Catahoulas) were among the most enervated and brutal in the South, a tribe that destroyed itself for all intents and purposes by sacrificing its children when the chief's mud hut was struck by lightning (worse than the Natchez).

And Roy Boykin loved women. Over late coffee and fig preserves he'd regale my mother and Mrs. Taggart and Aunt Helen with stories of our frontier women. And he loved especially the one about a certain Mrs. Dwight, who, when the British revolt against the Spaniards became paralyzed, decided that flight was the only solution—*flight through a vast wilderness, occupied by savages, to the British posts in Georgia and Carolina. A more precipitate and distressing exodus never occurred. Leaving their homes which they had made comfortable by severe toil, their property which had been accumulated by patient industry; with no transportation but a few pack-horses, with no luggage but their blankets and some scanty stores, they gathered their wives and children, and struck into the wilderness. Fearful of pursuit, fearful of ambush, dogged by famine, tortured by thirst, exposed to every vicissitude of weather, weakened by disease, more than decimated by death, the women and children dying every day, this terrible journey makes the darkest page of our record!*

Blabber, gossip, and half-assed anthropologist that he was, Roy Boykin still had the great good sense to read and memorize the most remarkable historian that ever lived, the lordly J. F. H. Claiborne: *But the courage and perseverance they evinced, the uncomplaining patience and fortitude of refined and delicate women, at that period of suffering and peril, shed a glow of sunshine over the story, and their descendants, still numerous in Mississippi, will read it with mingled pity and admiration.*

Roy striding the kitchen and chanting, and the amazing thing was how my father and Henry enjoyed it as much as the women. (We had some excellent talk fests on Sunday nights during my senior year in high school, those nights before the murders and fires.)

The women and the men did love sterile Roy Boykin as he strode and cried out that *among the fugitives were the Lymans, Dwights, and many of the most cultured families of Massachusetts. The supplies they brought with them were soon consumed, and then they lived on roots, herbs, and whatever they could gather in their flight. Some of the Indians they fell in with seized their pack-horses; others, more humane, would divide with them their meat and corn. Having broken the only compass in their possession, they traveled by the sun and stars. They crossed the numerous rivers on their route on rude rafts bound together with vines. When they got to Bayou Pierre it was very high, with a fierce current, and to cross it on a frail raft was too hazardous. They tried various expedients and failed, and at last the most of the men threw themselves on the ground and declared they might as well die there, unless Providence opened a way to cross over.*

And Providence thy name is woman.

One man only insisted that, on the opposite shore, in all prob-

ability, Indian boats were secreted, and that if one or more would join him they would attempt to swim their pack-horses and make a search. No one seconded the proposal, until Mrs. Dwight said that she would venture. Her husband raised by her intrepidity, declared that he would make the trip, but his wife insisted on accompanying them, and all three plunged into the river.

They were swept down by the violence of the current, and were given up for lost; but providentially they struck a reef where the water was shallow, and finally reached the shore. After a long search they found an old Indian pirogue full of cracks and seams, which they caulked by tearing up a portion of their ragged garments, and then, constantly bailing, the travelers contrived to get over three at a time. And Roy was delighted to portray, by way of gesture and intonation, how liberal of spirit was this delicate lady, this immigrant, our early mother, who could go virtually naked before her men, when the chips were down.

Henry loved those stories, and Henry thought Roy's son had rejected those stories—and Henry's ignorance of Royal got April a shot at a second Husband.

"Pitiful sentimental hicks!" said Mary.

At one point on the journey—when, owing to cloudy weather, they had not been able to regulate their course, and had wandered out of their way into the prairies, they had been thirty-six hours without water. The pangs of hunger were hard to bear, but their thirst became intolerable. On the morning of the second day, perceiving no sign, they halted, leaving Mrs. Dwight and two others in the camp, and scattered in different directions in search of water. Late in the afternoon, one at a time, these parties came in, broken down with fatigue unsuccessful and despairing to press forward, to remain or to retrace their footsteps, either seemed inevitable death. THE HEROIC WOMAN, who had led the way across the swollen river, now staggered to her feet and said, "Christians never despair.

*I will proceed onward in the search and not stop as long as my limbs
will support me." Followed by two men and two women, in the
course of an hour, when they were nearly exhausted, she paused at
a spot where the grass was luxuriant and the soil spongy. "Here,"
said she, "we must find water or die." By digging a few feet, with
their hands and sharp bits of wood, the water slowly oozed up, and
thus a second time the whole company was saved by the faith and
fortitude of one feeble woman, at length, naked* [literally, the
record suggests], *and emaciated from sickness and famine, the few
survivors reached Savannah. Doctor Dwight and his wife returned
to Northampton, Mass. He was afterwards lost on a voyage to Nova
Scotia, and the heroic woman who had resisted suffering and inspired the despairing succumbed to the blow. Such is the nature of
those we love best. Enduring physical ills, reverses of fortune, pri-
vation and danger with more than the patience and fortitude of
men, but fading and sinking under the slightest wound of their
affections and their faith.*

That's what it's all about—it's about the Dwights, their physical
stamina and moral probity, and that fantastic walk from Natchez
to Charleston, the spiders, mosquitoes, flies, and snakes—and also
it's about Claiborne being strong enough to write the long history
that would finally fix in Roy Boykin's emotions with the power of
myth. April's trap for Royal was wired by her father's love for
Roy's gift in articulating such true legends. Dumb Henry loved
and vaguely respected Roy, and he couldn't understand why Roy's
son wasn't the same breed except he wasn't Roy's by blood.

Royal'd lived with Henry at his place (with Henry, not April
and Helen) the summer after the accident, but he hadn't visited his
parents' grave that entire summer, and he had gotten boozed up one
night to the point he told Henry he was leaving the county and
never coming back because he didn't feel at home anymore—and
anyway, says Royal, "I'm an *adopted* child. I'm not really the son
of *those people* and I don't want to be a son of *this place.*"

That's it. That's all. His folks were killed the fall of his freshman
year, and by the next summer, his summer with Henry, he wanted

free from Bryan and all the deaths—Billy's, his parents'—all of
which is natural enough. It's simple as mud in your coffee cup.
Royal was no more than a frightened boy, a goddamned sophomore
at Tulane with his first varsity season coming up, who blew his
tender top the least bit—with the result that Henry misunderstood
and decided to murder the ungrateful little fucker years later.
It's the cruelest and clearest logic you can imagine.

*Daddy comes home in the afternoon when Aubrey and I are
planting flowers in the front yard, out on the terrace by the highway, and he tells me he didn't care what I'd done with Royal that
summer (which, as you know, was nothing to speak of). He says
that, and then he says that if Royal comes to Bryan it'll probably
lead to death. Royal's!* And she's got the gall to act surprised at her
daddy. She'd seen him sucking down the coffee and the cigarettes,
in excess. And she'd heard the gospel radio broadcasts coming from
Del Rio, in the middle of the night. She knew damn well that when
he went to chicory coffee by the hour in the nights, and started
smoking too many Picayunes, like Aubrey wolfing down jelly
beans, there was something wrong. And she knew what the wrong
was. Crazy Henry was jacked up and he was having some fine
conversations with his Indian, ole Kaw-Liga. Man, it was dooms,
conclusions, and despairs about the gospel and the wrath of God—
he was putting an edge on his mind. He was making up his mind
that something was serious—and that's a handsome thing to see in
a man these days—something important and serious enough from
time to time to keep a man from sleep and alcohol and women. It
takes character to sustain a proper hatred.

A man needs to burn like that sometimes, and I'm not talking
about anxiety, because anxiety's not true fire. It's a confusion looking for an idea or some excuse, and Henry already had a clear idea
of what he meant to do, and Henry doesn't make excuses. His vision
was sharp to him, like a hot pin for a boil, or a welding torch, and
precious and hard as a diamond engagement ring. Henry was aiming himself in the direction of Royal, and you can be sure that April
knew it, desired it, desiring to sit above the game again, a goddess
who controls all bets, she thinks. Henry's eyes were so cold they
could freeze Wild Turkey or Neat Jack—and that did frighten her

with recollections of the belt he sometimes used to use on her—but, still, in a way, it was a pretty thing.

Last month when Henry rediscovered his hate for Royal was similar to the time he went for his old friend Warren Ray at the Mill one morning. It was similar, but his desire was stronger against Royal.

Warren was having a big time with telling the story around the Mill: Henry Smith was keeping some woman, some whorish woman, in New Orleans. And Warren was embellishing the rumor in grand style, telling people that this woman is the kind who knows how to use razor blades and whips and cigarette butts for obscene and beautiful purposes—she's a nigger-and-frenchy type who prefers to be screwed between her big titties, says Warren. And it was some kind of discouraging pettiness and spite in Warren because he's not usually the kind who gossips much. Poor Warren was probably no more than jealous of the good times he figured Henry was having in the French Quarter, which is natural enough—and it was also natural enough for Henry to go after Warren with an old peavey one morning before the first whistle blew, and just when the nigras were wandering into the mill yard. It was when Warren was opening the kiln to get the freshly dried lumber out and ready for the dry chain that would feed those boards to Henry's saws. He went after Warren with that old rusty peavey, a weapon reminiscent of crusades and plagues and ritual dead marches, and chased him out from that terrifically hot and sweet-smelling kiln—chased him away from those ricks and around the acre of sheet metal mill into the lumberyard out front. He ran yelling and waving his incredible instrument until he captured Warren in the dusty corner of an empty bin, Warren crying and sweating for his life. Henry might not have meant to actually kill Warren, but he sure sent him to Hellfire before he set him free from the dust and chips.

"God damn you, Warren, you talk too much. God damn you for lying about a good woman." He set up a roar you could hear clear over to Nancy's Cafe two blocks over. He dropped his peavey and picked up a Lebus binder and a length of chain, and armed in both hands now, brandishing both chain and binder, he howled execrations down at cowering Warren. Oh Christ, Mary, how I love that old fucker. Henry in his starched Levis and his Big Mac shoes, and his frayed, starched white shirt he always soiled in half a day, Henry stopping Rumor must have been a prime sight to behold. He could never stand a merely fast and easy talker of any kind, especially when somebody's putting down a friend or a member of the family, and Warren and Daddy had worked together at Chalmers' Mill for twenty years. "Warn, if you got to know what it is down there, you come and see next time—but keep on talking about what you don't know about, I'll hurt you."

He told Warren that if he talked about his friends that way again he'd get hooked and sliced and set out to barbecue. And by that time the mill yard was filled with the nigras and Mr. Chalmers and my daddy, and everybody was laughing to beat the band, and the second whistle was blowing to start the day for good and all. The nigras loved it and Daddy and Mr. Chalmers didn't care because they knew that Henry had his reasons. The reasons you go to New Orleans are personal. Everybody knows that.

And Warren never again made up stories about a Cajun woman who was teasing Henry's rectum with a feather. After that particular morning Warren hoped to avoid all visions of Henry creeping across the mill yard in his brogans, pike and halberd in hand. Warren was satisfied that Henry was entirely serious in his defense of the New Orleans woman.

April knew the man was like that. My God, she'd been in the very room when Henry blew the shit out of the T.V. set the first time Sammy Davis Jr. was on the Ed Sullivan show, which is the most famous story they tell on Henry. Henry simply went back to the closet and got his twelve-gauge Parker and cut down on that black like it was the only reasonable thing to do. And it didn't even surprise her. She says she simply got out the dustpan and broom and went to work. She even had the wit to take the pieces down to the repair shop the next day, where the wreckage was on display in the window for more than a year. She knew they couldn't fix it, but she wanted them to see it; and the story got around so fast they didn't even need a sign to explain. People'd stare through the glass and say, "My, my," and "Man! Henry Smith really does hate niggers."

Sonny, I was so frightened I didn't know what to do. I was thinking that maybe I was going to have poor Royal's blood on my hands, but I've got to confess there was a sort of crazy meanness and desperation in the letter I wrote to him in Jackson—something like, "Dear Royal, we'd sure love to have you down and I'll cook some ham with plenty of redeye gravy. We'll have a wonderful time, but I do think you ought to know that Daddy has been talking about killing you."

That was the second letter I wrote to him and the one he responded to. How 'bout that, Sonny. He didn't answer the first letter I wrote to him, but when I came down hard with a true threat, he came right on home.

Sonny, I'm terrible because that letter I wrote to him gave me more pleasure than you can imagine, and he did write right back, on a piece of official note paper from his law firm: "I understand, and I'll be down Saturday night for that fine meal you suggest. Affectionately, Royal."

Sonny, I've been so lonely and it really is wonderful the way that things are working out, and I could hardly keep my mind on Aubrey for being so excited about Royal's coming. And yes, she is driven to tell me the whole damned scene, or at least the part of it she understands, and it chills my fat blood, baby, because she did know the boy was in deep irrational trouble with ole Henry. She knew the ole bugger is scrambled as hell and that she really might have to clear more mess out of the kitchen than just the dirty dishes or a blasted T.V. set if Royal hadn't been on top of his wits. Gray matter in the fatback, by God. *Sonny, Royal was late—he didn't make it in time for supper, which did hurt my feelings a little and it surely did upset Daddy even more. He called about four-thirty and said that he had a meeting he couldn't miss under any circumstances, and Sonny, he didn't even mention Daddy. I thought that was cool of him. I told Daddy I'd talked to Royal on the phone—and Daddy said I should of told Royal to bring his shotgun so they could do a*

*little hunting on Sunday. Oh, God, that was scary! Daddy as you
know never hunts on Sundays, and the humor of his voice was cold
enough to bite your fingers off. But oh my, I did feel relief that the
murder wouldn't happen in the living room or kitchen, or anywhere near to where Aubrey was. Dearest, sweetest Son, our lives
are terrible and out of shape sometimes. I got to thinking about you
gone off to Texas for acting foolish and about my own crazy
Daddy. I stood at the sink and I said shit this ain't no good.* And to
say such a thing she has got to be very, very sad indeed. She rejected her own husband in jail without hardly a tear, but finally she
discovers the miseries—took a long time but finally she got there.
She stood at the sink and saw nothing but acres of hot, green time
beyond the window, acres and acres of fleshy grass and weeds
going on forever and ever.

*Oh Sonny, Sonny, but when Royal finally did come, he was
ready. He was slick and smart and a sight to see. Royal Carle Boykin had on work clothes! Khaki slacks and a denim shirt cut off
short-sleeved with some pinking shears he borrowed from a Jackson secretary. He'd obviously bleached out the shirt just before he
came. He'd surely had to use the automatic dryer at the coin
laundry at his apartment in Jackson to make himself look more like
mere folks. He sort of strutted into the room. But it wasn't exactly a
strut either. He came in looking terrible and benevolent as a
preacher—and he was walking curiously because he was feeling
obviously rather boneless in the legs, as you'd say. He wasn't any
S.O.P.-type Jackson lawyer, and he said right away he hated to
miss a fine meal but that he'd steel himself until tomorrow when
he'd appreciate it even more, and almost immediately he added,
looking straight at Daddy, that he was also sorry he was too late to
make a visit to the cemetery. He made it clear that the idea was to
pay respects to his parents. Royal looked at Daddy very apolo-
getically—but not like "I'm sorry I brought that up." It was more
to say, "Godalmighty Henry, I'm sorry everything has gone so
wrong between us." He even mentioned that he was sorry to have
missed Daddy on his visit a year ago—when he'd been in town for
your troubles and all.* Poor goddamned Royal had read the situation
right—he knew it was the graves of his parents and the fact that
Henry had this simple-minded vision of him walking around up in

Jackson in a white suit and a new Panama hat, being the big man, and probably sipping all the neat Jack he wanted at the New Capitol Club in the evening. He knew that Henry believes there are certain things that bind people together with hoops of steel, certain ties that can't be violated without killing the soul, and that when the soul is dead it is maybe best to get rid of the body too. Henry had those ties with legend-haunted Roy Boykin and his sweet wife Merle—living and dead—and he had them with Royal Carle, for better or for worse. Roy and Merle Boykin, lying in their graves and burned to a crisp—that was what was getting to be Henry's clear idea and the reason he wanted Royal dead, and somehow or another Royal knew it wasn't all pig shit and madness. Royal'd made it a point to run into Henry a time or two in the Quarter. He'd even met the woman Maria—and he knew that Henry was, for all his pleasure in that seedy demimonde, a man eaten up with feelings of guilt. Henry knew damn well that gentle Roy wouldn't ever have understood how his friend could let himself be a *model,* and he certainly must have had bad dreams of shame where Merle would turn from him in disgust.

"Henry knows best," says Mary. Mary cherishes my one original Maria Santillo—a small picture in which Henry is depicted as a fireman. It's a very realistic interpretation, with all the detail of an old Texaco ad, except that Henry's browless, lashless, and silky, scarred face is done in the same red as the hat. All red, except for the clearest and wisest blue eyes you ever saw. "Henry knows best, because he hates the past," says naked Mary, Blake-lover, standing before the painting. "He's Bryan's one true revolutionary. He hates the Boykins and you because you don't know how to live."

My God, it does take patience to live with women, especially when they're so firm and wrong at the same time.

. . .

*Sonny, it was something to see the way they shook hands at
the door like the dearest old friends and Royal asking Daddy about
himself and everybody at the Mill before you could say Jack Robinson—then he excused himself and went right on back to our bedroom to see Aubrey for the first time in a year, asking me how we
were doing, and saying it was too damn bad about you, Sonny, and
did the little fellow know how to handle a peavey and throw a pass
yet. All that with Daddy left out in the kitchen and suddenly I was
deeply afraid that Daddy was going to kill Royal. Seeing Royal so
close at hand and spanking clean the way he was, it really drove the
fear home again. Sonny, you couldn't imagine a sweeter boy than
Royal Boykin was when finally he got to our house, and you could
see that Daddy wasn't clearly lined up on Royal right away, which
offered at least a little hope.*

*That is, I didn't know if Daddy knew which way the night was
going until I saw him go back to start the coffee, and then he came
out just when we're closing the door to Aubrey's room and asked
me to whip up some nice fresh coffee cake, and by that time he was
grinning like a possum eating grapes and you know how ugly he is
while smiling with his face muscles all screwed up.*

*Anyway, Daddy had Royal set down in the kitchen as soon as
we came up from Aubrey's room. And there they were, Royal
lighting up a Camel and scrubbing his hands through his curly red
hair—he had himself slouched down in the straight-back chair same
as Daddy. Royal was trying to smoke that cigarette, but the finger
and thumb grip made it plain enough how unnatural it was. But he
never choked.* The kitchen is the only room that's not loud and
tasteless.

*Then for a minute Daddy let a stillness fall over him. He was
quiet as Christ on trial.*

*Sonny, I was so proud and scared and happy I thought I'd pee
down my leg.*

And she was no doubt in the same state while writing this brave
epistle—with the added excitement of wondering how I'd react to

it all. And she'd be unhappy to know that on first reading I reacted with wonderful disinterest. I never figured the bastard would actually marry her.

And I won't believe it until it happens.

Sweet April was exercised—hell, I wouldn't be surprised if she took up novel writing, which is an acceptable vocation for a lady back home.

Royal puffs away for a while. He was niggerlipping and looking at me mixing up that cake, but it wasn't many puffs and looks before he wheeled back to Daddy and yelled, "PRAISE GOD—Henry!— Praise God, to be back in Bryan!" I nearly spilled the pan of batter, and Daddy jerked straight up like he was stung. "Henry, you look fine—FINE, and I'm so glad to hear the Mill's going so well." Royal trickled smoke out through his nose like a dragon. "And April, you're still the Queen of the County—and right here in this good house is that fine little man down the hall for all of us to love and cherish. Nothing changes and nothing's the same. It's amazing. Why, jus' do look at you, Miss April. Very nice." And then he reaches over toward the stove and slaps me on the bee-hind, and he was smiling the broadest smile and showing the whitest teeth—not a stain to be seen anywhere. Royal was working it right on out. He was checking out all the emotions.

"Sweet Bryan and her pines!" he cries, and then he loudly hums a few bars of "In the Pines," in a Josh White sort of rhythm and voice. And then a sad look comes over his freckled face, his face falling and his now cool eyes staring strictly into Daddy's. "If only my own folks could be here now—right here—with Momma bitching at you, Henry. Her telling you for the thousandth time how you ought to get married again, and Daddy raising hell about how he doesn't want the Mill to start any damned Osmose treating plant to add to his worries. That would just about do it, wouldn't it?"

But Daddy wasn't changing his expression which had gone to stony once he got sat down and listening.

"Let me tell you," Royal hustled on, "in Jackson they think they've got something going with all their new buildings and a little industry coming in—but if you see it straight, it's just a dull town with a lot of rich bastards trying to get richer." Royal looked

real pleased with that, like he was absolutely positive he'd hit some profound chord in Daddy's soul. But of course he hadn't. In fact, Royal was saying some pretty silly things all the way down the line—and that getup he had on was looking more and more ridiculous, especially since his hair wasn't cut right, too short, and no sideburns at all—he was wrong about everything here and there, but under it all you could tell he wasn't finally a truly silly man. Daddy could see it too. Daddy was up against it good, but still he fired back. The scene was very acanthocladous, as you like to say, Son.

"Industry is money, and people need money," Daddy said, easing Royal back the best he could.

"Right, Right, Rayut."

"You got damned rayut I'm right," Daddy, conversationally, was on Royal like white on rice. "An' if it's so bad up there then why you working there? Must be something you want, something to keep your little ass up there so long before you come down."

"Hell, Henry I've only been there a month—and last year on vacation I did come down for Son's troubles."

"An' that don't count." *Daddy's skinned head was looking more and more ilke a big blue bullet stuck up between his shoulders. Son it was tight with ole Royal almost sinking like my angel cake does when I don't pray over it enough.*

"You're right, Henry, and I ought to be shot for not coming sooner—but you've got to admit I've got a real knack for doing the wrong thing at the wrong time—like any young man. And I'm sorry for it. Real sorry." *He squinted up his eyes as best he could and sucked on his cigarette with a contrite look.* "I've got a lot to learn." *Sonny, that was when he really began to pour it on. He put his head down on the table and pressed both hands to the back of his neck, and when he looked back up there were real tears in his green eyes. It wasn't a real Jordan, but still there was a drop or two at the sides of both.* "I've got a lot to learn," *he says again—*"And about practicing up in Jackson instead of here at home—well, that's another thing. That's the price I'll have to pay. It's the way I'm learning what's gone wrong—who's robbing whom and where the money's going. That's the one good thing I've done for all of us!"

Daddy says, "Oh shit. Sheeit. Royal Carle, you don't fool me none, you're a slick little bastard, but you don't fool me, no more than Bilbo did. You a goddamned Communist!"

I was falling in love with both of them for what they were doing to each other, and I swear to God at that point I almost wished I could have seen them fight each other with knives or something so I could have loved them right to death.

Daddy was still leaning across with his face shining and his proud flesh tight—and Royal rocked in his straight chair, working to maintain his small control.

Royal said, "Now I figured you'd feel that way. I knew it. Damn right. I knew it—and I don't blame you one minute. Hell no, but you'll have to hear me out."

"You're a goddamned niggerlover an' a Communist who don't believe in God, that is what. But I'm listening. I'll listen for a little while." Which, of course, was incorrect, because of all our crowd it's Eugene who is the only true and bona fide niggerlover. I'm the only one who never had to fight loving niggers, the way the others did. If they treat me as equals, I dig niggers. Bobo hates them, and Royal and Stream don't know whether to shit or go blind over the matter, but I have *always* dug niggers.

Methodism, if you fall in with the liberal preachers, will help to develop an inclination toward niggerloving. But mostly it was my crazy parents—they taught me that niggers was people, just like us, and created by the same God. Daddy and Momma both believed that the colored peoples had run into a string of bad luck. (And the only other man I knew who also shared that opinion was the Sheriff.) I asked my daddy once about the niggers and he says, "They are down on luck, but that'll turn around before long." My daddy is a smart man. He knows more than *Time* magazine. Bullish R. S. Joiner figures he's a pilgrim and a stranger. So does my mother. They paid a dollar an hour, in secret, to our Ollen, our maid who came in one day a week, but I am *not* the way I am because she let me look up her dress. It's really not quite that simple.

But I wish to hell she hadn't! It would be so much easier to deal with Mary if she had not. Delicate and hairy Mary with her existential itch and Freudian sebaceous cysts on her back says my Leftish tendencies are founded on no more than all those afternoons

I lay as a child on my back on the linoleum, long Ollen, with her red panties on, stepping over me.

Not so. It is much more than that. Much, much more, though Ollen was rare indeed, something else, a lean and coal-black nigger girl who showed me, after I discovered it was O.K., legal, accepted, appropriate to hug her when she came through the screen door, things I only had dreamed before. My daddy at the Mill, and Momma gone to the Jitney Jungle, I'd, logically, sprawl on the kitchen floor at twelve years of age and re-lax, just spread there, and she'd cruise the room while scrubbing the stove and cleaning the refrigerator—she'd hike up her checkered cotton print, she'd prance— PRANCE—she understood that nigger stride and word. It was wonderful, full of wonder, and once she, a clean girl, set the whole thing down on my bare tummy for just a moment, before she rose and danced away into the hall.

These days and times it takes a lot of proof to prove that Ollen was not the single fecundating matrix of my liberalism.

HA!

But had it not been for family and church, all that remarkable synesthesia there on the floor would have revolted me—it would have made me a Super Bircher and a Klansman had it not been for those other influences.

Ollen, surely in exile now, gone to Chicago, please come home and prove to other boys that the mysterious side of life is not always terrible.

This is a hard part: what I mean is that the way Ollen was was mysterious, but it wasn't quite ugly or taunting, and the story of it isn't offered as some kind of rite of passage. Long tall Ollen, who put her bush down on my bellybutton, probably did cut a few new grooves in my brain, and certainly the telling of what she did is just a little cloying and/or unsavory, but I must protest that the influence of her pirouettes and leaps and splits was essentially salutary. She worked hard for Momma that one day a week, for a year or so, and then she quit (and I don't know why), just faded away into the quarters the way they did back then.

I was, from the beginning, and still am a niggerlover. Me and my spade buddy Slater Jackson have tried to get our minds around the word. Slater says it's simple as people liking different things unless they're taught not to, which includes different skin colors and different builds and features—all that good stuff about *natural curiosity* your liberal types make so much of—but none of those ideas finally wash, none of it explains why Royal and Stream, both raised about the same as me, have always been so nervous about the race problem.

"They lack your *sensuality*," says Mary, lovingly. Using that word and deep image to her. And I'd like to accept whatever it means, but I'm afraid the problem still remains unsolved. Those guys are just as *sensual* as I am. *Niggerlover* means something that *sensual* doesn't—*Daddy was feeling in high spirits now, and every-thing was coming to a head, the core was pooching up against the top of the boil. You could tell it. Daddy was a happy man.*

And Royal had himself under control again, his voice rising in those smooth bell-like tones I admire so much. "That Communist business is simply false and I'm not here to pull your leg in any way." Which part about the leg was a plain protective lie. "*I'm here to make amends for something I only vaguely understand.*"

Both men had all the gears and wheels moving, and Daddy's head was glowing like one of those semi-human machines in a science fiction movie.

"*Royal Carle Boykin, I asked you down here to kill. I meant to kill you hunting in an accident.*"

Plain, strong, handsome talk from my Daddy. You could see the directness in it, the honesty and old-time masculine strength. It put even more of the spirit into Royal. His eyes popped wide open—he flung his arms up in the air, and then he leaned back and he laughed and he laughed up from his heels. It was the joy, joy, joy from deep in his heart, and it was great to see him enjoying every breath of it. It was an attitude that damn near routed Daddy. And, Son, you shouldn't have wanted to destroy the town, but you did have strength while trying.

"That is wonderful," Royal cried out. "I mean it. It's the most wonderful thing I've heard in years. It's what the Yankees never understand." *And he pounded his little fist on the table, pounding both hands at once with sweat pouring out all over him, and knock-ing the cups from their saucers and sloshing the coffee all over.* "Here you are hating my guts more and more all these years—and *you 'would' kill me. Goddamn right! Because of what I said about my folks and then leaving like I did. And now you've got me. You knew you'd get me sooner or later, and, man, was I scared. Man, you scare the hell out of me."* Royal was in the main vein. He was living and dead, rising and falling. He was crap and gold, the golden entrails of a porcupine, and the Kingdom of God was coming in.

"You a Christian?" Daddy blurted.

"Hell yes. I'm a Methodist and a Democrat."

Daddy clamped his hands down on Royal's shoulders—his poor old scarred hands without any fingernails. And he started yelling this time for sure. Yelling and rising and leaning into Royal's screwed up face: "YOU HATE ME and you hate your dead MOMMA and your dead DADDY—and you hate GOD."

"I don't do it. I don't do it." Royal was actually pouting. He was pouting and talking just the way a child does. But Daddy wasn't listening the way he'd promised. He was straight up and he was getting shriller and shriller. "You hate us ALL." Then what was saddest. "You GOT to hate us. You GOT ... TO ... HATE." Then Daddy sat down again and put his face down into the warm, sticky coffee. He choked and he sputtered. "Goddamn you. God-damn you for taking my hate away." And then he fell back in his chair, shaking his head back and forth, looking like he does when he comes in from work on a hot day. Daddy was all done in and gone down, but he was peaceful. Sonny, he was a peaceful man, and Royal's face was almost the color of Daddy's, and he was biting his lips and rubbing his eyes, and his face was full of love. And then the boy with eyes like stars, and teeth like pearls, and hair like coils of golden wire, he crawls up from his lair (his warren?), he surfaces and explodes, revealing his inmost self, like one of those fishes with stalky eyes from the deepest depths—that boy attempts to emerge from the very Marianas Trench of his soul. He really can't make out Henry. He really can't finally comprehend how ole April, barelegged and barefooted there in the kitchen (stunned with apprehension over her batter), wants him to wed. Royal Carle is most understandably not suffering *ataraxia à outrance:* "Henry, *I'm learning to hate again. But if you got to kill me, go get your gun and do it—because I've got nowhere to go if you want me gone that much. I mean it, Henry. You just think about it. I came back to the*

state to practice and to think about politics. And just how the hell am I going to make it if my father's best friend—the man who in the heart's most essential blood is my next of kin—goes around telling people I'm a Communist and all." Sonny, it was beautiful the way he said it.

And Daddy again is dealt a serious blow. He says, "I never did say nothing to nobody but April here." And that was the truth, as you know, because Daddy's not about to do any talking out of church. It perked Royal up right away—he figured it might be worth his trouble after all to go on talking for his life and vocation.

"I mean if I can't get your respect back, I'll sure never have a chance with the other people in this state. You got to try to trust me. You got to," and Royal's almost begging—he's up to his feet and moving from my stove to the window and sink like he's pleading in front of a Hind's County jury.

"You tell me why I got to trust anything about you, Royal Carle," Daddy said softly. He's tired too much to continue thinking of murder. "I may not be able to kill your ass, but you tell me why I got to trust a man who comes in here in them fakey work clothes and new shoes, and shows he'd say damn near anything to save his puny life."

"If it's going to be this way I wish you'd gotten me out hunting. I wish you'd shot me before I knew anything about all this hatred in the family. That wouldn't be any worse than this shit. I do wish to hell you'd gotten away with it." Royal bends over the sink and turns on the tap so he can suck some water out, his mouth being dry and also so he can gain a moment's time. He splashes handfuls over his weary face and then stares at his reflection in the window. And it comes to me that none of this is necessary and how Royal is definitely being put upon and suddenly I was furious at Daddy for being such an old damned fool.

I said, "Daddy, you've said enough and there's no good reason why Royal has to put up with all this carrying on." I say, "He's come down here to see me as much as you." My intent being light sex and humor. But I'm obviously out of order, because Daddy doesn't even modify his expression, and Royal gives a fast hand wave in my direction, which is an obvious sign that he's got more to deliver. He says, "I've got one last story to tell," and, Sonny,

you know how bad Royal is at stories. "One story—then do what
you please with me.

"*It was just this spring, before I came back to Jackson. I was
in New York City just messing around and thinking about where
to go, and going to plays and museums, and I was thinking in terms
of Cleveland or Denver—when one night ole Stream calls me at my
hotel in the wee hours. We'd been writing and in a mild way he'd
been encouraging me to come home. But it wasn't having any effect.
Well, Stream is selling his text books in the Jackson area and he calls
in the middle of the night to read me an obituary!*" And it surely
must have been a much better tale when Stream told it, because
whatever Stream's not, he is a good man with a story, being so
sentimental. Lord God, the pit of juicy despair Stream must of
been in the night he was compelled to call Royal. Has himself a
hard day trying to move his anthologies with the professors, passes
out three, four fifths, and gets not one adoption, poor booger—
starts reading the rancid *Evening News,* and finds Mrs. Walls.

Stream's not exactly a failure even though he did have himself a
Woodrow Wilson and a Danforth when he got to Vanderbilt,
after Southern and Millsaps, to work on his M.A., and then had to
give it up after a semester of straight Incompletes.

Having been raised by a Methodist preacher, he is the one
among us modern enough to have the classical identity crisis, the
only one. He's making it as a bookseller even though his style is
somewhat unorthodox. He's doing well by doing such things as
fainting in a professor's office.

He's a passional man. Every goddamned human he meets is a
potential *Belle Dame Sans Merci*—he sweats the fucking program
instant to instant. Stream *believes* in books, whole books, tables of
contents, bibliographies, pages noting errata—and once, on a bad
day, he entered the office of my dear teacher, Mr. Burger, at
Southern. What a meeting of minds! Stream believed he was in the
office of an English professor, when, in fact, he was in the office of
a history professor, Mr. Burger, A.B.D., V.U. He, Stream, had
decided on the hard sell—the hard soft sell—the soft hard sell—he
stepped into Burger's cubicle, the door open, and questioned,
"Have you thought about *In Memoriam A. H. H.* lately?" and then,
not waiting for an answer began to recite:

> *"A time to sicken and to swoon,*
> *When Science reaches forth her arms*
> *To feel from world to world, and charms*
> *Her secret from the latest moon?"*
>
> *Behold, ye speak an idle thing.*
> *Ye never knew the sacred dust:*
> *I do but sing because I must*
> *And pipe but as the linnets sing.*
>
> *And one is glad; her note is gay,*
> *For now her little ones have ranged;*
> *And one is sad; her note is changed,*
> *Because her brood is stolen away.*

Stream's version is that he was seized by an access of pity. Seeing that tiny room lined with scholarly periodicals (he didn't notice their titles) and what looked to be many worn first editions, and noting the fellow had on the most anachronistic sort of white ribbed socks, he figured this angular and brooding fellow might appreciate a little Tennyson. What he didn't calculate was his own reaction to his own recitation.

He felt himself becoming flushed as he toiled into the second stanza, pausing dramatically at each end-stopped line, and, as he rolled his eyes up to the fluorescent lamp, he realized the light was frantic and various, a tight gyre that included the entire spectrum, but he was completely surprised to realize that he was fainting as he said, "Her brood is stolen away."

Which he did. He did faint. He folded down in the position of Eastern meditation at the very knees of Professor Burger, head to floor, and had this event taken place early in Burger's career at Southern he'd have been distraught, but this was during his last week, and five years in Hattiesburg had taught him to forsake surprise of almost every kind.

"Rise up," he admonished, in balanced concern and humor. Then, "Get up, friend, I'm not even in literature." And Stream rose, did get up, but not merely because the faint was ever so slightly an act, but rather because his head had cleared somewhat.

. . .

What a curious meeting.

My worst friend Stream and my great teacher Burger met under the aegis of good Alfred—and they went on to enjoy dinner together, and talk of me. And Stream regretted he'd never studied with Burger during his (Stream's) two years at Southern. They talked about Nashville. They got drunk, crying out against the barbarian Mississippians—which caused, within twenty-four hours, the guilt and shame that forced Stream to call Royal. Hell Yes! Stream finds himself in Jackson a day later, fails to sell books at the very college he graduated from, and is seized by a profound fit of chauvinism. He even forgets to buy himself a bar of Ivory large enough to carve on with his pen knife back at the motel. Stream carves soap to ease his mind.

"It's the obituary of this woman—a Mrs. Lula Walls, same as in the old song—who died at Gomar, out from Corinth. I didn't know her, Henry, and Coldstream didn't know her, but he called me all that way from Jackson to New York to read me about Mrs. Walls, who'd lived to be ninety years old and left us ten children and thirty-two grandchildren and sixteen great-grandchildren. She's buried at the cemetery at Gomar, Henry—and she lived at Gomar all her life. She never had an extra man in Memphis or Nashville or Tupelo. Ole Coldstream read it out and says 'How 'bout that, Boykin—Lula Walls finally lost her beauty and her tempting ways, for Christ's sake. Gets you in your Jesus, don't it? That agrivatin' woman Lula Walls is dead!'

"And Stream wasn't being disrespectful, if you can imagine it, Henry, my friend. He was calling because he loved Lula, and he made even evil me see that woman with her flat old breasts and all those children and children's children. I can imagine her being photographed in her casket, in the 19th century way, the box held at a comfortable angle by her sons, and all the others in the family are gathered around outside that tiny, clapboard Primitive Baptist church. Ah, God, Henry—and they all had to stand so still so long, still as Lula, for a good take, which has caused 19th century faces to seem sterner than they really were in real life. Having to hold still so long to have their picture taken made them all seem

mean. And one child remains a blur off to the corner. He is moving and playing in a blur forever. I could see her leading the children of Israel out of captivity. I saw her at Mount Zion—and I saw her leaping as a young girl in her spiritual body out of the grave at the Second Coming. Mrs. Lula Walls, for the love of God, Henry— Lula Walls who spread her legs for love or lust a thousand times in the past—but maybe for not that at all, maybe just because it was her responsibility to give a man his pleasure. I could see how all the children of the earth should be standing at her gravesite and some- how praying for her benediction—because Lula, who is in the ground now, must not be lost from the memory of man. She's got to be remembered by ME, and by YOU, Henry, and by April here. Lula in her plain gray dress and with her hair pulled back in a strict cruel bun, Lula with her papery skin falling away to reveal all the bones of her mortality, she must be remembered—as 'my' people must be remembered. Goddammit, Henry, you say what you want to, but it wasn't silly that I felt like bawling in that sterile hotel room in New York City when Coldstream put the screws to me. It was a feeling a lot like I'm feeling tonight. Stream says, 'Royal Carle, you can't practice in Cleveland, Ohio, because it doesn't exist—think about it—nobody in their right mind could believe that Cleveland, Ohio, is a real place—and if it does exist, if there's any proof at all that Cleveland, Ohio, locates itself actually some- where on this continent, it amounts to the fact that Cleveland is where the ladies come from who tell you which wash is whiter on T.V. Come home to Lula!' cries Stream."

Now, this is Sonny reciting, now—*I take pleasure in seeing an army general, at the foot of a breach that he means to attack pres- ently, lending himself wholly and freely to his dinner and his con- versation, among his friends; and Brutus, with heaven and earth conspiring against him and Roman liberty, stealing some hour of night from his rounds to read and annotate Polybius with complete assurance. It is for little souls, buried under the weight of business, to be unable to detach themselves cleanly from it, or to leave it and pick it up again. I order my soul to look upon both pain and pleasure with a gaze equally self-controlled.*

Ain't that fine. Let's hear it for Montaigne.

And Royal'd love to be just that sort of people.

"*Stream said, 'Royal, if you don't come home, I hope you die in the cradle in Los Angeles. I hope you die in the cradle on some polyethylene bitch, and when you die I hope they burn you to ashes and put you in a pink plastic bottle, and put you on display at a blue bar in San Diego.' Stream put a curse on me, and I feared it. I do fear it.*"

"*That's a good story,*" *Daddy says,* "*and I come near to believing it, but . . .*"

"*'But' is right,*" *says Royal, interrupting.* "*Now you listen to me, Henry.*" *And Royal has stopped walking about the room.* "*I know the other side of it too. I meant, by my story, to point up how it is, in a lot of ways, easier for me in Mississippi, if I don't get my ass shot off. I know the place, and I can get things done. Shit yes! Politics maybe. In plenty of ways I can make it easier here than anywhere—but that doesn't make my love and grief and honest sentiment any less real. Henry, I'm back for good and you can do what you want to with me.*"

Sonny, I think I understood my Daddy best of all right then (including the wreck and the scars and my own sweet, insane mother), because the truth is he had to take what Royal was saying, and Royal's rhetoric, as you say, was bound to work—including all that foolishness about Lula. He sounded just like that damn fool Roy.

He had to accept the truth that was in it, and he couldn't kill Royal. Royal was after all Roy and Merle's son and in some true way Royal'd proved he did love his people. For a little while Daddy was hearing old Roy's voice again—some goddamn story about the yellow fever wiping out New Orleans in the days of French rule— it was the same wild spinning of tales that had been Daddy's solace for so long. He had to take Royal's word almost as much as he'd always taken Roy's, and that was going to keep him from killing Royal Carle Boykin. But I could also see how nice it had been for Daddy while he was planning the murder. The idea murdering had made sense out of everything in the world he wasn't understanding, and I knew that Maria down in New Orleans had her work cut out for her, because I wasn't ever going to be able to help him again. Royal was breaking him. Royal was destroying my own father. God love Daddy. Putting Royal out there in the cemetery next to his people with Dallas Ewell watching over them all would have been such an easy way.

   Sonny, don't think it's too strange that I'm trying to write this out like a story, although I know I'm doing it badly, and without the real sense of how it all meant to me. But it is important to me that you know, for those documents that got us legally divorced were really just so much paper, and you know how important it is to me you don't have to put out any money—though I do appreciate the toys you've sent to Aubrey, and so does he. It's a curious thing, because the way things are now I manage to feel the family is closer together than ever before, and not entirely sundered, and that's why I can spend the best part of a busy Monday trying to tell what happened.

   I really don't know what the future holds, but I do know it won't do for you and me, or Royal, for that matter, to make up a future in our minds that's not tied to the past. Right?

   I agree with any reasonable person that says it was crazy of Daddy to collect photos of all the presidents before Franklin Roosevelt, and to paste them up on the flags in his room with Julia. For certain it is true that Thomas Jefferson never had it so bad.

   Julia Pastrana probably never did exist. It's probably just a made-up picture—made up by hateful people like Daddy and Foots Magee. They added the beard and hair to the picture, or maybe it's just a picture of some poor deformed Negro child whose parents weren't apes at all, and who should have been helped by The March of Dimes—but if you look at the life Daddy's had to lead it's not hard to understand how he gets fooled by all kind of fake things. He didn't choose to be himself any more than we did. And you got to admit he's been patient with you and me. And why? Simply because he knows that love is hard work and usually a mess that nobody in the world can accurately predict. He's the one person who didn't get upset when you killed Billy and Foots.

   And you don't like Aunt Helen, and that's not hard to understand, but you do know very well that if she hadn't been around I'd of never been raised at all.

   And, Sonny, don't be so goddamned stupid about practical mat-

*ters like the human soul, because it's obvious as the big nose on your
face that Helen has been in love with Daddy all her life, and especially since Momma died, when she naturally got it in her mind
that she herself should rightfully be the one to take her incompetent sister's place—and then to have Daddy go and let her do
everything for us without ever thinking for the first time of marrying her.*

*Daddy may have him a good time in New Orleans, but it's really
not very hard to see why Helen has been so grieved about it. And
you know it!*

And that's just like a woman: she's telling a firsthand story
about a man who has saved his life by way of Odysseuslike cunning,
but the thing that finally dominates her head is a goddamned
woman scorned, scored, a thing that happened when she wasn't any
more than an ignorant wee tad.

And like she's got to explain all that to me! Like I don't know
the hell her old man had to come through before he fell into the
scented lap of Maria. And the truth is I've got a fair share of
sympathy for that bitch, Helen. She has desired me jailed, hanged,
and de-balled a couple of times, but I'm capable of understanding
her reasons. I got magnanimity.

Yes, sir . . .

Less than a year after April was born, her mother went to bed,
or to be accurate, she began the long process of going to bed per-
manently, her last and most comfortable grave being a fairly expensive casket that got slipped into a hermetic Clark Grave Vault,
a wondrous expense for Henry in those days and times. It all happened long before I knew April, but from all the times she talked
about it I learned how much her mother's failing has to do with
the way she is. April heard Helen tell of that woman's weaknesses
so often she decided to be an entirely different kind of person, not
at all like her mother. All of which has got to do with how it came
to pass that Henry was so close to the Boykins, and why he feels
the way he does about Royal (or *did* feel), and why I feel the way

I do about all these goddamned people. They are worthy—as Mary, my present lover, is worthy—but Mary can't see it.

The only brand of legend and myth that's got skin on it for Mary is some kind of contemporary bullshit about her father not being able to get beyond Full Colonel because he's in the bag so much, which drunkenness is the result of many ultra-modern-type affairs and the Catholic piety of his constant wife. Which legitimate pain I'm not about to condescend to. Never. And sending her to that fucking convent school, where they tell you to shower and bathe without looking at or touching your tinklepotty, is surely bad news. It's a worthy story. But she, for all her *Cahiers de doléances*, has got no right to put poor Maylene down as simply a moron. Mary, Mary, Mary, lover, you prowl the tangle of my considerable belly hair, and you pleasure yourself and your *belle chose* upon my Elizabethan prick, so why pick on my past, and the past of my past, the way you do? The world itself is an old and good sweet thing. It's worthy and worthy of your consideration and affection.

Maylene Smith, mother of my first wife, she was a study of pure reason, if reason, as Hegel suggests, is proper adaptation to perceived reality. But if Plato had had his way (and surely Plato is the devil in all the myths)—if Plato had had his way about the State, the world would of never have had to put up with Southerners (neither Negroes nor Whites), Jews, Mongolians, and, generally speaking, we wouldn't have had to put up with most of the squalor of human history as we've known it—no Machiavellis, no Montaignes, no Cromwells, no Maylenes.

You can imagine Plato's revulsion at Maylene Smith, mother of April, wife to Henry. Pale, pale, with a Buster Brown haircut suggesting a profound admiration of all things depilatory, she married Henry because he seemed the nearest thing to a flayed body she'd ever met, and that was even before he got burned, years before, of course.

But then she found out that Henry's flesh was, in spite of all he could do to arrest it, entirely alive and capable of swelling and distending. Maylene Smith found that the world made some pretty incredible demands on a slight young hairless woman (in the late thirties) who had somehow grown to maturity with the idea that her breasts were only to feed babies (maybe) with.

April and Aunt Helen believe in that interpretation of Maylene, but I don't. For having never known her at all, I'm sure of my position on the matter: Objects, Objects, Objects, Objects, Objects. It was objects that put her in bed, and finally in her grave, objects and the way the light falls upon them.

I certainly do tire of the way that Stream, Professor Burger, and Mary Ann rave on about modern ontology in such a way that it sounds like the misery of light on objects was just invented last week to explain twentieth-century intellectuals. Not so. Its provenance is the primitive or semicivilized mind, and Maylene is the female troglodyte who finally just squatted down and stared at some Precambrian rock until she died.

I can easily imagine a cave man who stops in the middle of his throw to contemplate the point of his spear. He stops short and wonders how that stick got shaved. He lets down his arm and fingers the point. He sits and stares at the whole shaft. And then he slowly retires to his back, stretching his dwarfish body across the grassy plain—he stares into the sun until he is stone blind. It's been a long time going on.

Maylene was the most unself-conscious creature to ever pad around on God's earth. She was prime Cro-Magnon, but it was, I believe, the stillnesses that broke her down. Stillnesses invaded all her pots and pans at about 2:00 p.m. on November 15th, 1940, and they were what finally began to completely tear her down and wrap her around with the bleak bedclothes of a perfect despair.

The best way to see Maylene would be with a stereoscope—or whatever you call the device that shapes one object pictured from two slightly different points of view into a single 3-D image. Let's play like we've got a whole stack of those pasteboards with pictures concerning a day in the life of Maylene Smith. Let's play like it's one of those bad days when she's got pads and pins and belts hitched around her sensitive lower abdomen (it's her first period after April's born), and the baby is crying again because she wants solid food in spite of the fact that doctors made you drive a tad half crazy for months before it got any in those days—two, three months of torture for both mother and child. And of course little April's on the bottle, the goddamned bottle being the only truly scientific method of feeding in those days, or so said the County Health Clinic, intending no harm.

I see a howling baby soiled and sweltering in an unvented wicker crib—all that smell of Carnation formula and yellow baby shit, and the razor smell of baby piss, all quite vividly evoked by this down-shot picture slotted into my trusty stereoscope. Maybe what I need is a stereopticon: image, dissolve, fade, and then new image. Anyway: there's the gossamer hair stuck flat against the soft skull by sweat that's also beaded up along the baby's upper lip, all in glistening 3-D. Only Maylene's knuckles can be seen—they're clenched to showing her veins and bones—her left hand clenched to the edge of the crib. It's quite a dismal shot, and also dismal is the drone and whirr of the paddle-bladed Emerson fan which oscillates hopelessly across the room. But even that's not enough. It's also important to know how the world has been to Maylene before the baby came.

Maylene and the swine, Maylene and the chickens, Maylene and the milk cow, Maylene and the buzzard tree.

But don't expect any of those easy bucolic visions: depraved rednecks, sodomy, incest, and so on: because her life wasn't the most common sort of grinding poverty and rural life during the Depression. Her people, the Willys, had an acre garden and kept animals, the women did, and the men ran a wildcat sawmill, strictly rough cut; they hauled the logs out of the cuts and draws with mules. They did O.K., like my people, but they did leave Maylene watching the animals too long—just standing there at the pen or in a field looking upon those benign creatures. It happens that way now and then in big families with lots of girls: one's left to drift, and Maylene simply stood in sun and shade too long, whole days when time ran through her body as slowly as the water in Steele's Bayou. She grew up without much ability to enjoy the nervous actions of human beings. The only radical activity she could understand seemed to be the weather. Even a small tornado that roared across her pasture once seemed to have more reason to it than all those humans down the path at the house. The air became still as green water in a slough—the air and sky *were* green, and from the southwest the emerald and black clouds stacked and rolled her way. But she didn't retreat down the path to the toolshed, or farther to the house, where all the other women had run. She, a young girl, merely hugged the loblolly and watched her Jersey cow rise up in slow circles, its teats awash in the loud wind, as loud as a freight train (I'm satisfied I don't exaggerate), and then settle down on a knoll unhurt—Maylene could understand that sort of going-on, though it was the silences of animals on a clear day across the field that she enjoyed most of all, and the way the animals didn't have to worry over their young much. Christ! And I know another story Henry told me about Maylene.

He told it when I visited him and Maria that one time right after I was out of The League—the cows and the mockingbirds, and the buzzard tree—perfect happiness in sunshine, perfect misery in rain.

Henry came home one afternoon from the Mill and found her sitting on the front steps. She was staring damn near directly into the sun blazing over on the edge of the brake, and behind her, in the house, the baby was setting up cries so terrible and shrill heaven itself must have heard them. And heaven that afternoon was Helen who'd heard the shrieks a quarter mile down the road at her place, Helen who, while Henry was running across the back yard, was struggling to release the child's head from the crib slats, which new crib Helen herself had bought so the baby'd have more air on it. The child hadn't been wiped, changed, or fed the entire day because Helen was gone shopping in Bryan. And Henry found Helen crying softly and tugging at the slats. Henry pulled opposite ways after rubbing some White Rose Petroleum Jelly on April's cheeks, and Helen pushed her loose. She picked April up and soothed her. Helen pulled that child of her own sister up against her small breasts, and then she turned on Henry and cursed him: "Why'd you marry Sister? Why poor Maylene? Sister's hopeless. Sister's never *done* nothing and Sister never will ever do a *thing* for you, Henry."

With Henry's wife, her sister, sitting stupidly out on the porch and within normal earshot, Helen shifted the baby to her shoulder and pressed herself against his work clothes as best she could, his body, his manliness, by God. She actually reached around and grabbed hold of his skinny buttocks and pulled him to her. She rose to heights of bravery in practical love my generation can't often reach. She pledged her love to her brother-in-law right there on that bare, hot, cypress floor, and she was rejected.

She offered him a reasonable alternative to the squalor he was in. She'd keep it clean—no more egg-lacquered dishes for him to do at night when he's beat down, no more compostlike laundry. It was a sane deal. She offered him a sane woman who'd never let the dust cover up the objects of his life, who'd never let the first dish loiter at the sink. Helen would of moved in with them that day if he'd just reached around her with one of his arms while she stood there. Divorce Maylene, marry Helen, murder Maylene with aspirin and paregoric, lock her in the shed and slop her like an animal once a day—ANYTHING to change it—Helen would have gone along with it. Which has got to be in the great tradition of frontier women.

Eugene, says Henry, *I didn't know what to do. I couldn't get her ugliness off of my mind.*

Helen's ugliness! She was so thin that loving her in bed would set up a clatter worse than the day Ezekiel's bones racked themselves together in the vision. Bone-thin and hawk-faced—and Henry was in love with the rounds and hollows of that poor little woman sitting in the falling light out on the steps. He drew himself away from Helen, never touched her with his hands, and walked out to where Maylene was sitting with all her indelible silences.

"What's wrong, Maylene honey?" He said it softly as he let himself down beside her and put an arm across her shoulder. "Maylene . . . our baby coulda died in there . . ."

"I seen birds sit on an ole cow's back a long time . . . the ole cow never was bothered with no bird"—she said it like she was in a dream, and Henry didn't answer for a long time.

Finally he spoke sharply: "Wife, I don't understand what it is you're saying."

"I say I don' want to do with you or that baby."

"Got damn it, Maylene, I ain't no cow."

Maylene began to hum to herself and Henry went to his truck

and drove away for the first time, which is a natural enough thing to do when the sort of thing that should never happen does happen. A woman like Maylene is very damned unusual. So why the hell did she have to happen to him? When he'd stood up and faced Helen, she was standing like a ramrod in the doorway, her face as mean and devoid of clear emotion as his was.

Helen took her nutty sister and her sister's baby across the field and brought them to her own little house, and there they stayed. When Henry returned he lived to himself in the house he'd built for his wife; he slept alone in his house and left his wife and child to Helen.

But mostly I see Henry, as a young man with his thick curly hair pulled straight back without a part, and smooth Maylene there on the steps, one raggledy-assed Plymouth Rock hen pecking near to one of her bare feet, and the old cow never bothered with that bird that was sitting right on her own back . . .

Wife . . .

Wife

Wife

His great mouth, seeming to smile, opened wide as he spoke; his voice was harsh—not unpleasantly so, but as if it had hardened that way after years and years of speaking—and went on monotonously, with the effect of being able to go on forever.

Mr. Lenin had a good woman and Mr. Smith didn't.

But sitting alone there on his porch and watching the distant figure of his little bride off across the dock field did create a curious sort of revolution in him. Being crazy the way she was, or at least the way he thought she was, he chose to never love on her anymore. He'd walk over there and talk with her in the evenings, and often as not he took meals with them, but he never once stayed an entire night at Helen's house, and he never tried to carry Maylene back to his house, for any purpose. Sometimes they'd walk off toward the edge of the woods together, and every now and then they'd hold hands (they were young people) while talking about the silences she'd observed throughout the day (for he had grown relatively tolerant of that foolishness): the hairy pig was a gray stone in the wallow, and, yes indeedy, the buzzards that hunkered in the one dead tree were gentlemen.

. . .

How strange it is. The only thing to make me cry so far this summer is the thought of Maylene and Henry. The *tolerance* of that man—to walk out in the evening with that beautiful girl, to handle her nice breasts and pretty butt with his hard eyes, to get knots in his belly from thinking of her useless snatch—to suffer those conditions and emotions is tolerance out of mind. Dear God, the way her eyes did shine when the big drops of rain burst on the water of the pond—the way she'd squeeze down on his horny hand with her blunt fingers when the thunder churned off toward Louisiana, and the way she'd smile up at his face. Was that a happy time for him, or worst of all?

And what comes next is so gross it made Mary almost run out on me. "I hate all that Mississippi bullshit you come from." Bosh. Smokes dope all the time and has the gall to condescend to people who came to the spooks naturally.

And so it is that Helen claims Maylene finally went on to bed for good and started dying in earnest when lightning struck that buzzard tree in a storm one morning.

That pattering of rain that never wakes you up. It actually soothes the sleeper. And then the BLAM that brought Henry straight up off his sheet. He peered out the window through the vague early morning light, out through the veils of rain, but he could see the tree that was split and on fire, and steaming, and he could see some black forms scattered around the burst pine. And the he saw a worse thing, a woman in a gown who ran to the tree and picked up a black form. Goddamned Smiths! Goddamned Willyses! And then there was the bony woman running after the fleshed one and then he realized that he himself was outside and running toward the both of them. The rain that was coming down by then was a bitch and full-fledged chunkmover, and he was still in his briefs.

"Maylene, put down that goddamned bird!" She's standing

there mothering that huge ripped bird, kissing its warty head and beak. Blood and gore and rain, and those great wings broken and splayed, a dead fowl bigger than your famous albatross, and she's shaking the goddamned peeled head of it like it was some demon prick she loved beyond good sense. Which is the part that Mary can't abide. Poor girl can't stand events so obviously symbolical: that seem so obviously symbolical to her. As for me, the scene isn't symbol at all—it's just one helluva way to start a rainy day: worse than toads for breakfast.

"Take it away from her, please, Henry, take it away from her!" Helen was terrified and crying.

Goddamned excessive Smiths! Willyses! Boykins! Shit. I come from sane people.

April tells how her daddy slapped her mother then, and how her mother did drop the buzzard. He slapped her good and hard and the poor woman ran whimpering back into the house, Helen and Henry there in the rain with the steaming tree and two, three dead birds. And Helen joined The Church to survive the birds.

And he never spoke to Maylene again, says April by way of Helen, and he's spoken very little to Helen, his servant, since that time either.

What is curiously grotesque to me is that both April and Mary Ann have got essentially the same opinion of the scene. What say, Martin?: *I remembered, revered Father, among those happy and wholesome stories of yours, by which the Lord used wonderfully to console me, that you often mentioned the word "poenitentia," whereupon, distressed by our consciences and by those torturers who with endless and intolerable precept taught nothing but what they called a method of confession, we received you as a messenger from Heaven, for penitence is not genuine save when it begins from the love of justice and of God, and this which they consider the end and consummation of repentance is rather its commencement.*

Mary Ann. Mary Ann! Don't leave. Stay to imagine it. There she is—Helen—utterly exposed again. She's dripping wet and standing in boiled buzzard entrails. Her soaked nighty is showing off her skinny titties to the man she still loves, the man who, because she's meager and ugly in the flesh, won't take her to bed, marry her: whatever it is they want. The women . . .

Just what is it you women want? Tell me, Mary. Tell me before I die. Let's draw up a fucking treaty. Please, please let us all come to terms with what's wearing us down, destroying our great civilization.

Mary Ann, I tell you this: it is my belief that I should seek out Julia Pastrana, famous apewoman, for I sense in the dark cells and prisons of my honeycombed bird bones that she and I could, in the confusion of our blood, establish a better race than the one that now exists: Zeus as Archaeopteryx: Leda as Lady Neanderthal: I in my jipijapa hat and she with her linen bonnet on: we'd surely make it all fresh and new again.

It happened in Bryan. It happened ezakly the way we all have seen it through our several optical devices, and it drove the man away from the two women who loved him. Stupid as it may seem.

And Helen grows older and thinner and uglier. And Maylene is a long time dust.

Well. And why is Royal going to marry April?

"Everything is true to you, Royal Carle, every damned thing in the world," said Daddy.

Royal looked at him with a smile beginning to form. "It was that way a long time. But I'm seeing the lies again, and I'm hating the lies. You're showing me the truth again." But I think it was me who was hating right then. I hated Royal just a little for being so smart. Just a little.

"I want some of that coffee cake," Daddy said, trying to get himself to smile too. And I take some pride in the fact I got the cake made. Justifiable pride, as you say. Justifiable homicide! Good Grief! That girl maintains only my worst habits of phrasing and wit. *Daddy says, "I'll sit right here an' eat some of daughter's cake. You go on an' tell me some truth, Royal Carle."*

They both took some, and Royal, he actually smacked his lips over the sugary crust. He liked it. He really liked it, and he was sputtering to talk some more before he'd finished swallowing. "By God, Henry, I will tell you a truth. Henry. I'm going to marry your daughter maybe." And, of course, in *this* letter I thought the marrying business was a metaphor—the final trope, the *coupe de théâtre,* to win the argument with: Beulah Land and Lula's Land, the Married Land. Ain't that funny, Sonny thought, ole R.C. finally getting across his figurative Jordan. Royal in the role of both Isaac and the Lord High God. Which shows I've not been working for the Unitarians too long. Literal-minded Joiner is what's needed.

"*Henry, I love your daughter maybe.*" *And he fixes that famous smile on me and pops the question right after a sort of cough-type laugh,* "Will you marry me, April? Surely you'll marry me. What about 'that' for a truth, Henry?"

Sonny, it gave me a real shiver. It was a crazy way to do it, the thing Royal did, but no matter how much off the wall it was, it worked. It achieved the reconciliation we all wanted. It was the reconciliation I'm sure you'd want. And let me say here and now I think it pretty bitchy of you not to answer my other letters. And you may ask how I'm so sure you're receiving them. Well, I'm just sure, that's all. Shame on you, Son!

I'd sent her my address, with a note saying I'm O.K., so her intuition ain't exactly intuitive. She's worthy of a psychological study: "The Reasonable Woman as Visionary."

Anyway, Daddy ate his slice of cake and then lit himself another Picayune, stinking up the air with that awful smoke. And his final statement went something like this: "You do that, Royal. That's just fine with me. You go on ahead and do any damned thing you want to, because none of your talk is gonna make me trust your ass. You still some kind of bastard, and all this palaver won't cover it either. But you do try hard. I got to grant it. You marry her tomorrow or whenever you want to. She's been married before, and to a better man than you," *which I'm sure will please you, Sonny, true or not.* True! Quite true. The only person outside of Davis Benton, the Sheriff, who stuck by me, by me and by the niggers, was Henry, Henry who was supposed to hate niggers worst of all. I'm positive he actually approved of our accidentally killing Foots Magee. But enough of that. Henry's final lines were, "*I'm going to New Orleans in the morning.*" *He got up to the cabinet and poured himself a good big glass of whiskey, and he drank it down right then and there, and he didn't flinch. Daddy went off down the hall to his room and his pictures and his record player and radio. But he never turned on a sound. He slept a couple of hours and then snuck off to see Maria.* Henry has got to hate living in that room she added on for him.

What a night it was! Me and Royal sitting there eating the rest of the coffee cake and sipping on Luzianne, and talking softly about how it all seems to have turned out all right. He laughed and said maybe we'd better court awhile to make it look right around town, and in Jackson, but he did have his hand on my leg before we'd been talking long, whether he's serious or not. And we checked on Aubrey, who's slept soundly through it all, and all things considered it was a very pleasant evening and night.

Sonny, it hurts me to tell you how fine that night last week was, but I'd be dishonest if I didn't. And I know I haven't gotten it written up like Mr. Claiborne would, or Henry James, but I've tried for the "mystery of history" like Professor Burger used to tell us. I've been writing on and off the page, like he said the good historian does. We're all having a good life, aren't we, Sonny? Understand what I'm saying, try to understand.

Love
April

I understand.

4

MAYLENE WOULD have been my mother-in-law! Mary noticed that
in any considerations of Maylene I never seemed to have the famil-
ial tone—she noticed that Maylene as mother-in-law had never
actually occurred to me. "Maylene would have been your own
dear mother-in-law!" Says that and fires up the Tappan for supper.
It gives one pause, for one must internalize such a realization to
make it a felt truth—something all wool and a yard wide. One
should be able to do better at defending the mother of your own
child's mother.

Did Henry marry a mentally deficient woman, thus proving
himself to be a threatened and inept monster? No. The answer
is no—for Maylene could play the piano a little and had a pleasant
singing voice. She even played in church sometimes, and she had
a high-school diploma. She could write some English. She seems
to have been especially talented at math and science, and she read
the county paper every day, and the *Post* every chance she could
get her hands on it—and she was interested in raising horses. In
fact, Henry says he encouraged the idea of raising horses, but that
takes money, and at the time he didn't have any to spare. Wasn't a
damn thing wrong with Maylene except that her plain people
inadvertently raised her into the psychology of a rich and culti-
vated person. Something like that.

What Henry saw when he looked at her was a pretty little
country girl—but actually she had a fancy sensibility. She should
have been just another Mississippi farm girl, but actually she was
the shepherdess in Boucher's *Pastoral*. Henry wanted genre paint-

ing, but she was all baroque on the inside. She may have spent her childhood contemplating cow patties but her soul was meant to be at home in the *Fête at Rambouillet,* by Fragonard. I'm almost positive that all those years of languishing in the south forty caused her to see the average pine forests as paths and wombs and caverns of sensuous and reasonable fecund green. I'll give you five to one that's what was the matter, Mary. She should have been Fragonard's lady on the velvet seat of a delicate rope swing—a lady kicking off her slipper for that lecherous fellow in the dandy pants. Which fellow is looking up her dress. Nobody really wants to live the simple life.

Henry couldn't grasp that—not back then. It took Maria in New Orleans to make a decadent of Henry. He had to be burned and painted his own self before he could understand.

Henry had the right idea. He wanted a family, and that's the kind of worthy goal that seems to have gone entirely out of fashion with the youth of today. Most of my generation would rather marinate their brain cells in gin or blow their minds on bennies, or other kinds of dope.

To hell with young folks. I'm twenty-five, with the responsibilities of educating young men and women, and I'm making a second serious attempt at making a woman happy, and these are equally difficult vocations.

But it's the old ones on our mind now.

There's no possible way Henry could have improved his lot with Maylene—a person who never gets plugged in on normal human time won't ever come to anything, no matter how hard you try.

Even if Henry had been able to say, "Goddammit now, Maylene, you come on and step your little tail right on out from that picture frame and fix my scrambled eggs"—move off out here in Real Time and away from that static prospect of hogs and blue bottle flies, all captured in a scene among the rotting melons—ain't no still goddamned shred of grass hanging eternally from a Jersey's mouth can ever equal the booming and buzzing of the good old-fashioned *human* real world. Even if he'd known how to say it and charm her out of all that foolishness, what then? What if he'd been able to change her from STOP to GO? What if she'd actually quit being a seer of stillnesses and, paradoxically, also a proto-coquette. What a flavorless gain! What a loss!

But Mary says I'm messing around in her domain—the Enlightenment. She says that Maylene could not have possibly *related* to both Fragonard and Vermeer. She says it's a contradiction in terms. Well Billy be damned and etc.—so much for terms—because it's all a matter of point of view: objective or subjective. From the outside she looked like a Vermeer or maybe even a bleak Hopper —she *looked* that way. But from the inside she *felt* herself to be a Fragonard. She *desired* Fragonard and Watteau. I think I already made that clear. Which of course explains honky-tonks.

At which point Mary starts throwing plastic plates and saucers and cups at me, and she's amazingly accurate, especially in sailing the plates. Whooooeee, she looks so fine in jeans and bandanna bra. Mary, be both my bandicoot and bandersnatch. Bop me. Noggin my noggin all you want, but later, my little mouse, I get in your pouch, sweet marsupial.

Such talk will calm her mind.

Art History 2013. Hot damn, it turned me on. Maylene is the *Young Lady Adorning Herself with a Pearl Necklace.* Adoring herself. Which pearls she got out of that pig wallow she's always watching—the wallow where people are always throwing their pearls right before her new eyes—eyes as warm as egg yellows exactly ten seconds after you turn the burner on.

In Jan's fine picture it looks like the girl is checking herself out in a little mirror on the wall, but we know better. She is *not* looking at herself and she is *not* thinking about those oyster frustrations she holds in her little fingers, and she is *not* Julia Pastrana looking across the Queen's table in London with an eye to figure out which of those creatures is her real father. Truth is—the girl with the ermine fringe upon her garments is Maylene, and Maylene is looking out a little mullioned window, looking, dear friend, at her buzzard tree, and she is calm. That delicate gaze is on those birds beaded up on those limbs like dirty oil on a piston rod, and she is calm, self-satisfied, and beautiful.

To make shrimp teriyaki in Fort Worth one must marinate at least a pound of deveined green shrimp (shelled) for at least fifteen minutes in bland cooking oil and soy sauce and pineapple juice—and then, if your lover has begun a tirade on passion, loyalty, race, religion, ambition, and death, you cool it all for ten minutes before dumping it on his goddamned head. Which Mary did, and I don't blame her, much. I am, however, irrepressionable, as it goes in blurbs: Henry! Henry, with your dork seized by a lady from a *fête galante*, you did your best—but be more gentle. Bite her lightly on the ear and tell her a sorrowful story. Cry quietly in her ear, "Buzzard, buzzard, buzzard. Dearest Maylene, I'll never shoot another buzzard on the wing, the fifty-dollar fine being more than we can afford." Buzzard, buzzard, Maylene—don't that make your clit quiver, Maylene? But now I am undone. I'm covered with shrimp and shame and rice, and I don't smell too good, and I'm hungry enough to eat what's spilled over my head and shoulders and books and papers. I *would* eat it if it weren't for Mary's sincere invective against me.

She can cook and she can sew, and in the evening she doth blow.

But Henry never did learn to do Maylene right, and she stayed nervous, and she got April under one of those pump-a, pump-a worthless screws that come to nothing except mean babies. Poor Maylene, finally withering away in Helen's guest bed. Poor Henry, who ran to the Boykins seeking something moderately normal.

And Helen actually did have Vermeer prints in Maylene's room, on the very wall by her dying bed—*Maidservant Pouring Milk*, *The Music Lesson*, *A Lady Writing* (and what a shame we don't have Maylene's letters), all the most famous prints—and Helen's logic was impeccable. Pictures to encourage Maylene to the very end—images to encourage her in Education and Industry.

.   .   .

"Sonny, Christalmighty, Jesusgod, Hush Puppy, Chitlin, Nigah-lovah! Sonny, STOP." That's what she says, and, "Stop torturing yourself!" Which ain't no good line. "No amount of *construing* will make it better. You fucked up. You lost your fucking wife and you lost your fucking child. Face up to it." Mary certainly lacks a proper sense of play.

This new woman of mine, because she was raised all over the world, though mostly in Formosa, has got what is called a Standard American voice. It's more like she was born in Des Moines than in Austin. It is shrill and flat and hurts one's ears. "You don't know shit from Shinola—as . . . you . . . say—about painting. Let it be . . . as . . you . . . say." And I do hate to see a woman cry, but finally it won't impede me.

Pride, Maylene, plain sensual pride is what you suffered and died of (although the clinic called it measles and neurasthenia)— Pride, the pride of a swollen sow, and so she did die and get buried about two weeks before Pearl Harbor. They say she died of measles, neurasthenia, and complications, and the sunshine glistered on the vault nobs in a fashion that would have pleased old Jan, and certainly the light of God will remain with her in the ashes until Judgment Day. And what shall Maylene's heaven be? Cowbirds and winged pigs, black angels dancing a sacred minuet? Bertrand Russell doing the Memphis Shuffle?

It's mid-July and Mary has gone to Galveston to visit friends. She says she won't come back until April and Royal are married and I've got my sense back. O.K.

II

April's marrying Royal Carle Boykin soon, and he's a good man in spite of being a smartass—or at least that's what I would of called him before I went with the Dallas Bulls of The NFL, before I learned what I did with that red shirt on. And I did say it to his face plenty of times. I had to straighten him out sometimes when we ran around together. I helped him out.

But let there be credit where credit is due. With Henry and April, in the kitchen, he took a calculated risk, he damn well diced for his future, and maybe even for his soul. He's coming right along, and he called on me again last night.

Royal called last night, called me from Jackson, and he was suffering on the long-distance line—he's high on Rebel Yell, which ain't Turkey, or even green Jack, and he has been unfaithful. *Double and triple unfaithful,* he says. Soon to be married to my wife (on August 15), the engagement to be mentioned in the state papers (and also in New Orleans) next week, he has been out with a Jackson woman. He has carried on with her! I was tempted to tell him to tell it to April, but of course that would have been foolish and no fun at all. Ding-a-ling, his voice a dingbat thrown four hundred miles: *Son? Hullo, this is Roil.*

It was lovely. I said hold on a moment and got the whole jar of frosty Gibsons out of the fridge, and then I eased down in Mary's Day-Glo chair. The air conditioner was a-drone and I was very much at peace before the body of the talk started.

"Hey, Son, what the hell's goin' on?"

"____"

"Whudder we doin' to ourselfs? Son? Are you there, Son?"

"Yes indeedy. Rave on, Royal. Rave on."

And he said he didn't mean to be out tonight with a woman so shallow she's convex, but what's to be done in lieu of late movies on T.V. and Jax beer—and how shall one live in a city that has no desire to become a Padua? *DALLAS,* he shouts—*all they admire is DALLAS—but, Son, these Jackson women are the most beautiful in the world, they are the most profoundly sexual and decent creatures in Western Civilization—they're woeful peckernappers —bands and cadres of toothed vaginas. Son, they work at loving like it's a correspondence course in shorthand. They're trying to improve their lot! Raunchy has become no more than a way to build character. Raunchy is merchandise. They debase ole Billy's death!*

I told him that women had done that sort of thing for a long time, and I pointed out that April's not so different herself.

NO, NO—NOT DALLAS, NOT CLEVELAND . . .

This ain't like you, Roll. Not at all like you, and the boy says he is changed, and he's sorry he shit on me last spring. He says me and my niggers weren't crazy after all, and just how many people do you know who'd run the phone bill up for nothing more than old time's sake and because they feel guilty about how they're living their lives. Royal did, ole muthahumpah Boykin did just that. He says: *I come back here because I thought that bad as it is there's people sensitive enough to change it sanely . . . but it's a city unworthy of any descent from the entrepreneurs of twelfth-century Bavaria. Son, it's a harsh place, but it now lacks or never had the true gift of great self-serving greed. Son, a small greed is the worst. Son, it is desirous—but it is lacking in profound cupidity.* Something like that.

Royal, relax on the Wilbur Cashish sociology. What about the women? For I knew it was the Jackson women that had cast him back to April and Bryan and Henry.

Right, right. What the hell's the South about if it's not about women?

Lula? April? Maylene? Helen? Jackson women?

"Do you hate me, Son?"

"Nope."

"Son, if there's any chance you'll evah come home to the family, I quit right now . . ."

"No chance at all."

"She's O.K., Son? She ain't no *bad* woman?"

"_____"

"Son?" Beg, sunnavabitch, beg!

"Yes, indeedy," I answered evenly. "She's O.K."

"Good, good."

I told him that any man in his right mind would take a chance on April and Aubrey and Henry and a load of birdshot in the back of the head and neck rather than consign his fate to the Jackson women. Seek your bride in Bryan, Collins, D'Lo, and Yazoo. Seek not in Jackson—or any place in urban Texas. Enough.

"You never did intend to go East or West, did you?"

"Never."

"Did Stream's call really shake you up?"

"Damn right!"

Royal's problem has always been virginity. I'm damn near positive he'll enter his marriage essentially a virgin. Maybe there was a whore once or twice in New Orleans, an obligation to his fraternity, and maybe there was some lady in cotton undies up in Nashville during law school—but never a Polly Roberts, a Modene Grunch, an April of the silky pudenda—none of your essential down-home-type fucking. Royal's what's called pure, in the good sense.

And now he's calling me because he's carrying the burden of his near sin.

He and Stream, who's still working his textbooks out of Jackson, got themselves a couple of excellent girls from a local bank and they set out to act the roles of proper bachelors—a last fling for Royal before he finalizes the deal with April, wherein he'll be most surely committed to steady sex, and loving, and fathering, and I'm not suggesting that R.C.'s queer—never—because he's always enjoyed his fair share of titties, all the baleful extremes of petting, no doubt—but when those two girls got drunk as coots and began to attempt the casual and mass media brand of seggsuality, deciding to take a nude plunge in the apartment pool at 2:00 a.m., Royal turned loud red as a Pall Mall package—in direct contrast to Stream, who, though nervous as Jim Eastland at an NAACP picnic most òf the time, is, finally, a wild man, a crude voluptuary, which is more to his credit than anything else I can think of.

Stream, who's buttless and never had much definition in his muscles, is delighted to strip on down to his candy-cane Jockey briefs. Stands there on top of the Formica coffee table and reads "The Force That Through the Green Fuse Drives the Flower" in a wretched, nasal imitation of Thomas and then does the Sabine women bit with his naughty, naked date right on out into the pool. Whoopee, and to hell with anybody in the stockade who might be up that late to see it. Stream's a gifted drinker. He's always able to reach a level that charms without cloying, excites without offending, depending on the company. A man who faints on Tennyson is capable of anything.

But Royal can't drink well at all. He goes from nothing more than a warm stomach to deathly ill without benefit of vision between, and sitting there engaged to April, imagining what Henry'd think if he saw the scene, he's suffering a state of fierce consternation.

His date is Ruth Motor, Edna's third cousin, who is originally from Hot Coffee, and she is crazy about F. Scott Fitzgerald and Hemingway, and loves also good ole Kahlil—she is a really decent woman, except for too much spray net, and she is positive, after good oysters and beer earlier in the evening (and after a good production of *The Rose Tattoo* at the Little Theater)—she is positive that this amazingly suave Mr. Boykin will dearly love the wholesome frolic she's got in mind.

"Royal, honey, cum on," says Ruth, kicking off her genuinely expensive Ann Hickey shoes. Royal and Ruth had been selecting records throughout most of Stream and Dora's strip, selecting, stacking, and playing records to both encourage and distract the ritual. A matter of distraction to Royal, a matter of encouragement to Ruth—Dora and Stream getting bare to the strains of Tannhäuser. *Oysters, Tennessee Williams, Dylan Thomas, and Tannhäuser: Son, there's got to be something peculiarly Southern about all that.*

Ruth's saying, "Stream's cute but you're better built," while whipping off her stockings and working her toes up and down in the deep pile.

It's not all that easy or even reasonable to turn down the Ruth Motors of the world—and after Stream and Dora gave up their naked poetry and galloped off to swim, Royal let down his defenses considerably—he drew Ruth down to him on the couch, kissing her eyes and telling her to keep her clothes on until the bedroom and the dark: "Keep your clothes on, Ruth, for the present. Please?"

"Sweet shy Royal," and then she bites his nose, reverting to some habit she'd learned in Hot Coffee. *I tried to laugh it off by*

*telling her she'd have to admit they looked pretty silly bare-assed. I
told her that seeing her clean knees and looking down her low dress
at those wonderful big bosoms was super and a helluva lot closer to
the spirit of modern love than being a goddamned exhibitionist.*

*Kiss, kiss, kiss—and Son, I was almost crying out of raw . . .
excitement.*

"Am I ugly, Royal?"

"Ugly!"

*Son, those stockades they live in in Jackson are fearful—god-
damn gates of wrought iron—buzzers and bells for admittance—
all that phony aristocratic bullshit—tier on tier of rooms full of
pretty people, and not one of them in true love . . . and, yeah, who
the hell am I, "Moon Pie Boykin," to knock Ruth or anybody else
who lives in the motherfucking Regal Arms Apartments.* Un-
commonly common language for R.C. *Who am I to knock a clean
girl who keeps up a nice room or two and cooks a fine lasagna?
Fucking-A, as you say, Son—she's superclean—she's hot—she
reads PLAYBOY—eat her and she tastes like butter ripple ice
cream or fried rice. She douches or whatever they do. She . . . is
. . . so . . . pretty. She's prettier than OUR April . . .*

*I took her up the carpeted stairs to Stream's room—where
Stream's got the bottom part of a department store mannequin suspended from the ceiling with black panties on—the damn thing
swings lightly, pushed by the breeze from the air vent up at the
ceiling. It was Stream's smelly bed, where he beats off all the time,
and I started telling her about my parents.*

*Goddamn, Son. I told her the whole thing. I even told her about
Henry and April, and I think I even mentioned you. The room
smelled of Scotch and soiled clothes.* Soiled clothes: a very Boy-
kinean expression. *And it wasn't much better than doing it in the
pool.* Body ash/chlorine. *She was down to skin in no time and I was
talking about Momma and Daddy trapped in the car on fire, with
Henry burned out on the road and all bunged up. I kept on thinking that I'm not the kind of people that does things like this to Ruth
Motors. I'm sitting with all my clothes on right in the middle of that
seamy bed and I've got her laid out across my lap so I can work her
at both ends like she's a dulcimer . . . Son, I was my father. I was
romantic, garrulous, and humane. I'm talking about my parents*

*screaming in the goddamned car—and Henry down on his knees
watching Momma's face pushed against the glass and then the glass
breaking and Momma and Daddy spilling part way out on the road.
Shish ke-bab. And Mother's foot also stuck out the little back window. Shit. And I brought Ruth off—she's popping around like
bacon in a pan—and I brought her off while I'm jabbering hysterically about Daddy reading Jack London. I told Ruth Motor that
Momma smelled like grapefruit and Daddy like pine oil. And then
I take off my clothes! We wrap up in Stream's grubby purple sheets
and I go on talking. Stuff about okra and trying to reconcile myself
to you and Henry and April. Ole Ruth, she hung in there and
listened and said it was wonderful, but didn't I need some help myself, meaning to make it . . .*

Goddamned Royal. He should *not* have mixed personal history
—any kind of history—up with simple screwing, for as Augustine
points out: *He who praises the nature of the soul as the sovereign
good and condemns the nature of the flesh as evil, truly both
carnally desires the soul and carnally shuns the flesh; for his feeling
is inspired by human vanity, not by divine truth.*

Women like Ruth ought to have a law on the books that will
let them bring the Royals of the world to trial for a breach of sexual
contract. And, Royal, don't give me any yogurt about how that
loving, with its complex-type confessions, is sufficient, the equal of
a roughfuck. Not so—and baby you put down that sort of foolishness with April and she'll cut out with every latent heterosexual
redneck in Hinds County.

Ruth may not have minded that easy dawdling you gave her—
but that action without a good pneumatic assault on her brand-new
diaphragm is worthless—it's goddamned criminal. Women like
Ruth, without a proper liberal education and without a culture
that provides a duenna to instruct in matters social and physical,
are wonders of self-preservation. They're revolted by the thought
of abortion—the destroying of a tiny baby—and they fear the
abstraction and spooky chemistry of the pill, so they set their
fragile, residual Calvinism on the bathroom shelf next to the Arrid
spray, and then they go get *fitted*. I suffer to think of it.

The city of Jackson ought to raise a statue of Ruth with her
hair piled high, of Ruth clutching her tastefully designed contra-

ceptive purse under her long, round arms—for it's Ruth who's hauling that city kicking and screaming into the inevitable and healthy wantonness of the future. Let them design the statue in such a way that, to accommodate the moods of custom, her plastic clothes can be changed from time to time, and also her hair. Let her be continually various and beautiful—let Baptists from Clinton and Arabs from Vicksburg also worship there . . .

There are two things I have always observed to be in singular accord: supercelestial thoughts and subterranean conduct—or so go *Essais* by tough Mr. Montaigne.

"Royal, why all this stuff?" And he's quiet, and he's trying to answer correctly, but can't.

"Because of what I'm doing."

"Go on and marry her."

"I guess I'll have to." Which did finally piss me off.

"Why *have to?*"

"Son . . . you . . . know . . . why."

Because she's mine. Because you told Henry, the summer after their deaths, that you finally couldn't consider them to be your parents, since you're adopted—you're staying with Henry and taking meals with all three of them that summer at Helen's—and you try to have an *understanding* with Henry. Jesus! It's a wonder he didn't murder you on the spot back then. You're working at the Mill with me and you say this town can't be your home since they're dead, nor any part of the state. You tell me and Stream those deaths by fire have made you a citizen of the world. My. My. You stand on that same front porch where Henry left Maylene— Royal stood there and said that life was *mysterious* and that his *destiny* was otherwhere—freshman bilge. Said stuff like that to Henry.

And now he tells me he don't know why he's marrying April!

"Yeah, Royal—it's because you'd like to be a grown man. Go to hell, Royal. I got lessons to prepare, books to read, about Mars.

Read Rilke, or Gibbon, or prepare to go to Mars—for there are no other alternatives."

"Sonny . . . you're being mean."

Mean. He calls me mean.

III

At first I saw it off at a distance—this crowd of little pecker-wood buddies of mine is gathered around Royal and they're having what looks to be a friendly conversation with him, except you notice how the little tappers are keeping one grubby hand on the right hip of their jeans—and how they're scubbing the left foot in the dust. They're studying something out—they're tyros of cruelty and violence. Royal's erect, his hands easy at his sides along the seams, and he's not quite focusing on any one of them. In fact, he's looking at his feet one moment and then he looks off past them —he's looking in my direction, but he makes no sign, no signal of any kind.

1006767 × 11 = 11074437 is going on in his head, while they're saying a teacher's pet is worse than bird shit. I'm watching from the bicycle rack off across the playground, and I damn near pedal off—but then I noticed they form this circle around him and start marching away toward the end of the lot and the creek, where the grove is, which grove is the place for serious fights and punishments at James K. Vardaman School in Bryan.

Not a single yell or loud outcry from any one of them. Those mean little somitches are telling him he's broke the rules of conduct, that he's an asskisser, that he's a brown-nosed bastard for smiling the way he does when he gets so much praise from the teacher, and *we* are gonna make you pay. Bo saying this, and Stream, as usual, acquiescing, and Carl Phillips and a few others.

It's a wonder they didn't take all his clothes off and make him run from the tree to the creek naked, like the Germans made the Jewish women do, leering at them, back in World War II. Advanced in their jealousy and hatred, they were capable of damn near anything short of killing—and they probably could of even done that if the wind had stirred off of Steele's Bayou from the southwest, in the wrong way. They cut him—they cut Royal with rocks so badly he still has a patch of scars on his forehead, his chest, his arms, his belly, which to this day he calls the Marks of the Beasts. They tied him round and round with the good ole Cascade Baling Rope they got from Coldstream's uncle's icehouse, and then they stoned him. It may still be shocking news to some people that children have evil in them, but it's not shocking to me and R.C. He was bloody on his freckles—bloodier than the Knoxville girl—bloodier than the boy who killed the Knoxville girl for doing the mess-around, in the old song.

Hard white sky and hard ground at the mimosa tree—and Stream and Bo and Carl moving across the hot rocks to put the hurt on small Royal. They were barefoot and vicious, and even Royal's bravery was probably a species of barefooted viciousness. It was noon, a prime scene, and they'd got him away from the schoolhouse on the day vacation begins. They were at a safe distance, out where the bayou bends around the grounds—kudzu, willows, mimosa, and even a patch of canebrake.

Bryan's school is an old W.P.A. Romanesque structure in which one child hanged himself in the coat closet at recess in 1948 because Miss Torrance the day before asked him how it was at home—her knowing goddamned well his momma was selling wet skin for beer money. He—Darrell Fisher—cried a lot, and she was down on him for it, had made him go to the coat closet every time he cried—she'd told him he could come out of there when he's done with tears. She did that sort of thing to Darrell. That humiliated and terrified little chap managed to get his own belt and one from somebody's coat hooked together. He got it over a pipe at the ceiling and, with his own cowboy buckle under his chin, he hopped off a chair. It not only strangled him—it also choked him, and the belt buckle with rhinestones made his throat bleed. It's a cozy sort of Second War event but when I saw them moving in on Royal Carle it crossed my mind that he might do the same and then there'd be another hot room where we'd have to look at a little child, with bulgy eyes, dead and limp and bleeding in our midst.

I never told Mary about this one, but I'm the one who found Darrell. I was checking on a decay snake (Kate, I called her) I'd stashed in a jar at the corner of the long shelf. Dead and limp in our very midst, and Miss Torrance, she puked immediately and we all sent up quickly a considerable amount of groans and screams until the principal and a man science teacher finally came and got him and gently lifted him away.

If I had my way I'd tear that building down. If I had my way . . .

It wasn't any reason they had to put those dry women in those rooms with us, women who hated the meager signs of sex they saw in us, hated so much they beat us with pine staves for nothing more than sticking our boyish hands under Edna Motor's salty bottom. Grab-ass in the grammar schools is heartbreaking.

What I remember is how in some inarticulate way I knew that Royal had beaten them with his colors and silences. Once they'd accosted him he never spoke another word, except for little squeaks and shunts of pain that shook him when the pebbles started getting on to stone size. He's dressed neat as a pin in jeans and a starched denim shirt—and the bruises caused by the rocks were exactly the same color as his blue clothes, and then the blood comes sparkling and spurting from about his head and face, and belly and arms. With his pale freckled skin and the clothes his momma got at Sears put together against his red hair and blood running the way it did, I couldn't help thinking he was an American. It struck me then, watching them batter that child for no other reason than his superior ability and intelligence, that his reds and whites and blues made him an American, yes Lord.

Which was pretty perceptive of me at that age.

Silences, and all the teachers at a final meeting up in the front of the school, the mimosa tree shaking, and the assassins quietly picking up bigger and bigger rocks to kill him with. It was very goddamned simple and symbolical and primitive, and I'll never in my life tell Mary about it. They were creatures who'd long since forgot how Royal'd bragged on his perfection at multiplication, division, and subtraction. Their minds and bodies had all the rationale of lemmings pouring over the cliff into the bitter sea.

.   .   .

"Cut that out," I panted up and yelled. "Cut it out right now or I'll tear all your ears off." Why, they turned to me as if they were all in a dream, Stream saying, "Huh? Sonny?"

I'd run all the way from the bike rack, a thundering (relatively speaking) sprint at 115 pounds, in the fourth grade. Bandaged to that mimosa, Royal's bleeding like a stuck pig, slumped.

"STOP," and they all quit and stared at me. Sweet, sweet Jesus, they were a miserable sight. Nine years on the earth and already they had learned the sickness of failure. Little boys who couldn't even throw a baseball correctly, they had been swinging their arms, smoothly releasing stones at just the right moment with a good whip of the wrist, and stepping handsomely toward the target— they were getting it done in good form. Failures make your teeth ache, but it coordinates your bones and muscles. And when they turned to me their eyes were innocent: *If he survives this he's O.K.: Let's see how good he really is. Is he really our leader? Son, it . . . is . . . a . . . pain . . . to follow another boy.* "Git." I said I was vast and high and cool, and curiously, I didn't count in the ritual at all, except to stop it—I hardly counted at all—I was too big to be of any importance—I was not even in their world. Being too mature for your years will do that sort of thing.

They stared and quit and wandered off in different directions, utterless. They each went to their own house because what they'd done made them want to be alone. They were having rise good solid stunned emotions that make you want to hug yourself in solitude.

Royal cried that time, and he thanked me cordially for helping out. I could see I was on the right side in that affair, because that little boy's tears fell down like bullets on a brass plate—they fell like hot lead that's poured down through the wire of a shot tower.

Clearly—I could see then, even then, how life was likely to be, grown.

Royal cried that time and he thanked me cordially for helping out—Royal tied with Cascade to that mimosa tree, and pulling and shaking until the little pink flowers, those pufflike things, were sailing down on his attackers. As I charged across the schoolyard it *was* a curious sight, that mixture of delicate tree and its shower of beauty and the goddamned barbaric act that was going on in its midst. It was like the Confederates in the vales of Pennsylvania in June '63—those ripe Dutch farms and the Army of Virginia bringing waste.

Shit fire and save matches, let's listen to the great Abiezer Coppe—*and methoughts there was variety and distinction, as if there had been several hearts, and yet most strangely and unexpressibly complicated or folded up in unity. I clearly saw distinction, diversity, variety, and as clearly saw all swallowed up in unity.*

What I mean is I recognized my man that day, as a child, recognized that if Royal could stare, though bloody and sliced, calmly back at our buddies, he was the kind of person to stay close to.

In the fourth grade he shot a fierce finger at Stream, Bobo, and Carl Phillips, for at noon, with the blinding sun above, they cast stones at him—*and it hath been my song many times since, within and without, unity, universality, universality, unity, Eternall Majesty, & c. and at this vision, a most strong, glorious voyce uttered these words, "The Spirits of just men made perfect," the spirits & c. with whom I had absolut, cleare, full communion, and in a two fold more familiar way, then ever I had outwardly with my dearest friends, and nearest relations. These visions and revelations of God, and the strong hand of eternall invisible almightinesse, was stretched out upon me, within me, for the space of foure dayes and nights, without intermission.*

And before he is grown he has one way or the other done in every last one of the boys that threw at him on that day. When they walked away across the powdery dust of the yard at the James K. Vardaman School in Bryan, Mississippi, they might as well of had targets drawn on the backs of their shirts, for his cold eyes, however full of tears, were set and aimed against them, against all the dumb boys save Sonny—*and the time would fail if I would tell you all, but it is not the good will and pleasure of my most excellent Majesty in me, to declare any more (as yet) then thus much further: That amongst those various voyces that were then utter within, these were some, "Blood, blood, Where, where? upon the hypocriticall holy heart, & c." Another thus, "Vengeance, vengeance, vengeance, Plagues," plagues, upon the inhabitants of earth; Fire, fire, fire, Sword, sword & c. upon all that bow not down to eternall Majesty UNIVERSALL LOVE—*

I'le recover, recover, my wooll, my flax, my money. Declare, declare, feare thou not the faces of any; I am (in thee) a munition of Rocks, & c.

1649. Man, ole Coppe, he understands Eugene Joiner, and ain't no reason in the world why I can't finally be, like Professor Burger wants, the Ultimate Radical Historian, though my first practical acts failed.

Go up to London, to London, to Jackson, Dallas, Houston, that great City, Write, write, write, write. *And behold, I writ, and lo a hand was sent to me, and a roll of a book was therein, which this fleshly hand would put wings to before the time. Whereupon it was snatcht out of my hand, & the Roll thrust into my mouth; and I eat it up, and filled my bowels with it, (Eze. 2:8 & c. cha. 3. 1, 2, 3) where it was as bitter as worm wood; and it lay broiling, and burning in my stomack, till I brought it forth in this forme.*

And now I send it flying to thee, with my heart, and all Per AUXILIUMPATRIS.

Maybe sometimes just a little thing like running Caldwell Bobo over Coldstream Taggart seven consecutive plays in a high school scrimmage game, when Bobo is a bull that grew up to be a D.I. with no college education, and Stream's a lanky boy and Preacher's Kid who's dying to make first team his junior year—but tough tiddy, because Stream, pitiful or not, is the one who produced the Cascade Baling Rope they'd tied Royal with. He'd been one of Royal Boykin's tormentors nine, ten years ago, and Royal, who's calling plays on our old-fashioned Tennessee System Single Wing, saw to it that one Coldstream Taggart's spirit got broke, to say nothing of three of his fingers on the sixth play. And of course, to be objective about it, it was just good leadership, his exploiting such a weak position as Stream's. It wasn't the clean and Protestant wind blowing across the wide valleys of Bohemia in the fourteenth and fifteenth centuries, not pure, yet carnal at the same time, like a large nipple, that Taste of Possibility, that recognition that you can, Yes Lord, put The Man down!—it wasn't the invention of the laager or the Taborite wagon-fort—it was nothing more than old-fashioned scorched earth, and we pounded the shit out of Taggart. Bearing down on him, God, the terror in that fool's eyes—Stream—me at pulling guard that afternoon in September and thundering out around his end with Boykin (Got damn! We *knew*—we knew and remembered that mimosa tree—we knew exactly what we had to do)—Boykin, not huge, but by then hard as pine knots, right along with me—Joiner and Boykin and Carl Phillips, the fullback, all of us leading big, mean Bobo right on over Stream's hole on the sweep. We sillioned up the Bermuda grass, we homed in on his fragile form, and we passed right over him—Ruppachucka, Rappachucka, Ruppachucka. We broke his soft ass up, we popped his skin in many places, cleat marks he'll never lose, and when the play had gone all the way in to score, we all looked back, with considerable pleasure, on bony Stream, who was tossing and jerking in pain like a flounder on a gig. Give Stream some credit though—he put on enough weight to make first string the next year, at wingback. He was a damn fool to ever try and make an end. He put on some weight and kept the courage he already had.

But what the Boykin did to Bo to get him back after all that time was even more appropriate and terrible, an index of his subtlety in vengeance. Stocky and mostly insentient Bobo thought it was dandy to grind down Stream—but he'd forgot what R.C.'s motive was. He didn't know he was included in the self-same recollection.

Boykin fought Bobo for no good reason, and nobody but me, who never mentioned it, understood. It was absolutely the only fight he was ever in, unless years later, his tenuous participation in Joiner's Revolution counts as a fight.

．　　　．　　　．

That same junior season, late in the schedule, Bobo accidentally stepped on Royal's toes while walking back to the huddle. It's Monday and we're in sweat clothes running plays in a desultory fashion. We'd won easily Friday night over Crystal Springs; we simply weren't required to put out until Tuesdays—but, like the old saying goes, any time you fuck around, you get hurt—and Bobo did come down clumsily and hard on Royal's foot. There was instant response. Instant. Royal yelled, "Damn!" and when dull Caldwell turned back to apologize, Royal let him have it, a direct shot flush on the nose. Royal put all his shoulder action and body weight into that blow, taking a step of a full yard forward as he delivered the dreamed-of blast against Bo's face. Then, when a cry and a fan of blood spews out and the palms of Bo fly up on arms confused as much as if they'd been unstrung and mishandled by a drunken puppeteer, then was ezakly when Royal crashed a left and a right to both sides of Bo's rib cage, fracturing a couple, and putting Caldwell out for the last two games, including the one for the championship.

Bip, bam, thank you mam!

Royal *can* understand how Henry feels: how it is a sore place persists for years: *in this hour of vengeance it behooves us neither to show pity nor imitate the mercy of Jesus. For these are the days of fury, of terror, and of violence.*

A man's got an obligation to remember the great lines and speeches—the handsomest of the skeins and rhythms, though I can't remember where that last one comes from.

Bip, bam, and Bo is kneecrawling and crying in the grass. He's retching up all the water he shouldn't of drunk before practice.

It shocked them all because Royal's always been noted for an even temper, and when he stands over sick Bo and starts apologizing, saying he just overreacted to the pain in his foot, there wasn't much anybody could say to him.

He apologized to Bo.

He turned and apologized to the whole team for showing a bad attitude.

He told the coaches he'd understand if they kicked him off,

broke his plate in punishment—and he was probably praying they *would* kick him out of football, which game was always a misery to him, for eleven years. He spent, all the time hating it, eleven years under the helmet.

He unsnapped his chin strap, removed his helmet, and headed on into the dressing room. It was fine! It looked exactly like he was suffering a most profound confusion and grief.

Dreary Monday—after a dull day of poorly taught English sonnets and lousy goddamned presentations of the history of the pyramids (we were told that a hundred thousand slaves built those things, when, truth be told, it was about four thousand volunteers who loved every minute of it and sang praises to all their strange gods as they toiled)—Monday, and now, with a slow November rain pattering the dying grass, we had to watch all the order and reason of a long season collapse. Coaches Morgan and Topp had the looks, wide-eyed, of virgins under the first influences of Spanish fly. They said things like, "O.K. let's shape up," and, trying to make a joke of madness, "You people are gettin' so mean we don't need no practice." Damn few "people" laughed.

Had we been in pads they'd of called for a full-scale scrimmage. Shit yes, a goddamned roothog scrimmage, full speed, to cure all the ills of puberty, to solve the wrath of all times past—and what I remember is the bold red of Bobo's blood, and the yellow of his puke, on the green and brownish matted grass. Poor Bo—he later fought in the Asian War, but nothing ever broke him more than what Royal Carle did to him in bleak November. It was a famous event and nobody then or since has been incautious about romping around on Moon Pie's cordovans. He's quick and really knows how to hurt a man.

Royal's done some good stuff, but he never led the people in a fight, and he never played in The NFL. He never led the People against their cruel oppressors—he never stood side by side with Slater Jackson and roused the coloreds to seek their true identity, he never climbed upon a communion table to curse the tyrants in a loud voyce: *Thus saith the Lord:*

Though you can as little endure the word LEVELLING, as

could the late slaine or dead Charles (your forerunner, who is gone before you—) and had as live heare the Devill named, as heare of the Levellers (men-Levellers) which is, and who (indeed) are but shadowes of most terrible, yet great and glorious good things to come.

Behold, behold, behold, I the eternall God, the Lord of Hosts, who am that Mighty Leveller, am coming (yea even at the doores) to Levell in good earnest, to Levell to some purpose, to Levell with a witnesse, to Levell the Hills with the Valleyes, and to lay the Mountains LOW.

April's taller than that goddamned Royal Carle when she's got heels on, and Aubrey, he'll go to seven feet maybe—*High Mountaines! lofty Cedars, it's high time for you to enter into the Rocks, and to hide you in the dust, for feare of the Lord, and for the glory of his Majesty. For the lofty looks of man shall be humbled, and the haughtiness of men shall be burned down, and the Lord ALONE shall be exalted in that day.*

Hills! Mountains! Cedars! Mighty Men! Your breath is in your nostrils.

Royal's the man, but he won't take it all. Aubrey won't ever in a hundred years look like him. Aubrey's large even now, and he's got my bitty ears and my big long nose, and he's hung, too. I'm nicely built (like a Greek god all over)—Royal's flat-faced, a miniature Kenworth with six forward gears—he's 5 feet 6 inches, and nobody who comes up close to them and takes a long keen look will ever believe he's Aubrey's real daddy. By God, they'll be the funniest looking family on Capitol Street, except for April, who is beautiful and probably kind these days, since she's got her a loving and patient man.

IV

I'd garrote the bitch if I came upon her now—I'd lay her open from cerebellum to lumbosacral plexus and let the blood run from the Old Capitol—sand-blasted and high on State Street—right on down that long, wide way, on past Reb's Tobacco House and a million eight-page Bibles, until it reached the I.C. station.

"My, my," the bemused fellows in the Desoto Trust Building, where Royal works, would say, "My, my—there's blood down in the streets again. Wonder who's down there lettin' the blood today."

"Hell, it's jus' ole Joiner, that goddamned Bryan County Redneck at it again. You know, that *bad crowd* we're always sufferin' with—that same bunch of Populists and Visionaries (madmen all) who tried to seize control down in the boonies last year. Full vicious men!

"Reckon we better get out the dogs—the cattle prods—the bull horns—reckon we better get in touch with all the Reasonable Civil Rights Groups—and best we call the lawyers that work for the President's Committee. They may be outside agitators but they still pretty reasonable fellows—and—Jesus Christ!—we better try to get out the Guard and a few thousand Federal troops.

"Most curious: murder and riot, but not a single Major Network's around to cover it."

No. Incorrect. Missed signals and a lie, for I wasn't ever able to really hurt her. When the Foots opened fire on my Brigade of Brothers, when most of us ran—both necks *and* niggers—ran from the traditional gunfire of repression—when, at dawn, at the tag end of the battle, I imagined I saw her way off down the street at the wrecked icehouse with Stream and Moon Pie—even then—when clearly she'd forsaken me, I couldn't hate her enough to really hurt her. Not even when she didn't visit me in jail.

Women—rather than fight them, I'd best go up to Jackson with all of them, with April, Maylene, and Julia Pastrana, and Ruth Motor. We'll all go. Both the quick and the dead. All the women and also Stream and Bo—to campaign for Royal Carle Boykin: Your...Next...Governor.

I'll M.C. and introduce a fine new singing group to the crowd— The Wearps—Maylene, etc.—who'd sing such good stuff as "More

Than a Hammer and Nail" and "As an Eagle Stirreth Her Nest,"
maybe even "Springfield Mountain."

One of those fierce afternoons at the corner of Capitol and State,
everybody sweating to beat hell, but most especially Julia—little
humane and silver beads dripping from her beard. Ruth would sing
rather in the style of the Andrews Sisters—clean and modern, except for her hair beginning to melt a little, like cotton candy at the
Spit. And Julia, yea, Julia, Julia, she'd add tones dark and bloody,
like Goya's final dreams—she'd sway and twist in her saturated and
intricate brocade—her voice would be a perfection out of Gypsy
Caves, her vowels all Roman, and she'd sing lead.

The Wearps. Let's hear a round of claps for The Wearps.

Let's hear some claps for April and her alto from the Methodist
choir in Bryan, airy and light, light and airy, but if you tend to it
carefully you'll hear the resonant sounds of your own hungry heart
when love has got you in her hands.

But Maylene will sing not at all. She'll merely whistle as mysteriously as a cardinal. All my pretty ones swaying together in the
impacted August sunshine. Stream a chill tenor, Bobo a murky and
cruel bass.

And then Boykin in starched denim strides forward from behind
the Doric pillars, where he's been quietly paring his fingernails,
raises both chubby freckled arms. The crowd falls silent. He sidles
up to the mike. He speaks: *My fellow Americans, my fellow
Mississippians, I have been called many things during this canvas-
sing—I have been attacked because of the company I keep.*

*My distinguished opponent has attacked me as one who has
dangerous and ugly and "strange" friends. But I ask you to look in
your own hearts when he goes on that way—for who among you
does not keep a "strange" friend in the very parlor of his heart of
hearts? We all do! You live by the side of the road in this great
land and state of ours long enough—you try and be a friend to
Man—and I'll tell you for a fact, you gonna goddamned well have
some very "strange" folk nigh. It's a Truth. PRAISE GUD . . .*

Hot damn! Royal's got 'em grabbed—they're his log, and his
speakings are a canticle they know, his various utterances are a
cant dog locked in their sides. It is the very pinch and cut of truth.

They froth a little. *There are those among us who would do away with "strange" people. They would cast out the strangenesses within—and they would deny their entrances from without. No ingress or egress of any strangeness would they allow. My fellow Mississippians, my fellow Americans, would we have it so? Think of our forebears who fled the state during Reconstruction, fled west, and then returned, unable to live in a land without niggers. Think of our own nigras who have fled north—only to return home because they missed a white drawl and clear-eyed bigotry. My friends, we have been—and we must remain—a people who cherish and nurture all manner of Strangeness.*

That vast throng, mostly a gathering of the relatively unstrange (for we must remember this is Jackson), has become somewhat listless and seized by mild midsummer neurasthenia. They have begun to question the candidate's logic. But of course the Bryan brain trust has prepared for this—the speech has been carefully shaped. Hell, it would even please the Irish Mafia.

Hold on! Hold on! I know. I . . . do . . . know many of you "enjoy" modern plumbing. You "enjoy" good motels, credit cards, and the Medical School. You call it "progress." And indeed it is . . .

Many of you would rather not turn the entire state into a Civil War pageant and museum, gaining earned increment by selling tickets at all roads and bridges at the state line. I do not blame you. I would not see these fair counties turned into a bloody Disneyland, however lucrative it might become.

I offer no reaction that tries vainly to reclaim the whole past revisited. But neither do I offer merely a madding rush into the so-called future. No! Neither do I offer only the so-called present world of today with its fuzzyheaded, imprecise, and oftentimes effeminate postures, virtues, and vices. No! Again I say no, sir, we won't put up with that.

You say then to me, what is it then that you DO offer? A GOOD question.

Yes, the answer is . . . Progressive Strangeness! Strange Progress! Let it be said that they are "masters" of a Strange Progress down there.

Ah, but I see some smiles before me out there. Some of you are saying to yourselfs, this is a so-called tease, or josh, or even a so-called put-on. It is no such thing at all.

Now listen . . .

To achieve this strangeness and valid progress we need give up but one thing—which is of course the habit of killing each other so frequently.

The die is cast, and I shudder and chill even here in the ravenous sun to hear it spoken so plainly. The Wearps let out a hummmm as he speaks it. Two, three hums to hold the crowd in line. The crowd which is now offended by such obviousness.

Stay? Stay! and he increases the pace of his speaking—*I know that all of you are thinking it is impossible to consider either strangeness or progress outside the so-called normal condition of violence.* He pauses briefly.

But, my friends, I did not even suggest we should do away with "violence." In fact, I offer an INcrease of violence.

And now you suspect me of supporting the CCC and the W.P.A.—the so-called Youth Corps. You have visions of "healthful exercise," tree planting, ditch-digging, hoeing, liming, dunging—you are near believing I'd accept such things as that as satisfactory avenues of violence.

No, my friends, for though those activities are worthy, and a little strange, though they foster health of mind and body, I would never suggest to you good people that they are adequate to our needs for violence, that they are violent enough to break our habit of murdering our fellow Mississippians, and other Americans. Those solutions are worth including in any just administration, but (and pardon the expression) they are a wee tad lily-livered.

Hummmmmm

Tradition! Progress! Strangeness! Violence!

Yeah, yeah, Amen, and so forth—a few in the crowd are finally warming to our man.

Would I do away with your riot and drunkenness? Would I take the paregoric away from your maiden aunt? Or your mother? Would I take Piper Cubs away from Delta planters? Would I do away with . . . with . . . "The Sporting Life?"

I wouldn't do it.

. . .

My friends, it fills me with an unspeakable sadness to consider the possibility of hot summer nights that offer no possibility of genuine, misery-making excess.

And there are those who would make a Des Moines of Jackson —insurance salesmen—and there are those who would make a Kankakee of Hattiesburg—runners of shirt factories—but we, I pray, will never shout "Kamerad" in defeat to such like, ever.

And what does the other party offer? Dullness! Wholesomeness!

Fellow Democrats, listen to me . . .

And while all this foolishness is going on I am reading the minds of two ladies up front in the crowd, obvious members of the La Leche League they are so healthy-looking: *She? I see it here in the program—she, the odd one is a Julia Pastrana, Mexico City and Pearl River County. Mexicans are worse than niggers? That woman singing common measure up there is a nigger!*

And: *OHGOD—Fred has this document he brought home from work, and it asks the significant question: Can the Negro and Ape mate and produce offspring? The answer is YES! and it says further proof of the close link between Ape and Negro is the fact that no White person has ever mated with an ape and produced conception—she, it says here, was trained to wear clothes and was taken care of by the Catholic Church in Mexico.*

Also, in conversation I pick this up with my eagle ears—"Sweetheart, except for the girl who's singing alto, who's nice-looking, that's a strange crowd up there. April Smith Joiner Boykin, it says here in the program. The one whistling has got some talent, but she don't look quite sane."

"Rat, rat—she looks like a picture of cousin Flo, in the nineteen-thirties—she's the one still locked up in Whitfield."

Long the argument has raged—is the Negro an ape, or some kind of subhuman?

. . .

Royal, carrying on—*Never will we submit to a state where there are cotton fields in Sunflower County with no cropper shacks at all—no culture without a no-neck in East Istabutchie driving a 1958 Mercury automobile so fast the chrome and fins start sloughing and flaking off in the high wind will ever satisfy a great people. Plug the holes in that shack, put safe tires on the Mercury— let them stay a little while ... they are our heritage.*

It could of been that way—Royal could make a talk like that, but it wouldn't pay. What I mean is the blood must run. Stepped in once, twice, many times, the Mississippi River is a bloody water. Stop the killing? Ah God, the fancy cannot cheat so well—and I've learned my own lessons the hard way, under fire. When I took all my personal history, and theirs, and put it all together, and when I rolled it all up in the grief of losing my game (football), adding to that gruel all I'd learned from a great teacher or two (Benton and Burger), I still went out and did some violence that led to killing. No doubt about it. Which wasn't fancy. Killing, Royal, is definitely here to stay.

But Royal will try to keep our language slow, strange, liquid, and pure. NO GHETTOS—THE BRAVE MISCEGENATED SOUTH. "Hush, Son."

Royal will teach us to sit up long into the night and sing gospel hymns and spirituals in our thirty-thousand-dollar houses. Some outsiders consider Power in the Blood of the Lamb to be a Metaphor, but we know better. We know that we are the Goat: lust and violence, lecherie and drunkennesse. We are the goat turned Lamb, and when our mixed blood has flowed sufficient unto Grace, we will, praise God, have saved the Whole Nation. Our goddamned South will never stink of peace—our peace *will* at last be aggressive and terrible, will come to us only after black balls have whomped against a million blond snatches, and vice versa [< L, equiv. to vice, abl. sing. of *vicis* change + *versa* to turn]—Well, why not?—for those great Bohemians Žižka and Procop should (though they really are not) be our mentors—Žižka and Procop should be our heroes: E. P. Cheyney, *The Dawn of a New Era, 1250–1453,* 1936—J. Herben, *Hus and His Followers,* 1926—F. G.

Heymann, *John Žižka and the Hussite Revolution*, 1969, J. Huizinga, *The Waning of the Middle Ages*, 1924. That sunnavabitch Boykin has never read enough.

But let us imagine that he has learned to deal with paper money and other mere symbols in the years since the mimosa flowers fell across his scored and bloody shoes, his goddamned Buster Brown *bundschuhs.* He'll beat the *condottieri* for fourteen years, but then somebody'll mow him down with a bank note or a ballot. And when they do destroy him—the old fox, the Royal Carle—they'll do it with his own wagons and chains and medium bombards.

It's Luditz and Kuttenberg now, but Lipany is coming—and God forgive me for comparing Royal to Žižka, because Royal won't really ever tell his troops to make a war drum out of his own skin after he's dead—which is exactly what Jan Žižka did for *his* Bohemia. Let's hear it for Jan fracking Žižka who made a drum of his own skin, in the fourteenth century. How is *that* for your resurrection?

By Christ, it's what old meatheads should do with their dead flesh. To hell with giving your own sweet corpse to science! Billy Rath and Bill Wallick and Red Grange and Sid Luckman and Jim Ringo and Big Daddy Lipscomb—that great fucking American— they should be torn, scored, and flayed—they should become one of those big drums that get pushed into stadiums on little carts. The goddamned game is unsymbolical. To hell with the anthropologists who would make it so. As leave call screwing symbolical as football. Boom Boom Boom millions and millions of fathers explaining to their sons that the sound they're hearing over T.V. comes from the still sentient skin of Great Americans. In this I do not jest. BIG DADDY LIPSCOMB!

"Hush, Son." All the women say it, rightly.

V

Royal was meaner then. You can see it in our class picture. Him with his eyes like a black-footed ferret's, or a nutria's, eyes demanding change. His eyes were very mean back in the sixth grade when we ran off our social studies teacher, Miss Gresham. One of the few nice ladies we ever had.

He sticks up his porcine arm from the front row where he's sitting strictly in plumb—and he asks her if she can name all forty-eight states straight through. He said he wondered if anybody could do it without a hitch, and Miss Gresham, because she was off guard and at ease, drifting, said sure she could. She looked perky and pretty in her ballerina-length seersucker, and all of us enjoyed the good way she smelled the hours she taught us—"Evening in Paris" for us kiddies . . .

She was the first white woman to ever excite me very much.

But could she name the states? Hell, I'm surprised Royal didn't ask for all the capitals to boot. She was smiling and tilting her head back and forth, trying to do it alphabetically instead of by the map in her head—which map in your head is the only way, the map in the head, not that Alabama to Wyoming idiocy—and never trust the ones who don't know their geography and history: she left out New Hampshire, Connecticut, Oregon, and South Dakota. Missing South Dakota, that's what got Royal irked and started pulling some of the rest of us in behind him. Miss Gresham was making it easy for him to round us up for his kiddy-matinée insurrection. The goddamned pitiful thing was she believed she'd got them all O.K.

Royal never mentioned the ones she'd missed. The room became very still. You could smell the chalk dust and the finer dust on the window blinds, and all of us children were strangely soaked to the bone in that fearful knowledge you feel in your skin the first time you hear and understand the springs squeaking in the early morning in your momma's room.

And damned if Royal didn't tell her it was O.K.: "That's not exactly right, but it's O.K., Miz Gresham." They'd swapped places.

That little chap with all his freckles bunched together and looking so goddamned earnest, even the least bit saddened, wasn't about to let up—in the midst of some headlong compulsion or another he's going to see to it that *facts* get their due in our classroom.

And would she have a go at the presidents? No dates needed.

Miss Gresham might not have been the most flawless flesh in the world, but even back then I knew she was being taken advantage of. Her eyes were widening a little, the daydream fading. All the young teachers taught in a sort of Mel Torme and Eddie Fisher mist—but Royal was burning the dew off her tender grass in a big hurry. In essence her mind was spotless, having been exposed to not much more than the *Baptist Record* and whatever else they read as education majors at Delta State—she was the kind who— since I think I'm right in remembering she was originally from the panhandle of Oklahoma—must have thought a great evening, when she's a child, was shooting jack rabbits for bounty money, to go to the picture show with. And there she was, in a slow ground fog, trying to teach the smartest class of pupils Bryan, Mississippi, ever turned out.

She was, in the most elemental sense, outclassed—and on the presidents she scubbed her sweet ass along the chalk tray and got a line on it. She was trying to believe it was all in fun and in the best interests of education. But finally the presidents broke her down. God, she fooled around and left out Van Buren, Taft, and Mc-Kinley (while noting that Cleveland had had it twice)—she went along naming them cool as you please with no more than a *let's see now* between, until she realized the little bastard Boykin was after her.

She might have lost her metaphysical cherry to a Camp Sheldon Soldier (for surely an Oklahoma cutting horse got the meaningless real thing), and it might of seemed her soul was gone to a joyous nasty hell when his prod went deep, but when she saw and under-stood the vain squint in the cold eye of twelve-year-old Royal Boykin, she'd learned about a helluva lot more than sex. Trapped in a child's eye, she learned more than a whole goddamned brigade of pricks was ever about to teach her. Right there in her own schoolroom, full of patriotic posters and good advice on how children can save their permanent teeth, she found out that *losing* is a helluva lot worse than being lost. If she'd suffered amnesia and had awakened in the arms of some stud nigger sergeant in Detroit City, right after the great riot of '44, she'd of been better off than locked up with R.C. If she'd campfollowed across the entire width of Poland, the close weave of her skin covered with lice and groady with disease, she could of cursed or prayed to God, something fine and extreme, but who, what soul, can ask in good faith to be delivered from the curiosity of a bright child? Real sin would of been a blessing—but she had no way of understanding the vigorous mental depravity she'd been pushed into by Boykin. No way at all.

All us pupils gave her bleak stares and sullen hanging faces with nascent smiles at the corners—then giggles—when Royal was saying, "Miss Gresham, you left out three presidents, and they are Van Buren, McKinley, and Taft."

Maybe I read myself into her, but I don't think so. I've been mad, but never dumb.

She'd got the message—she couldn't finish it and fell apart, crying and streaking the powder on her pretty face, and shaking the padded shoulders of her cheap suit.

Miss Gresham scubbing her hands up and down on her skirt at the hips and yelling and bawling at us. She stopped dead still and cried out, "OOOOOOOOO . . ." And then she ran down the side aisle to the door, and swear to Betsy I expected Bo to trip her.

It shouldn't have happened. She might have been vague while thinking all day about the corporal's seely instrument, and all his other doings on her tidy little ole bunnybody, but all things considered she'd managed to say some interesting things along the way about national parks and koala bears and salmon. She hadn't been an entire disaster as a schoolteacher. She'd treated us permissively and kindly as she would have her own children, but educationwise it was all wrong, and Royal knew it, the little snot.

It's one of those hard things to judge. She wasn't much teacher, but then again it was Royal's meanness that was the real evil, even though he told me he never meant to drive her off completely. He said he felt he ought to point up her incompetence in some dramatic way in order that she grasp it and understand the necessity to correct it. Christ! *Incompetence*, he says, in the sixth grade.

She was a young teacher and she wasn't fired for missing presidents and states, and certainly not for crying—it was for telling us, and Royal in particular, at the door, that we were mean and would spend all our eternity in hell for such meanness. She might as well have taught us all to be Communists or that the world wasn't created in 4004 B.C. as do that: "Y'all go stray-ut to Hail—y'all mean and thoughtless—y'all go on stray-ut to Hail." Weep, weep, weep.

Bundschuh! Bundschuh! Bundschuh!

It's curious. I feel more guilt for that day than almost everything else. By God, I hope Miss Gresham is having herself a good life.

VI

If Mary stays in Galveston much longer I'm going to start doing impure deeds. Actually I ought to burn all my volumes, quit thinking about squamous things, and cut out. I ought to go play ball or something.

I'll leave her a note that says I've turned over a new leaf—I'll tell her to stuff re-form and/or revolution right up her pretty, bumpy bottom—small bumps and some runkles—*she's got runkles on her but she's pretty*—I'll tell her I'm giving up school and talking and writing and study of all kinds, and I'm going to the Pacific Coast and be a longshoreman with Eric Hoffer.

Mary, I done quit the soft mental life and I'm heading for California and training camp. You won't believe it, hon, but since you've been gone I've bought me a new size-huge jock and a size-huge sweat suit, new sneakers, too, and I been doing laps at the T.C.U. track. I'm under three hundred pounds and I'm feeling like maybe I could make it again.

Babe, it don't cut no oleo with you, but it's true that every team in The League would be proud to take another look at me. I never was fired or let go on waivers—I wasn't sold or swapped for a fucking draft choice—I got hurt and quit. I got the actual letters from the Bulls saying they want me back. Ain't no goddamned assistant coach ever came padding down the hall to tell me to come on with him, AND BRING YOUR PLAY BOOK. Nobody ever said Joiner had a bad attitude. When they cut down to forty-nine players, I was there—when they cut to forty-three, I was there. I was there on September 9, when the final forty were home free.

JOINER WAS NEVER CUT

Shot at and missed, shit at and hit, but never cut.

But I won't write that note. I'll just leave. I'll just leave, noteless, and go to Jackson to visit the bride and groom. After the letters and the phone calls I'd like to face them meat to meat, especially R.C.

Hell, I don't even know for sure where it'll take place—the wedding. Probably at home, even though not many people are there who'd enjoy the ceremony. But maybe in Jackson—probably at Royal's new suburban Presbyterian church, for, as I've said, surely R.C. has become a Presbyterian in Jackson, though he'll always be a Methodist at heart.

I wouldn't go to the service itself. I'd just make the party afterwards, that small but gracious affair at the Hillyard Country Club. I could head on over there, and he'd take twenty, thirty good minutes off from the other company so we could have some conversation about all the things we've done for each other.

He'd try to act like he never called, like he never knelt at his pussy Princess phone and cried out to me. I ought to crash that goddamned party—be nimble among the potted ferns and rubber plants—I ought to swing easily into the queer indirect lighting of the River Bar, stride in, and cry in a level voice, "Royal Boykin cheats on his woman! Ruth Motor—I tell you . . . there's this woman Ruth Motor who . . ."

But I'll be suave. I'll nod to Helen, who'll be dressed in purple, a tasteful frock the color of nux vomica blossoms; I'll nod and she'll shit a brick: stramonium: henbane: ipecac. And Stream, on seeing me come back, will swingle and twitch like he's on squill. Last thing I told Stream was I'd come back and get him some day. Say a thing like that up in the nose nasally to Stream and he *stays* nervous—starts memorizing Melville. *I'm gonna getcha* . . . Anyway, Royal'd stick a glass of Turkey in my fist and want to know

how the hell I'm doing over in Texas: "Son, this stuff about giving
a Classical Education to culturally depraved [deprived] children
is *fine*. Rhetoric is important, Son. Right?" Big back slap. T.V.
and the Junior Chamber'll do that to a good man. "Without History our civilization simply can't survive. Son, the average student
today don't know who Charlemagne was!"

"No shit!"

"And I think it's pretty amazing that school in Texas will take
you on . . ."

"After what I did?" says I with violent humility.

"Yeah—but I guess you proved you didn't start it?" Bleakly,
seeing I'm bunched up around the brows.

"The school is experimental."

"Well that's great. Hell, you don't even have a teaching cer-
tificate, do you?"

"Nope." He's a goddamned academic snob, he is.

The little bastard. He's quietly pissed that I showed up. Bad
form. The call and April's letter should have mended all wounds.
Lula Walls should of covered all his crimes. There is nothing so
bothered as a man who's trying to mix dignity and sincere cam-
araderie in the same pot. It'll give a fellow diverticulitis sure as hell.

He expects me to be reasonable and understanding as he is. He
craves (he says) all my stories about how my students who, though
exceptional (up and down the scale), have done especially well
with a male teacher.

He'll be amazed to hear that a sociologist in Austin is considering a thesis on my effectiveness as a teacher. He's happy (translate
embarrassed and *jealous*) to find that *Look* just might do a feature
on me: Ex-NFL Star and Revolutionary Scholar Makes a Legitimate Comeback Slap Dab in the Middle of the System—gimme an
L, gimme an I, gimme a B.

It's not every kid in any kind of grammar school who knows
about the mechanical clocks and astrolabes the sixteenth-century
Persians used, not every tad gets the straight skinny on the use of
perspective in Canaletto's *Stairs of Santa Maria della Salute*.
Royal, I've taught the laws of congruent and isosceles triangles to

little people who are said to be low down on the I.Q. scale. I've taught crude calculus to near idiots: an old Western tradition. And I could, given another chance in Mississippi, raise Aubrey better than you.

And we teach practical stuff at the U.P.S. Shop and mechanics and electronics—we get the little mothers ready for the great world. Calipers and squares and plumb lines—I've given a little talk on the flying buttress—arch and strut and buttress—while showing kids how to build a trestle table for our refectory. At the U.P.S. we don't always teach the same goddamned subject. We mix it up. And I've done about everything but coach.

Royal'd unbind his tux from his ass and be frank—he'd want to know if it hurts the ole ego to be doing that sort of thing after being in The League. R.C. wonders how I can stand teaching tiny tots after I had such a great future as a tackle. And, yes, madrafact I can (most of the time), being as it is that I'm the subject of three dissertations in criminal sociology, a regular walking rehabilitation project. That's great for the ego.

And don't you need to lose a little weight, huh, Son, for the old health's sake, for old sake's sake, as we say in Ireland and Southern Mississippi.

We'd get around to how this thing probably is working out for the best, and Royal'd smooth back the kinky hair on his temples and tell me I really should visit Aubrey whenever I want to—he'd say that, knowing goddamned well I'm not about to see any of these people ever again after this terrible night.

I'd maybe wander by April, who's short and stately in her super-delicate blue chiffon, stopping very briefly to shake her hand, since there's no help . . .

Kill! Kill! Kill!

Royal'd come right on over to me, where I'm standing amid ferns as thick as some primordial swamp. He'd come to me because he would want me to understand that in the course of human events Sonny's woman, his sweet and hairless April, is destined to end up under R. C. Boykin. He'd want me to know he's got no power over it. He'd say, "Come on, Son, let's take this bottle out to the twelfth green and get bombsville." And off we'd go, arm in arm, singing "Power in the Blood" and "Beulah Land."

Give the bastard credit. Even now he can fake those songs. Hank Williams—godalmighty, we'd sing some Hank, and Royal'd claim there's something *peculiarly Southern* about us sitting there in the grass getting piles together (wet grass and cold stones being just the things to give you piles, says Coach Topp) with all that racket going on back in the club—us wandering out there beneath the summer moonlight that's spilling down on the North Jackson ticky-tacky—and Royal's actions, sir, are cruelty out of mind, abject cruelty. It's sentimental horseshit and condescension, for he knows damn well the fucking yeoman past is dead as Lee's lieutenants, and us with it. I ought to lift the green flag right out of the cup and stake his head down to the hole with it. It's *peculiarly Southern* how he'd say, "Have a cigarette, Son." He carries them for his loyal friends, though he doesn't smoke much himself. He's my assassin any way you cut it. Takes my guts and heart, and now he wants my lungs—eats me head to asshole the way you do a pig. And the worst of it is he'd cry before it's over. A face-to-face confrontation would do him in.

"I love you, Old Cock, Old Son." Then he'd get up weeping and stalk around me like Ganymede around Jupiter. I don't pretend to understand his mind. He *would* rather be out there with me than in the smoke of his own wedding party, April or no April. He'd really try to whip up a funk. He'd weary and get bistre circles around his eyes, but he's not queer: "Sonny, make a go of it this time. Do the great, fine work you're capable of . . ."

He's still upset about the revolution.

"Goddamn it—I joined in a fight some poor beat-down people were having. They'd had two of their people murdered, and that kind of shit has been going on too long."

"All you did was kill pore Foots."

"Lord God, I'm sorry. I'm sorry it came to more killing. I guess. But it put some life in those niggers."

"You were drunk or something."

"Bennies and beer and rum. It was a good ole religious high."

"Pass the bottle," says Royal. He'd have to drink on that, and he'd have sense enough to know what I did wasn't entirely abnormal.

I lean hard on him: "Man, you wouldn't be marrying that fine woman in there if it hadn't been some trouble . . ."

"Which would of been O.K."

"You don't want her?" Hope rises eternal.

"Yeah. I want her."

"Why?"

"We've been through all that," and he says it in such a way to suggest I'm supposed to respect his wedding day, and night. "Go to hell," he says in a downcast voice that's almost a curse and a hiss. "I mean it, man. You've clomped around on my life for twenty years. You're a damned murderer, and now you got the gall to rebuke me with questions when I've been very, very good to you."

"You'll do it tonight."

"Of course . . . of course." He walks out across the green and looks at the moonlight down in the sand trap. He then stares out across the course toward the river and the airport light glimmering over the swamp. He's in a mood, while I'm still seated back on the green, humming "Careless Love" and patting the folds of my peanut belly. I'm so bloated and sick with being bloated I wish all my shirt buttons would pop off into the chicken's mouth the way the fatman's do in *Smilin' Jack*.

"Have you ever made love to her?"

"No." Forcelessly.

"Turn around so I can hear you." And he does turn.

"No . . ."

"Why?"

"Because up till now she was *your* wife."

"You'll do it tonight?" I'm surprised to hear the tremolo of a whine in my voice.

"Yeah, man. I'm gonna take her nighty off an' ball her eyes out." Royal says that. He's gonna take her down to her bare nothing and do it. He gonna bang her bod. All of it. But her nipples don't look nearly so much like coolie hats anymore, since Aubrey. Royal's the kind who sits up all night reading Alan W. Watts and

Marie Bonaparte. He will not be pleased until it's clitoridean, spiritual, and vaginal simultaneously. But he's going to find out that all she requires is that he be sincerely horny. If he's truly horny it'll please her. And as for all the detail work, I've already taught her that. It'll come out real good.

Best I not go to Jackson—best I stay right here and read *The Renaissance Idea of Wisdom.*

But I did pose a good question. For without my little war he'd of never got her. Beating her up and tearing up Cantrell's Stand and trying to kill Stream wasn't particularly good for our marriage —but it was the niggers fucked the kitty. But I do not regret it. Not for one minute.

Let him live with the irony—and, Royal, however much I miss her and treasure the memory of our times together, and our little boy, I'm not sorry I got mixed in with Slater and his good people. I did exactly what I had to do. The time had come around for me to be an *active* niggerlover.

And I'm not saying I was hot to trot for Slater's boycott at first. Hell no. I like Slater, always have—drove the ice truck with him—and he's a lean grainy nigger with those yellowish flecks in his eyes, even when he's young. He's always a sort of stooped and bony mother—tall and with an axlike face. He might even be a Watusi, or part Indian. What the hell? And by the time I'm in high school it's clearly correct for Slater to vote and go to a white school, all that good stuff you get with good law—and I wouldn't of done much more than maim him if he'd made off with April— but I do admit the boycott he got up did deal me an awkward blow to the emotions: you might say it complicated my attitudes, be- cause it changed the looks of things.

I didn't like seeing the Rangle Grocery close, and I didn't like the demise of Chalmers' Five and Dime, and I damn well didn't enjoy the end of Betner's Drugs. It's like a gouged socket and there's a sort of spiritual glaucoma afflicts a community when a boycott begins to thrive—and just because those fool merchants won't put in the nigger checkers and salespeople.

Both sides were making me pissed. It was a lovely perfervid ambiguity right up until the fucking necks—that *bad crowd*—started the burnings and killings in earnest. You can expect a nigger church or two to get burned every three, four years, but when those Pure-White-Race-or-Bust people burn down three, four a year and then get unsubtle about murder, you take a second look at the political diastole and systole, you decide maybe that things aren't so ambiguous after all.

And Royal is cruel enough to say the boycott caused it: *The goddamned boycott "caused" Foots to blow up Roosevelt's truck —it caused him to shoot Jubal.* He said that to me after it was all over, and he'd say it again in Jackson. It is amazing how we'd be having this supererogatory and, by God, supercilious conversation while sitting and lying butt to gut on the green—*our revolution is a bourgeois revolution, therefore the workers must open the eyes of the people to the deceptive practices of the bourgeois politicians, must teach the people not to believe in words, but to depend wholly on their own strength, on their own organization, on their own unity, and on their own aims.*

I'd recite that to slick, callous Royal.

"Very pretty, very pretty," says he.

"Damn right it is, and just because we shot up the courthouse and lost don't make it any less so."

"You didn't have a plan."

Which is incorrect: "Did too."

"Goddamn it, Son, you're a white man who is trying to be Muddy Waters and Big Joe Turner and Hank Williams and Bilbo and Vardaman all at the same time—and Marx and Engels and John Reed and Martin Luther King. You've got some kind of emotional and intellectual hard-on."

He's sitting on my belly, in the role of the victor by this time, but enough is too much. After he's done heaping scorn on me I'd have to cast him off—I'd have to thrust up swiftly my deeply swathed rectus abdominus—I'd have to bounce him off my belly, and when he's risen three or four feet above the grass of the green, I'd snatch back my legs against my torso—much power still remaining in the rectus femoris, the iliotibial bands, the vastus lateralis, the gluteus maximus, the biceps femoris, the sartorius, the semimembranosus, the gastrocnemius, the vastus medialis, and of course, the Achilles tendon—snatch back and then belt the sunnavabitch into the stars—I'd cast him far out into the tail of the comet Ikeya-Seki, and he'd cry unheard beyond the orbit of Pluto.

I never lived in a shack that smelled like cornmeal and piss— being like that because the meal and fatback was what you ate and because, especially in cold weather, you did your business through the holes in the floor. I never was a nigger who came back years later to the open field where once his house was—a nigger seeing only high weeds where his shack had stood and fertilized the ground. I never was very social with them—but I'd wanted to be, and would have, had things been different. But neither had I spent all that much time with the really ugly necks, except to drink with them in the tonks.

And none of that makes any difference, because I'd seen plenty to do what I did. I'd beat up my wife and I'd wrecked a tonk, and I was up on b and b, and I was miserable because I wasn't in The League any more—but that didn't make my feelings for the nigras worthless, which is what Royal's set on believing.

I ended up at the M.E. Negro church that's burned, and all these people are crying and singing over the deaths of Jubal and Rosey—and I'd seen Jubal get it. It wasn't outside my domain, as Royal put it. Hell no. I'd seen them all before and I knew a lot of the names. And I knew Slater very well, and I'd sat around with Jubal more than once at the icehouse—him playing his guitar with a bottleneck on one finger . . .

I spoke to the coloreds and told them how it wasn't going to be this way forever and I recited some Coppe and other stuff, which they didn't follow all that well.

Royal: *yes, yes, the killing of Jubal and Rosey—deplorable— deplorable—but can it really be that riot and anarchy served their memories?*

Yes, yes, and you weren't the one who saw him shot, and, man, some people have got to be mean to shoot a man who's singing.

It was the noon after I finally split with April, and I'm just sitting in the car down in front of Betner's Drugs, which is about to go under from the boycott I thought—and there's this ancient nigger, ole Ju, out front of the place with a couple of Beatnik-types. They're singing hymns and protest songs and it all struck me as a little bit revolting, and then I was revolted at myself because I was revolted by the Beatnik-types. What most upset me was how these outside agitators had sucked in this handsome old nigger.

That sort of thing was on my mind, but I was also staring at the sun's reflection on the dusty pane, and I was thinking how crazy it was when there's a fine unpolitical storm out in the Gulf not far away—and I was also considering the remarkably puerile idea of going in and buying some Trojans from poor beleaguered Dexter Betner, the idea being not so much political as petty and sexual—the result of some fantasy about going to New Orleans and balling my eyes out for the rest of my life. I was hung over and Lordy it seemed odd for those cats to be singing with Ju. *It's a kneeway journey home.*

Ju's a fat bald man with tiny gray tufts nearby his small close ears, and he didn't see too well. He's mashing and slapping his guitar through some blues song I don't know too well, and this vague boy and skinny girl are trying to pick and sing along with him, but mostly they are faking it voicewise like Dylan does.

I was definitely getting mixed feelings right up until the time I see those kids' eyes pop wide—up until the time their eyes pop wide and their mouths drop open in true fear, and they drop their instruments, all of which happened in a great hurry.

You got to realize I was very hung over and sitting in a warm car sweating and thinking about an estranged wife mostly—I simply didn't have all the circuits connected. It was like my whole head was full of hairy and thirsty cilia (especially my mouth)—so even when the guns went off, blowing out the window of Betner's and knocking down Ju and the boy and girl, I couldn't quite get the meaning of it framed immediately.

First thing I did was rub my arm across my smarting eyes and feel vaguely irritated. Boom Boom Boom—and my body is saying what the hell's all that—and why can't they leave me alone at least in the middle of the day . . .

. . .

It just wasn't the place for such shit. There wasn't anybody paying attention to the songs but me. There wasn't any crowd at all, Benton having told the locals to cool it and pay no attention. But there it was, after the booms. There's bottles of suntan lotion all broken and dripping in the shattered display, and there's these people floundering around on the sidewalk.

Somebody'd eased by in a car and cut down on them. Hell, they damn near cut down on me, a couple of shots actually hitting my front fender. But by the time I'm awake and halfway out the car door here comes Benton and Mayor Jernigan and Dexter. Everybody is there and the ambulance siren is tearing my head off as it comes toward us.

It was one helluva mess. The kids are all gouged with shot but you can tell it's not mortal. They're sitting and crying and holding their chopped hands to their mouths while their jeans start getting sour with blood. It wasn't them that caught the force of it—it's Jubal, who'd been sitting in a crate, and he was demolished.

Hell, if it hadn't been for his guitar over his chest and belly he'd of been ruined entirely. He was driven backwards into a pile of wood and his poor head was almost gone.

It is the one thing I try to keep entirely out of mind as much as possible—it was so ugly. I've never even done more than mention it to Mary: Jubal hardly had a head at all, but he did still have the broken neck of his guitar clenched in his fist.

Benton was furious that I hadn't seen who did it. He's asking me while the girl is saying they had stockings over their heads, and it was a pickup not a car, and she thinks she's got the license plate. But Benton wants *me* to have seen it.

I told him the goddamned girl'd seen who did it, and up yours, Davis, and leave my ass alone. I actually had an inclination to draw back and hit the Sheriff, which he noticed. Suddenly I felt terribly sorry for him. His face was collapsed and his eyes on mine were batting open and shut at a terrible rate and he was liverish in color, not pale—he was blue like a kind of drowned man, and he said in a loud voice, "It's happened!"

. . .

And when Foots got killed that very night I had a vision, but it wasn't as bad as seeing Jubal all messed up in the guitar wood and strings and plate glass. The vision was wretched but it wasn't the vile thing they'd made of that old singer, and Foots' death, because he was more or less whole physically, and because he asked for the grilled cheese, wasn't so bad at all.

Just as Foots got hit in the cross fire I saw him catch a bullet in his teeth.

It was a tour de force. And it was a large bullet.

He opened his great mouth wide and bit down quickly, and there it was between his false choppers, a bullet that looked about six inches long and about three in circumference. He stopped dead still in the rainy dark and turned his head slowly from side to side, then moved his head up and down, very slowly, showing to all that he, Foots Magee, had done it, had caught a large bullet in his teeth. His eyes were wild and his smile was expansive and excruciating, but also there was pleasure and pride and maybe even a little Joy in his demeanor.

Foots bit his bullet and glowed in the wet dark for an instant. Which was a lovely vision indeed.

Royal—you thoughtless sunnavabitch—you never saw that nigra's brains running off of Betner's bricks, and you never saw Foots in his glory, and you never really roused a people to resist. You never did any of that, and you have no right at all to call me foolish for getting involved.

They got married today. August 15—the day when practice starts. Sobeit.

And Mary's back from Galveston, thank God.

A man ought to be able to change his life.

5

STILL, IT was The NFL and I was good enough in some ways. I was big and fast enough. Six feet seven inches and trim at 280 pounds, and solid. It wasn't this soft meat and chicken fat I've got on me now, and breathing hard all the time, and not so much of the booze and cigarettes, and other trash that Mary Ann brings around the place. I wouldn't ever have made one of those T.V. ads, even if they'd asked me, because it's a good way to be a bad example to the kids. The players themselves ought to put a stop to it?

The Game is Big Business, but shouldn't there be some attempt to save a little of the illusion of manly health and vigor that President Kennedy tried to keep before the people?

I was big and fast enough, and I could block. During training and exhibition season I blocked hell out of some of the best men in The League, including Coley Sellers who was with us then—the Bulls. He's with Denver now, and it's a shame to see a great man like that let go on waivers and end up in The AFL.

It was almost the worst thing that ever happened to Foots Magee, whom I did help kill, and who was indeed one of the true Bryan greats, and just a dozen or so years ahead of all my crowd.

Foots was so mad the year he was made a free agent and ended up in Philadelphia that he played like an animal for three more years, which was three years too long physically, and which didn't do his soul any goddamned good either, because it wasn't his salad days in Detroit no matter how hard he tried.

It could of course have been worse. He could have come along later and been one of those old NFL stars who ended their days in the *early* AFL. Or he could have gone to Canada . . .

You flip the T.V. from channel to channel and the difference is clear as a bell—The AFL with a lot of flashy individual play—but also with too much red-dogging and too many bombs early in the game—flashy play and niggery uniforms—a lot of fun to watch—but not that solid class, that sure combination of finesse and weight and power and speed and quickness you get with a couple of NFL clubs.

And Foots, he sure as hell played three years too long. It left him bobbing and shaking his head the whole time he was pumping gas at his cousin's filling station in Bryan.

It's not very frequent this sort of thing happens—but that good man—God bless his dead hide—he took too many shots to the head. He spent too many years under the helmet. He's a center and during his last season he started missing his audibles, his automatics. He couldn't shift gears in the line—he forgot what the quarterback yelled out as fast as it was said, and Christ, he fucked up some plays.

Being punched out is a terrible thing, and every athlete suffers it once in a while—a series of rapid-fire *déjà vus* while moving up over the ball—Foots remembering plays from his champion days with the Lions, perfect punt snaps and great blocks on the sneak—memory and history being man's worst curse.

Let's hear it for the Post-Historical Civilization!

He dropped back in the path of a pulling guard a couple of times, and that's, by God, just about the most embarrassing thing in the world.

Aesthetically, you don't have much when you see two offensive linemen knocking each other out. They're likely to fine you for it. They're likely to break your plate.

. . . likewise also other sinful folk: the people high up in the stands with their whiskey and women . . . Jeesus . . . sleek women and feeling their knees and snatches . . . Foots was sick on hate and yet when he was dying he wanted a grilled cheese sandwich—dying in my arms and saying "Gimme a grillcheese . . ." *Like the*

sea and the river unquiet and unquelled in evil. Let's hear it for Peter Chelčický: *As waves of the sea against other waves, quarrel against quarrel, pride against pride, hardship against hardship—in one place they have slain one another, in another place challenged one another, as desiring to slay or rob another, and thus is the most mournful sound of the sea to be heard.*

Slater leaned in beside me in the rain and said we better get us and the body all the way on the other side of the truck and out of all this shooting—I think I loved Watusi Slater that night, but it did piss me off bad that he wasn't showing any profound signs of grief for Foots, and I gave him a hard look to suggest my displeasure.

"That man's been dead for years," he says to Foots Magee. "Now let's try and save ourselfs." He squeezes down on my shoulder and says, hauling up the thick words from deep in his throat, "He's the one shot ole Ju, and he probably killed Rosey. Remember?" We each got hold of a sweaty and bloody armpit and pulled Foots around the truck, but he was dead already, I'm pretty sure.

Waivers, the goddamned waivers. I'm glad I knew when to get out. It's the American way. You get in there and do the best you can and if you do good you go around looking like it's easy, and you never admit you were scared shitless all the way up. But if you see you're just another jock in the game, you get out and go on to something else. It makes real good sense. Guns in a rainstorm sound silly. The sound can't carry right.

When Foots was with Detroit he'd come balling back into town in his red, goddamned Pontiac convertible. He couldn't really afford it even with what he was making then—which wasn't all that much by post-T.V. standards—but he *was* some kind of happy man, and until he got worthless he laid just about everything in South Mississippi. And some Delta women to boot. No more than a couple of grand for an NFL championship game. Jesus!

And he was generous to everybody—especially old friends and

his people. He got his old man a new shotgun, and he got Mrs. Magee an automatic Maytag—but on the night he died of bleeding he was paunchy all over and mostly the soggy fool. A goddamned pitiful, drunk fool is what most people thought he was by then— gone crazy hating niggers and everything. Shit, you'd think he'd of learned something from all his colored friends in The League—but when he collapsed full of shot and shell he'd long since forgot all that.

All he had left was his legs and even there he couldn't trust the gastrocnemius and semimembranosus, and, Christ, from deltoid to rectus abdominus he was all gone down when he died.

His pectoralis major was nothing but tit.

But I shouldn't talk, considering the condition of my subclavian artery.

Foots never learned anything while out in the great world. He was predictable, which is *pure* worthlessness. Him and Stream as far apart as Mercury and Pluto, but just the same at heart, both terrestrials. One bone-coarse, the other bone-sensitive, and neither one of them able to change. So it would be them I do harm to—kill one and damn near maim the other.

But even toward the end Foots was an attractive enough man so long as he kept his clothes on, which he didn't always do while working around the pumps. And even near the end he looked O.K. until you checked out his eyes, which were gone from being good hard ones down to sullen and vicious—especially since his head dawdled around on his shoulders the way it did. He'd left all his character in The League—that vicious man, Foots Magee—all the skill that would let him snap the ball on punts with his head up, when he wanted to, his vision clear to block. He, and the beauty of it, was able and quick enough to wheel to the flank to pick off the biggest defensive ends in The League as they rushed.

And Foots was a womanizer of the first water, specializing in the kind who dye their hair black and wear split panties and briefs, like Mrs. Weatherford. He took it all for granted—and he never once thought of trying to be a good example for children—he took his 6 feet 3 inches, 260 pounds, and 18-inch neck for granted in those days, all that vast molding of flesh and muscle, like the *Prometheus* by Rubens. He didn't realize that the forearm shivers and booze would finally pluck his liver out—pluck his liver and fuck his head up. Hell, even when he was in decline the women loved him.

He'd been a fine man.

In the old days everybody'd gather at Nancy's when Detroit or Philadelphia was playing, everybody sitting around the Cafe watching the T.V. set and drinking Sunday beer, and sometimes you'd miss a whole quarter after Foots made a perfect punt snap or a terrific block. Somebody was always primed to tell a story on him —usually something about his women—and most frequently a variation on the time he bet Sheriff Benton (and others) he could make it with three at once at the Moss Motel.

He was a football player and he could also sing songs. He was *talented*. He was a coordinated, talented man, at his best, and he never once in his heyday in The League showed the mummernem guilties. Most necks—even after the sweet smell of success has come their way—still show the guilties in their eyes: shit built in by mummernem.

Man, if you don't know, I cannot help you!

Foots was infantile and always capable of joy. Get his randy ass a little high and happy in his glory out at the Second Stand and he'd take the mike and start belting out some first-rate versions of Hillbilly and Rhythm and Blues. When he did "Little Momma" or "Wild Side of Life" the goddamned place would come apart. I've seen him do "All Night Long" so good, and tearing off his polo shirt in the process, so good there's ten, twelve hysterical women down on their sweet knees in front of him. With their pretty heads thrown back and their long hair washing back and forth across their dainty backs, and swinging their titties in time with Foots' voice, they were completely and gloriously depraved. And what the hell could their dates do but drink more Jax and pray for a split lip on the sax player—take some hexamethonium?

.   .   .

And what the hell is at the heart of such carousing? What is it makes a man seek out that funky shit? Maybe a man just can't stand the feel of his entirely healthy body breathing the cleanest and most odoriferous air in the world all the time, maybe he's got to have himself a place of Weatherford-type ordure to hunker in from time to time, so he can remember what his body's all about, and where it's eventually going.

It's strange. Goddamned perfectly clear winter night, the temperature in the forties, and the pines green and lovely and grave outside—how come we go inside and wrap us around with all that fucking neon? Drink all that beer? Dance to all that music written to hunch time?

It's what I can't understand about Davis Benton: how he can encourage that life, how he could bet Foots he can't make it with the two Westerman sisters and Maudine Terrell. Those three women came in a claque and took a booth under the Regal ad and assaulted many beers with unmitigated excess—right up until the moment ole Foots made his move to the mike.

Had Foots paid them to do it? I doubt it. The legend says otherwise.

Everybody starts yelling for Foots, including this high school kid who's the regular singer with The Boonies. Foots flings up his arms at the bar and cries out: HAVE NO FEAR—BIG FOOTS IS HEAH. Hot damn, that tough mother in his weenie jeans comes loping across the floor to a bombast of cheers, and about the time he's toed his Acme's up on the base of the mike, those three women *are* dropped down in front of him—even before he starts singing. The sunnavabitch made the bet early in the afternoon, at Nancy's, and he really couldn't be entirely sure the quail'd show up. But you never do know. And they did. Those dirty women came.

I wasn't there, being too young for the Stand when Foots was in his prime, but I got the truth from a hundred people.

And the smile he had on his face the second before he stroked into his first song was the sublime face of Power. I kid you not. It crosses my mind every time I hear that story told: *Foots Magee had the Power*.

With Delmus McCoy going down on the piano and little Leroy Rivers (in fact a Cajun nigger) on harmonica, it was close to gut-bucket. Foots does a job on "Popcorn Man" that is truly carnal. He makes up verses and then shouts back to the band to glide on into "A New House," which he does with much body motion. *I got a whole lot of lovin' locked up inside.* The Stand rose to the occasion that night. *My baby don't wear no furs—two towel sets, him and hers.* Everybody on their feet and swaying back and forth with Big Foots and the three women he couldn't have exactly counted on to come around. They've all come a kneeway up to where he's at, busting out their hose, and now they're laying hands on him.

Foots was magnificient right on down the line, and what I couldn't free myself from was the true fact that, yes, by Jesus, most women would, after that kind of action, crawl his handsome ass. Bryan Mississippi, My Home Town: *I'm gonna buy me a pistol as long as I am tall.*

Cantrell over behind the bar saw what was happening and he was scared the whole place would break out in a flaming and positively illegal orgy. *Let copulation thrive.*

Foots sang out his set, then went off with the girls, and there were many cheers, though not from Benton, the loser. Benton was trying to look disappointed. He didn't cheer. He merely smiled.

What kind of man makes a bet like that?

What sort of man wins such a bet?

Foots' exit was ugly. He grabbed a Westerman girl under each arm and jogged across the room with them, Maudine chasing after. He ran with his knees rather high and actually banged one of the girls in the face a little, causing her to cry out. Foots is yelling, "Oink, Oink." It was ugly, and I hear that almost everybody laughed at the Westerman with the bloody lip. It was ugly and it was sad—and Mary says the saddest thing is how I still think of it as ugly and sad: *If you'd tried to be nice to those girls they wouldn't have understood. It would be the old story of the nice boy and the whore.* Except, Mary, the Westermans and Maudine *weren't* whores—nor was Polly Roberts—and, Son, if you don't watch out you're going to try to solve the entire mystery of human depravity, which is a rather large order. Son, you're going to try to explain what's so evil about nice girls, if you don't watch out.

It was ugly to see the Foots who was so robust and masculine while singing turn into a giddy mean child, a goddamned hateful child, so quickly, a tease. When he's going "oink, oink" he's got his freshly mouth pulled apart to show his fine square false teeth— he's making the sound with just the movement of his tongue—and he's running awkwardly in his boots, all of which was *ugly*.

And betting money on making three women—it's absolutely sickening. And it *was* especially bad because Davis was in on it. Davis bet against it, but he was pleased to see Foots win. The goddamned Sheriff admits grinning in spite of himself as Foots and the women passed through the door.

Going out the door of the Stand one of the Westermans kicked her dress up and showed her bare butt under the split briefs—and that really makes me sad, because it doesn't sound at all like April with nothing on under. It's not the least bit similar. Those hose and garters and briefs on the Westermans were a terrible profanation of the female backside. It wasn't the happy way my daddy and Maisie were naked either. And I'm not putting down any of your liberal B.S. about the glories of the nudist colony. One's a honey pot and the other's an autoclave. Necks and Libs: Fuck 'em all!

Onward.

Foots actually got those women to the Moss Motel, and he actually did it to all three one way or the other. He kept the whole bargain. He turned on the lights and left up the shade so Benton and a couple of other guys could look. Hell, I'm surprised they didn't film it for a skin flick to be shown over at the Red Cat on Saturday afternoons.

Benton told me all about it, and I said I was surprised a man of his caliber would go for that vulgarity. I kept after Benton about that night for years. I wanted him to know how disappointed I was in him. But it wasn't until the summer I killed Billy that he finally blew up at my prickishness.

We're going off down the bayou road to drag for bodies and he brings the truck to a skidding stop—immediately after I've mentioned seeing a Westerman sister the other night, and just before he figures I'll want to talk about what a dirty guy he was to make that bet back then. I'd never seen him angrier, including the night with Billy.

"You still think that's bad do ya? You tease Billy Weatherford and rob him and make him look bad in front of his wife and you can say my peeking was real bad . . ." He was gripping the wheel and staring past me out the window on my side. He was bitterly angry, but he was having some extra thoughts about it too. "And don't give any crap about my *motives*, either."

"Why not?" I asked, and I was nervous, very nervous.

"Because I ain't in the motives business. I'm in the acts and consequences business—and it didn't harm nothing to do it. Nothing!" he shouted, and then drove on, blowing dirt out the red ruts behind us.

The Sheriff hurt my feelings. He'd finally given me tit for tat, but he'd really hurt my feelings, and I was damn near in tears before we got to the bridge.

"If I didn't do dirty stuff like that ever now and then I'd go flap crazy." He said that almost to himself as he parked and just before he got out and started hauling the grapples out of the bed.

I told him it was the ugliness it did to Foots that hurt most. I said it damn near whining, and mostly lying.

"You may feel sorry for Foots—but mostly you want me, the Sheriff, to be Simon Pure," says Benton, his voice trailing off, while he starts hauling that miserable gear down the bank to the boat. "I'm a fool sometimes. But I'm not a young fool."

And finally it was the Sheriff who really did Foots in—and it was when Foots was most vulnerable; it was when he was finished with ball; it was when he was pumping gas and mixed up with the race problem. During Bryan's first demonstration, it was Foots who got the donkey's tail stuck to his bottom.

He's in the deputy's car. Fooled, he's fooled and Davis had to do it to see that the common weal was properly served.

Here they came, more than a hundred niggers led by ole Slater, and marching with their little protest signs toward the courthouse to get the right to vote—and there sits Magee in the patrol car protecting them: Foots Magee, the leader of Magee's Raiders. Our Ace Patroit and Champion Commie Fighter was precisely out of action. The bitter irony.

All those months he's been drilling his two dozen out-of-work mechanics in a fallow field away from the eyes of Earl Warren's law, and now it's the locals get him. All that time getting ready for those same Communist niggers who are marching safely past the car.

II

It wasn't the Foots who'd sung the great medley at the Stand, the Foots happy in his game and the winner of the most famous bet ever made in Bryan. Foots had found the bone-and-marrow hatreds —and I suspect it comes from being left out or dropped, from never having it or from losing it. Or from being close to people who never thought of *not* having it, and certainly never thought of losing it . . .

Magee's Raiders weren't taken all that seriously until some churches began to burn and a body or two showed up in the bayous. There's always a lot of talk about killing this or that nigger or agitator, but it rarely comes to anything. Wasn't any absolute proof they'd done it, except gossip and their own words around the service stations and tonks, which of course they'd deny if they were hauled into court. And we don't worry about courts too much in Bryan. Thank God.

.   .   .

It's exceedingly difficult to get the blame established about that body we gathered in on the grappling hooks.

Yes, sir, working around in the bayou with Benton did wonders to develop my social consciousness.

You float in the most wonderful and palpable stillnesses across the heavy brown water, and you really don't expect to find any of the missing persons you're looking for. Now and then a jay barks, and up ahead you can see the deputy's boat casting around for the same thing you are, but nobody expects anything to happen. Passing strange—because the cars parked back on the bridge seem to be natural as grazing cattle, and the few spectators gaping after you seem to have only the most normal sort of meditation on their minds. It's hard to believe those boys gawking away up there are joking about how nice it is of Slick Fletcher and Foots to feed the fish with niggers all summer, or maybe they're saying the goddamned coons oughta know better than try and swim with trace chains around their ankles.

There's something fine about drifting along in a boat and drinking beer, no matter what the reason for being there is. You stroke and break the water from time to time, and it seems there's nothing so lovely as the meaty green rosettes of water lettuce or the purplish flowers of what's maybe mad-dog skullcap over on the bank. You can't believe the hook's pulling down away there through anything but weeds. Dragonflies jab along low over the water, quick creatures the great Otto Lilienthal must have seen before his eyes moments before his glider crashed in 1898. The slough! The slough! The long political bayou and slough. And ugly salamanders in the shallows with their bloody and feathery gills. *Zupp* goes the beer can being opened, and I'd long since forgotten the other time I dragged the water with Benton—the day several years back when I criticized him for watching Foots bugger the Westermans, the day we really didn't catch a thing.

The day we actually got the body was the summer after my junior year in college and I was married and getting a fine bookish education from Burger and company at Southern, and I was completely unprepared for anything except snapping turtles and gars.

Benton gave a pull on the rope and said he had it. "Here's our man," he said. "It must of been caught on a snag," and up it floated right beside me. And I don't mean to suggest he was the worst kind of drowned body. He didn't have the bullae yet and he wasn't soft as the one over at Natchez that was swollen to 400 pounds and soft as dough with his eyes gone and shotgun-sized holes in his cheeks from the fish. And he wasn't all shrunk up like the salt-water mothers are. Our blunt three prongs were mostly in his clothes and he didn't seem to be weighted.

"Start the goddamned motor, Joiner," and I did. He handed me the rope and I let the fellow drift back in the wake as we headed up to the bridge. Putt putt we went and still it wouldn't have been so bad if Slater hadn't been there leaning on the pilings. It was Slater and some white boys and Rodney Kloninger, the county coroner, and the motor of the deputy's boat that was following us in. Putter putter.

Benton's out of the boat and wiping his sleeve across his mustache when Slater says, "I told you they dropped him off. It's them Raiders."

"Shut up, Slater," says the Sheriff, but it's not said the way you badmouth a nigger. That's clear enough. He said it that way because he wasn't ready to think of murder quite yet.

The white boys had smiles like Henry's sardonicus. It was a couple of Tanksleys and a Magee, one of Foots' cousins probably come to gather talk.

Kloninger says he's been down maybe eighty hours, and Benton says that's long enough, Rodney, and he's your man as of now. Rolled over he turned out to be a nigger I didn't remember seeing before. He was, said Slater, Buster Doleman, from Simpson County, who'd volunteered to help organize the voter registration.

"He don't look shot," says a Tanksley rather lightly and just before Benton pulls out his pistol and tells them to get the hell away and gone or he's going to shoot their fucking heads off. Benton was exercised, and all that was growing on the dead man's head was a little design of algae or something at the hairline.

.   .   .

It's not a pretty scene to imagine but it's important for getting perspective on Magee, and the Sheriff. It helps explain why Benton treated Foots the way he did a couple of weeks later. Doleman wasn't shot or weighted and apparently the autopsy didn't show anything else to indicate the usual kinds of violence, but Benton was satisfied he'd better be cautious about Foots and the Raiders. When Slater told Benton there's to be a march, the time had come to get the hooks in Foots. It was the first summer the Movement got to our piney woods.

"Foots, we're needin' you to help with the niggers." It's the Sheriff calling Foots down at the Gulf station, and I can imagine how ole Foots' heart must have leaped—him without honor for two years. Pumping gas and half-witted from too many years under the helmet, and now a call from an *authority*, like a goddamned glory breaking through a high-piled nimbus of despair.

"I'm ready, Benton. My men are ready," says Foots. "An' we got guns." Talking that way and completely forgetting the day when he'd been a professional and a little of the gentleman: all those interviews on the pregame show, where he's dressed in a dandy three-button tweed suit he won for being the outstanding offensive lineman during the big exhibition game in Chicago.

And if Benton had been less smart than he was, Foots' arms could have been much trouble. But for Benton, the defender of our *colored citizens* (as he calls them), it was an easy straight to make. Benton swivels around in his chair and diddles with the air-conditioner knob: "Man, you don't need your own guns. You'll be deputized and armed by me and the county." Whole racks of rifles and shotguns right there in the patrol car. "Just park your trucks behind the jail about dawn."

Just park your trucks behind the jail at dawn. Benton tooled his sentence just right for Foots. One-hundred-proof Red Ryder it was, and I can see just that punchy man at Nancy's—she's open all night—having his coffee just before the dawn of the big day, and he's saying he sometimes misses the taverns in Detroit City and wishes it would snow more often in Mississippi. For a little while he can believe his life still has meaning and promise.

Five, six semis bomb past and for one morning he's not heading back to pumping gas, and back to the eyes of businessmen who come by to talk sports occasionally, and back to niggers who always buy a dollar's worth—black niggers pampered by the government he hates. *Just park your trucks behind the jail at dawn.*

I'm positive that when the Raiders picked each other up that morning they didn't have a single nigger, living or dead, on their minds. Anyway, it's no goddamned fun to shoot a nigger if nobody respects you for it. They were merely pleased to be at the beck and call of some kind of power and virtue, and all of it of course in fact no more than a bad joke I doubt any one of them has yet to fully understand.

That drowned nigger—Doleman—had him a little garland of aquatic life around his head—and I couldn't help thinking it was a shame he didn't stay down longer, so he could slough off that black skin. Kill a nigger and resurrect a white man . . .

It was an odd parade through Bryan that day. It was a mix of dandy new nigras like Slater and Civil Rights workers, bloodless Eastern-type white boys and girls (so-called Beatnik types)—not a solid, healthy-looking Polack in the whole crowd—and they were protected all the way from the quarters to the courthouse by the state police and the city police, the Sheriff's Patrol, and Magee's Raiders, who were neatly sealed up in those air-conditioned patrol cars.

Benton told Foots that if the niggers and Communists got the least bit out of line they'd roll down the windows and blast the mothers to kingdom come, legally: *So who cares if they meet up with the mayor and sign up to vote? They'll never have their way by it.* And Benton sold that crock to Foots and company, knowing full well that from that day on *niggers is people,* like Uncle Earl Long said, and the Sheriff wasn't against it.

They marched along pridefully and fearfully with signs that said REMEMBER BUSTER DOLEMAN and ALL AMERICANS HAVE THE RIGHT TO VOTE.

Seems sort of quaint these days, don't it?

I went to Slater's house the night after the body came up, and he said he'd been to see Doleman's mother and all the old lady had to know was was her child castrated, which he wasn't. He didn't have any shoes and socks on but for the most part he looked normal enough. Slater and I sat out on his shack porch, *his* momma inside fixing midnight eggs for us, to go along with our beer, and he said Mrs. Doleman was relieved beyond words to hear her son wasn't mutilated. Whoooeee!

Mutilated. It *is* important not to get yourself mutilated! Or maimed.

It was the first time I ever made a social call on Slater, but he seemed to take it for granted—like he was waiting almost. He's a sullen man basically—but he's not without the wit: *Jerner, you see a few more dead bodies you be a real man.* Shit like that—but he's not all political either—meaning that he knew I was a niggerlover at heart and sick from what I'd seen, and visiting him because I wanted to just be human in the middle of the night with a Negro acquaintance. *Me and you going to have nice houses someday, and we're going to drink better stuff than this ole beer. We're going to remember all this misery like it was some kind of bad dream* says Slater so peacefully it sounded true.

That really tore me a new one.

But it's not the easiest thing in the world to say what a torn new one feels like, because it's not easy to imagine Doleman's death. I never saw it. Rodney Kloninger and Dr. Saucier figure they suffocated that man with maybe an oily rag from the pickup. But they didn't kick his ribs in or shoot him or cut his nuts out, none of the usual things. They're getting pretty sophisticated and there I am in the rank dark with Slater, and what I want to ask is how was it with

Doleman, and how does it feel to be you right now—and what about this march that's coming up tomorrow?

I did manage to ask of the march. He said Benton would take care of it.

Benton'll take care of it—hearing those words from that strange Indian-looking Negro gave me a feeling almost as strange as trying to think of Doleman gagging because he's got a mouth full of rag and grease and his heavy nostrils pinched closed by Magee's wonderful opposable thumb and first finger. They made me feel about equally bad.

"Benton's pretty good to you people?"

"He don't like no kind of dead people," says Slater by way of talking more niggerish than usual. And I felt curious because at the time I couldn't figure out whether the Sheriff was fancy or fried. I was wondering how he *really* felt about the niggers—and it was like Slater read my mind: "Sheriff has got him a pretty good idea about fair play, that's all."

"Which'll do for the time being?"

"Damn right."

I had a hard time with the eggs and I had delicate disjunctive twitters in my head while thanking Mrs. Jackson. I said, "Thank you, Mrs. Jackson." And the dings started in my head because my voice sounded curious to me. She was nothing but a mammy.

The next day I was out front of Nancy's to watch the whole thing. Slater waved and I waved back. I'm standing there with Stream and Royal, and Stream says we ought to probably be marching ourselves. I said that there was something to that statement, and Royal said nothing.

Well, what the hell? I got involved soon enough. And the true pity of that day was seeing Foots so full of pride and hate, his face dry and red in the cool car—there he sat protected from the noon sun in Bryan while the future of the South and also the United States went sweating past outside, and he never knew how far away from all of it he was.

If Foots hadn't put his vision into action by burning those churches and probably killing Mr. Doleman, he wouldn't have had enough reputation to warrant the care Benton gave him during the parade. Foots should have stayed out there in the scrub fields and pines and drilled forever like Chiang Kai-shek.

III

Davis was dee-lighted with himself. You might not think a fellow who likes to peek in motel windows can be austere and civilized— you might not think a sheriff who gets a kick out of watching Foots waving his distended dick in a lighted motel room could be considered a bastion of order and justice—but it is true. A man who even enjoyed the sight of Foots shooting an occasional finger in the direction of said window—which finger from Foots was to say he'd won the fracking bet, see!

Davis Benton has got himself a congratulatory call from the Governor: *The smoothest-handled demonstration of the summer, and a damn shame they didn't get it on T.V.* "Which shows how dumb about some things even a governor can be," says D. Benton. "*All they wanna re-poat is vilence . . .*" says the Governor.

"Right, Governor," says D. B.

But it wasn't the call that pleased him most—as Slater had suggested, while forking up a band of rubbery bacon—what most pleased our mustached and bald lawman was putting down Foots. Benton says he couldn't care less how big a man Foots *was*, because he *is in*sane, and nobody is *safe* with Foots and his crowd around. Nobody!

Benton cracks open a Regal and passes it to me the evening after the march.

The pole beans are better than ever and the okra, best of all, is perfect. He's just put a border of tire halves along his driveway, has painted them white, and Bessie, his Titianesque wife, has recently stuck a simulated green frog on the nearest loblolly—and also lovely was the new pink flamingo they've got set up on his one leg next to the thrift bed. He's a peaceful and happy man (the Governor having just called) and he's pleased to see me come driving up. He's a man who's just about to bust to indirectly praise himself.

"Son. I'd like to make me a list up right here and now—with your help—and on this list we'd put the name of every bad actor in the whole goddamned county." He wipes the suds off his grenadier-type mustaches. He gives a long meditative look up at the nimbus that's folding high over his precious house, and it's painfully clear my hero is ass-deep in his pride. He even puts the can in the grass so he can fold his hands over his chest. He was so peaceful and cruel and relaxed I figured he'd just melt away and become the dew. "Son, I'd make me this list if it was legal and I'd send it to Mr. Hoover at the F.B.I. and the Attorney General of the U.S.A.—I'd figure a way to get every one of them in *jail*." He says *jail* and sits bolt upright and actually extends his long arms so he can clap the hands. "Name the bastards! Foots. Slick Fletcher. Dallas Thurston. Shit, half the people at Stone Creek—Henry Smith—and—damn right—even ole Chalmers at the Mill. He don't much look the killer, and troublemaker—but I got it on good authority he's doing a helluva lot of loose talk that gets the rest of them people up in arms."

Oh my. Christ, the evening was serene, and I didn't much give a rip that I was missing supper. Hell no. For the Sheriff of Bryan County—my friend—was into some good stuff, and in the fall, back at Southern, I could tell Professor Burger that not every peace officer in Mississippi was entirely vicious. And then I could go on and tell Burger that maybe we better fear the *good* sheriffs more than the *bad* ones.

Goddamned Benton was being a fool and messing up the security of the moment. He should of been easy and graceful about his success. We should of been talking about the odors of Bessie's positively antebellum honeysuckle over in the trellis. Davis should of been sustained by a fervent and quiet confidence in his own wisdom—and I don't mention the honeysuckle just for detail work. There is no pride or honor, no idea or theory, worthy of that kind of evening. No past event has the right to intrude on the security of such a green dusk.

Security! That's exactly what he was tampering with. For, friend, there are some dusks in the summertime so abundant and lush in all their greens it'll break your heart with peace of mind. I mean we ought to have special names for all these shades of piney-woods green, the way Eskimos have all those words for snow. Rather than making a petty list of humans to lock up, we ought to have been making up phrases for green.

Let's hear it for Bug Green—the color of new needles and the minuscule creatures that crawl a legal pad on such nights—as come after such evenings—it's a green for doubters and temporizers, Doubters' Green (sometimes called Pea Green, or damn near yellow), the green of men who suck a lover's breast too long, causing pain all around.

And Black Green, Hardnosed Black Green, of the long needles at a distance across the road—Securest Green, and Rankest. It is so stern a color nothing watching it can fear anything—it is so strict and calm the doubters gain courage and praise its harbor and protection. Man can't be afraid of anything in a green decline—no man could ever fear death even when the creatures are making that breathing and grinding sound all around.

What I should of said to Benton was something about how, mysteriously, his control over the politics of the day was similar to the spirit of this falling evening. And he should have understood. And would have. But I didn't.

"Davis," says I, making myself restful in the Augustine, "Davis, maybe that's a piss poor idea—maybe not all those people are guilty of crimes quite yet. Like Henry, who never has actually hurt anybody."

"*Yet*," he retorts. "But he is capable of killing me and you and Bessie, and April. Right? He is capable of killing all of us—because he's so exercised about all this race shit." Davis at this point offers a significant pause and draws on his Regal like it was the required long draught at the Pierian spring. "Nigras, Chinamen, Arabs—it's no difference to me so long as they work hard and don't try to marry your daughters." And he was entirely serious.

"How about the activist-type niggers and the muthawhumpin' Eastern collegians? They on your list?" I chew me a blade of Augustine.

"No." He bites King Edward clean in half.

"No?" asks Joiner, seditiously.

"Because the niggers have been shit on too long—and because those kids who walked along with them was decent sorts in spite of them sandals. Don't quote me." He drags his horny hand across his skull in search of a new knowledge bump. He eyes me like if I tell this stuff at the Stand, he'll say I'm a liar and ought to be locked up—crazy damn Joiner. "Son, I thought you was a nigger-lover like me."

"That what we are?" I was getting peeved.

And so was he, the conversation having taken a long turn away from the green trees. "I'm trying to find out where we're *at*. And I think I know. The Federal Government in Washington is where it's at! Don't quote me."

I flopped back in the low grass and emptied the can. I felt vaguely that me and this good man were not done with our troubles. "Davis, I got to get my ass on home to the women. Davis, you're the best sheriff we ever had. You lie to the voters about what you believe, and you're a goddamned pervert, but you *are* the best sheriff we ever had."

"What's eatin' you?" Bleakly now, confused by his one friend he considers liberal as himself.

"You just might be getting a little simple-minded about this law business."

He is very, very disturbed, and his voice is down to a hissing whisper—"Son, there's very little of life that's all that *un*-simple, once you get the hang of it. Like Smith," and he wants to whap me goodbye, mentioning my friend and father-in-law. "Smith's all tore up and confused by Roy's death and living too much alone, and that slut in New Orleans. He's got too goddamned much at him at once."

"Got damn . . ."

"Yeah, shit—and wouldn't it be nice to fight with ice picks and not get stuck? Wouldn't it be nice to have the fun of looking for dead niggers and never find one? Trouble is—as you known, boy—is you *do* find it. Next man you kill, it might not be so easy to clean up," which wasn't fair one bit and he damn well knew it. He knew damn well the pussywhipped bastard was going to his boot for a pistol, and he knew damn well I never meant to break Billy's face.

"Come on now . . ."

"But maybe it *was* pretty funny to be stealing and then get caught and then to see ole Billy go to his boot. Maybe you breathed sweet air just before that goddamned fist of yours tore his head loose." He twirled at a mustache tip and looked malevolently at me.

"Not so."

"Bullshit," and he was jumped straight up and standing over me. He was way out on a rage—"You think I don't know—you think I haven't wanted to shoot Bessie and the kids a hundred times— you think I never considered how really easy it would be to actually get rid of Foots and all that crowd. It's a goddamned pain in the ass to round up those rats, and then to have him in my own cars so the law can be maintained. Sonny, I been pulling dead meat out of wrecked cars for ten years—tore-up men, women, and little chil- dren—I pulled the Boykins loose from their burned-up car. I feel like a fucking buzzard sometimes. I feel like them goddamned gars and turtles that eat holes in floaters . . ."

"DAVIS," the sound of Bessie from the front stoop. "Davis? What you picking on Son for?"

IV

Finally what was wrong was my reactions, because I was fast, damn fast. I could do the hundred in around eleven, in full equipment. But still and all I couldn't cut it. Those bastards want you to run like the wind and be quick as a goddamned cat, which I wasn't. Fast but not quick, and the difference is the difference between on and off, baby. I wasn't what you'd call brilliant in the agility drills.

Camelwalking forwards and backwards, side to side, dancing nimbly through a grid of ropes, raising the knees high and prancing through a course of tires, and then performing a series of somer- saults in a straight line—I wasn't what you'd call a regular Martha Graham at such stuff. Never quite foolish-looking but always just a bit disappointing.

I may not of been the best going, on somersaults, but I didn't get plowed under at thirty-four like Foots who'd of been senile before he was forty, and playing with his pecker in public, pissing on the cement at the same time he's filling your tank with gas.

No, sir. I've been out of The League going on three years, but I ain't pumping crazy gas and staggering in the mornings. Foots, he bobbed his head and spit all the time. Spit and bobbed his head and hated niggers and lived in Bryan, Mississippi.

He was a graceful and terrible man—godlike in body he drifted up to the line and bent to his task, gripped the ball along the laces and snapped with one hand, even on punts when he wanted to— Foots had it all, in the body, for a long time, twenty damn near perfect years under the helmet, sixth grade through ten years in The League. But he was all worn down on the night we killed him.

And you take Royal. He's got a bridge in his face like Foots did. In a great performance XL Rodgers of LSU took out R.C.'s front teeth, in Tiger Stadium, in Baton Rouge, and I wonder how Miss April's going to take to that.

But she probably won't care: "Royal honey, don't forget the Polident. Keep the ole legal breath sweet."

She'll adjust and forget, being the painfully sane woman she is.

I made the team all right. I got my fair share of clean blocks, but it wasn't always the crisp way they wanted it. I could nullify a defensive charge most often, always jamming the head straight in bravely, and never using the shoulder first like kids do—but I didn't always move them out quickly enough. I couldn't always translate that speed on the forty-yard dashes into your great five-yard bursts that are necessary on the running plays. You float back on up to the line with the play and the count fixed in mind, drop down, and then it's like you're not even in your own body anymore. Your external physical self becomes a tank or a Taborite wagon-fort—it's like you're driving one of them big earth-moving cats—your humaness, the sentimental meat and bone of you, is high up in the cab, behind glass, behind the mask, and you're scared the sunnavabitching thing you're driving won't crank, won't jump at the signal, the cue, won't get off from the light—you're like a greasy boy his first time on the drag strip—everything below your neck turns into one of those old La Salles that had no pickup but on the open road would glide along at eighty miles per hour without a wiggle. I was fantastic on downfield blocks, but Mojack—Christ, in early practice out on the coast, he's one defensive end I had one helluva time keeping out—and the traps were worse because you got to get to the bastards before they realize they're meeting no opposition. Fast is not quick, and I never thought about it until I went pro, because at Southern I went both ways, offense and defense when they needed me, and quick enough, All-Gulf-States three years and I could of done it in the Southeastern or the Big Ten.

And I almost lost it—Lord God, six months ago I was panting like a hound while climbing stairs, and once, early in the morning I hurt from my belly straight up the gullet to my perfect teeth—the pain started in my asshole and fired right up into my mouth, and the fracking palpitations, and not being able to get my breath, and peanut butter . . . angina pectoris or some such balefulness is what it was—the first signs—and small pains in the left arm, like being frogged real bad—from being anxious and fat, and no exercise except screwing. But I'm doing better now.

Some running and lots of dynamic tension and less Jiff and booze and ben. Boykin's careful about the body. He's mighty serious about the human body.

April was the kind who encourages you. She's the kind who says, "Sonny Joiner, you look great!" at the breakfast table over Big D., when we're set up for the end of exhibition season—she'd say that—with my face sunk-in and gray that way it gets from exhaustion, and hollow-eyed—and my hands purple and puckered from being cleated—even after half a day off and the night in bed to ease the soreness. "You're a fine-looking man," and she sips at her Luzianne.

I got to hate all that encouragement.

They were getting by me now and then on the pass blocks which I was really good at most of the time. Dropping quickly back and butting, keeping the lane open, and setting up the cup of protection for the quarterback. It was lovely on a good day, the air weightless and cool and every line on the field strict as geometry, and the fall smells distinct. Like a dance. You swing back and spot the defensive end driving across—Mojack—and if you're lucky you jam head and shoulders and elbows and fists and eyes into his chest, snap up to a high block, and send him sprawling.

Now and then it worked that way.

Angina pectoris. It was the sort of thing that killed Bill Wallick in the fifties. It's not just I'm a young man afraid of death for no reason: because it happens; it happened to Wallick, who was the best pro tackle that ever lived.

Teams studied the Rams' game movies just to watch Bill Wallick, so they could see it done right. He had it all. He had tremendous power and speed and he was always just a breath ahead of the snap. He often ran straight over his man in the line. He ran over linebackers. He ran over halfbacks. He could of been a great fullback had he wanted to. Bill Wallick. Sul Ross. Los Angeles Rams.

Cutting along at twenty-seven thousand, flying from Chicago to New York, the greatest players in The League now—great athletes like Morningside Robbins and St. Claire Granville—still talk about that man. The films of Wallick are still shown. He's the Bogart of pro football, a goddamned collector's item.

The best The League has now will brood and talk about what it was that Wallick had, and assistant coaches who played with and against him treasure their Wallick stories, releasing them when a storm brews and shakes the sky over Pittsburgh, lashing the plane with hard rain and making the landing fearful, or during the off season in a Tulsa cafe—how it was that Big Bill Wallick was a strange man who worked logarithms in his spare time for fun, and a terrible drinker—thirty martinis in one party at Long Beach, California.

One sportswriter with a residuum of mother wit called Wallick a visionary tackle.

Sunnavabitch, Wallick was fascinated by the Möbius strip, a goddamned amateur topologist he was. He'd make himself a

Möbius strip while flying east, he'd bring along his own construction paper and tape, and then he'd cut that single strip along a line
drawn on it, and he'd chuckle because it didn't make two strips, but
rather a single two-sided strip—and then he'd cut another Möbius
in thirds to make two intertwined strips. He got good deep pleasure
from such easy things. He brooded peacefully over the surface that
didn't have another side, a spectral surface, as the Rockies passed
below, and Wallick also believed in numerology and was addicted
to cards: poker, cribbage, bridge, old maid.

I'd of called him the Platonic Tackle or the Saint of the Interior Line, for he never married, and no man ever easily met his
gaze in a game, those pale blue eyes that always seemed to bend
around the man he faced. He was always studying the calculus of
a perfect block, studying while in the process of playing, his body
a harmony of infinite instants, and even his elementary physics was
perfect. Listening to the count, imperceptibly he began his explosion from his tight three-point stance—he was well in process
when the ball was moved, and he was never offsides, not one offsides penalty in his entire career. At 260 pounds he wasn't terrifically large and now and then a few giants would beat him once
or twice with mere mass and strength—but soon he would master
their style.

Christ, I myself have seen the films of what he finally did to
Marion Hatfield.

Hatfield had all the moves on defense. He had cypress arms and
tremendous lateral action—he was strong and he was smart, and he
took the measure of Wallick for an entire quarter. It was a cruel
duration for Big Bill, until he realized that fierce Marion had little
feet, for all his gifts. Marion would be vulnerable low down at the
ankles: Hatfield could be cut down. Wallick's solution didn't produce the most elegant-looking results, but other football players
and serious fans understand the effectiveness of what he did. Wallick simply started high in a three-point stance and fired out and
down and even back up a little so quickly he removed Marion from
his fragile base, Marion falling on top of Wallick again and again.
Five, six times Big Marion told the head linesman to watch Wallick
for offsides, but they couldn't find it, and finally Marion was shunt-
ing away or moving off the line, both ways hurting his game.

Magnificent!

The greatest topological and drunk master of elementary physics the game will ever see. The plane geometry of yard-markers and first downs, the parabolas of passes, all the mystery of the game's motion was to him a vision, an absurd possibility for human energy and grace—barbaric struggle in Wallick's game was raised to a vivid if not eternal abstraction. Never married and never hawked much tail I hear.

And he fell dying in the shower after the sixth game, with the Bears. I heard it was like he suffocated, and an awful thing to see, with all that pain gripping his arm and chest, Wallick thrashing around on the shower floor. He'd had the signs that something was coming, that the Goddamned Butcher Man was going to get him soon, but he didn't stop, he didn't stop when now and then the pain was obvious, and obviously not the normal pain from blows and weariness, but none of all that courage kept him from looking pitiful and foolish while he was clawing at those slick shower tiles.

Baby, when they write you blocked like Bill Wallick it means it was your day; it means that for one day you were a great football player. And don't let those intellectual bastards fool you, because to be Bill Wallick ought to earn you more than some slick obituaries on the sports page. It ought to set all the fag poets in the country to writing odes, like ole Pindar, because, by God, class and guts is class and guts whether it earn you a laurel wreath or just ten grand a year. And I know some history; which shows the Greeks were brutal so much their women didn't even go to the games. But still you hear this shit about the *amateur tradition* and how great the Olympics are, when everybody knows but us Americans that that's a lot of B.S. We play against *pros*, good pros and good men, in those Olympic games; but still we like to think our boys are so goddamned simon-pure, which they aren't.

Amateur is liking it, loving it, whether you get paid or not, and here in America we *pay* people for being good; and Bill Wallick was a fucking pro. He loved it and he got paid for it, and he wasn't any whore either. He was the best there was at a hard job, and what it all amounts to is that he ought to be remembered forever. Some say he was a cold and brutal man, but I never saw where he killed anybody. He's better than a general who kills people.

V

She knows the game. I taught it to her when we were at Southern together. April watches things real well. She never cared much about it—but she learned it and she liked it—just like she's probably going to learn some things about law and politics now she's with Boykin. Because he's the kind to make a wife keep up: the senators from every state, lame ducks, incumbents, torts.

She'll act just like it was the hottest mess of ideas she ever got stuffed in her pretty head. She'll get all stewed up—or at least act like she is—about what happened to the mystical Henry Wallace or to some honest sheriff in Hammond County who got voted out for being decent to a nigger, like what'll finally happen to Davis.

When we were married the only thing she read were some novels, her favorites being the Brontës—which seems strange, considering how unromantic she is. She read novels and the *National Geographic*—she's a goddamned bug on primitive customs and tribes, and she used to worry about the possibility of having sagging breasts in old age. She worried until I taught her some exercises to keep it from happening. I should have told her her titties were really too small to ever sag too much.

She studied when she wanted to, and read for fun when she wanted to, while living in my house—but married to R.C. she'll have to *apply* herself. It truly pains me to think of her rising in the morning with those beautiful small eyes looking like piss holes in the snow from staying up half the night reading *Economic Issues and Policies*.

Harrington, Hobbes, Coppe—Royal will teach and be ignorant. Incapable of either decadence or debauchery, he will never enjoy the peace she offers. He'll never enjoy it the way I did. *Howl, howl, ye nobles, howl, ye rich men for the miseries that are coming upon you and there's a most glorious design in it . . .*

And Royal won't mind her being an *aficionada* at football. He still likes the game well enough to take her to one now and then.

"Royal, honey, wasn't that a fine rollout." and "Got damn, Royal Carle, honeychile, what a helluva red dog!"

He'll drink his Fitz from his silver hip flask, but her knowledge won't give him the profound pleasure it gave me.

Per non dormire—per non dormire

She's the most basically keen and intelligent mean person I ever knew. She once told Coach Jakes that Charley Ray was flexing up on his right foot just a little on plays when he was going to pull—tough Charley, the last of the great watch charm guards. And it made a difference because the Lafayette linebackers had been keying on Charley and racking up our outside running game. The point being that the incompetent spotters in the press box, with all their fancy phone arrangements between them and the bench, they didn't see what April saw. They didn't pay close attention to detail, and when we saw the movies on Tuesday night, there was Charley, in slow motion, arching that foot when he's about to pivot.

We're standing outside the dressing room, everybody snug in light sweaters and ready for the party, and she's got an arm around both me and Jakes—a little photo pose for the gentlemen of the press, sports page human interest for the *Picayune*. Standing there between us handsome brutes, and exactly when the pix is being shot the third time, she says sweetly: "Coach, maybe you better tell Charley to quit pointin' his moves."

"Huh?" He's smiling down at her and she's smiling up at him to make a nice picture.

"Charley was giving away the sweeps." Pop, pop go the flash bulbs.

"I think you're 'bout right," says Jakes pleasantly, dismissing such irreverent female interjections. "You're a good fan, April."

She meant no harm, and certainly she didn't mean to harm Charley—it was just one of those prideful little confessions of expertise we sometimes make. It charmed all the journalists, and it should have. Here's this slim, pretty girl who just as well might be showing a knee and saying fup fup be dup be dup, foop foop be do, but rather than that she's showing how the game is really the important thing.

The caption said something about how the *Sweetheart Gives Advice*, but they left out the particulars, thank God.

And it was a sad thing to know that Charley was sitting back there in the dark sweet smell of Tuff-Skin and alcohol, and he's having to watch his mistakes being run over and over in slow motion on the bright-assed screen. Jakes is yelling again and again, "Let's look at that goddamned little toe dance just . . . one . . . more . . . time." He keeps jumping out in front of the screen so the moving frames get muddled on his chest and shoulders and head, and it is very strange to see the movies of a football game being flashed across a furious human body—he's yelling, damn near hysterically: "Christ! Ray, don't you LIKE sports?"

I guess the only thing that got Charley through the ordeal was knowing the assistant coaches, who'd been spotting, already'd caught worse hell. We'd barely won (21-13)—but dammit I'd made ten personal tackles and had blocked very well, a grade in the high eighties—and none of that got mentioned when the fuss over Charley got rolling in Jakes' turgid brain . . .

Any player will tell you it's hard to imagine anything worse than seeing your mistakes run over and over—backwards and forwards—in slow motion in a dark room, with your peers looking on, the *in*sane coach with his pointer on your one position in the line, again and again.

In olden times it was sometimes said that football was a game that really didn't test the individual. They'd go on about how every mistake a baseball player makes is vivid and obvious to everyone, and even more so in track, because it's one man against all others, and there's only one winner. Some oddballs would even say that even a game as silly as basketball was easier to watch, easier to observe errors in. The idea being that football was some kind of impacted action with what seemed to be three dozen people all piled together so you couldn't tell it when a single player was fucking off. Which is like saying that the individual bodies in Rubens' *Defeat of Sennacherib* are unimportant—like saying that perfect horse's eye in the left foreground of the *Victory and Death of Decius Mus in Battle* counts for little.

Some people never learn to look at anything.

And none of that ancient criticism of the game was ever really true—but nowadays it's absolutely un-true. Mr. Edison and all of modern technology have taken care of that. The camera has made the individual in football the most vulnerable of all athletes, for on the field there is the least illusion of security, especially in the line, but all one has to think of is Tuesday night—the thought of the glowing screen on Tuesday night destroys all security and leaves a fellow naked at the seat of judgment. Goddamn coaches, like a committee of French judges, study those films hours and long hours. Shit, nobody in Hollywood ever saw so much film as a diligent football coach.

In slow motion you can point quite easily at the extravagantly lifted heel; you can see the slight relaxation of the hand that's in the grass; and the inclination of the body toward the direction of the play. I swear to God that from my guru squat on the mats on the front row I could actually see the glint of pleasure in the line-backer's eyes.

Forward agony is bad—but backward agony is even worse, backwards and forwards, and wrong every time, but at least all motion moving forward seems normal, even beautiful, the sensation being that the world and time and all the bodies in their rocking and drifting motions are more graceful and honest than you ever imagined—all things toiling wonderfully in the slow calculus of error. I'd love to see a conversation at a country club party in slow motion—every gesture, every nose rub indicating dubiousness, all the social tricks of all the liars would be so obvious.
LIARS LIARS ALL THE FILTHY LIARS OF THIS FILTHY WORLD

Mary Ann approves of my exercise—she even likes jogging with me at the track because it makes her abdomen stronger for loving—she approves my efforts to regain health, but she also claims the ben I'm taking for aid tends to make me a tad paranoid. Maybe just a little. But vision, too, is a purge, and vision itself will make the strongest man a tad suspicious. Liars! Liars! Liars! Makes a fellow feel real good.

But backwards is terrible and ugly and awkward. *Live* spelled backwards is *evil*. Reverse the picture and all the fearful symmetry of the dance and play is destroyed. When the pile, after the tackle is made, explodes slowly upwards and backwards, and the players, because the mind wants them to be moving forward, seem to be straining foolishly and helplessly against the force that implacably returns them to where they started, you know how perverse all recollection finally is. An eternity of Tuesday nights and awkwardnesses would be hell enough for any soul.

And I never liked that goddamned Jakes much. He's a loud, big, hairless bastard. Naked, he's pink and ugly as a skinned squirrel. He don't smoke and he don't drink, and there'll never be a nigger on the team so long as he's there. But still I respected him awhile because he was always good to me—*Joiner, boy, you got great power. Use it! Use it! Get in there and knock somebody down!* And he even admired the academic grades I got, since it was good P.R. *Joiner makes Scholars All-America*—he really dug that shit. And he liked April, my wife, right up until the night she ratted on Charley.

We may expect that in the course of time changes will be carried out in our civilization so that it becomes more satisfying to our needs.

Jakes isn't nearly as smart as he's got the reputation of being.

He should have known I wouldn't be first-rate pro material. But he didn't. He thought I'd be great. He said I was the best he'd ever coached, and he pronounced it to all the papers, and then went on to say that furthermore I was probably destined for the Hall of Fame.

I disappointed him.

That sunnavabitch, he let me disappoint him.

After the Sun Bowl game my senior year, he told one of those ratty-looking Texas reporters that he figured Joiner was the best college tackle in the land and that it was *criminal* that Joiner hadn't made more All-America teams.

Truth is I made second string on *one* All-America team—a team chosen by some oufit called the Council of Christian Players, and what was crazy was I don't even know how they got my name. April says it was because I didn't smoke or drink much in season (sneaking around most of the time when I did), and because I always made such nice talks at church groups and at the Lions Club. I admit it. I'd go to such places when asked, blithering on about how sports is essential to the liberal education—how it's part of a great Western tradition. Only thing I can claim in my favor is how I talked more about the Greeks than Jesus—that and the fact that what I said was true.

"It's because you're handsome and articulate, Son." And what about manslaughter and my performance at the Graham Revival?

"They didn't know about that," says April.

It was all a fluke, and she didn't understand when I told her the worst thing I could think of was making an "all" team on account of some virtues that didn't have a goddamned thing to do with the game itself.

"Sonny, you're a good man *and* a great player, and it's wonderful that some organization takes that into consideration. Even if they are Christians." Such pap creates the urge to kill. I mean it. The human animal is often driven wild by drool. DROOL LIES DROOL pap. *Joiner is only dangerous when aroused:* one reporter said that.

She meant well, and I guess Jakes meant well, but if I'd really been all that good I'd of made somebody's *first* team, one of the wire services; or one of the teams chosen by the big magazines, like *Look*.

I got *mentioned* everywhere. I was Honorable *Mention* Consensus All-America, which is like making the All-Gossip team.

Mary kisses my neck and rubs my back. She says that all the All-America stuff was secondary and that the *playing* was the important thing, which is a change of pace for her, however predictable. She wants to hold on to her man, and I want to believe her in the worst sort of way because it was all very good awhile with the weight of the pads a light burden indeed, and the balanced security of the cleats, and the *compleat* knowledge that April, sleek as an otter in a tiger's mouth, would be there with her terrible love for me when the conflict ended—I lived within and acted out the language of romance back then, for no man ever took more pleasure in the flesh than I did during our perfect college marriage.

6

YES, WE MADE OUT before we were married—but we didn't do it all the time and any place—what we did was discover a fashion of loving that fit us—and what we worked out was one helluva lot saner and decent and hygienic than balling on back seats at drive-in movies or in the college parking lot behind the stadium. Never once did Joiner cast down a rubber on that five-acre tract of asphalt for the poor nigras from Buildings and Grounds to sweep away in the morning. But that's not much to brag about, considering I owned a Volks my first two years at college, having sold the ghoulish DeSoto that reminded me of Billy.

Let's see? For clear gain and virtue is the fact we never merely petted much. No arduous fingering did I offer April. My father early told me to avoid the meannesses of frustration. "Son, buy a rubber, maybe two, and do it proper. Get a room, Son, get a room." It was just about the only advice he ever gave me, and he didn't wink when he said it. He considered the care of a woman a serious responsibility, and my mother has always been a pleasant woman.

From almost the beginning we took little trips to New Orleans and Jackson to visit friends and see the sights—we always told Helen we were staying with the family of some friend, and I always gave her a phone number in case of some emergency. April and I got a kick out of that, because it was a way to be honest and thoughtful in the midst of a lie. We didn't want to get dangerously out of touch. We just wanted to be safely alone.

In N.O. we stayed with Boyce Stuart, and in Jackson it was Terrell Simms, neither of whom existed—old friends from my one summer at the Philmont Scout Ranch. To get clean and inexpensive rooms at the Pelican and Stonewall motels we were entirely satisfied to chance getting caught in a lie.

Had ole Helen really needed her Maylene's child—like if her gallstones flared up—she could of found her. And she wouldn't have missed us just because the voice at the other end said, "Stonewall Motel. Can I help you?" She'd of known in a flash, and she probably wouldn't have thrown a hissy fit either, so long as she knew it was all a secret. Helen's spent her life keeping books at the Chalmers' Mill and she knows the value of occasional deviousness, and she never really hated me until she thought I was insane, which was a long time after the Stonewall. She'd of put the call through to our room. She'd of told us she needed help, in a strict voice, and that would have been that.

We got away with it all and, wonder of wonders, we did keep it secret—though I must admit I told Royal, to keep from getting a disease, and he was proud of us and never told.

Sociology: maybe the sociology is important, though that's not exactly the right word. It wasn't so much April didn't have any female friends as it was she never made *close* female friends—except for Pauline Robbins when we were in The League. She could twitter in the halls of Bryan High with the best of them, but she wasn't the kind to enjoy pallet parties and loose talk about girlish sex. Bananas and candles—most of the girls from Stone Creek were that way—they knew from nothing about candles and bananas. They never got very well integrated with the relatively uptown habits of Bryan girls (their exaggerated imitations of Jackson women)—and anyway she was only there one year before we went off to college together. Or: the other girls were spooked by her because she lived with her maiden aunt who was reputed to be weird, and who'd converted to Catholic. Or: they'd heard stories about her awful-looking daddy who didn't even live in the same house with his own daughter, a man who looked exactly like the devil and went to see queer people in New Orleans all the time—buzz buzz.

Maybe it was no more than being my girl that called her out and made her separate. Which proves I'm not so hot at general sociology. O.K. The point is I never made her notorious or gave her a bad reputation. A neat intelligent girl with a close mouth and a strange family and a giant boyfriend is finally too complex to get a bad reputation in a simple place like Bryan.

Let me celebrate again, in detail, the way she was. Loosen your kidney belt. Take off your girdle. Park your bike. Prepare to enjoy the Higher Raunchiness.

In those days she'd say something like, "Sonny, you got real class. You're just wonderful." Meaning aren't *we* just wonderful. And then she'd scrunch up against me as I fired that ridiculous Volks up the hardroad toward Big J. And what haunts me is how I had a comfortable maturity back then—how I'd manage to double-clutch in my peg pants ordered from the Tall Man's Shop in Brockton, Mass.—how I'd manage to ease that toylike car up through the voracious and scented dark, toiling securely along on those bitty wheels—how I'd manage all dips and turns with equanimity while she's giving me a rolling hand job. I'd pressure the accelerator deep into every curve, resisting forces centrifugal and desperately trying to accentuate the shrunkenness of the centripetal.

I wasn't the kind to take her loving roughly. I never failed to take her out to eat when we were in Jackson (Jackson mostly, because Helen thought of the Crescent City in terms of sin and Henry—oftener the Stonewall than the Pelican)—I always took her to some good place like Primos or The Capitol Beer Lounge: fried chicken, fried livers, oysters, sometimes a helluva slab of beef. The only proof for the existence of God I accept is the Gustatory Proof: Only a Supreme Being could create chicken livers and oysters.

She loved to eat. And then a movie at the Lamar. It was fun to know that after the show those slick Jackson kids would be going off to park at the airport or somewhere equally semipublic, while the children of the boonies were driving confidently over the Pearl River Ridge to tryst in Rankin County at the everloving Stonewall.

We'd see those Jackson athletes and their dates at the theater, and the boys always seemed a little soft and a little pious, like they were more interested in their letter jackets than in their women. It's really a little pitiful how rich city boys always seem to affect the sullenness of necks. It's like they don't quite trust their good fortune, energy, and good health. Bad faith. An American boy ought to stand up straight and smile a lot, but those Jackson boys dropped their eyelids and had bad posture. No pride. They looked like a bunch of big Mexicans.

She was brilliant.

I always signed in as Gene Jumper, Mobile, Organizer, and they never questioned it. I've always been oily, dark, and heavy-bearded. No questions. And we had us a special suitcase we always carried. It was an ancient leather thing with metal bumpers on the four corners. It was mine, and the same one my folks had carried to Gulfport on their own honeymoon. April. It was mine, but April always took her soft things and tomorrow's dress out of her own bag and mixed them with my clothes before we were very far up the road from Bryan. It was good to see her wrestling that old suitcase in the back seat of the Volks. I'd look over at her calves and part of her thighs, and her shoes always slipped off while she was repacking. It's a good thing to remember. And the manager was always pleased to see us up from Mobile. He always cut a winsome eye across the washers we wore for wedding rings, and the Bryan County tag was big as life on the back of the car.

Ah God, those were the nights. We played.

Since I'd been taught not to be greedy with women, it wasn't any trouble for me to enjoy the horsing around ole April delighted in, and a delight is the right phrase for how she was, most of the time. We'd turn on WOKJ for R&B first thing—we'd put down the suitcase and immediately start to dance around that small room with all our clothes on, like at a prom or armory dance. We'd slowdance and bop, the air conditioner droning behind and under the beat of the music, and we were a multitude while dancing that way alone together—we were all the decent, raunchy lovers in the world, and that kind of action would go on maybe half an hour. We didn't snatch, we didn't tear. We were great hunters, professionals, stalking our sex, our sexes, our magnificent differences. Stonewall, praise thy name.

Pride: Vanity: what the hell do they mean? Was it pride and vanity I felt when I collapsed on the tufted spread of that strange motel bed and thought of how what we were doing was so much better than what our friends suffered? Wasn't our rubbing in the cool musical dark of the Stonewall better than all your sitting-position screwing going on back at the college, in the parking lot behind the stadium? Wasn't it better to put it off for weeks on end, preparing, in delightful anticipation, to make a proper sexual odyssey? Was it not surely better to sail between Charybdian Helen and the Scyllalike Dean of Women to gain at last this port where Penelope is ever young and honestly horny, the way a good woman can actually be? Fucking-A it was.

Friend, it was perfect solitude, sanctuary, and privacy—no goddamned coaches and cameras anywhere around, no Benton to peek. You stretch your upper body flat on the motel quilt—head, back, and butt on the bed itself, while your stocking feet crimp up and down on the carpet—do that, and you become the perfect easy rider. Listen to your girlfriend pee (she goes to the bathroom after dancing), fight off the shadow of embarrassment, and you can damn well believe this is what being grown is all about. She never turned the faucet on.

Stretch the arms wide and stare up at the dim squares of the ceiling, the only light being the inch shaft from the john, where the door isn't completely closed. Stretch forth, relax and stare, and you'll be so full of yourself it would take fifty Calvins and a whole herd of Savonarolas crashing through the shuttered windows to make the guilties come. And then we'd talk awhile.

I'd get up and pop us both a beer, and then she'd prop herself at the head of the bed. She'd sit with her legs laid over my shoulders, having taken off only her stockings and shoes. She'd commence talking about our friends. She'd go on far too long about all

the reasons Stream drank too much, opining, in an almost dis-
embodied reverie above and behind my head, that Stream wasn't
ever going to satisfy his daddy's idea of service to humanity—and
why is it Stream can be so cruel sometimes, inventing things like
pig parties?

It wasn't easy to lie still and be patient while she talked and
wiggled her satin legs against my bare arms. All her jabber (however mellifluous) about the uglies in the fraternity house basement
was pretty hard to take.

I learned pretty early that pity was an occasional mechanism
of her loving—a sad movie, an armadillo run over on the highway,
some terribly bleak story from real life—let the images of pain and
humiliation wander in her mind and out her smooth mouth awhile
and it wasn't long before she'd be up from the bed and in the
shower getting ready in real earnest, continuing to chatter while
the water pattered over her—give her time to consider life's little
tragedies (except for personal stuff like Maylene and her own
father) and she'd be genuinely aggressive about wanting to make it.
She'd be the perfect jockey rider, crying the joy of being healthy
and pretty. "This *is* good." Oh terrible wheel of fortune.

Stream and all the pigs—maybe he did me a service by causing
a sad story for April to mull. Redact, redact. Redact the pigs.
"Stream says it was charity," says I, stretching my legs into the
air beyond the bead, exercising the teeming belly muscles. Report-
ing on Stream's most recent extravaganza.

"The hell it was," says she, and gathers her legs away from me,
pulling them up under her chin. She's pondering hard: true uglies,
crude women, harelips, hunchies at a proper party—a keg of beer
and first-rate vegetable hors d'oeuvres. We did it all up brown,
never letting the girls know they're there at a nice party because
of their obvious wretchedness.

Stream, the idea man of his fraternity house, convinces the
brothers that a pig party would be a radical moral act and a helluva

lot of fun, which is the worst kind of tepid existential bullshit.

I was in the first session of summer school to take my course in the English Revolution from Professor Burger, and under those circumstances who am I to fuck with the bourgeois machinations of those petty somitches at the fraternity house. I ain't no fraternity man. Hell, I'd just dropped by for lemonade.

"Sonny, sweetheart, Stream is sick. He's a very unhappy boy," her voice muffled by the pillow she's got on top of her knees. "I ought to bring *him* up here."

"I thought *I* was bringing you."

"_____"

"_____"

"You should of stopped it."

"Goddammit, it all turned out O.K."

"And they'll catch on. They'll go to night school and catch on."

Stream pulled it off by way of blood oath and deep conspiracy. He's been reading morose shit like Sade and Kafka and Sartre all summer—and he's taken to growing long hair and burns and muttering a lot—but on the day he springs the plan there's an air of peculiar authority to him. Carl Phillips (our old fullback, who didn't make it at college ball), Morris Thompson, Doyle Morgan, and I are sitting with our feet on the balustrade, but Stream is walking in slow circles on the other side of the porch where no chairs were; he's biting the waxy rim of his cup, and it's obvious he's big with an idea. Which idea, when he finally offers it, comes out in an apparently spontaneous monologue about how everybody is too influenced by appearances and probably the dogs and pigs of the world were really great people.

At first I thought he was into some kind of Humane Society spiel—I figured he'd go on with plans to protect the ibises and shoveler ducks—but finally it winds around to a statement in favor of unfortunate girls—*and wouldn't it be great to give them their innings? All the girls damaged by fate and genetics*—and aren't they all women below the waist, where it counts?

He'd gotten a reputation for this kind of harangue, and he was tolerated, admired, because there was often a plan for *fun* at the end of it: like the time he carried on about conservation and eventually led the largest tree-planting expedition in the school's history, planting more than a thousand pine seedlings in the girl's athletic field in the middle of the night.

He'd collected them legally from various forestry stations, legally but under somewhat dishonest premises, having told the rangers they were for some undeveloped university property.

It was a great success. There were pictures in the papers: *A Strange New Forest in Forrest County*, joked the *Hattiesburg American*. All Stream and his buddies got was a reprimand from the school officials. The boys had to pull out all the trees and take them to the agriculture department so they could be used correctly, but the extra work was nothing compared to the reputation they got for being wonderful, crazy guys. Shit! I hate pranks. Useless goddamned labor.

And once, after he'd done a chant about the waning of ritual and tradition, he started working on some zany matins for the co-ed dorm. He got a band together—he looked up the exact time of sunrise—and he actually marched to the co-ed dorm, with the best horizon, just before a cloudless dawn. Cymbals! Drums! Trumpets! Actual practiced flourishes and rolls to get all the women to the window. Sousaphones! COLDSTREAM TAGGART AND FRIGADELTANIG GIVE YOU THE SUN. And damned if it didn't show its burning edge at the far horizon of pines exactly when he needed it.

It was a great hit and on the occasion of that prank they received no punishment at all, for none of the girls would tell exactly who it was. Ole Stream got to be quite a cutup in college. P.K. P.K. P.K. So much so his daddy made him go to a Christian college his second year.

Wouldn't it be great to have a pig party? Man, those silly boys were ready. And Stream created both rule and retribution. 1) Pigs must be collected the day of the party. 2) They cannot be co-eds, and better if they aren't even from town—*outfroms* being most prized. 3) Major birth defects will be given special honor. 4) The pig judged most piggish will win the pot (they all forked over ten dollars).

Right there in the late daylight they're gaining momentum,

they're turning over all the rocks in their heads, and all kinds of moist creatures with pussies are slithering out: *Saprolegnia ferax, Cymbella lanceolata, Tabellaria fenestrata:* they're in an infantile dither of remorse and vengeance and affection. No doubt about it, there was some affection in all that dipshit prurience, because Stream kept saying it was a moral idea, a way to knowledge, like conservation and Morning Prayer.

"Sonny, are you with us?"

"No." I could feel the vodka in the punch.

"You goddamned meathead." And there wasn't any moral or charity in calling me a meat. Plain bitterness and jealousy. April.

5) Every precaution will be taken to see that brothers not involved are absent from the party, but if any should appear during the evening, nothing will be explained. Nothing! If anybody comes and wonders how all that ugliness showed up at once, it's to be laughed off as coincidence, as nothing more than bad luck hawking tail. The pig party is secret! 6) Every man at this party is a gentleman, every lady will be treated like Miss America, Miss Mississippi, Miss Shrimp Festival, Miss Suet . . .

Six rules.

Retribution: anybody who speaks of the night for ten years will get the shit kicked out of him by Joiner. Simple as that. I made it very clear that I would seek them out, though they flee to the ends of the earth, if any breach of faith occurred. I told them I'd kill anyone who hurts the feelings of a pig.

"I'll get me a basket case," cries Morris Thompson. "I'll *wheel* the bitch in."

They sat up half the night making plans.

And April's on my mind the whole time I'm an accomplice to Stream's stinking prank—which obviously I finally was—I'm wondering why I'm involved in such gross foolishness when no more than fifty miles away is my wholesome truelove. While Stream and company have withered arms and port wine stains in their minds, I'm planning my next vacation with April, with pretty, pretty, pretty April who's sleeping alone and thinly clad beside the ancient oscillating Emerson fan that's moving the heavy air back and forth over her clean body. I was imagining how put out she'd be with what we were planning.

In the perfervid yet chilly dark of the Stonewall: "Were you attracted . . . to any of them?"

Good question, my dear. "No?"

"Yes you were."

"Yes, I was—to all of them."

"Which is like none."

"Not really."

I feel her sliding down beside me, smoothing herself up over the escarpment of my torso, mussing her dress, arranging herself high up on my chest. "What made you want them?" And her Chesterfield breath is beginning to smell a little excited—even though it doesn't yet have that ovate and pearly white odor of puréed mushrooms that is the absolute signature of a hot woman. Which lovely scent she never had until she brushed her teeth and rinsed her mouth, with water. Goddamned mouthwashes will cover the good smell worse than cigarettes. Let's hear it for good breath. Brush your teeth with soda and rinse your mouth with pure water.

"Well, babe, there *was* this one deep-socketed, long-necked, stringy-haired woman. Bony—Christ—she was so bony you'd have to wear hip pads to bang her, like Helen."

"Sonny!"

"She was tall and she was lank and her high breasts were convex, and she wore pointy falsies. She's so cheap-looking you could buy her with a bus token." It was a good lie to tell her.

"Was she *afflicted?*"

"Not unless common ignorance is an affliction."

"Sonny, we're awful."

"Yup." And whatever rise I had on went plumb down. April, too, went limp on me, and we breathed slowly together in the mean dark of the Stonewall.

"Didn't they realize they were out of place?"

"Everybody was drunk, including me."

Everybody wore the mortal face of drunkenness, but, strange as it seems, no vileness was aimed at the girls. Those boys had been

really alive for a couple of days, and the likes of Carl Phillips and
Morris Thompson aren't the kind to be easily seized by vision—but
for forty-eight hours they'd been possessed by something luminous
and terrible—each fat leg, hairy and so doughy white, like a floater's, each narrow forehead and bushy brow was joy illimited. They
sought them in drive-ins, malt shops, tonks, pizza parlors, evangelical churches, and Jitney Jungles, burrowing backwards through
all their personal rabbit warrens, where sister, mother, cousin, and
maiden aunt hunkered damply on the straw of every bend in the
maze. Terrified of all the self-contained and perfectly beautiful
Aprils, they could now strike back at every clean limb, and at all the
scented breasts, and at all the cruel spit curls below the pearly ears.

Little Morris Thompson, lawyer's son and mechanical engineer
(from Pass Christian), obsessed with his shortness and bowed legs,
the one who always said he wasn't inferior because he knew he was
inferior, Morris sought out and found the hugest daughter ever
born to a welder in Laughlin County. He got her at a prayer meeting on Wednesday night, choosing her for her pink cheeks, tent
dress, and 198 pounds. *Pray Your Weight Away with Dr. Peale*—
but after her third Black Label she did a bop to unhinge the cosmos,
shudderings and sea changes of gyrating flesh that quite inundated
the small continent of Morris. Morris, who once crouched on a
chair outside a rat hole in that very house, crouched patiently with
a filed fork wired to a broom handle, and after a vigil of nearly
three hours—actually stabbed the mother, which was no small
accomplishment.

Morris and Carol Bell danced the night away, for both of them
at last—because of Stream's existential itch—were free to be themselves, in Hattiesburg. Only the vague and bitter motive behind
that party could have let little Morris wheel and cavort the way he
did that night.

As I made my rounds as dateless host there were many things
to see and hear while I was carrying that bowl of vegetable goodies
—little tomatoes, celery, pickles, and carrots trimmed and sliced in
thin strips—we'd even filled the trough of each celery stick with
cheese for the girls. Most couples danced, but a few went off to the
smaller rooms of the basement for talk and necking. Propped
against the door jamb of a small ponderosa room with a simulated

leather couch in it, I heard: "What's these?" A coarse female voice.

"Shrimp. You never ate shrimp?" asks Fred Treadwell, the son of a dipsomaniacal doctor from Biloxi.

"Maybe what you need's oysters," says the coarse voice in a teasing fashion.

"How come?"

"Mountain oysters, honey. Bull balls, Freddy!"

"You from Texas?" and then there's the clatter of the little plate and sounds of furious lovemaking that causes me to imagine exploding hooks and eyes and also an extraordinary flak of girdle parts. For a moment I couldn't tell whether Fred was loving on her or beating her up for being from Texas and teasing him, but finally I satisfied myself it was only a fizgig and her fellow having fun. I'd gotten tight.

And it did seem like fun for a while to tread the linoleum of the house basement with bowls of Fritos and small tomatoes, but at last I came on Stream in a dim corner, where he's with a lady, an absolutely flawless lady with a patch over one eye.

Clearly Stream has not played by the rules much better than the others—for none of the girls were really crips—there was fat and bone aplenty, but nothing absolutely ruined except for that one eye. Most were just a little ugly and rough. Stream had got the only maimed one, but where he cheated was in her class.

I crouched to join their conversation, offering my wares and casting up an observation or two about the rhetoric of Leveller tracts, and Stream's lady was graceful right away. She said I made a perfect hostess, making her joke in a charming and affectionate manner. She took some celery and didn't fear the crunch.

My head was suddenly reeling. Was I short of blood from squatting? She's dressed in what appears to be a soft blue with a low bustline, but the sleeves are long and fluted. I stood up to gain my breath again and found myself asking her to dance. I gave the dishes to Stream and told him to play waiter while we were gone.

She smelled, for all the smoke around, like far fields in the sunshine, heather and clover, and like the fresh water of a brook as you lower your head to drink. She was a college girl, proving Stream had broken his own rules, a student at Mullins and the daughter of Stream's mother's best friend, and I'm positive she knew damned well exactly what was going on at that deplorable party. She talked of the countryside and the mountains in Virginia and said it was probably more interesting than Marion County and Columbia, where she came from. She stood on her toes and kissed me on my Adam's apple, and I was suddenly in love with her; and I grant you that the recollection of that girl is awfully sentimental, but any vulgarity or austerity of style would make this report a lie: the part where we're dancing, and what came later.

Such keen features, such a fine authoritative nose, such a honed chin, and her one eye had long natural lashes. I wanted more than anything in the world to put the spiral horns of the addax on Stream. After that kiss from Eden I was sure she'd cut out with me. I could take that tiny waist away from Stream, and the smallest wrists I ever saw in a dim light.

"Will you go out with me?" I asked in a voice one might use while inquiring as to whether the market had any brains or tongue.

"Of course." Of course! Holy Jesus God! Of course! I wanted to cheer. My goddamned eyes were filled with tears.

"Now?"

"Yes." And she pushed her stropped face into my coiled chest hair. She pushed her intricate self hard against me. She was honestly and suddenly hot. She was proffering silly lines in a way that proved romance can sometimes be true and wonderful. We were characters in the *Alexandria Quartet*—we were ass-deep in a believable piney-woods worldliness.

"I'll want it all."

"I want it all."

Mary, back from Galveston and trying to change her ways (she's putting on a crisp dress from time to time these days, instead of always walking around in those butchy jeans, or butt naked), admits it is possible for such a brief encounter to be completely meaningful, in spite of the gothic element introduced by the empty socket. And Mary may be the most consistent argument against sending pretty women to graduate school. Reading good books at Mullins may make a young lady more imaginative and sensual, but I'm almost sure they'd never praise a student who talked about the

mothering gothic element posed by the mothering socket. Bungle-
some and hypertrophied crap like that comes later, after they've
gone professional.

*It has been the custom heretofore that no man should be al-
lowed to touch venison or wild fowl, or fish—in flowing water,
which seems to us quite unseemly and brotherly as well as selfish
and not agreeable to the word of God. In some places the authorities preserve the game to our great annoyance and loss, recklessly
permitting the unreasoning animals to destroy to no purpose our
crops, which God suffers to grow for the use of man; and yet we
submit quietly. This is neither godly or neighborly; for when God
created man he gave him dominion over all the animals, over the
birds of the air and the fish of the water. Accordingly it is our
desire, if a man holds possession of waters, that he should prove
from satisfactory documents that his right has been unwittingly acquired by purchase. We do not wish to take it by force, but his
rights should be exercised in a Christian and brotherly fashion.
But whosoever cannot produce such evidence should surrender his
claim with good grace.* Which is how it ought to be, if not the way
it is—just emotions, just heads, just hearts. Fuck the law. Which is
stupid. But I cannot and will not ever believe that law's the answer.
Royal, forsake your midnight mischief at the tome—quit the bed
of our wife—go forth and preach, for the end of the world is at
hand. Graham is righter than most—God, if he was only a Populist
—I'm sorry I tore his pulpit down—and Dianne was rightfully
mine that night at the pig party, for Stream had no right of title or
deed or will (least of all will); he should have faded away in a
Christian and brotherly fashion, but he didn't.

He comes out into the main dancing room, having foisted off
the vegetable goodies on one of his brothers; he leans against the
knotty pine and begins to tap his foot, while looking sorrowful as
a possum dripping a litter from her belly.

"Stream'll understand. He only brought me as a favor to my
mother." She paused into a casual stillness, releasing her hand from
mine, her right hand from my left, as she gently slipped the thumb
of her left hand down under my wide belt behind. "He's afraid of

the patch," she says. She says, "Coldstream Taggart is a damn fooool."

April. Ding. Ding. The Stonewall Pelican. Loyalty? Fucking loyalty. A delicate girl, even smaller than April, hardly a hundred pounds whose eye was knocked out by her daddy's Big Wheel Yazoo Mower, whose green patch is not offensive, the strap tucked up and under a glossy black cascade that would put ole Bill's Dark Lady to shame.

"Let's go," I said. *Violate friends, trueloves, and all the reasonable rules. (I'd suggested a seventh—avoid fucking pigs at all costs—too complicated, problems later—a seventh practical rule that was never agreed to.)* And I wasn't about to go to the stadium lot, and I wasn't going to a motel, nor could I feature the forest floor as a proper place for it. This house itself would have to be the place.

We climbed the three floors (four, counting the basement stairs) of that bad house and ended barricaded in an attic room that was used only occasionally by a brother doing graduate study in library science. He's gone that night to court his fiancée in Bay St. Louis. Jesus. I was a very happy man, and *she* was a happy *girl*. I placed a big square fan on the librarian's locker at the foot of the bed, aimed the big mother straight across the tidy sheets (and there's a pile of rope on the floor below a small dormer, a fire escape for the intelligent librarian)—I'd already secured the door with a straightback. Privacy! Goddamn it, a man and a woman in heat need privacy. Nothing on film.

I stripped, and I've never been so proud to do it. It's hotter than hell except on the bed itself, so I stripped with alacrity but without unseemly haste. And so did she. A man gets laid maybe four thousand times in his life, and often and well by the goodwife, but only once or twice does he achieve sublime voluptuousness—and no number of position books is about to make said voluptuousness a regular thing with said goodwife every other time even.

As I stepped out of my particolored shorts I realized that the heat was really oppressive. But then I looked at her.

I was Martin Luther with his nun.

She, Dianne, was shorn of all her pretty garments. She hadn't even needed help with her zipper, and she had the hairiest box I'd ever seen. It was like a boiling pool of licorice. Black wires! It was also like black wires.

You're worried about the socket. Well, she kept it patched throughout, but no amount of socket crud could have ever made me squeamish with Dianne. Her single glistening eye was joyous. You know what she said? She said, while standing in that fragile hump of clothes: "You actually did it. I was afraid you wouldn't." And then she looked me up and down. Up and down, but it wasn't the look of the butcher, the baker, the candlestick maker; it was a look conveying only the most natural and reasonable appreciation for the most perfect MALE body she'd ever laid her eyes on. But most of all she evidenced a simple (simpleminded?) appreciation of the fact I did bring her up there and did it—took her away from flimsy Stream—walked all those narrow stairs up, up and away from the girl I'm sure she knew I had stashed out somewhere.

She gave me the confidence to flex.

And no other woman has ever allowed me that. Not one. Nor April, nor Mary. Blast away with the piledriving ass; that's fine. Work their little bitty titties up to reasonable size and tell them to swing them in the breeze, and they're delighted; but never once did they say, with either eye, *Sonny flex—enjoy your Godgiven human body, for I admire it.*

With her single glittering eye she approved the chains of tendons my body wore, and getting there is half the fun—more than half sometimes—because with Dianne the deal wasn't so much the fucking as the goddamned sincere recognition of almost spontaneous Romance. There wasn't any way in the world we could make it right on that short bed, with its metal head and foot, no matter how much wind I got to blowing across it. Maybe I could of put the mattress on the floor, arranging the fan some other way. Maybe get on the bed and have a chatty little conference about sexual gymnastics under duress—but anything like that would have stanched the drift. That girl wasn't a promiscuous sexual-athlete type—she's a nice, normal woman who found herself at a weird party where she meets a good ole boy she likes; really likes. She wanted the pleasure of recognition and I'd already given it in spades before we ever got in bed.

We were plenty hot. Don't get me wrong. I spilled my jeans and shorts on the floor, then rose slowly like when you're coming up from touching your toes. I pulled to full height and touched the low ceiling with my head, and smiled an uncomplicated college smile as best I could. It was the flexing of a ballet dancer, and would I could have done a splendid leap onto that bed without bashing my head and crashing through the floor; I would I could have done it without crashing naked down three stories until I lay naked on the basement floor amid a mess of carrots and gawks.

What I actually did was great, if I do say so myself. I stepped across the room and dropped to my knees in front of her, which put us just about eyeball to eyeball. I told her I cherished this moment and that she was very possibly the most beautiful naked girl I'd ever seen. It was a generous line, but I felt a little devious about it since Momma and Polly Roberts and April were the only competition she had. She understood, however, and recklessly threw herself into an abandon of embraces. I kissed her patch. I kissed her eye. I kissed both titties. I kissed her belly button and her snatch. I turned that little girl around and kissed her spine, and then carefully, oh so carefully, but without the awkwardness of any physical hesitation suggesting indecision, I placed my body on the bed. "Honey," I said, "crawl up on top of me." For I couldn't bear the idea of having the bed collapse under the type of screwing I do when I'm on top.

Enough. The rest of it was pleasant and obvious: a tight pussy, a loving and competent slow screw until she cried and bit her lip and did a push-up off my rib cage at the very time she crimped her cunt and came, or whatever, as I had already come some minutes before, with visions of Joiners in the Shenandoah Valley of Virginia.

No Texan or Yankee ever threatens a Mississippian, but Carolinians and Virginians always make us feel a little inadequate; so the idea of my children born to a Mississippian who chooses to live in N.C. or Va. seemed like an interesting way to improve the blood strain.

. . .

And getting dressed was also fun. In fact, I think that getting dressed was the most intimate of all. It was the vanity of children, but nevertheless it was probably a more significant test of mature courage than what was done in the heat of passion.

There ought to be a word for the pleasure one feels while watching a relatively satisfied lady dress. I couldn't take my eyes off of her. There wasn't a breath of actual lust left in me. I'd already rendered every ounce of body and mind I commanded, but watching her glide back into her things was incredibly gratifying. It was almost the best part.

I hurried into my rough garb and finished her zippering. I slowly locked it at the top.

"Thank you," she said.

"You're welcome," I said.

For all Stream knew we'd only gone for a walk or a drive, doing nothing more than hugging and kissing; it never would have entered his mind we'd made love, and certainly not in his house. He's not happy about our going anywhere—I'm supposed to be shepherding his zebus—but he never suspected the *grande passion*. As far as I know nobody in that fraternity ever suspected, unless maybe the librarian noticed a musk about his spread, and he'd of had to be damned sensitive to catch that musk, because there weren't any stains. Dianne straightened the bed before we went down—out the door and down the stairs again, returning to the party. Thank God there was a john on the first deck (a tidy one for guests and parties)—thank God there wasn't a soul on the second and third deck that night.

Man, I do not like to get caught in such shit, and in this case I knew damn well April'd hear about it if I was suspected of anything really irregular. What we did was hustle out to the front steps to sit and wait for Stream, who was sure to show up before long; but probably not before he could savor a little lover's talk. And it's a good thing their house mother was on vacation: it's terrible to think of all the things that can go wrong: twisted knees and ankles, dislocated shoulders, the usual broken bones, crushed nuts, bad grades, cameras, preachers, politicians: Loki and the

Midgard Serpent are always ready to ruin the brave and the beautiful.

Dianne was peaceful and she didn't make the usual demands. Hell, she didn't even suggest I visit her at Mullins, which bothered me until I realized that Taggart had mentioned I was taken. I asked if she had a boyfriend in Virginia, and she said she did. She said she was secretly married to a medical student in Richmond. Whomp! Just like that. It was like a double-yolk egg had been deftly cracked on the top of my head, but not a rotten one. "I really needed some loving," and the way she said it changed the runny feeling into a sense of grandeur. When she said that, we changed into an eagle and a dove, and I was tempted to say that I was secretly married, too. Why not? I might as well of been. But I couldn't lie, because she'd actually done the ceremony with a J.P., and that makes a difference. Damn right.

What did worry me was that maybe Dianne was involved in some kind of *agreement,* some kind of modern marriage, and anything as strange as an *arrangement* would have made a hash of the entire adventure.

"Y'all have an understanding or something?"

"No. No, we don't." And she squeezed down hard on my knee. "I guess I'm just a fallen woman." But it wasn't like she's going to slash her wrists or do something really stupid like confess to her husband.

"You sorry you got married?"

"No . . ." and her voice was insecure, but not because the answer was a lie. Rather, it was a way of telling me how hopeless it is to reject the past, or command the future, for that matter. "We'll probably get married again at home next summer, to make it right for our families . . . and get some things." She squeezed again and set a practical smile on her face. "Let's just sit still until my date comes back."

"God damn!"

"You mad?"

"Hell no."

"Then shush." The Great American Shush, though rendered more humanely than most.

. . .

We apologized to Stream for going off for a walk together, and staying so long, but it turns out we've got mutual friends in Memphis. Dianne and I apologized but it was mostly just a ritual, and not obsequious at all; and Stream knew we'd struck up an attraction, but he's satisfied it didn't come to much.

"Have a good life, Dianne." It was a line a fellow once said to me when we'd been hitchhiking all day. One of those lines when you team up for a thousand miles but then go off in different directions at Memphis. And a damn nice thing to say.

"Have a good life, Son."

And that was that.

What does it have to do with April in the Stonewall, or Royal, or riot, or race, or football, or revolution? Mary says the fact I never told April about that part of the evening proves a) that I never had anything very profound with my truelove, because b) she was beneath me socially and intellectually. Mary says I'm a goddamned hateful redneck snob who'd sell his mother for status.

Leave, damnit! Leave for good and all. But she doesn't. She just falls on our bed and cries and cries: *ladies ladies ladies—Joiner you and your stupid LADIES.*

Bull Bull Bull—because the thing with Dianne is nothing but a good story, one of those hopeful and life-giving incidents that happens from time to time—just like the Stonewall and April—just like some of the good times with Mary—just like the tree people.

See the Yo-Yo go up and down, see, see, see the Yo-Yo with momentary Dianne, but that's not exactly what we want. Tier by tier, stair by stair, a whole stadium full of fuck scenes—see the Yo-Yo on his raunchy truelove at the Stonewall.

. . .

Stricken by wild pity, April retires to the shower, and I feel guilty while the water's on.

That Virginia woman's on my mind and I was a little sorry I couldn't tell April how Dianne managed to make me more than merely comfortable and hot, how she had made me proud of my powers. Which isn't to say that April denied them. Quite the contrary. April took them for granted.

Outside the shower in the dim light she's humble, girlish, a little stooped, and putty-faced, almost contrite, but her hair's not wringing wet like Mary's is so often. Walk the dog. I'm a meathead in Paradise, and when she spatters herself with talc and cologne it almost breaks my heart. Goddamned Dianne wouldn't ever do that outside the bathroom, but April does it at the dresser, showing her naked front by shadow of reflection. And Polly Roberts never bothered with extra odors when she's ready. April. April at times like that showed her true self, and exactly the part that Royal admires. April doesn't have the famous sexual V. No hairy box has she. It's only a bland I with fuzz all around, all around, all around.

Is April naked finally no more than the standard American cocker spaniel? No indeed. And that's the wonder of it. Without Maylene and Henry and Helen and all the Bryan County clabber, she might have been—she might have been your classic, dumb-assed, whimpering bitch (and she's not the pregnant squaw I saw shooting pool in an Oklahoma tavern once either). She's a practical girl who is satisfied that she deserves the pleasure of making love. To which very little can be added.

She went at me like I was steak and potatoes and a mixed salad with French dressing, but she didn't gorge, and it wasn't antiseptic, because there's nothing sterile about a decent girl with a profound need, hankering. Maybe she dreamed of stallions in fields, and maybe bulls with vasty dongs were in her mind the while—dark pulses and niggerish foreskins—but I doubt it. All that business about thrumming, ungrammatical, archetypal emotions being the essence of the spontaneous nitty gritty is probably true, but you rarely think about it that way while it's going on. April, I believe, is a sexual nominalist.

·   ·   ·

And then she'd sleep. I'd kiss her hair and say, "Honey, I'm going to walk a little."

"Fine, fine, but be careful," and then she'd drop like a mimosa blossom settling on a stream. She'd sink into the rest of the blessed, while I prepared to walk the roads of Rankin County.

II

To hell with Žižka, Hus, and Winstanley, all them Europeans, however much they illuminate my weighty theme. I invoke now the spirit of Andrew Jackson, that sublimely lucky sunnavabitch, that great American (for he took advantage of every break), that Super Neck (though his soul was gentry): ole beak-nose, ole birdy-chest, Mr. Aches and Pains.

> *Rude his sun-burnt men*
> *In simple garb of foresters are seen—*
> *But mark—they know with death the bead to sight,*
> *And draw the centre of the heart in fight.*

What incredible bullshit! What essential myth! What basic history! But of course it was really niggers and Cajuns and dandies won the fight at New Orleans. Those lacy Creoles could out-shoot the yeomen any day of the week. They did it. They challenged the rude hunters to a shooting contest and won. They did it in New Orleans soon after the battle—they were tired of all the unjustified fame and praise that was falling on the Kentuckians, which praise made it look like they, the men of the city, were nothing but a bunch of inaccurate fruits.

Hell, the woodsmen didn't even bring enough rifles to the battle. It was halfbreeds and fops that saved the spirit of the Union. The confidence of the Union was saved because of city people, and because General Gibbs on the English side stayed in his strict formation and got slaughtered by grape and canister while waiting for the 44th to come forth with fascines and ladders to scale Andy's mud wall that stretched between the river and the swamp. Gibbs, he stood too long in one place. So it was Gibbs who let his brave lads get gored—*The Conquerors of the Conquerors of Europe* were defeated because Gibbs and his lines, like dull heroic couplets, were moveless. And anyway it was early on a foggy morning, so *nobody* could see to aim. Actually it was the cannons that did it, cannons and plain luck.

Nevertheless: O Andrew, I invoke you now. I needed you with April, and you were there more often than not. You stood by me and got an eyeful when Dianne tested me. You served me well at the pig party and the Stonewall, but you forsook me at the Knee and in the tree. And I need you now with Mary. I need for you to honor and toughen my story. *And you, too, my fair and beloved country women, whose first honour is in the gentleness of your nature, will you not unite your sympathies and tears over the grave of that man, who, above all others, was the most devoted friend and admirer, might I not say romantic, that woman ever had?*

Who so prompt to defend and protect her rights, or guard her from injury and insult?

Whoever cherished or exalted more the purity of the domestic and social virtues, so infinitely more important to human happiness than all others? Whose valour was it that protected our mothers, and wives, and daughters, from the savage tomahawk, and a licentious soldiery, and one of our richest cities, with its Beauty and booty, from ruthless invaders?

Whose, but Andrew Jackson's?

After my arm got broken and damn near ripped out of the socket, I went to visit Jakes over at Southern. I wanted a rec from him in my dossier, which he was of course pleased to write, in his deathless run-Spot-run prose. I told myself I wanted to see him for the rec (the idea being to coach and teach somewhere the rest of the year, but *somewhere* turned out to be Bryan of course and what I did was work at the Mill)—I trick myself—for actually I just wanted to visit with the man, and maybe see some of the players, my old mates.

Jakes and I sat there talking about old times and also about how the Bulls might have a shot at the title since the defensive line's getting tougher, and we agreed that Morningside Robbins (the Negro I'd played behind in Dallas) was the best offensive tackle in The League, even though he's aging—*But, Son, you'll be better than him in a few years. Maybe even next year when the arm's well*—says Jakes—and it's clear as hell he's hoping I'll get the hell out of his paneled office—his goddamned brand new office I helped him get by playing brilliantly for three years. No doubt about it, he wants me out of the very office where my own face is hanging on the wall behind his pussy blond desk: an actual tinted individual-head-shot portrait, one of the Hall of Fame portraits commissioned by the Southern Touchdown Club—and there aren't but fifteen of them to this very night.

Jakes is vaguely interested in the pro-ball lore I've picked up beyond the Magnolia Curtain. He's especially interested in a fantastically huge hanging dummy we—the Bulls' offensive line—call Fat Lady. It's rather like a boxer's heavy bag except for being so much larger. Six feet high and ten feet in diameter. Jakes is always looking for *advanced devices*. He's interested in anything that will *im*prove his sophomorish offensive line, because what's really on his mind is the game with State in Jackson Saturday. He'll never get a shot at the Florida job unless he wins it, which species of crude ambition isn't entirely unmanly, right?

But what I remember most about that last visit with Jakes was how I brought the talk back around to pro ball a second time and asked him if he considered Robbins the equal of Bill Wallick.

Beautiful. Jakes went dumb and stared at me a full three seconds, maybe ten, with ignorant fuzz in his eyes. "Hummm." He rocked back in his swivel and pondered the neat tongue-and-groove joints in the far wall. He's trying to remember who Wallick is, and, by God, he doesn't have the foggiest idea. "Maybe so, maybe so."

He says it very seriously while pinching his chin and eyeing a plaque over in the glass case. "Maybe he is . . ."

Maybe so and maybe he is, my ass. He showed me he was a small man for good and all right then and there. He wasn't big time. He couldn't possibly be dedicated to his game if he didn't know who Bill Wallick was. And he didn't get the Florida job either. He's still at Southern, and hot damn to that!

It's like if Boykin didn't know who Learned Hand was. It's like never knowing about Procop or Ben Tillman or James K. Vardaman. And who's Babe Ruth or Jimmie Rodgers or John Keats? Who's this poor soul, General Gibbs? Andrew Who? Piss on Jakes. I finally did disappoint him, but he disappointed me worse. When he lied about knowing Bill Wallick, he was dead for all I cared, and dead without honor.

Mirrors in bathrooms and locker rooms, pictures on placards, portraits hung on sterile walls, wallets full of photos (lemme show you this one of my little son)—all the images that bleed the soul away—and still the peoples of the world wonder why their civilizations are botched in the teeth, as it were. It would be better to carry around little dried collops of human meat. *This here piece of jerky is actually a chunk of my darling baby . . . wife . . . best friend—I cut it about three years ago, but it's still he . . . she . . . it.*

That morning I got free and shut of Jakes I never saw anybody else but Moody Pravis the trainer.

I stepped into Moody's office, where he's reading some professional literature—*The Compleat Jock*—and I say, "Moody this is the worst day of my life," a line I always said every day before practice when I was one of Moody's boys all those years. We talked ball about twenty-five minutes—we had a damned pleasant visit—and Moody don't give a rip who coaches. He has survived three already, and he'll be whistling and taping at Southern when five more fools have come and gone. Moody Pravis, he's bald and runs the whirlpool machine and tapes a man in less than a minute—and when he sees a fellow admiring himself at the big mirror, he says, "Whoooeee . . . Uhhh! This game'll sure mess a feller up. Why, I remember just last year you looked real good..."

.   .   .

After I left the Stonewall, wherein Sweet April was sleeping soundly, her female body contemplating unconsciously the yeoman service done by my prod, I went down the Rankin Highway to drink some beer at a place called the Knee (from cypress knee), and there it was—my picture up behind the bar. It's one of these football schedule placards with little oval pictures (paper cameos sans relief) of the players laid out along the top above the dates and places and prices of the games. It's a cardboard ad, and I resented it being there to remind me of how hard I was going to have to work to get in shape by September 1. I got me a Country Club and meditated on that pix that's stuck up among the beer nuts and Fritos and peppers, and even a big fearful jug of hardboiled eggs: Eugene "Sonny" Joiner All-Gulf States Tackle: the gleaming smile of my pearlywhites: the top of the seven and the five showing, in a honky-tonk: and Dianne Harvey on my mind.

Be with me, Jackson...Beowulf...Clovis.

My confidence hasn't faltered many times in my life (though there is that single massive exception that ruined everything)— but there in the sleazy Knee I felt pretty woesome, with Dianne's shade skulking my mind's fen.

I wondered what she'd think of me if she could see me there alone and disgusted with my malt liquor.

She'd probably be sorry she let me screw her. She'd probably run home and douche with a strong solution of Borax or quicklime, cleansing herself for the splendid medico she's married to. She'd do that—or what's worse she might get sentimental and reject her decent husband again, desiring once again to ride the funky ole draft horse: giddup, Eugene, plow. Pull. Which won't do for an image. A mule?

Christ, was I ever jealous, which is a fairly rare emotion for me—foul, corroding, miserly, tendon-slicing jealousy that makes the flesh feel pulverized and the soul feel pickled, makes your balls feel like those dead eggs up in that sorry jug. Balls-eggs? *You ain't nothin but a meathead at a third-rate school, a second-rate team, and that girl so happy and punched out back at the motel couldn't care less about Gibbs and Jackson and the battle of N.O....*

Jackson he was wide awake, and wasn't scared
  of trifles [truffles?],
For well he knew what aim we take with our
  Kentucky rifles;
So he marched us down to Cypress Swamp;
The Ground was low and mucky;
There stood John Bull, in martial pomp,
BUT HERE WAS OLD KENTUCKY.

The "Hunters of Kentucky" was on my mind along with April and Dianne and Professor Burger, who could still believe in all that folderol, being from Canton, Ohio.

Jealousy? I had the companionship of good mates on the team—the respect of my mentors, athletic and mental—and Stream and Royal and Benton and Bobo were still the friends and enemies of my youth. Bryan was home, though my parents were gone two years to Memphis, blaming me (and I've never felt comfortable in their home at White Haven, even though it's like their other places: small, tidy, smelling of Pine Sol and oil paint), and history and football were visions enough for any intelligent, modern man. Jealousy? Jealousy is a version of loneliness, and loneliness is a cheap word, a shrill self-pitying blurt I hate—*O where is the horse and his rider, O where is the giver of gold*—but jealousy *is* loneliness, exile—and so it was that I discovered the first gate of exile long before I entered her city proper, which is Fort Worth.

And jealousy is, most seriously, the killer of pleasant rhetoric.

My little oval face, behind the bar and the stooped, toothless, and grimy tender with his plaid vest on, smiled down with a wholesome, benevolent, and understanding smile that said there wasn't necessarily any hostility between funky music and good health, between peanut butter and good conditioning, pig fat and angina, April and Dianne. You can't *prove* cigarettes cause cancer and heart disease, said my cameo face (except of course it wasn't in profile) above the cash register. You can't prove a better woman than April wouldn't have moved you under different circumstances. Son, you don't even have to marry April . . . you don't *have* to. No, sir! *Boy, if that Dianne girl don't want no*

*Fritos and beer and Johnny Cash as a steady diet, she's not for
you.*
Goddamn it, face, *I* don't want that stuff as a steady diet!

*So he marched us down to Cypress Swamp;
The ground was low and mucky* . . . .

Goddamned "'Ring of Fire": God damned Redneck götter-
dämmerung. *Eugene don't admire the honky-tonks too much* is
what my reasonable momma used to say.

Andrew Jackson was an orphan. Boykin is a bastard, an actual
illegitimate child his people got at the Home in Meridian, and
on the night I told April about the pigs I, too, felt like an orphan
and a bastard, and swine. I needed the iron will of Jackson, but
what I got was tree people and troubles with Cheryl—the tree
people, the locally famous Tankersleys, and they were in high
fettle. Wasn't any doubt they were high, Andy. They're so low-
down they're the highest people in Rankin County raising hell on
a summer's night, and it did me good to hear that clatter of
chains and pails and cans and actual music—midnight mischief
to cure the sociological blues—Mississippi cum Virginia women
—and I wasn't about to miss whatever joyance was going on off
through the sawgrass and bitterweed and elderberry and dock.
They were famous creatures destined to cure my blues, or so I
thought as I lifted off the bar stool soddenly.
    Four generations, and all the social service organizations
around the Capitol City couldn't get those goddamned people
down from their houses that rose in tiers and levels into the leaves
and limbs of three water oaks. A storm was rising in the southwest as I checked out in a brisk jog toward the bridge, and a
jogging drunk is crucial pain.

    I'd actually seen several Tankersleys on an earlier afternoon
when April and I were sunning on the east beach of the Pearl—
their beach. One man and a couple of boys came popping south

in a rowboat with an outboard. They beached their craft and then climbed those railless stairs that rose at least thirty feet at a terrific angle into the branches and leaves. They didn't say anything while they pulled the boat toward the small bluff—and they didn't say anything, even to each other, as they moved almost like acrobats up to their loft. Each fellow balanced himself with a string of catfish he held and swung before him rather like a censer, and when they disappeared behind the burlap cover that served as a portal, there was still no sound at all, and nothing to be seen. It was strangely disconcerting to look across that distance of hot beach and up into those splendid trees, knowing humans were up there (and lots more than the three we'd just watched) but hearing and seeing nothing. The banter of the city off to the west and cars passing now and then back on the road seemed reassuring—it was downright comforting to hear humans and machines going about their helpless blather, for people really ought not sleep in trees at 4:00 p.m. "All of them must be asleep . . . babies and children and grown-ups," said April, respectfully.

But, friend, on the night of the storm they were ripping and tearing. I turned off the highway and began to run along the path. Those flickers of light and those muddled yet somehow racking sounds off through the woods were surely signals and calls from a safe harbor, for the storm was about to break. The ground would indeed be low and mucky soon. And certainly I was rushing toward some powerful essence of *strange*—certainly there would be naked redneck women careering around the trunks—Bessies and Pollys, Westerman and Weatherford women, all fleeing Tankersley satyrs—because those people were known moonshiners and fierce drinkers—everybody knew they owned the largest portable still in the world, a still real and mythic as the famous swamp lions of Bryan County. As I thudded along that dark, wide path, I imagined a scene worthy of Italian actresses in Tennessee Williams-type movies. Goddamned Burt Lancaster would be swinging through the limbs—he'd be making brash, successful leaps from house to house, from tree to tree.

. . .

But what I actually found was work: industry. It was the damndest vision of excited and useful labor I've ever beheld, and after the first shock of it I wasn't the least bit disappointed.

It's a whole crowd of humans both in the trees and on the ground. But the first thing I saw when I broke into the clearing was a wad of half-naked children cleaning fish on a split log. They're going at cat and bream with spoons and old knives, and there's also four, five more catfish (big horns, big whiskers) hung through mouths and gills on the near tree. The big fish are fastened and hooked to the tree on straightened coat hangers, and the older boys are skinning them. The whole crowd is swilling down R.C.'s and Orange Crushes and fighting around in the dirt when they feel like it. Fishguts, fish heads, fish blood, that fine old garrulous and humane reek of *fish*—and it's bright as day from all the lights that are strung around on poles and branches. These people are robbing Mississippi Power blind.

I wasn't disappointed. In fact, somewhere between the first thunder back at the bridge and the moment I entered their company, after running at least a hundred yards along the wide path, I'd completely forgotten my downtrodden feelings about April and Dianne. When I saw that first child notch and then break off that first fish head, I was mostly gone from other trouble. Andy Jackson and Robinson Crusoe: great men!

Joiner was being treated right. The dogs growled and the littlest tads drew back when they saw me rein up in the light, but it wasn't so much they were frightened as it was they were interrupted, or so it seemed when I first burst in.

"WaChont?" asked one of the large boys whose hand and pliers are done with stripping the skin off the biggest fish—which boy's eyes narrowed a little but then relaxed.

"Nothin'." And I offered up a smile.

"WaChont?" came down a gravelish voice from up the tree.

"Not a thing." And what worried me most was how it seemed quite possible they'd all turn back to their riot and let me stand there with nothing to do. I gazed up into what must be called

a Redneck Rose of Heaven, levels on levels of tree people who
were washing and painting the firmament, tattered people in
Mississippi fustian (and surely they were all drunk as coots on
something of their own making—sundry liquors—white liquid
light extracted from all the luminescence of all the naked bulbs
they'd strung the oaks with—moonshine no moon shone on—
and a mellow wine the women surely made in earthen crocks
they wedged between the crates and rough walls) who were
scrubbing the sins of the world away.

Such fine dreams the odors of raisins and oranges must have
raised!

On the first level a Maytag pumped and thudded with washing, while men and women scoured pots and pans and scrubbed
walls and floors with great brushes and sponges—real sponges like
you get from Tampa.

"Looks like you people mean to make it right," I shouted up,
growing more fearful of being left out. No answer. But within
a minute a large wicker basket is lowered to me—it's a splendid,
yellow wicker basket being lowered by way of a glossy new
rope. It settled at my feet and was full of white things, underwear
and sheets and pillowcases for me to hang on the line, clean
clothes to be strung out on the several lines they'd spanned between the trunks: an honest offering from on high.

I stumbled on treacherous roots (but didn't spill my burden)
and went to hang that sweet garb—no murrain this season, no un-
clean plague on the tree people: three pins for the sheets (but use
a single pin to fasten down the different pieces), and there's a
great beating of thunder off to the southwest where it always
comes from, unless it is a hurricane.

Poor people work when it's cool.

And the next load was mostly jeans cut short for summer—
I was fully integrated—as the children continued their chores
with fish, sending them up in pails—there was a lot of stuff going
up and down—nobody was paying me any mind, but they *were*
letting me help out. As I turned in my space in the light I noticed
three tree houses. But when the second load was in my hands I
noticed the nicest thing of all: a gift: a goddamned Mason jar of
their wine was cushioned by the blue heap, and it was half full.

I'm in with the wimmen! But at last I'll finish my night's work and a barechested and bony man, pinch-breasted as Andy, will swing down on a water vine and shoot my ass off about the time the kids send up the last pail of fish. I will have served my purpose. They've got refrigeration up on those limbs! And April's surfacing fearlessly from her first deep sleep.

Exile, Exile, was on my mind even back then. Mary. I drank too much beer at the Knee, where my own face bore down on me, and too much raisin wine beneath my tree; and when an old man of maybe forty-five, who looked like an unscarred Henry, was suddenly standing by me at my clothesline, having appeared soundlessly and barefoot around the trunk, I started—I sprung straight up, leaping with only the thrust of my feet (stiff-kneed), and pins fell out my mouth.

"You a mighty bigun to be doin' that," says the wropped elder.

"It's what I got offered to do." I said that.

"You almost too goddamn big to go up," he muses, while tapping a middle finger rapidly against his chest. He's sending coded messages to his lungs and heart?

"What are the *men* doing?"

"Paintin' mostly." He looks almost kindly on me, for obviously he has received an affirmative reply from within his bone box. He's toothless (came along before tree people started using fluoride) and he's trenched in the face (the marks of rural ben?), but I please him. "Cumon."

Praise old men—and I'm in and up—ah. Dante, the Rose of Heaven is become a Water Oak. Mary, it's a kind of Saxon Jacob's ladder, for unvarnished pine is the color of golden stairs, rising into the lit fecundity above. I put the extra pins into the basket and tugged the rope so they would know to raise it, and then I followed the elder to those stairs.

On the first floor is the Maytag—ruppachucka, ruppachucka —in what seems to be an all-electric kitchen. There's even good water that is lifted in buckets from the well set off in the woods, buckets of pure water that rise at a slight angle on a chain, like the chairs on a ski lift: a goddamn Rube Goldberg: or maybe a crude series of Goldberg Variations on poverty. Whatever, it got the water up. All you do is use the crank above the stainless steel sink and up the buckets came (more like a cistern device, cistern cups, really, than buckets from a well) and very little seems to spill. I tested the floor, noting its gaps, flecks of towheads from below, and moved toward the ladies. My inclination was centripetal and toward the trunk as I followed that old man weaving lightly and lightly up so high (ten feet at least)—and a nimble old tabby he was, buttless, horny heels like Nick hisself—Christ, I was getting giddy and timeless.

A fleshy, freckled woman, in a gilliflower print, was slipping wrapped fish into an ancient fridge with the motor on top. A fish head from the ground below winked up through a gap with a cold disconsolate eye. "What about when the storms come?" I asked of a girl who also appeared from around the trunk, high in the kitchen, as both May and Tag went chump-a chump-a. Surely later and even higher that girl and I would make it, glowing with St. Elmo's fire above the thrashing Pearl. High in the top-gallants of this tight ship I'd fuck her precariously on a spar —Bloom Bloom—and the storm was bearing down on Bovina as I began to climb a permanent ladder up to where the men were painting.

"Storms don't matter," she answered, but already I was going up again. We passed through the second deck; the living quarters (low tables and chairs—Mississippi Orientals); we proceeded safely up another ladder to where the men were. They were obviously looped, but they were slapping on paint with considerable care, while Zenith sang Country and Western to every killdee plover in the county. Old Man introduced me to Jerome and Harold and Sim, near, high cousins probably. All three were stripped to their brand-new colorful shorts—all three, though of slightly different molds and obviously sprung from different parents, were muscled like runners of middle distances.

The one called Harold says, "You too big to be up." Harold seemed nervous about having me there, but the others were easy enough. Sim poured me a whiskey, fetching cubes from a Styrofoam chest. They all remained very still until I'd taken a sip of my drink. "Good stuff," I said. "Thanks for the hospitality." I smiled. They smiled. And then they went back to painting the gypsum boards.

It was the sleeping quarters—mattresses (no beds) were stacked across the room, which was relatively spacious, about twenty by twenty, though the tree trunk in the middle took up some space. It was a bare, wildly colorful place, the only furniture being what seemed to be about ten red boxes (more boxes than proper chests) arranged around the walls for storing clothes. The windows were small and set against the low ceiling, like in a Nissen hut, but they were well-fashioned—everything was well-fashioned in the tree house—and there were a couple of electric space heaters stashed in one corner. Also, I was delighted to see that this high up, with the wind beginning to rattle the acorns, there's a wider roof and even gutters—a corrugated metal roof being the best imaginable for loving in the rain.

I'm gazing around when Harold hands me a can of paint and says to paint the bark. So I took up the brush and began to paint the bark pink. Paint the bark? "Ain't nothin in that paint to hurt the tree," said the old man, understanding . . .

. . . LIGHTNING. Webs and slivers of fire in the sky. I was terrified. But I was working hard to cover the bark's irregular ridges with pink.

"Ain't no way to condishun the tree fort."

As drops began to fall like shot in a brass brazier, as the smell of the fish cooking in lemon and butter began to fly up from below. Work for the day is coming. The whitesky and devilish sun is rising over the Atlantic, rushing to meet the sundering storms of the West.

How did the tree house look, objectively? Three big water oaks form almost an isosceles triangle, the closer trees about sixty feet apart, the far one about a hundred from the others, and each tree has three levels (though maybe the far one I never got to had an extra deck for storage): a kitchen level, a living level, and a bedroom level. There's more room in a tree than one tends to imagine. Each story is sturdy and fitted securely to big limbs, and here and there are struts and braces to the ground. On the living level of my house one wall was exposed to its boards (careful re-

pairs constantly going on) and clearly they had done good work
—studs and lintels were cleanly joined—double studs at door-
ways; and up in the sleeping quarters, where I worked, the rafters and joists and plates were exposed, and all the boards were
beautifully joined. The ridgeboard received the rafters securely,
but still I feared the storm.

Actually only the close trees, which were nearest the bluff
and parallel to the river, had kitchens and the cisternlike pails
that swung up water from the well in the woods. Only two
houses had fresh water and the metal troughs to carry dirty water
away from sinks and washing machines, troughs to run the dirty
water down the bluff.

And the kitchen I saw was clean, for all the work going on
in it. The shelves (set into the walls, not the tree) were covered
with wax paper, and they sheltered quite an assortment of modern
products for the lady around the tree. The Tankersleys were definitely clean necks; in fact, if they hadn't had such bad taste in
colors, I'd of said there was a smattering of genius to them: but
it was pinks and purples and something like corruption green all
over, and, as I say, the night I was there was a time for putting on
new layers of horrors. They especially loved chartreuse.

They had everything but bathrooms. They had some showers down on the ground and running water everywhere, but the
crapper was still old-timey, a plain goddamned outhouse off in
the woods.

They did have the crocks of raisin wine—but no moonshine.
The men drank bonded bourbon just like everybody else in the
world. It's difficult to be cleanly objective about such people.

It is truly curious: when you discuss necks, people don't expect anything but visions of stills exploding and incest and awful
hostility toward other racial minorities, but obviously it's not always that way. And, no, I won't claim that the Tankersleys are
the solution to the problems of this great nation of ours, but their
kind is better than most contemporary reports would have you
believe. Maybe they shouldn't steal their electricity off the county
wires, and maybe the county shouldn't be so permissive about

letting them do it, admiring their antisocial rustic technical know-how. Who's to say?

But I for one believe that electricity is awful and impressive and that the ability to use such knots as the bowline, fisherman's bend, prolonge, and Matthew Walker should be respected. Maybe Dianne Harvey and Dianne Harvey's medical husband will think the Tankersleys merely quaint. Well, I say stuff a beady-eyed fish head right up your prophylactic, quaint ass, Dr. Harvey. You sunnavabitch, you think it's great to be able to circumcise a baby —but can you tie an underwriter's knot to take the strain off of electrical connections? I'd bet you can't! Nor could you skin off insulation the way a Tankersley can, so as to get the plugs and screws together right! And what about the use of rosin-core solder? I bet you'd use acid-core, wouldn't you, you dumb condescending shit? I'd like to drown you dead in a butt of malmsey quaint!

Up with quaint! Up with Regional Utilitarianism! Let's hear it for both red and white wires—insulation—let's hear it for copper shoes and asbestos string! But most especially let's hear it for fried fish!

I was positive that tree was going to get struck—balls of fire charging along the lines, incinerating all our clothes—the tree itself exploding the way it happens in forest fires.

What I did was climb back down to the living level, followed by Harold and his company of boozy painters. I entered that level redolent with white slabs of fish prepared with lemon and butter. Immediately my girlfriend handed fish to me on the sort of plate you get out of a detergent box. Immediately I sat with the others on the floor to enjoy a feast in the middle of a stormy night, all of us bone dry in spite of that blaster, that chunkmover. Those goddamned people! *What will be her name?*

For she was there. Andrew, Rachel, your Rachel, never looked better than my dearest beauty of the swamps did that night, while outside sheets of liquid fire were surely destroying all the rest of

humankind. April had surely already been blown to smithereens
—surely by now she was only a cinder sunk in a tide of fire that
rolled southward toward Bryan. Surely this girl squatting across
the floor from me was the last female I'd ever have an opportunity
to love. *You must love that girl,* I thought to myself, while wolfing a perfect hushpuppy (just enough onion inside), while watching her devour an entire pone. *Love that girl—serve her right tonight or your soul will find either Oblivion or Hell.*

Daddy, I've tried. Shit, I've tried to treat my women right.

And she wasn't ugly. She was stocky and wheyfaced, and she
had carrot hair. She had a round face and what looked to be little
pink eyes, which eyes were the only ones paying any attention
to me.

Those other birds were busy with talk of preachers and the
price of fish—and the worth of all this stuff they'd stolen from
discount outlets. I was eating apocalyptic catfish with a crowd
of fucking criminals! Criminals, however talented.

Buzzards, jackdaws, rooks, cormorants, pelicans—but only
that child's eye suggested I was still on the scene at all. Her almost blind-looking eyes skewered me thoughtless so bad I had
to look down again through the gaps in the floor to where the
children on the ground were also eating mindlessly, and fearlessly. A yellow cat and a feist dog were policing the grounds.

How come they took me up and then talked to me so little?
I'd heard they rarely had visitors. I'd heard it at the Knee.

And the storm passed over. "You too big to bup," said the
one called Sim: and that of course was what was wrong: I *was*
too big to bup, but I was also too big *not* to bup. I'd come crashing up the path—and whether I liked it or not—and whether
they showed it or not—these people were scared of me—those
basically rancid men were placating some water sprite or storm
troll. They were scared. They'd let me hang their clothes and
paint their trunk and eat of their food because they were scared
of me—for they were a small race of people. That bolt of insight
shot through me painfully.

"Ain't like living in no ground house," says I, wiping my
mouth with what is no doubt a napkin filched, purloined, stolen
from Gibsons. But I got no answer. I got wan smiles from ribbon

lips, but no words. The storm had suddenly passed, and my welcome was over. They weren't hostile so much as obviously nervous, finally. It was as if those rabid motherfuckers were afraid
I was one demon who didn't know the rules. Didn't I know the
party was over? Didn't I know to make like a full-torqued triskel-
ion? GO, said their mucky hunters' eyes, and also the eyes of the
fat lady across the room: the mother of them all? She'd been
rocking back and forth while the storm was on. She's seated on
a big striped pillow, and she'd seemed the only one besides me
afraid of the weather. But when it stopped, her eyes, too, said go.

So I went, with the girl. Up with Dianne, but down with
Cheryl, and going down those railless stairs with Cheryl Tankersley took a helluva lot more courage than going up to the librarian's room with the Marion County Cyclops. "Thank you, folks."
And I rose with her (I merely gestured rather aimlessly with one
paw)—we rose together and slipped from the living room. We
climbed down the metal ladder to the kitchen, passing a middle-
aged man in long johns I hadn't seen before—her father?—because she suddenly hurried. She took the long stairs to the beach
rather than the ones to the ground—that fat child literally ran
down those precarious stairs.

I stood amazed at the door and watched her flee. I wanted to
follow after her by way of scooting down on my seat, figuring I'd
fall to a truly ignominious death if I didn't. But my fear of being
backshot was even more acute than my acrophobia. Would that
tribe actually let me escape with one of their women, and a mere
slip of a girl? Though I hadn't seen any guns, which was odd. A
corner in the living room was crowded with fishing gear, but no
guns? *And draw the centre of the back at night?* For as any good
Jute knows: the wages of bravery is death. Doom.

But finally I stepped out the door and down those stairs as
swiftly as possible, negotiating each as if it were a holy station, and
the farther down the dimmer light, until, at last on the beach, only
the washed moon above illumined the boy and girl—as we trod
along in the wet sand it seemed entirely wonderful that those men
back in the tree let us go so easily. Back in the tree they were
talking blissfully about politics by now—Ross, Charlie, J.P., Big
Hugh, all the great names—and they apparently didn't give a damn

about what we might do in the false dawn, down by the riverside.

Such excellent water over our toes, such excellent gentle breezes that whispered behind the rain. Walking along the beach (I'd taken off my shoes), I felt wonderfully relaxed. I was holding the girl's hand but assumed she'd vanish before I reached the bridge. I was thinking what a great experience it had been, and one I could share with April. April must have wakened in the storm . . .

"UmSherl," said the little girl, tugging on my arm. My God, she looked like a fat baby. I must have been crazy in the tree.

"How old are you, Cheryl?"

"Old enough," she answered, with tender conviction. What else did I expect her to say?

"How many years old?"

"Fifteen."

And do you have a husband in Asia or Germany, or at Parchman Farm?

"Honey, I'm a married man."

"Yur a *bad* main . . ."

"I know."

"Yur a *beug* bad main," and her drawl was filled with raunchy tolerance and humor—it was an innocent sluttishness that sickened me: an image of a scourge of pussies rose before my mind: The Pussy Whip!: *Each thong of the scourge had a different shape of pussy tied securely to its end. It looked as if the Apaches had scalped a representative of every race and nation, and the handle was burnished arabesques of silver and gold, and the knob was a big toe with a long jade nail.*

"God bless you, Cheryl." I meant that. I wanted to free her from whatever vile expectations she'd conjured. I wanted to dissipate my own lewd vision. I think I wanted to join a monastery. Haul myself on hands and knees to the gate—cry to the brothers: *Brothers, I'm here—I'm scourged—I'm wearing a crown of snatches for humility: curly snatches, kinky snatches, snatches both fair and brown, snatches tight, snatches huge—brothers, I'm tonsured . . . let me in . . .*

. . .

What I did was turn her down, as it were. I picked her up above my head and then lowered her for kissing, face to face, which pleased her greatly. She squealed and kicked her thick feet and begged to be loved on more, but, thank God, the kissing and hugging was almost enough. My little butterball, my little reeking biddy, she was satisfied to be hugged and kissed and fingered—which took some doing with her body off the ground throughout. I told her this was the most exciting night of my whole life and she's the best ever but I just can't do it now but later maybe and goodbye Cheryl goodbye goodbye—I brought her off and tongued her teeth—all of it with her lifted off the ground. The muscles of my upper body shuddered as she whirled and cavorted back toward the bluff and stairs.

Both my arms ached terribly as I walked back to the motel. I ached all over.

Back in the Stonewall, April remained asleep until I turned the shower on.

"High lonesome?" I heard her ask.

"A goddamned *fine* high lonesome."

Guilt? Shame? I scrubbed intently and worried that my right index finger might rot off in retribution for faithlessness. I wished I'd taken her, Cheryl, down on the sand, by the lapping dirty water, for then I could have imagined that in the future some son of mine would be poling home to a bower in the trees—a boy of five about to drink his first wine in the midst of a summer storm. They'd of named him Grendel Tankersley . . .

I got in bed and kissed my truelove on the cheek. "I love you."

"How come?"

"Because you ain't no ugly . . . because you don't live in no tree."

"I live in a cool cave with Eugene Joiner."

. . .

And in conclusion a note on Time, a note on Bergson: *There was this farmer out in his orchard feeding his hog. He held the heavy hog up so it could reach the apples on the tree. He lifted his hog higher and higher. Fella came along and said, "What the shit you doing?"*

Farmer said: "Feeding my hog."

Fella said: "Don't that take a lot of time?"

Farmer answered: "What's time to a damn ole hawg?"

7

JAKES. Jakes was good to me while I was on the team, but he knew all along I didn't like the way he treated other people—like Bo Mitchell, who was a Southern's best tackle in ten, maybe fifteen, years outside of me. Jakes put some bad shit on Bo about his hand and the unicycle business. Bo gets cleated in practice through the hand and this green strandlike thing pops up through the bloody hole, and he's also been stunned on the play, by the worst lick a man can get, an elbow to the Adam's apple. His hand is numb and then he's spitting and hacking and blowing blood and pulling on his bloody green string showing from the hole, which makes the fingers of the bad hand snap back and forth. It was an ugly wound.

Spitting muddy blood and knock-kneed from being punched out and working on one hand with the other like the world's grimmest puppeteer—then finally, after he's eased from spitting up from the throat and focused on the goddamned curious antics of his digits, the thing he's doing broke clear in his mind and scared him. He's standing in a wilderness of sun with the dust settling and everybody watching, and he was bawling, knee-walking, crawling, and bawling: "Got damn hand, got damn . . . hand!" And pulling and snapping his fingers into his palm.

I started for the manager to fix it because I think I've done it—I thought I'd cleated Bo, who's on my side of the scrimmage—when Jakes screams a helluva lot louder than Bo did—Jakes is yelling for Bo to get the hell off the field if he can't take it without so much bitching and moaning and the rest of you men get back to busting ass, etc.

Jakes was standing not twenty feet away from us on the sidelines and he could see all of it. Jakes could see that Bo was hurt pretty bad, and it upset him. Jakes was truly unnerved by the grotesque sight of Bo staggering and falling around and fiddling with his gored hand—but he didn't know anything to do but yell and scream out worse than Bo and try to be the hardest roller of all. Jakes is too sensitive to be great at coaching. Jakes was genuinely sympathetic with Bo's busted flesh, but he reacted the wrong way, and he never thought of apologizing. He could of apologized to Bo in semiprivate after practice—he could have drawn him aside at the door of the coaches' dressing room the way the great ones do when they've fucked up, slapping him on the small of the back and protesting that everybody gets carried away and acts the fool sometimes, in the heat of battle. He could have been affectionately ambiguous, suggesting that both of them had carried on too much out on the field. Bo would have understood the meanings.

But what he does is add insult to injury. He puts Bo with the red shirts for two weeks, and then doesn't let him play in the next game—but by that time he's confused and has half forgot why his best lineman isn't with the team. Jakes tells the press that Bo can't play this week because his hand ought not to get hurt again so soon, ligaments and all.

Nobody believed it. We had our open date the Saturday after he got hurt, and by Wednesday of the next week he'd already scrimmaged with the red shirts against the second team.

Damned great Bo—gawky but strong as band iron, and fast— he worked hard his two weeks with the shirts. He made him a doughnut bandage with sponge and adhesive so he could do his best with those characters. He wouldn't even let kindly Moody help him out in fixing the hand. Jakes holds him out of a game after he's led the shirts to a victory over our strong reserves on Tuesday, holds Bo out of the Georgia game and is convinced there's some kind of reason to it. There's still some kind of feathery and clotted moral moth beating itself to death in his hard head, and Mr. Jakes remains true to it. You almost got to give Jakes credit for it, because toward the end of the second week he's putting decorations on his errors, saying how good Bo is for the shirts, the reddy reds, how he has definitely been a good *influence:* as if it were worth something to be a good influence on that bunch of cripples, never-wasers, and stars-in-waiting, especially near the end of a season. Bo had character. He had never once condescended to the shirts. He kept his peace like the good man he is.

And one of the gentlemen of the press was heard to tell Jakes his ass was mud if we lost with Bo out—Stanley Goodich told Jakes everybody knew Bo was tough as nails and only carried on that way because he'd been belted and tramped so hard in the pile—in a stupid blood scrimmage no decent coach would put a winning team through after midseason.

Goodich was the best writer any state paper had, his column being the best for facts and statistics and also unafraid of a little satire. In a mean articulate whisper we heard him and Jakes going at it on Friday when we're going out to fart around in sweats: "Coach, this is the damndest bullheadedness I ever saw. That boy's been a saint to take this crap." Goodich hissing out of his twisted teeth and between puffs on unfiltered Kools.

"Stanley, go ahead and write me up. Make a joke out of me. Go head . . ."

"It's *not* my intention to hurt the whole team. But what I'm saying is I'd do it now except it would fluster ole Bo—and *will* do it if you lose." Goodich was so mad he started coughing behind the closed doors—and he was right in knowing anything written during the week would have hurt us. It was bad enough as it was.

It was a buzzing of dim misery in the air the whole week before Georgia. They were the toughest we'd play all season, an S.E.C. team and a good one that had only lost to Tennessee. But when I spread the word that Goodich had put the hard truth on Jakes, we took heart and went on to beat Mr. Butts and his crowd from Georgia. We clobbered them 35–33. We beat Georgia, and Bo was on the bench in his street clothes cheering himself hoarser and hoarser as we went on to victory without him. When we were about to take the field (and I'd won the toss), I said in a loud voice, after the prayer, "Let's get it for Bo." Yeah, yeah, HELL yes, says everybody, including Jakes, and he didn't show any signs of realized irony. None. He steps back to where Bo is handling the phone at the table. He slaps Bo on the arm and repeats after me, "Get it for Bo." Big honest smile, too.

Christ. I was laughing loud enough for the whole stadium to hear me when we lined up to receive the kick. I cut my eyes up to my bride and she's giving me vigorous V signs with her fingers. She's sweet and sweet, while Jakes has gone to his standard game-day grimace and is already pacing in front of the bench. He'd had himself a very bad ten days whether he knew it or not.

Then the next week, against Memphis State in Crump Stadium, in the fourth quarter and after a brilliant, nerly Wallick-like game, Bo gets high—just stands up because he's tired and thinks for a second that the flow of the play is going the other way—but it's a reverse and he gets it fast on a double-team from both a halfback and a tackle who catch him at belly and chest and drive him clear off the field, Bo pumping all the way, backwards. He gets tripped up finally and dumped right in front of Jakes. Jakes says, "Christ, Mitchell, you look like you're riding a unicycle. You oughta join a circus." Then he benches Bo.

Jakes does have flashes of brilliance.

In some obscene way Jakes must have thought that one bad play vindicated him for all he'd done the weeks before, which is stupid beyond belief, because Bo'd been brilliant. For more than three quarters he played with a controlled fury that looked like reckless abandon—on defense, where he played most often. He nullified all blocks and jammed hole after hole, and he threw the Memphis quarterback for five big losses. On offense he was artlessly perfect, attacking with outdated cross-body blocks at scrimmage, attacking often very high with his spastic splay-footed and knock-kneed charge—he shielded and leg-whipped—and sent up great huzzas each time he made a tackle, each time his team achieved a long gain.

Bo's an intelligent and self-conscious, clumsy athlete who delights in the freedom of the game, and he was in high dudgeon right up until the minute Jakes put the unicycle to him, and even that didn't bother him much, for he was satisfied that everybody realized it was only a momentary lapse in an otherwise flawless performance.

But Bo was "Unicycle" Mitchell from then on.

He was Unicycle Mitchell although he played in the North-South game in Montgomery and in the East-West Shrine game at Kezar Stadium for the crippled children, games I went to and played in with him, when we were All-Gulf-States together, and Bo had two good seasons in Canadian ball before he started selling insurance in Hattiesburg. Where it's still Unicycle Mitchell, by God. It's what he goes by with all kinds of people. He might as well put it in the phone book:

> David "Bo" "Unicycle" Mitchell
> 210 Forrest St.
> 443-3073

And nobody remembers what happened in the dust of that one scrimmage when my cleats punctured Bo's hand, and damn few people recollect how Jakes didn't know what to do with the bawling of a giant competitor who's frightened by his odd wound— nobody remembers *that*, but the play when Bo got dumped on his ass on the sidelines in front of Crump Stadium's thirty thousand, that *is* vaguely maintained in the minds of hundreds of his friends and clients because of the horrible name Jakes put on him.

"How the hell you get a name like that, Mitchell?"

"Well," showing chagrin and pride (he's too goddamned ductile, too willing to defend from the mudsill), "we're in the fourth quarter at the old Crump and I've played pretty . . ."

And Jakes ran that play in slow motion backwards and forwards ten times on Tuesday like he did to Charley Ray when Charley's giving the plays away. And who's laughing the hardest? Who's damn near to split open and rolling around convulsively on the goddamned mats? Charley, that's who: "Whoooeee, look at

Uni go!" Man, we all raised some hell. People have got real short memories.

A responsible, grown man just can't like walking around in Hattiesburg, Mississippi, being know as "Uni" or "Unicycle." He couldn't like that even if he was walking around in *Petal*, Mississippi.

Puts one in mind of Malatesta's lines, great lines to remember and ponder, whether they're true or not: *Man, like all living beings, adapts himself to the condition in which he lives, and transmits by inheritance his acquired habits. Thus, being born and living in bondage, being the descendant of a long line of slaves, man, when he began to think, believed that fucking slavery was an essential condition of life, and liberty to him seemed impossible.*

Maybe Bo *likes* his nickname, maybe it's worth money to him. Who in hell knows? But it's intolerable when the wrong things get remembered.

I'm going to remember to remember Bo as the man who played another great game for the Shriners to raise money for the crippled children, and I'm going to be happy for him he's not in Foots' condition. Bo's successful, while Foots used to have crying fits in the sunshine in Bryan, because of debts and women. I never had to draw down reasonably and shoot Bo dead.

II

I was ignorant of a lot of things, but I wasn't dumb. I sometimes wish I was. Because if you're dumb, really dumb—stupid with no brains—you probably have something that's permanent and secure, unless they make a supreme effort to confuse you.

Polly.

Polly who sometimes sets up in my mind harder than any of the others, because of things that happened both before and after I killed Billy, and Polly is the only one that Mary has sympathy for.

Mary feels that Polly's really the only one who never had opportunity, and then of course there is the fact that Polly's the one girl who died, dying of truelove for Andre—which style of dying should in fact repel Mary.

. . .

There I was, driving all around the edge of town like a caterpillar on a cup lip, looking for a place to park where she wouldn't be afraid of getting caught by Benton or raped by some nigger who has just finished killing me... *The true way to break down the race barrier is to eliminate the sex barrier, and the great tragedy of our age is the inability of free white men to get together and create an organization on a National scale for their protection and his security. White people have built fine swimming pools in their parks which was to be used for white folks only. Johnson's Civil Rights bill made every pool in America a Negro pool. No white man with any respect for his wife and children would put them in a pool with a gang of Venereal disease ridden Negroes. If Johnson and his Supreme Court can turn the pools over to the Negroes, which he has done, then he can dictate to you in many other ways. He has put the Negroes in your business, against your will, he has made you serve the Negro, and in this way he has placed you in involuntary slavery. The Supreme and Federal Courts have turned law maker and together with Johnson's edicts and proclamations they are in complete control which gives them dictatorial power and you are at their mercy. Now dont get me wrong. There are hundreds of thousands of fine, honest, patriotic Jews and Negroes, who are a credit to the nation, and I would not do anything to harm one of them. I have all the respect in the world for them. But by the same token there are Jews, Negroes and white trash who would do anything for prestige, money and power. It was Jew lawyers who helped Thurgood Marshal put over the school integration bill in 1954. It was Jew lawyers who helped put over the prayer edict in the public schools. Jews helped build the NAACP and a Jew has been the head of the NAACP ever since it was organized. Today a Jew heads this outfit, and its legal adviser is a Jew. The motion picture producers are flooding the screens with sex, homosexuality, abortion, and nudity, and they are catering to the lowest forms of obscenity, and Jews produce almost 100% of these filthy moral destroying cancers and they call this entertainment.*

It was a Jew who promoted four human freaks with sheep dog hair and turned them loose on the world. It was two Jews who gave

*birth to Communism in Russia which has taken the lives of millions
of humans and is rapidly spreading over the world.*

Sheep dog hair?

*IN NEW YORK A WHITE MAN AND HIS WIFE WAS
WAITING FOR A SUBWAY TRAIN. THE LADY WENT
TO THE REST ROOM, THREE BURLEY NEGRO WOMEN
FOLLOWED THE WHITE WOMAN TO THE REST
ROOM. SEEING THE WOMAN ALONE, ONE OF THE
NEGRO WOMEN GRABBED THE WHITE WOMAN. ONE
OF THE NEGROES LOWERED HER DRAWERS, AND
THE OTHER TWO MADE THE WHITE WOMAN KISS
THE NEGROES BLACK BEHIND. Open up your purse. Get
this appeal to other Americans so they can know the truth. Send
$1.00 for ten copies. Many people should order more. Do it now
before you forget. Wont you do this for the protection of your
home and your family? Please excuse any mistakes. Its the message
that counts. . . .* which is the sort of thing you found around in the
bathroom at Polly's house, and worse. She and her daddy went to
Pure White Race meetings all the time, but I refuse to believe it
was such events that made her loving so remarkable.

What caused her problems was the dark Syrian blood she had
in her, her mother's. Her mother and daddy seem to have been
O.K. for a few years, acting lovingly, but the increase in niggerrid-
ing among Winston Roberts' friends finally brought ruin to the
family. Winston's dark lady got shunned so much by old friends
she took to drink and messing around with a coon ass from Bogalu.
Not even Holiness people would have her after 1954. And considering all of the above, Polly did pretty well to make cheerleader and
grow up only moderately sluttish and insane. I offer praise to dead
Polly!

We finally ended up down on the pitcher's mound at the Little
League baseball diamond on a blanket. I was tooling along the ridge
and when the moon broke through the clouds we saw that children's field like a garden of geometrical love just below us. Polly
said she thought it would be a funny place to sog.

That little, old-fashioned, and harmless word inflamed me because I had a good deal more than *sog* on my mind—and I could tell by the way she said it she had more, too, on her mind. We parked behind the bleachers, then rushed onto the infield and fell to it even before we got to the outfield where we were heading.

She was saying how it was all new to her but that she loved me and it was good—she does this fantastic job, she really throws a fuck for Sonny, flips onto me and says, "Oh roll, sweet baby, roll!" Flips back under and we hardly miss a stroke, while I'm gearing high and low, switching the dog on from time to time, for strong low-gear power, and so as not to hurt her on the relatively hard ground of the mound. She services the hell out of me and she makes it. God, I struck out a hundred times before I ever gave pleasure like that again, and it was all because Polly took my talent and experience for granted. She figured I'd do right, and I did. I hung in there and trusted our mutual enthusiasm to carry us through, to get us home free and finished, and I wanted to disbelieve all the rumors I'd heard—I wanted to believe she was my cherry girl. She believed I was an old hand and I wanted to believe that she was pure, or at least choosey.

We were great and when I zippered up my khakis and she arranged her somewhat dusty dress, we stretched out on that earthen hump just as vain as the two greatest lovers the universe ever shed moonlight on.

Yes, I resent most stories of initial tail, but certainly mine is extraordinary. Because it's not always a nigger whorehouse in Vicksburg with a lot of your pimply buddies standing out in the oily hall listening to faked sounds of passion, sounds that are really fear, delight, and viciousness but nothing easily got into the thick word passion—and it's not always in the back seat of a '54 Plymouth with a girl who's hot as an August noon but scared to death of getting knocked up—and it's not always that cool routine in some French Quarter or Dallas or Village apartment with a skinny modelish woman who of course has long ago put on her diaphragm or taken the pill—it is sometimes Eugene Joiner and Polly Roberts —Ole Son with his trusty bag on at the kiddie pitcher's mound in Bryan. It's not always bad or casual or any of that. Because for me and Polly it was a goddamned good time while it lasted—it was fine right on up until the moment that sunnavabitching energetic park attendant turned the lights on. I gave her the good deep shivers and there was a proper quailflight out my ass. So fine.

Sex, Death, and Ambition is all there is to vex words on, maybe. But what theme is it that accounts for how Stream had such good eyes for deeper characteristics and I didn't? At sixteen Stream cast a cold eye on Polly. He'd already read her clearly. No matter that she's already a cheerleader, no matter she has slim legs and natural brunette hair, no matter Polly is a goddamned racehorse the way she moves in the school halls in her black ballerinas, no matter at all, for Stream observes how she chews bubble gum from time to time, and he hears her bad grammar from time to time, the way she pronounces fork with two, three syllables, and he knows her old man is a wild dude crazy with booze.

And Stream seemed to understand the meaning of her cries and yowls when one of our boys got hurt in a game. She'd chew gum like the mischief when somebody was being hauled off between the shoulders of the coaches or a couple of mates. Stream sensed how she especially craved a sweaty boy's body when he's bloody and being carried from the field wounded. She'd rush out around the bench and touch the player's shoulders with both olive hands. To Polly, every beat-up kid who is cleated, broken-armed, nutted, and bleeding at the mouth was her daddy coming home from a bender in Pascagoula. Stream knew all that, but I didn't—and he believed Carl and Bo when they said she was part nigger and a punchboard, which was mostly lies.

At sixteen I thought she was *handsome*, one of Momma's good words for girls I took out: *She's a slender and handsome girl who has bad times at home. You treat that child right, Son.*

Momma never said Polly was *wholesome* the way she later did of April, but what she did say was high praise enough.

And it was Polly who provoked Daddy's talk on manners, taste, and tact in relations with women. We were working the garden on Saturday afternoon, and he never suggested that I should do it to Polly—or even that I could. He just starts talking about things in general, and it was genuinely heartwarming. He knew I was treading the banks of the scented swamp with Polly, which saddened him. He wanted his boy to ply all the white water and fly in all the gales, but he wanted me to avoid the foulest sloughs, of which there were plenty. His phrase was *miserable situations:* "There's no damned point in *looking* for *miserable situations,* Son." Then back to dropping beans in his brown paper bag. He said it required great skill to take pleasure and avoid pain while in the company of women. He said that Polly was smoked—*she's a nice girl, but she's bad smoked.* Plop goes a bean, and I didn't entirely understand.

The park attendant turns on the lights just as I'm giving her this delicate kiss of thanks (a kiss she considers more congratulations than thanks)—and off we go, she with panties in hand, and me leaving behind one shoe I'd scrubbed off during the struggle of good loving, but, lordy, even all that was funny because I'll never until I die forget the way she hurdled the Little League fence, giving me this beautiful view of her sweet ass in flight. In flight, hell, *aloft*—"Ass Aloft"—how about that for your art object, Stream? She even beat me to the fence. She could of been a great athlete.

There we were in perfect seclusion, the moonlight shifting in and out of the clouds, the frogs in chorus down in the sloughs, everything the loveliness of darkness and distance, then—Pow (one bulb bursting and sprinkling glass when it's turned on)—Pow—and the world's lit up—all the stark objects are right back on top of you: vertical fence slats, horizontal bleacher seats, the strict scalped edges of the infield. It came as such a shock I wouldn't of been surprised if suddenly we'd come to and found ourselves doing it right in the middle of an official league game, with the stands full of parents and brothers and sisters cheering us on, and the participating Little Leaguers looking on in wonder and awe and maybe some plain terror. Thank God I'm an only child—and we were long gone from that field and pulled into the Choctaw Drive-In, breathing hard, before we spoke more words. Giddy in the stopped car and munching fries it came to her: "It's Clarence threw the light." She wiped her mouth with her whole palm. "He lives off down the road." And she wept. Because Clarence Walls, caretaker and runty winebibber, was her father's best friend, and he was sure to tell.

"Don't cry," I said. "That sunnavabitch will never talk." And

I meant it, and he didn't. At the Choctaw, and faced with Polly's unhappiness, I performed even better than I had while fucking—I slouched deep in the seat, sipped my Pepsi, and told her I'd never been treated so well, and Polly—excuse my French—you are one helluva woman and I love you. What else? "Ain't nobody going to talk bad about you." I did us all proud: me and Polly, and Momma and Daddy. I always wanted to tell Daddy how I handled that event, but I couldn't. Stream may see well from afar, but I can pull it off up close.

Spiritually, calming Polly's fears was wise and good, but her easy mind set loose her nervous body again, it detonated further desires, and I had to pull to the back lot of the Choctaw so I could plunge again, sitting position, which was heartbreakingly raunchy.

First was the makeout and tonguing and biting, and I was in a fever to destroy her on that front seat. We were very hot, to the licking stage. I have licked dead Polly all over. She's the first pussy I ever ate. And it wasn't easy in the front seat. Grotesque, well maybe, but fuck you, Mary. It may look funny in retrospect, but who was looking? Nobody. I'm large but I managed the hell out of that front seat—I muffdove like a pro and finally gave her a proper normative dose, while sitting.

The front seat! What I finally did was slide myself onto the right side, scrunched down, my head against the top of the seat. It was then I said, "Look for something on the back seat floor. Climb over me and look for gold on the back seat floor, honey— look for a mess of golden honey on the back seat floor. Climb, goddammit, climb—look for golden honey." It was the first time in my life I felt I had some wit to me—she did as she was told and I pulled her pussy damn near clean over my head—all the while working with a subtle motion of the tongue. While crying out for pleasure she banged her head on the roof: I continued on. I pulled her cheeks apart and tinkered with her anus with my first finger. Man, it was natural. It was ezakly what a natural man will do. WILL DO . . . FUCKING-A. ARE YOU HAPPY, LADY? GOD DAMN YOU —BE HAPPY. . . . Be Happy . . . be happy . . . and she slid back over my head and settled in one of those positions of meditative love the yogas speak of.

She was crying again, but this time it wasn't your shame that was blasting Polly. It was surely celebration of the essential easy riding we were doing at the Choctaw in Bryan. I fucked me some Polly—Praise God—I did fuck some Polly, Billy's Polly, Everybody's Polly, and when I coughed up my second wad she was sanguine. Which is maybe why I could kill her Billy with such zest years later—maybe the swing, watermelons all around, against Billy's head was informed by what we did so well that night at the Choctaw. Piss on the Little League diamond—that, sir, was small change compared to the back lot of the Choctaw.

More on Polly. She was the worst best dead woman I ever fucked. She had herself a Bryan County, United States of America Need. While I was eating, and while she was digging El Dorado, her pussy slapped back and forth—it cried out Fuck in Anglo-Saxon the best ever. Polly. Dead Polly. Dear Andre. Dead Foots. Let's hear it for *onomatopoeia*.

And the next morning I put it on Clarence Walls.

After all of that I carried myself down to the hut, in the pines, of Clarence Walls, the next morning. It was some kind of pain, genuine pain, to rise from the bed after four hours' sleep and go to the hut of Clarence Walls. But I did it. I hammered on that shack, yelling "Clarence Walls, get your ass up. Get up!" and up he rose from a yellow sleep, cringing.

"You told anybody what you saw last night on the diamond?"
"Ump?"
"You did throw the light, didn't you?"
"Yup," and he grinned almost.
What I said was: "I'll kill you dead if you tell a soul." I stood tall to utter those lines. I rose to tippytoes above that small man. "I hear of one word you've ever spoken against Polly and I *will* kill you. I will, with my hands, destroy your body. O.K.?" I was

tired and I was in a rage. "You embarrass Polly and I'll hurt you."

"I won't say a thing." He clawed with both hands into the fly of his long johns.

"This ain't no drunk dream standing here."

"Right, rat, rat, rat," said Clarence Walls, studying me in his morning fear.

Mary Ann, my mistress now, she doesn't understand these things too well, even when I get her out of the shower long enough to talk them over. You try to tell somebody what went wrong, what you're feeling and knowing, but they don't want to hear about it—they'd rather read some awful thing like *Eros and Civilization* by Herbert Marcuse. They don't want to hear because they think they've already been there. They've not been there so long as me.

It's like the Chinaman I heard about who worked all alone up in the mountains and invented the bicycle without any help from anybody else in 1930. Poor bastard, high and remote, like a tiny person in a landscape painting by Tung Yuan. He'd never heard about bicycles before the one he built—the whole concept coming to him in a vision, though derived from his understanding of the little cart he pushes dung around in all day. And that bicycle was a crude bugger with wooden wheels, and no chain and no sprocket. Just crude axles—a crude pedal attached to the front axle—but, still, he's excited as hell and goes wheeling off down the mountain into town for the first time and runs into a whole world of bicycles.

Think of the nights he must have prayed at his kitchen shrine for the success of his marvelous vision and invention—and now here he is tooling along through the streets of maybe Yinchwan with bikes everywhere, elegant, metal goddamned bikes with rubber tires and complex sprockets and chains, and all the people laughing at what a funny thing he's riding on. People laughing to beat the hinges off of hell because he's riding something those Yinchwanians wouldn't even go so far as to call a bicycle . . .

And what's so sorry is that he did invent it—that goddamned Chinaman did invent the bicycle.

And what I resent most about Polly is she made me threaten my first man—she made me threaten a man with death.

8

My first plan was to go on ahead and eat myself to death—more and more peanut butter and saltines and whole milk—great gooey loops and curls around the fork and spoon, and crackers grinding in my throat, until the soothing milk comes down to wash it all away. I figured to make five hundred pounds, then die in bed like a swollen floater on a slab of beach. Trouble is I don't like the way I look and feel after about 320.

So the second plan was to fast, to diet, the abstinence route, which project was charming in several ways. I do like myself thin, at about 245, and I could of course pass through that weight while going down. And I fancied the idea of announcing my cause to the papers. I fancied calling a press conference to say I wasn't going to eat until all the whales (especially Blues) were safe again; or maybe I'd say I was coming out against some shit like Repressive Desublimation; and once I considered dying to point up the total lack of creative discipline in the Modern World of Today. Being almost incapable of abstraction, I've always felt guilty about my lack of causes—the lack of them, or the inability to serve the few I almost believed in, like marriage and football and niggers and friends.

But I never would of made it as a faster. The papers would have read:

JOINER FASTS TO DEATH FOR CAUSE—BONES WEIGH 210 LBS

How the hell can you fast to death for a good cause when you've got fat bones?

But Polly, yeah Polly, she thought up an imaginative way to do it for the cause of Truelove—she actually managed to be novel and precise about her way out . . .

·　　·　　·

I suspected right away with April that she had too much or too little going on in her for me to get my mind around. Sometimes anybody's eyes were like hands and worse on her—but she never gave me any real trouble. Sometimes I wished she'd be attracted to other men (like Morningside Robbins)—because I feared that her apparent lack of attraction to others suggested that her affection for me was faked.

She's a generally friendly, smiling woman with a face that always seems to be saying, "Here you go, sweet baby. Here's the titty to ease your misery." I wouldn't go back to that kind of young again for anything.

Her body. I never got bored with having her around the house both in and out of clothes. She has this fearfully perfect little hairless body—and one night in our apartment at Southern (this was before the Bulls, the Harpies)—one night when I'm standing behind her and she's down to her shorts and bra, she asks me to undo her like she sometimes would, and just for a second I thought I wouldn't be able to go through with it, and an easy three-hooker at that—but still I was Chet Atkins with arthritis, Segovia in the early stages of palsy. She was patient, said nothing, stared pridefully and vaguely into our big mirror, and finally when I got it off and tossed it on the bed, I thought I had survived.

But when she turned around and faced me bare, I cried like a baby; and not just because all that fine skin was mine, and had been for a long time, and not just because she loved me. Not on your life. It was because I was understanding that those breasts were truly something else, something or part of something I'd never fully come to grips with no matter how many nights I fed on and petted them. They might as well have been galaxies swinging a million miles out in space from me, something I only had an inkling of. That woman was on sidereal time and carrying something around in her that was terrible, and I couldn't entirely abide the fact that I had to stay so close to it all the time, whatever kind of time it was.

Look at a Van Allen belt sometimes, especially a big mother like the one around Jupiter—imagine looking down on top or up from the bottom, and, by God, it is the very image of cosmic pussy.

Woe and horror! *O Woe, confusion and horror, for there is little relation between our actions, which are in perpetual transformation, and fixed and immutable laws.* Very little indeed! *For the most desirable laws are those that are rarest, simplest and most general; and I even think it would be better to have none at all than to have them in such manners as we have them.*

And getting to know such female nakedness was like the time at the wildlife exhibition at the Spit in which I didn't participate. There were all these animals in cages too small for them. There was a peaceful-looking doe who didn't seem to mind what was going on or who was watching her, and here were little foxes so terrified they were crawling on top of one another in most pitiful fear, and stupid-looking possums (but calmer even than the does), old critters whose only claims to virtue lay in the fact their species had been on the earth damn near forever. But the thing that tied my eyes and set me down on my haunches was this one wildcat who's sitting up close to the front of his cage. He's sitting there boldly, and at first I thought he was just pissed-off for being locked up and stared at. I squatted in front of him and he stared me down right quick.

Standing there in that smelly cage with nothing but an empty peanut can for a watering trough didn't bother that gentleman one bit. He'd open his jaws and hiss a little, but mostly it wasn't because my kind had locked him in. It was more than that. I think that wildcat hated me not so much for being the kind of creature that got him in that cage and out of the woods and trees—but rather it was because I simply wasn't him. Him! It wasn't an association with pain. Strain, Son, go for it, catch the light. Yes, he hated me because he didn't sense anything in common between us. He hated the distances between us

> *My deare one*
> *All or none*
> *Everyone under the Sunne*
> *Mine own*

It was early summer, the Spit being in June that year, before the Bulls and the Bears, the Eagles and the Rams, and just after I'd finished my paper for Burger on "The English Radicals." I had a fresh degree, I'd commenced and I had a new pro contract. But concerning most important things I didn't know whether to shit or go blind. But I did refuse to spit that year. While Coppe, I think, with my voice, recited to my cat: *My own Excellent Majesty (in me) both strangely and variously transformed this forme.* Mad Coppe got in my mouth before that cage *and . . . behold! . . . by Mine almightiness (in me) I have changed in a moment, in the twinkling of an eye, at the sound of the trump.* I was yelling at him and smelling the pee smell and the difference, and it was something about him being conscious and having a mind of his own, and a world. A cat's mind a kingdom is. It was because that cat was understanding something (Benton's bodies down there with the gars?) hooked in the bottoms of all the rivers. He knew exactly what that drowned flesh and green water was, and he knew it wasn't he. I swear to God it was my one vision pure (no booze, no beer, no ben, so whatever state it was came from being in perfect condition by way of working at the Mill and running on the track, which extreme good health is probably the most awful high a man can have, being similar to faith in and grace from some religion or another), Vision and Prophecy, considering what Stream would put on me so soon. It was like the cat knew just how many hairs were on his body, and he figured he was the one who put them there. He was CAT, was a wildcat, stocky-built, tufted-eared, pure goddamned wildcat, for what it's worth *and all my forces were utterly routed, my house I dwelt in fired; my father and my mother forsook me, the wife of my bosome loathed me, mine old name was rotted perished; and I was utterly plagued, consumed, damned, rammed, and sunke into nothing, into the bowels of the still Eternity (my mother's wombe) out of which I came naked, and whitherto I returned again naked.*

I told my cat that, O bleak, bleak presentiment. Bone, marrow, and whiskers on his handsome face—like Žižka—he knew who the hell he was every time his heart beat. In a cage, in Bryan County— CAT CAT CAT—*because a great body of light, like the light of the Sun, and red as fire—as all Bohemia marches behind a drum of skin and is watched on from the sky by a cat's eyes. HE was red as fire, a Commie Cat, in the forme of a drum (as it were) whereupon with exceeding trembling and amazement of the flesh, and with joy unspeakable in the spirit, I clapt my hands and cryed out, Amen, Halelujah, Halelujah, Amen.*

And squatted there before the cages I did cry out in Coppe's words, though mixing them with others, Coppe's words from the *Flying Roll*, in Bryan, at the Fair, with people fairly nearby, people who were always willing to grant me most of my curious habits and performances. Yes, I was hunkering in a true inside hunker, heels flat and also the balls of the feet, arms hung down between the legs and the palms in the dirt, trying to meet the cat's eyes in a long gaze, because there were certainly all these creatures beside me living in a world of their own, creatures that cared very little for the world that I was in.

One of April's nipples whistled "Dixie" while the other tooted "We Shall Overcome."

And for a moment I thought I was getting drawn right into the mind and body of that cat, and it was like finding yourself on the earth before man appeared, and there were strange sounds all around, a language I thought I understood, but feared to understand completely, since better knowledge would likely kill me, or at least would change my mind so radically I wouldn't be myself, and might as well be dead *and so I lay down trembling, sweating and smoking (for the space of half an houre)—but at length with a loud voyce I (inwardly) cried out, Lord-uh, Lord-uh, what wilt thou do with me-uh?*

I felt like if I stayed down there any longer in the soft mud and weeds with the rain lightly falling I might keel over dead with the breath of the cat in my nostrils, and once dead I feared it wouldn't be even a human heaven or hell I'd go to, so I turned away from the cage, though still hunkering, and found myself staring up into the nigger mouth of Slater Jackson.

"I seen people crazy from animals," says Slater. "I killed one of them last year and it sure was good."

"Yeah, right, right," and I got up embarrassed as hell to think of myself seen chanting to animals, to think it was, of all people, wise Slater, the brave spade whom I wished I knew better, who saw me carrying on so.

"People in this town sure let you carry on." Which really

pissed me off, and made me think there was maybe something to the stories about how the niggers had a grapevine that covered the county, and super intuition.

"I don't do so much."

"You don't do much good."

I told him to go on, and maybe I walk in a trance sometimes, like I live in a tree, and maybe it's clear nobody *cares* what I do, because they're afraid, but, "Dammit, I don't *do* much. But I don't do bad, either."

"Look, man, you O.K., and you been right with me sometimes. But you could be so great. You'll finally get it all together, and you be of some use."

"I know you're pissed I didn't march last summer," saying it weakly, saying it, in truth, without much conviction.

"You did O.K. You came around and you did O.K.," and even Slater was seeming a bit sentimental.

"Then what the hell you talking about?" Knowing.

"Man, man . . . Son, you go on back to the creatures. You real good at that." And the black sunnavabitch walks off, walks off grumbling. He wants me for a friend—he wants me to help out on some practical shit in the community. He wants me to be some kind of super Davis Benton. He knew and appreciated how I was a niggerlover and he knew I didn't know how to have a Negro friend. But he was pushing too fast—he was a whole goddamned year early. I'm a goddamned gradualist.

And I'm not saying a woman's body is a wildcat, or *like* a wildcat, or that April was any kind of animal the night I had difficulty easing her breasts from their straps; in fact, what I'm saying is that we probably emphasize the similarities between cats and women too much, and between men and women, and between one man and another. My reason joggles. It's fine to talk of similarity, and then to talk of difference, but the real difficulty is in trying to understand what it is that's neither similar *nor* different. It's the awful unique and private part that counts and hurts, and it has neither sex nor species—and it may be evil, and certainly it's sociologically dangerous. Nor bird, nor beast, nor flower, nor man, nor woman, nor jet plane—that separate, terrible thing is like some brilliant being who's living and feeding on the glorious gases of Jupiter, or singing out among the double stars.

Oh my.

Earlier that day April wanted to know why I wouldn't spit: "Honey, how come you don't want to spit?"

"I've given all that up. I've set that aside."

"But you know how much the Dallas papers could make of it." And then she laughed because she didn't really think the idea was too cool.

"Rookie tackle is Champeen Spitter, huh?"

"Don't be so serious."

"Go to hell, goddammit," which was the first time I ever talked that way to her, and the first time I ever walked away from her. I walked away from her and Henry and found the cages, while the speakings were going on, found my cat, and got found by Slater, and finally got found by wretched Stream, who runs up yelling, "Polly's done it to herself and she had all the instruments. The whole band's!"

I can't stand it.

"Somebody found her in Steele's and Davis went and got her."

I said I knew she'd come to a bad end, and then I wondered about the instruments. All that hate literature and Billy and Andre. I told Stream she never had a chance.

II

THE GOVERNOR LOVES INDIANS AND LEBANESE AND CHINESE AND SYRIANS AND JEWS—ALL MISS-SIP-YUNS—the Governor said so at the Spit. But he didn't say he

loved dead redneck women, late lovers of Eugene, nor any niggers.
As we walked past the pavilion and the speakings he never mentioned Polly face-down and naked in the bayou.

Ruppachucka, ruppachucka goes Stream's old Dodge, while
he's telling me Polly's at the Parlor, and while I'm telling him it's
not the funeral home I want to go to. In my mind Polly and I are
still turning from the hard to the dirt road and down the fecund
declivity toward the diamond, and I tell Stream I want to see the
place she died. *I want to see where she died.* My god, the way she
smiled when I got hold of the elastic and pulled gently the panties
from her slender hips, and the way she laughed when I got them
tangled on her feet, her ballerinas already set aside on the mound,
and I also suffered an olfactory recollection of her cunt.

*The kingdom of Alexander either touched or was near unto
six seas: the Red Sea, Black Sea, the Mediterranean, Caspian, Aral,
the Arabian Sea.*

Dead in shallow water? Loving Christ.

I knew I was in for a bad year. I knew this was a true commencement. And Stream has a sure sense for solving problems about what
to do about the news of a death. He heard the news and came
straight to me with it.

He went across the entire fair grounds without telling a soul
before he found me standing at the cages. He knew perfectly well
I was having some sort of ontological and/or historical seizure, and
there was no doubt at all in his mind that I would be wonderfully
stricken by the news of Polly's death.

Pretty ghoulish, but not quite; for few men have friends who
have such gifts, the gift to bring the right pain at the right time.
Riding there by Stream I didn't know whether to vomit or cheer
for my round-shouldered doomster of a friend. We hurled along
through alleys of pine worthy of Corot, and we didn't even talk
while we went riding out.

And Mary wants to know why Polly (though she likes the *idea*
of Polly)—she wants to know why Polly is on my mind now. She
thinks that the deaths of Ju and Rosey and Doleman should obsess
me. And they do, they do, they do—but I never screwed Ju or

Doleman or Rosey, which does make a difference. And it makes a difference that she died when she did—during that terrible month before I went to training camp.

Stream began to slow down as we came down the slope toward Steele's Bayou, the bridge, and the county line. He pulled off the narrow shoulder, half on, half off the blacktop, and then we walked out on the bridge and looked down into the slow green water that couldn't of been less impressive. What the hell had I expected? Instruments?

Stream—and for once in his life he's not too giddy or grave—he tries to report the version he'd got from Benton—*Down there where the grass is matted a little is where I'm pretty sure they found her with the instruments—two electric guitars, one bass, a couple of harmonicas, and a tenor sax, and she was naked and face down in the water, half in and half out. And she seems to have stolen all the instruments. Go on. That's all I know.* And probably had that goddamned slime on her? *Right!* And she wasn't murdered or violated? *Benton says she wasn't.* My elbows were getting raw on the concrete railing I bent over, sand grains grinding into my psoriasis. Then a log truck came blooming out of the dusk and came onto the bridge and shook it a little, making me shiver a little, making me belly up to the railing like it was the most comfortless bar I ever drank at. Shit, it was gloomy and depressing and disappointing, because the literal place she died wasn't helping me remember her, or think her up. I wanted to feel all manner of wonder for the very grass that had borne the weight of her body at the end. I wanted to have the proper feelings so I could go down to the bank and rip some grass up for a keepsake, some blades to mash flat in my hardback copy of *The Mind of the South.* I even considered how it would be proper to kneel there and then prostrate myself so I could drink some of that green water that she'd gone down in. Bullshit! And I wondered whether Stream wanted me to feel guilty for her death, for some reason. I asked him if he'd told all he knew, and he said yes, and I decided that to suffer this thing right I'd have to get it from Davis myself, over beer, and without Stream around.

*It had to do with that cat Andre, but I'm not sure exactly how,
except he was double-timing* . . .

Is that all?

Methodism somehow saved Stream from Romantic Love and
any sympathy for it. Death shakes him up, but he fails to comprehend sexual sentiment. He's often dirty with, but never sentimental
about, women. So I went to Davis Benton to get the raunchy details
of the truth—I went to Benton's that very night—

*Son, I saw it coming a year ago in Bogalu when I was there to
hear her sing. She never had a chance. Drunk daddy and all, and
worst of all she's got this thing for musicians, and not wuffadamn in
school. I'd heard about this crowd she's in with down on the line,
so I decided to go and see it, and anyway I hear the entertainment's
real good.*

*Son, they got games of all kinds at the Club Karen, and girls,
and boys for older women. I mean old Cothern down there is inventive. Pays off and runs it all clean topside. Hardly ever a fight, and
no law with authority giving a damn, and they serve good steaks
and trimmins. A big roadhouse-type affair back in the swamps, and
Cothern builds him a fishing dock with a lot of cabins arranged
around this bayou there's no fish in to speak of, and a big long bar
in heavy wood, and it's got designs cut in it. There's animals and
fruits and vegetables cut all in it, but also if you look close you can
see in the dim light there are dirty pictures done in the wood too.
Cothern says he got it in Chicago. Like I say, he's got him a smooth
operation with straight tables and even this cafe set off to one end
that fixes steaks and seafood, hires a famous nigger cook from New
Orleans, and also gets himself a band.*

*Right! Right! Ole Bryan-beauty Polly, she goes down there to
get herself a job as a waitress after she flunks out of your ole "Alma
Mater"—she's through with the normal education, and anyway has
got to provide a few dollars to send her momma who's raising hers
and Billy's baby. But most important is the fact ole Andre, who
she's been on and off with for a long time (as you know), has lit at
the Karen. He's in the band. She's a waitress at first, but she's got
ambitions to be a singer. Beginning to make sense?*

The instruments?

I ask Bessie, how some women, and pretty ones, too, can go for these Andre-types. But she won't say. She won't say.

And God love you, Davis Benton, she never will, which isn't meant to suggest that she was out with an Andre-type the night we talked, or ever has been, though once she did hug and kiss me a little excessively when I came over one time and you weren't there. Bessie and I laughed or giggled to recognize our common hots, and that was that. But of course I never said anything about that time with Bessie on the night Davis and I talked about dead Polly.

Benton's my buddy, one of my daddy's few acquaintances; we go a long way back together, back to when I fished with him and Daddy as a kid, when Benton was between his wars, which wars and medals got Davis into law work. He ended a captain after Korea and liked to joke about how that "police action" made being Sheriff seem natural. Almost bold Benton, with his mustache (a mustache he grew in wars and so could keep without criticism from the community), he always trusted my head (or he did for a long time), he trusted me to try to be tolerant and reasonable, and really admired the fact we could talk some ideas from time to time. And I understood how everything was off the cuff, and how he rode niggers in public, and bad-mouthed the government like almost everybody else. I understood all that, and I finally even came to understand the way he was about women—how it was he had a deep-dyed dirty streak in him (which Bessie liked when it took the form of seeking entertainment, like going to the Stand or really fancy places like the Karen, and also probably when it broke out in bed), which dirty streak he needed to talk out with a friend from time to time. He figured I was a lot more cock than I was. He knew I was a church regular for years and came from clean people, and was serious about, then married to, April. But he also knew I drank and popped a pill now and then, and killed people. He figured I got my ass and didn't talk. You might go so far as to say I got to be a kind of therapist to the Sheriff—if being an absolute tolerant, loving, and honest critical friend constitutes being a therapist—which it does. Damn right!

And Bessie won't talk about Andre because she knows we men know how that sullen and womanish brand of hardroller is part of what every woman wants. Part. It's the mean creature in all us good men, the one that delivers the roughfuck when it's needed to keep the lady healthy. Yessir, it's the long-donged, sallow and bitter little whiner and woman-hater every good man will be from time to time.

But the kind that don't want anything else are bad sick. Any man who's that way full time is an Andre, is *worthless.*

This Andre person is "worthless." And worthlessness is an almost mystical quality, though deplorable, and worthy of baleful respect, when observed in its unalloyed state. *Son, I've seen the man recently, to use the term loosely, and if he wasn't so famous with women I'd say he's queer. I mean queerer than old man Chandler's third son, who decorates houses in Mobile. I've seen Mr. Andre bend over that bass violin and snatch at the strings with long, dirty fingernails. God damn, this Andre person is smaller than Polly was, and he can't even stand up straight. I mean he is "hunched," and like his eyes are bad, and has terrible long hair and ducks—but if he tried a beard he'd never make it, except around the chin a little. He wears a patent leather vest, and patent leather shoes: boots. Man he's 110 pounds of rompin' stompin' NOTHING, but that goddamned beautiful woman is in love with his scrawny ass. You see it comin'?*

He stands? I tell Davis I figure he stands, and that's correct, and Davis is very pleased that I know about something as dirty as standing.

Right. Right. This Andre person is exactly what some of these middle-aged women are all wet for when they show up at Cothern's nice ole Club Karen! It's all those rich women who do the fishing —in the cabins—with Andre's worm. Man! that's a bad place! All them titties and diamonds are just poppin' to get on down the path to the cabins with good-buddy Andre. And it's killin' our Polly to see him cut out that way, from time to time, to make his hundred dollars for whatever it is he does in those goddamned air-conditioned cabins. But I'll tell you this: no "normal" kind of fish bait was ever in those quarters.

Deplorable.

Right, and she starts singing with the band about this time too.

She sang some fine Country and Western ballads, and then some old-time blues songs—Hank, and nigger blues—and she was good. Son, that girl walked this town for years, and she was always so pretty, but there was something absolutely "perfect" about her, as Bessie said, when she was singing songs.

She never sang to me.

And she learned to sing for nobody but fucking Andre. And this Andre—the night we're down there—he comes into the night-club part of the place right in the middle of her act. He come back into that fancy room from wherever he's been doing whatever he does, and he sneaks up through the tables and relieves the boy who's been his substitute on the bass violin. Then—with her baby boy hunched over and thumping away behind her—she goes into the last song of the evening and cries it in such a way that my Bessie burst into honest tears. She's all broke up, knowing what she knows.

I'd lock him up. What? *I'd lock him up on "suspicion."* Of what? *Plain suspicion.*

And now you understand what she did, don't you?

My friend Cothern tells me the night it happened—just last night—he tells me she refused to sing when he came in late again. She walked her pretty legs right off the stand in a tight dress and bawling, and him not giving a shit. He was careless of our Polly.

You walked down through those weeds and saw her back and sweet butt and legs stretched out of the water, though her face was under. You understand some law then, didn't you, peaceofficer. Right!

And later on that night she stole the instruments.

That's bad. Theft is bad.

She couldn't stand what he's doing to her, so she stole the instruments, a lot of them, and started home. She's comin' home to Bryan, to her momma and Billy's baby. She's drunk as shit and high on some of them amphetamine-type drugs, and about dawn she cuts out with all the instruments. Cothern saw her. Cothern's worrying over his books and hears her banging around in the ballroom. He peeks in and sees her hauling all that stuff away, and he's so shocked he just lets her go, or he doesn't really believe she's going anywhere, until her Chevy cranks up and she's gone. I mean gone, and has it all in the back seat.

And that's what I know about it up until the niggers that found her called me.

Tell me about her dying, Benton. Don't just sit there in your goddamned straightback, cheap beer in hand, indulging yourself in another person's life—you get yourself back into that storeee and tell me—Reveal—how it was (in her head, her mind, her body, *bind, mody*) while she was achieving her dying in the dawn at Steele's Bayou. I commanded that of the Sheriff back then, I command it now. Raunchy peacemaker, tell it, son of a bitch, tell me how that beautiful Bryan woman died. He popped his eyes wide— he realized how reasonable was the demand.

She died of grief.

Put some skin on *grief*. What's grief?

She died because she'd lost her precious thang.

You admit that the Andre person could conceivably be a precious thang.

I think I'm right about the thing she died of—I ought to lock up that little prick.

Call it murder and make it stick?

Yeah. Something like that.

He tore off another tab top and slouched, tweaked the two ends of his mustache.

She must of taken them down there one by one. She probably took the bass violin down last. Right?

Right.

Took all that stuff down to the creek and started strumming her guitar. She's singing one of them ballads. "Wild Side of Life," the one from the female point of view. Right. She's sittin' in the high grass while the sun is coming up, and she's riding high on ole Andre in her memory—because of the pills. Go on, Sheriff. Right. She is imagining they got a high new house, and he loves her and she loves him—like me and Bessie—and there's sleeping children of their own in other rooms. She strums a tune on Steele's Bayou and then decides to suck the bottle once again; Pretty Polly, she had legs a man's half crazy to lick. You can say this after having seen her dead?

Man, she was pretty all the time. She drinks that bad shit again and feels a little sick. She's afraid she'll mess up that glossy black dress she's wearing, the one she used to sing in for Andre. She's got on this tight dress with all the sparkles on it—cut short—and slit at the hips—and tight at the titties—and she don't want to mess it up. It's tight and split on both sides up to where you can see lacy white garter.

Son, I'm positive we're right about the way it was.

We're right! Hell yes! Davis you may well be the best man I ever knew.

She takes all her clothes off with care. She does it slow and lazy. Because when I got there at 10:00 a.m. they were all stacked neatly beside her. She prized those goddamn clothes, and when she was clear of them she found herself sick and fell over and drowned.

Davis, don't be lazy yourself. Devise the whole scene. Leave nothing out. Especially don't leave out the nakedness drunk on Steele's Bayou at dawn, how, after folding and stacking the dear clothes, in high grass, she sat again, before she died. Man, do not leave out that.

Too much, Son, too much.

The good, just, tired Sheriff has had himself a long day, so he closes his eyes and rests his head on Bessie's table. He is—how shall we say—captured by dismay. *Son, don't pick on me. I'm the one that saw her dead. And you git it wrong, about drowning. Drowning didn't do it. I only told Stream because what happened is complicated. She's naked all right and her face was in the green water a little, but I don't think she drowned at all. Saucier and Kloninger think she hemorrhaged in the brain. She's the kind maybe whose blood clots easy, and she was taking the birth control for Andre. That's what Saucier said. I had to wipe the moss off of her face and some of her hair, but there wasn't any water in her. She's lying there exactly where she died because those nigger women on the bridge never touched her. Hell, they never even left the bridge.*

It's a bad summer when Polly Roberts dies of a broken heart, though Davis and the other authorities claim it wasn't in the heart, precisely. And I guess if it had been, precisely, it would be easier to take. For tonkwoman P.R. to die of a Broken Heart would have been so absolutely appropriate I could have dismissed her death as a disgusting exhibition of tastelessness. Yessir.

Son, you'd forgotten that girl. You're all involved with school and your goddamned football career, and the clean lovin' you get. Don't forget how it was me who was curious about what became of her, and it was me who went to Cothern's. And it was me who wiped her mouth off. I got down by her dead body with the niggers staring, and dumb-assed Rodney Kloninger chattering about how "odd" a death it was. I'm the Sheriff! I'm the one who saw that girl dead, and goddamn held her in my arms.

You never fucked her.

You never saw her with her clothes off. You never took her to the Clinic and called her momma. And what's gonna happen to Billy's boy now?

He's on his feet again and raging around the kitchen. He's yelling about how I talk like a Californian of late, and knows that crowd because he was stationed there through parts of two wars, or like a Delta faggot.

You so smart, you tell me!

I never saw her naked, but I ate her.

Sheeee-it

Which was a tawdry way for me to win that argument.

III

I didn't go to Polly's funeral. I drove over to see Professor Burger. I wanted to be a bully. I *needed* to intellectually kick the shit out of somebody, so I selected the most obvious victim, my great teacher, Burger.

What trade should mankind be brought up in?

Give over, give over thy midnight mischief!

Right. Right.

IV

All I wanted was the least security my plans for the future made some sense: to play pro ball.

Jakes and my mates at Southern, especially Bo Mitchell (the single-minded unicycle), they think being an eight-draft choice, even with an expansion club, is wonderful, the ultimate accomplishment for the American boy. Even Royal! Even Royal writes from up in Nashville and law school to say he's pleased, and also congratulations on the baby in the hopper, and isn't it a shame everything but the East hates J.F.K. *Son, I'm proud of what you're doing. I can be proud because I know you will learn from experience, the travel and all. I know that you will put that experience and money to good use in the future. Where will you be going to school during the off-season?* And so on, piously. He writes a friendly-type graduation letter, and includes a subscription to the *New Republic,* which is pretty funny and awful: a weekly douche of glib doctrine: writ to keep me from concentrating joyously from day to day on the passions of fame and fortune in The NFL.

He's *proud* of me, but he doesn't want me *caught up* in a mere game. It's the same old Boykin shit: when it comes to the real life, gear down, cool off.

He plays ball to get through Tulane (in a hurry, in three years) —Boykin *uses* the game so he can go on to another fancy school, for law. He *struggles* through V.U. Law by dint of *hard work* (at the Toddle House), by way of a tiny academic scholarship, and because Roy did leave some insurance. *He* is alone in the world, an adopted bastard. *He* never had abundant pussy and simple good times in college, and he hates anybody who did. Me.

No wonder he married April. It's a way of getting his lost youth back. Fuck him.

Poor Royal! Poor Royal and his teleology. He's embarrassed by how his daddy was a second-rate mechanic at the Mill, and a fool for history. He's embarrassed because Roy couldn't drive wuffashit and got himself killed, and also killed Pie's momma, and damn near killed Henry. Royal probably felt obliged to marry April because he felt obliged to do something for the man his daddy scarred. Boykin, you poor, poor country genius, you want to complexify me. You sit around the icehouse with Natural Law in your mouth—theories about the Unity of Being out of Père Teilhard's writings—jabbering about how snow fields and sunshine are one with the pines of Bryan. You did it three summers we talked. And Mary's right, probably, when she says Royal probably smoked grass in N.O., got his ideas the easy way and not from Chardin's turbid prose. Give that boy a summer night on the icehouse dock (plenty of cold beer and plenty of Fritos), but he ain't satisfied. All those midnight talks but he never ever saw fit to talk about the pretty flowers in New Orleans, or the ladies. He's thick with ideas.

I've never been lonely in my life.

But I have been isolated with my clean eyes. I've been inno-cent enough to know how stupid and anachronistic a provincial style can be. Yessir. So I didn't spit that summer. I would not spit, T.V. or no T.V., and it did seem to be something of a radical moral act. *Son, you don't "need" spitting.* I was pleased to think it. *Son, maybe you don't "need" football.* That, too, crossed my mind. It crossed and recrossed my mind like a camel caravan plodding back and forth across the Sahara Desert. *Maybe you don't need football* was strung out for months across the waste spaces of my brain. Promethean fires of camel dung! Oases of doubt! Which is worse than funky or lonely. Which is clearly an *idea.*

But I don't think it can be reduced to the predictable anxiety of going off to The League—training camp in San Diego—cosmic competition for the golden apples on the Great American Tree of Strife. I never let my balls gather much dew over that. There was a certain nervousness, a delicate, crystalline shattering of minor fears deep in the cells, like a gin hangover, and from time to time there was indeed the small voice of possible failure taunting from deep in the well—*Hear! O hear!*—but finally I also knew I wouldn't get cut in San Diego (or even back in Dallas at the end of exhibi-tion season)—I know I was evermore in shape, trim and sleek at 270. I never expected to beat out the likes of Morningside Robbins (one of the truly great footballs players), but I did figure to make them drop some low draft choice or some merely competent old meat like Coley Sellers, and my confidence proved not to be excessive. I *earned* my place. I got to be Big Side's understudy.

No, sir, it wasn't really the game that bothered me: except I wasn't positive I wanted it: except I knew for a fact I had to do it.

Davis. Davis, you mother, you knew but couldn't stop it. Back to Davis—Polly dead—her brain clotted—or maybe in fact it *was* her heart: *Son, you've got to talking with feathers in your mouth lately. You don't sound like yourself.*

My people had a dull, plain style, and my education is Methodistical Transcendentalism strained out of King James, Leveller tracts, permissive grammar . . .

An' don't blame me for how you are. I never went for church much. I never cared about the goddamned football . . . I'm a bad Baptist.

But only because directing traffic is demeaning to you. As a sheriff you make a great fucking snob.

I studied accounting at State. I went to college! Son, you've still got good people. Man, you oughta go see your people.

Don't you mummernem me, you filthy-minded Bessie-sucker.

I SAW MORE POLLY THAN YOU EVER DID. He's on his feet with his hands held high in celebration and praise. The miserable balding Sheriff knows he has been granted a vision of the awful power that drives our lives—more than the facts hung up on the mind's pegs, more than the animal cries of any insane crowd at sport, more than the pleasure of being drunk at the center of a juke's music was the stillness of that girl's body as it lay beside quiet guitars at dawn, by the bayou. Polly with her silent instruments and her perfect white body being stared at by understanding niggers was the kind of beauty granted to only a few of us necks. He did turn her over in his arms. He wiped the least slime from her mouth, and he stared lovingly at her dead and pendant titties. He covered that woman with his lawman's Ike jacket, and he wept for her. And when he put his arms down from above me, he was crying again: *I been where these people are at, Sonny. I've seen their bodies in life and death, and I never saw a death like Polly's before. She loved you, you dumb prick! She loved ole dead Billy. And she loved that boy with the bass violin. She was shaved beneath her arms and her belly was lined from her baby . . . she was a good girl. God damn you, Son, you go off and play your game, but I've seen more Polly than you ever did.*

And about that time Bessie came through the kitchen door: "Davis! will you lay off ole Son."

V

Plus ça change, plus c'est la même chose.

And there we were in Helen's house for the summer, for six weeks of it. We were in the home of Helen Willys who *worked*, who kept books at the Mill (still keeps them) for old Chalmers. Frontier-type Helen who lost her man to that Duroc-loving Circe, dead Maylene. Helen, stiff as horn, but essentially kind. Helen, the woman who raised April. April's mother? My mother-in-law? Not really. We were in Helen's spare white house (asbestos-shingled by that time) with the stump of the buzzard tree out back. We could see it from the bedroom window, from Maylene and April's little room with weary red roses on the wall. And the Vermeer prints, fading, still were there. It was the same as in Maylene and April's day, except for the King-size bed Helen got for us when we wed, and a window air conditioner, which was more important for the privacy its sound offered than for the cool its fan blew.

Helen loved to have us there. She deferred to us. She cooked for us. So long as April would chatter about recipes and flower arrangements and sewing, all was well. So long as I maintained a huge austerity and was appreciative of everything, all was well. Like some godawful desert bird, Helen twitted and hopped about her bitter house. Like a terrible dry thing, she soaked us up, and, like a cactus, she began to flower within the prospect of April's baby. She began to bloom. Miss Bones got compulsive and silly, buying enough comforts for an army of midgets, buying enough diapers to sop up Asia. She brought home a beautiful antique crib and filled it with presents and necessities for the baby. April protested, I protested manfully, fearing those mounting piles of white. But Helen only glistered and kept on talking and buying. It was predictable to be sure—it was an emotional thaw I feared I'd drown in, and damn near did, when April got caught up in it.

A small asbestos house by the side of the road, when it's packed with loss and hankering and unmitigated carnality can kill a man.

We most did it during the day when Helen was at work. But she knew. She surely knew, and encouraged. She smiled at us each morning as she sipped her orange juice, and it was such a smile as a roach might smile, if a roach could smile, or maybe a cricket.

"Y'all be good now." Helen slips a yellow, sharpened pencil through her bun and heads for work.

I did work. I took the six weeks to get my ass in shape and go crazy, while April was growing happier and happier. Yea, very happy. She was pleased to be at home. She was pleased to be knocked up. She was looking forward to Dallas in September— where she'd be when training camp broke. She was even more proud and pleased with me, and it was making me crawl the walls more and more. She hauled out boxes of Willys photos, old albums full of people who'd left for Arkansas ten years before at least, and she's especially de-lighted by pictures that show stern Helen and limp Maylene together as children. The strict stance and glare of Helen—the misty slouch and gaze of April's mother, Maylene. Uncles and cousins I'd rarely met, or never—half of whom were sod in Kansas or Arkansas or Oklahoma by that time.

People looked jaunty back then. Or they're so sad and stern. After lunch, and when Helen was gone to the Mill again, smiling like a fly, was when sweet April spread the pictures in their albums across the linoleum floor. The men wore train hats and battered straws, and bib overalls, and there were wilted dresses to the ankles on most of the women. God damn, they were sorry-looking undernourished people—strange people leaning against pines and

Ford cars—the which got April raunched up. She liked to make love after the old pictures.

How'd I act these times?

I acted very well indeed. You'd have to be a monster to ruin the happiest time in a young woman's life. And I will admit there was some kind of pleasure in staring into the spaces between Maylene and Helen in the photos. I'd fix on a house in the background, or the bark of a tree.

I kept expecting to perceive another creature in the gap between the figures of the women.

Sonny, those were real hard times, the Depression and all. And then she'd start to rubbing my back while I'm down on the floor on my hands and knees, still in the sweat clothes I used for the morning workouts. And probably it was the sweat clothes got her going as much as the pictures. Or the combination. Or something I can't quite imagine. Something red, white, and blue but blind all over.

She'd tread the house in her panties and bra, and she was showing a tummy pooch from the baby. *We're so lucky, Son.* And naturally I agreed with her.

What a perfect and sympathetic picture of the past she had (has). But—but—*we*, she and Son, were still alive, and young, with our lives ahead of us. *We* were going to Big D. *We* were going to be pretty people with nigger friends and lots of money.

Why so gloomy, sweet Son?

And I told her I wasn't gloomy. It was just I had to get the right attitude and in shape for training camp. She pops my jock and grins.

Son, you're such a fine man.

I got to get my ass in shape.

You so fine.

I was so fine my own family was gone to Memphis and rarely returned to home country. I was so fine my only favorite teacher thought I was a damn fool for going pro. I was so fine the only reason Davis could see for going off was money. I was so fine that goddamned nigger Slater made me feel like my pants were wet with piss every time I passed him on the street.

．　　　．　　　．

It was some hard pain and grit misery. It was the summer I put down my Claiborne and my Pollack (*The Populist Response to Industrial America*) and took to reading squirrelly stuff like D. H. Lawrence and Wallace Stevens, stuff that Stream put into my hands. I felt petty, lascivious, and terribly satisfied from time to time. So what that all the kids who worked out with me in the mornings loved me for all the wrong reasons, and most especially because they knew I'd killed my man? So what that Foots was always at Nancy's every morning (where I went for breakfast with Henry)? So what that Foots raved and raved about how great it was I'm going off to The NFL—Foots slopping his coffee and slurring his words, bobbing his head, then patting or slapping my butt on the stool? *Gonna be tough onna coast. But you be good. You big an' fast, you a real football player, Son.*

I'm gonna try and be as good as you.

You a real football player, you a goddamn jint, an' you can move. Pat Pat Pig Eyes Jowls Tics—*Son, man, I played a long time, a long time.*

I know, Feet, I know you did it.

And everybody in Nancy's put on a lovely earlymorning and understanding smile for me and Foots. Including Henry's *risus sardonicus.*

Nancy's, where the water birds and the gray water were still on the wall, I went there because I thought maybe it might please Henry. I decided he'd be pleased to pick me up at the mailbox each morning, removing me from the house of his women, which idea was a charming, romantic theory, but it didn't take long to see his mind in Bryan was on automatic pilot—even his work at the Mill. He checked kilns and directed the niggers like in an ancient dream and a vulnerable ritual. With Roy and Daddy gone from Chalmers', Henry was only doing time between trips to New Orleans. Royal'd seen Maria and Henry on the streets down there, and Pie said the old man looked (down there) more like a premature baby than a burned old man. Henry'd say, "How you, Son." And that was all until we got to Nancy's, where Foots was, and Davis, to name two. Sometimes Coach Topp was there, eyeing me, knowing I was starting to pay for all the bodies I'd busted up. I was making the big time and I was paying every minute I faced the jealousy and hatred and defeat in Foots' bad eyes.

Three days of that and I think I'd sworn to kill him, Foots. Maybe all the good I later did was by way of killing that wretched man Foots Magee.

Topp caught me at Nancy's door one morning just before I went to work out. Topper with his booze and bad heart and pitted nose, that great football coach, he pulled me aside: *Son, you aren't Foots. You're better.*

Thanks, Coach. And he was right. He wanted me to play well and like it for no more than playing well. Dear Topp! God love you, Topp. I should of said more about that good man.

But nothing so humane as Topp's words could sustain a man who had to work out with the young men of Bryan. They'd meet me there in the early morning. They got word I'm working out on the green grass just past dawn, and out they showed in various garbs. Little chaps in faded split jeans cut down to shorts. High school boys in official sweats Topp got for them so they could work out with me. It was Leon Taylor, Jack Strawer, Darris Bobo (Lurch's cousin)—it was the best from twelve to seventeen that Bryan had to offer, and when I stripped out of the khakis into my own Southern sweats, they were there, formed silently in a circle around me, ready and waiting—*Haarupp, Haaroop, Haaaareep, Forp*—I called it out for jumping jacks. I led them through knee bends and push-ups. I called cadence for numerous exercises, knowing how they loved me for killing. I did know that! And then we ran. Shit, did we run. Miles and miles—crunch crunch—on the Bryan track. I ran those boys until they dropped. I'd run up to five miles and all the time I'm hoping one of those idiot kids will drop flat dead of a heart attack. I ran until I was the only one running, until Darris was puking his fucking guts out on the grass, and then I'd say, "Wind sprints, anyone?"

.   .   .

Christ! it was a relief when Polly finally died. Die, Polly! Die! Rot your redneck cunt in the thoughtless ground.

It was truly good to bitch and moan with Sheriff Davis Benton. It was truly fine to get pissed enough to go off to Burger's, and finally to Memphis, on the Mississippi River.

Boykin, you creep, those weeks might of been vain, useless, and lascivious, but you, sir, will never sprawl on that King-size bed the way I did. Man, you don't even *need* a King-size bed! You been there since—kill kill—but it's not been how it was back then. My head on her tummy and the little baby (your Aubrey) just starting to stir around and kick in those mysterious waters. You, sir, will never have the pleasures of those particular circumstances: April striking my head and blathering on about how her daddy and Helen are wonderful fierce people, and beautiful souls, and isn't it amazing a life is under way under my ear, and, sweetheart, it *will* be a *boy* name of Aubrey, after grandfather Willys, whom we never knew, but know to have been a fine man from what Helen says and because he looks so warty, tired, and diligent in the sepia-colored photograph.

Royal, ole cock, put aside your *T.R.B.* Think of how you've missed all that.

Royal, she climbed my body that summer—was Son who put those dents in Aubrey's head. Hell yes! Was Son bit the top off your wife's clit, that summer. Tough shit, Royal. Was Son. Was. Was. Was. She and I were ravenous amid the artifacts of the past, in Maylene's room, beneath the crucifix Helen stuck on the wall after converting. ROYAL—LISTEN, MAN—WHAT'S THIS COUNTRY ALL ABOUT IF IT'S NOT ABOUT ROUGH-FUCKING? HUH? What it is, man, is about how you grow up big and strong and smart and White and do well and marry the pretty girl in town and make All-America, and then go on to Pro Ball—it's how you get yourself a lot of passionate feelings, derived from confidence in your success, and fall into an immense bed to fill a pregnant woman full of worthless sperm by way of said roughfuck, which, of course, calls for wet interludes of breathing and panting before you start to work her up again, reaching into that pool of honey and come, striving to get the honest bone again. Royal, are you prepared to suffer the likes of that? Probably you are. Good luck on your new job.

VI

Shame, shame. I never did thank Royal for his present of the *New Republic*.

But I did write a couple of letters to Professor Burger at Southern. I wrote and told that man about this fellow Foots Magee, telling this Burger how this fellow Foots looked like a beat-down Odysseus, or a character from a Dürer print: Nemesis: Foots with bit and bridle in one hand, and the chalice of success in the other— fat fat fat—sanguine and nearly naked Foots standing, teetering, on the great orb high above Bryan, Detroit, Dallas, and the whole world. Or is it the world he's standing on?

That wonderful profile by Dürer, his goddess, actually looks like Foots did, if you can imagine brown greasy ducks on the head of it.

Knight, Death, and Devil, and I did try to study in the afternoons of that summer, reading in my rocking chair on the car port, enjoying again the sweating after the fervid cool loving with April, Royal. *Mulier fornicaria*, the whore, and the Roman Church as the mystical body of Antichrist, I had that on my mind. Also Dürer's friend Pirckheimer, the humanist, with syphilis, before I'd drift back to Petrarch.

And in one letter to my teacher I began with Petrarch's words to Bruni, the papal secretary: *You make an orator of me, a historian, philosopher, and poet; and finally even a theologian. You would certainly not do so if you were not so persuaded by one of whom it is hard to disbelieve: I mean love.*

Perhaps you might be excused if you did not extol me with titles so overwhelmingly great: I do not deserve to have them heaped on me.

But let me tell you, my friend, how far I fall short of your estimation. It is not my opinion only; it is a fact: I am but a back-woodsman who is roaming around through the lofty pine trees all alone, humming to himself some silly little tune, and—the very peak of presumption and assurance—dipping his shaky pen into his inkstand, while sitting beneath a bitter buzzard tree.

Malice. I wanted to see whether Burger'd catch the buzzard tree not in Petrarch, and I wondered whether he'd notice the sentence I left out: *I am a fellow who never quits school.* He caught neither.

Malice. But something more. I wrote him those letters and taunted him because he'd never given me an audience.

Even Jakes would give me audience.

I'd taken four courses from Burger, over a three-year period, and oftentimes I was his best student. He chatted with me over coffee in the union, and there had been the usual conferences in his office. And by the last semester he was taking liberties with my nerves, liberties he should never have taken anyplace but over booze.

Stops me in the hall. "Joiner, you still going to play?"

"Yessir."

"You big turd." Then he glides off, which isn't proper behavior for one who hasn't performed the amenities.

It was a curious relationship, friendship. Dennis Burger knew I liked his style, and liked to read the histories he assigned (herein quoted) even better, but he never believed I took him quite seriously.

Not comfortable in desks, I'd sit on the waxed, dark floor against the wall with my clipboard. I'd take careful impressionistic notes and answer all the questions he asked me, but I could tell by the way he yanked his lobes and stroked his nose there was more than a little dubiousness behind his eyes.

Burger likes to scrawl on the board in big letters: CHURCH HISTORY IS NOT THE ONLY HISTORY. Or: HISTORY IS A BITCH. And one day during a lecture on The Twelve Articles of the Bundschuh, he rushed back to the board and wrote LUCK LUCK LUCK LUCK LUCK LUCK until he'd filled it up.

Usually I followed what he was up to, made some connection or another, and smiled a lot. Still, there were dubious pullings, or the blinkings from his weathered eyes.

Burger is more than one of your passionate jackoff-type teachers. He lined out dates and names and made the logics seem orderly when needed, and he knew I liked that orderliness.

Best was when he attacked "official history." Best was when he'd assert how Alexander was smarter than Aristotle, or something about how *they* didn't want *us* to praise the Stoic teachings that led Brutus to assassinate Caesar, and of course I loved to hear him praise Winstanley and Coppe to the detriment of tedious people like Bacon and Donne. All that, and yet he still wasn't a radical.

Some of our activist-types tried to get him out with a placard, but no go; and for all his steam in class he'd never even join a panel discussion or go to officialized bull sessions in the dorms.

Charley and Bo and I tried to get him to lead a discussion at the Athletic Dorm, but you'd of thought we'd invited him to view human sacrifice. He wouldn't do it—saying no while jogging in place. Which hurt my feelings.

I wanted him to talk about medieval games—tournaments and long bow contests and early games with balls—I wanted him to show some of the P.E.'s that ideas and facts could be pretty freaking interesting. And Burger would have made a good impression, because, though he's thin, he's also tall and has long hard muscles like a track man. He's very fair, with limp strawy hair. And he has weak eyes, if you pay attention. But there is no doubt about his masculinity.

Grant that he was trying to finish his dissertation on "English Education in the Seventeenth Century," but still that doesn't let him out of being chickenshit to his public—to me and Unicycle Mitchell. Burger should have been more thoughtful. There really is something awful about the teacher who enters your life only in the classroom, comes in and offers transports of detail and imagination, and then just fades away like maybe the whole thing was no more than a movie or a play. It's worse than how it is with coaches, and maybe the reason so many athletes don't like professors. A coach may be a dumb ox and have it in for you, but at least he faces you on your feet and eyeball to eyeball, and what you do makes a goddamned lot of difference to him. You perform badly and he's out of work, which isn't so with teachers very often. Goddamn teachers ought to make you learn and do well. *Class, this school is ranked 210th in archaeology, and that's going to be corrected this semester. You people are going to dig and dig, and you're going to dig right. I'm going to show you how to use your tools. You "will" learn how to recognize a chip of skull or shard. Potsherds! This class "will" find potsherds—because you are going to know how and where to look. Listen, we've got good mounds and bluffs, some of the best around, and "we" are going to make the discoveries. Patience! You goddamn people think you're archaeologists, huh? Well, I'll tell you what: you ain't got no patience! Our diggers were entirely unranked in patience last year! You "will" have patience. You "will" make discoveries!* Something like that.

Yes, the above is so, but actually Dennis Burger was more like the player-coach as teacher than anybody I ever met. Which complicated, as I say, the relationship.

Burger wanted to help me get the fellowships. In fact, he was pleasant and insistent about it from time to time in his office, saying I was probably the best major Southern had had in years—and he said the department head and others agreed—but always he was examining my face for signs of cunning and deceit and brutality, things that are disrespected where he comes from. Pushes a black text aside and says, "You come from good parents, don't you? I mean they're interested in education, aren't they?" He bumps his heavy glasses (horns and thick lenses) on his knifenose. He screws up attempting a friendly smile on his thin lips, and what he's saying is, you ain't no gentleman farmer's son, or boy of Klansman, nor son of any Oligarch. He's saying you're O.K., boy. But what are you? He should have asked about my people in an effortless way over beer. That way I could have told him all about how tough it is to sometimes come from good people.

All I said was, "Right. They care about education."

"Well, I want to encourage . . . cur, k-cur . . . I . . ." He could be stammering, confused, and shy. But then he calls me a turd almost as a parting shot, after three years together. No wonder I wrote those treacherous letters and finally drove over to gig him.

WHAT IS A BOHEMIAN? He lashes it across the misty board during our last semester. "Joiner, tell us what a Bohemian is."

From the floor beneath the east window, I cry out in excited voice: "It's a revolution any way you cut it. Both art and life . . ."

"Ha!" He liked that shit. Tit for Tat. We were close in class, the way he liked it. "Mr. Joiner, tell us about revolting Bohemians in Bohemia—like in the fifteenth century."

"Naw," saying it like the good ole boy I am. "Mr. Burger, *you* tell *me*. Make me see it." And I clapped the clasp of my clipboard three times rapidly, which was my best performance, creating laughter and good feeling throughout the wasp-infested, high-ceilinged room (the wasps up in the north corner, rarely diving), setting the stage for one of Burger's truly great hours. That small class, which included Bo and April, settled into musty anticipation as ramrod Dennis blinked and peered over our heads, seeing surely (on the mottled plaster of the back wall) the majesty, invention, and despair of early fifteenth-century Bohemia. It was like how you feel before kickoff, before the first contact.. It was a passionate aca-demic moment. And, glory be, Mr. Burger rose to the occasion, in his voice of mellow vision and security: *Let me tell you about Jan Žižka—Jan Žižka who makes the world-famous Henry V seem a buffoon in a farce. Žižka's victories at Lüditz and Kuttenberg make Agincourt seem a dottering performance by drunken legionaries. Žižka was, as Mr. Joiner suggests, a Bohemian in every sense of the word. He created a new warfare for a new idea. He literally created a new vehicle, a new machine, a new thing, to move, literally move, through space and time, the revolutionary ideas of Jan Hus.*

Once again the pivot to the board. Once again the grand scrawl: THE TABORITE LAAGER-FORT. A tank made of Jax bottles chugged through my head.

Žižka remembered the tradition of the laager in his soldier's blood. He remembered how the Goths had used a crude version centuries before at Adrianople, and he knew from daily experience how these wagons were basic objects in a peasant's life (like pickup trucks in Mississippi)—he knew the laager was sensual to the mystical rednecks of old Bohemia, making them good things to fight in, and, if need be, die in. Which made the fuzz on my back spark, and April uttered an OOOOO, softly, for she always thought of him as a wise and appealing man, a sort of golden-tongued Montgomery Clift. *A sensual place to love and die in, for a new religious vision.* He was so pleased to know he had us he paused a moment to light his Muriel—and I glanced at April, praying she wouldn't OOOOO again, for the wrong reason.

Žižka used his wagon-forts for maneuver and fire power. The practical implementation of the radical Hussite doctrines was the wagon-fort. Hus, burned at the stake in 1415, "required" the wagon-fort. A primitive Christian communism, a married priesthood, these innovations of mind and feeling, "demanded" the creation of a new "thing." At least a new and subtle method of using the old thing, the wagon. A religious vision that offered the Holy Wine to all the people, all believers, did require the wagon-fort. UTRAQUISM. The mere flails and scythes of the peasants were not sufficient weapons to create a new society. And isn't it strange that it was the peasants (led by the radical intellectuals at Prague) who made innovations in both theology "and" technology? Isn't it strange that we aren't taught this in "official history"? Puff Puff. Lobe pulls. Squintings. We write "official history" in our several notes, and had to admit that our medieval text hadn't done much with Bohemia.

Žižka "experimented"! In an age when the miter burdened the heads of Europe, Žižka stood, one-eyed on the free hills of Tabor and "imagined" the new laager. Finally blinded by an anachronistic arrow, finally losing his good eye (the right one) at Rabi in 1421, he gave wise counsel for battle out of utter darkness. He commanded from a profound night and was obeyed.

Blind Žižka required order—he did not allow the slovenly progress typical of his enemies, Emperor Sigismund's crusaders.

Students, the "condottieri" were sloppy, sloppy and heavy with feudal armor. The Pope's legions were fat and conservative, while the millenarians of Tabor believed they were called to prepare for God's return. Their hope was boundless, sustained by the day to day exuberance of their simple and practical—note practical—style of life. And I wanted to ask him if he really dug that Brook Farm shit—and is this lecture a tricky way to make us sympathetic toward Soviets, huh? I thought such things, but by then I knew it wasn't so. I knew that the emotions of a Taborite couldn't be compared to the busy juices of nineteenth-century Yankee intellectuals —and I knew that Russia never got in Burger's mind much: he'd passed them off as "brutes" in Western Civ: he was in love with the Bohemians because they lost. Which is probably unfair, because he does like Cromwell, who didn't entirely lose, in the long run. Maybe it was no more than the fact that Žižka got left out of the book, an error to be sure. And if that's how it was, I could go along with his lecture. But how come he never told us what kind of clothes the Taborites wore, or how they smelled, or how they took their sex? And why be so hard on the man when he's doing a pretty fair country job of teaching? Maybe he'd never experienced the kind of muscle memory required to pull out and block on a touchdown sweep, and maybe he had been excessive in his praise of these obscure Czechoslovakians, but none of that could obliterate the fact he was putting on a good show. A good show? So he fucks up a fact or two? I was beginning to feel like Royal when he went against Miss Gresham. Hell, teaching is ambiguous work, as I know from recent experience. Winstanley knew—and Burger knew, having taught it: *But one sort of children shall NOT be trained up only to book learning and no other employment, called scholars, as they are in the government of monarchy; for then through idleness and EXERCIZED WIT therein they spend their time to find out policies to advance themselves to be lords and masters above their laboring brethren; as Simeon and Levi do, which occasions all the trouble in the world.*

Therefore, to prevent the dangerous events of idleness in scholars, it is reason, and safe for common peace, that after children have been brought up at schools, to ripen their wits, they shall then be set to such trades, arts and sciences as their bodies and wits are capable of . . .

Now, there's a lot of hash in all of those words—mine, Winstanley's, Burger's, anybody's—but one thing I know is that what you do for a living is important. Maybe it's the only important thing. You can teach a child about bees and birds and God and why things die, but if you don't instruct about vocation, you've done the next thing to nothing. I feel like Chaucer's Pardoner when he tells the pilgrims that all he has said is a lie within a lie within a lie, and that only Christ's blood is truth: which was the truth for his day and time. Chaucer: the one English poet I can really admire.

See the wagon-fort. See it run, children. Down with scythes and flails. Up with modern-type handguns and crossbows. New weapons to be fired from loopholes in those newly armored carts. Put pikemen, twenty or so, between the carts, Slater, to fend off cavalry assaults. Go, Prof, go—make us a picture show: James Mason as Jan Žižka: *Žižka observed that the handgun was finally the weapon most effective against the feudal knights, so a good third of his soldiers were, in fact, provided with handguns. The feudal armor could resist the crossbow bolt.*

And, no, one must not forget the medium bombard, which bombards blasted the entrails out of popish princes. Let's get a closeup of *that:* one young German or Italian with breastplate crushed back into his chest by a hundred-pound stone fired from one of them visionary bombards. Let's hear that poor cocksucker as he cries and pukes inside his twisted helmet. He has been unhorsed. Momma! Momma! It's the same in any language, in any religion, at any time! He is unshriven of his courtly loving—hellfire sluices down his groin—Momma! Fade out. But it's all in a day's work for our nimble and freewheeling Taborites. They ain't got no armor on, they ain't got no pope, and they shoot dead with stone balls the boys who do. They strike terror into the hearts of knights in armor by grinding across the battlefield with considerable speed (note: the laagers are linked together with chains—they are pulled by terrible chiliastic studs and mares)—and as these wonderful fel-

lows charge they sing "We are the Warriors of God," by Jan Hus.
A wasp strafes the room and I got April's silky flanks upon my
mind. I got my imagination's mouth upon her goose-pimpled
withers. Remarkable flowers in New Orleans are sprung from
dykes. The weather will be warmer—
*One-hundred-pound stones against the feudal cavalry. It was
the family as an army, and when Žižka died of plague his soldiers
called themselves "The Orphans." And when Žižka died, at sev-
enty, he required that a battle drum be made of his skin. Think
of those poor Germans! Defeated again and again by a blind man,
and now they hear the reverberations of a dead man's skin as the
laagers are brought into line.*
What's a dead man's skin sound like? Bump bump? Boop oop?
The legend of Žižka's skin is O.K.
No wonder decadent Europe shuddered!
The great thing about Dennis Burger was how he rarely raised
his voice, exclamation points being more a pause than an increase
in volume. He was a great teacher, and subtle as the fracking snake.
In Mississippi he preached *against* the Pope and *for* the proto-
Protestants, but he never mentioned how Taborites and niggers
were rather alike. He was quite satisfied to make us sympathetic
with a bunch of Bohemian yeomen we never knew existed before
he told us.

*. . . but the battle of Lipany came, in 1434, when the moderate
Praguers turned on the revolution and defeated Procop—Žižka's
successor—with the very tactics that had defeated the Crusaders.
In a fratricidal battle, Žižka's great general, Borek of Miletinek, led
the moderate Bohemians against the radicals. The slaughter was
terrible. Miletinek's men faked retreat and rout, then turned to
slaughter the faithful—led by Procop the Great—slaughter the
faithful who had been drawn from behind the wagon-forts.*
*And what was gained? Very little. A Bohemian Church for a
while. A liberal mass for a while—the chalice passed to all believers—until in 1620 the JESUITS took that too.*
So much for Bohemia . . . and he quickly strides out of the room
like he might be all choked up.

VII

I wasn't about to go to Polly's jumped-up funeral, though at break-fast April said I should go to it. "Considering how close you once were, you maybe ought to go."

April wasn't going, but I should—she thought I ought to go back down into Preacher Morris's church again, that goddamned blond basement, to watch the worst trash wail, keen, to see Polly's truly *in*sane Daddy probably blame it on the niggers and Catholics —Andre being probably a Catholic with nigger blood in him.

I wondered would Polly's Syrian momma come up from the Louisiana boonies for it. I wondered if they'd even tried to get in touch with that poor driven woman I'd heard had birthed five straight sons to her second husband, or third. I'd like to have met ole Polly's momma.

Wiping away the sleepy dirt in bed that morning beneath Helen's cross (a scrawny Jesus in His drooping misery), I had a blip-type vision that maybe also hairy Julia Pastrana might wander reeking down under that ground into Christ's Gospel Church, to grieve Polly. I rubbed on April's pregnant pooch and pondered how the ape woman might stump forward in her heavy female shoes (with hooks and eyes), blubbering to be saved, spattering her brocade. What wonderful theological debates she would raise! Davis would be there. He'd be soaked through with lascivious senti-ment, but at least he'd vote Julia human and a creature with a soul. "Grant this nigra salvation, so we can get on with Polly . . ." The mortician would set her hairs all wrong.

I tried to imagine Burger among the howling evangelicals, but couldn't.

I didn't go with Henry that morning and I didn't work out on that day. When I finally got up with the distant cannon fire of the coffeepot in my ears, I'd decided to write a careful letter to Burger —write it—mail it—then wait a day or two before attacking. In the kitchen, Helen gone to work, April pottering about the house and probably waiting for me to love on her on the linoleum among the family photos, I set to writing on the yellow legal pad, at the little trestle table, with my trusty yellow pencil:

Dear Mr. Burger—

You say that my writing is similar to Winstanley's—something akin—while adding that unfortunately there is also a taint of Methodistical sermonizing in my prose (I refer to your notes on my paper entitled "Toil"). But, sir, do you actually know what taint meat is?

No, I doubt you do.

Well, sir, taint meat is that small space between the pussy and the asshole—*taint pussy, taint ass.* Onward!

Taint right for you to call me a turd the way you did—for nothing more than not going on to more school. Taint right at all. You cursed me without understanding. Sir, your *geist* (ghost) lacks *scheide* (cunt?). Something of the sort. The ontological situs of cunt is, sir, certainly as perplexing as the situs of any ghost; though, of course, my German is, as you know, limited in the extreme—nothing more than phrases from a dog-eared paperback dictionary and some trots. But by dint of hard work I've learned some things *you* haven't—like how Luther was a horror.

Back to *geist* (ghost) and *scheide* (pussy)—well, sir, you'd have me unsheath my dork and make a fracking righteous sword of it, wouldn't you? You never said it with decent candor, but that's what you've been about. Right?

You said I might *serve* my best ideas better by giving up football. You did say serve, you presumptuous sunnavabitch. You were and are clear out of bounds. You don't know diddly squat about me; you got no rights in the matter.

Now.

What you don't realize is there's no *geist* outside the *scheide.* None. Vicious Martin would have us believe that Spirit (*geist*) is to sword as Word is to sheath (*scheide*. . . snatch), which is a complex if not lousy fucking metaphor—suggesting we go around lopping off heads with our spiritual swords, our spooky dicks, as it were.

What *did* he mean, Mr. B?

I say put the *geist* back in the *scheide,* and let it stay. Heah? Constantly and Loyally.

It won't work but it's as good a plan as any. And, by the way, I never did have any *ideas.* It's goddamned un-Southern to have ideas. Ideas is Platonic and our weather isn't made for such.

We're actually Slavs of a sort, like you've suggested in the lectures, but mostly we're more pre-Christian than anything else: lots of little ole gods all around. Praise Vodyanoi, god of swamps, sloughs, mires, and mill ponds: Mike Vodyanoi, Pittsburgh Steelers ... I've seen him often in Steele's Bayou.

God damn you, Burger, I'm a niggerlover true and blue—no matter how they themselves might not think so. I come from good people who know there's damn well trouble enough in the world without making up more over skin. Right? Right!

I'm going to love my little son when he comes. I'm going to make good money and receive praise for good work in The National Football League; I'm going to gain some normal wholesome fame, which is a worthwhile and manly thing; then, maybe, after a few years I'll consider serving, another way. Maybe it'll be more school then. Maybe I'll get degrees and carry signs and set the world on fire. But, sir, for now, all I want is the clean tail of my good wife, and good food, and lots of money to go to the picture show with. Also, I do admit I like to pull the laundered jock up my legs, and the helmet down over my head. And I like the heft and stink of my shoulder pads—and, damn right, I'll admit it ain't half bad to be knocking people down, on the football field. Man, I've worked hard to be a good lineman, and you, sir, ought to have respect for that.

Luther! Shit! He killed more people than I ever thought about. I've only killed one up to now, a necessity which also was an accident.

Here's your Luther, Teacher—*and even though it happen that the peasants gain the upper hand (which God forbid)—for to God all things are possible, and we do not know whether it may be his*

will, through the devil, to destroy all order and rule and cast the
the world on a desolate heap, as a prelude to the last day, which
cannot be far off nevertheless, they may die without worry and go
to the scaffold with a good conscience, who are found exercising
the office of the sword. [Lord Lord, Land Lord!]—*they may leave*
the devil the kingdom of the world and take in exchange the ever-
lasting kingdom.

Now Now!—*Strange times, these—when a prince can win*
heaven with bloodshed, better than other men with prayer! Yeah
God—all you little princes can pull up to heaven on a rope of
knotted blood—take your *geists* out the wet word and punch a
bunch of peasants dead. Right! Right!

Strange times, strange times indeed, Brother Martin, Brother
Burger.

He condoned the slaughter of Müntzer's peasants behind their
wagons at Frankenhausen. That somitch was the first Platonist with
a Prince Elector to pay his bills, and, Mr. Burger, that caused
trouble—that caused a right smart of trouble.

You stare down on us in that classroom like a bird gawking
down from a barn, like the raven, like the crow, like the buzzard
from the buzzard tree—and you just can't wait for one of us to take
your blather seriously and get our asses killed.

I'll tell you what—which is, I've done it in a way already before,
and it didn't do any goddamned good. None! Except for the solid
pleasure of it, which was in the doing merely of a prime violence. I
tore shit out of that pulpit right up until the Police and three
Subaltern Evangelists showed up. Burger, you wouldn't have been
pleased to see it.

Billy Graham and his wrong Crusade received a little revolutionary assault from ole Son a long time ago. I knew, even as a boy,
the by God enemy, and did attack. I come from clean, sane people,
so I know what isn't, and what isn't is a big jumped-up choir loft
and pulpit for a chap who never should have become more than a
decent pitcher in the Sally League, or Cotton States. Maybe even
something really useful like a good Medical Doctor. He's a pleasant
fellow and entirely sincere almost, it seems, but he really, when you
listen to him carefully, has hatred for this world: and that's a sin
the likes of which he never thought to preach against. He preaches

with a brightly painted tie on *because,* he says, *the birds are brightly colored*—but after a while you realize it's angels he'd like to have the colors of. He claims the colors of the natural birds, then preaches how the lice infected everything that flies way back in Eden time.

Hell, he even waved away a decent storm. He actually believes he did. An actual thunderhead drew up from the southwest, as they are wont, threatening the stadium with decent rain and lightning, but Billy actually believes he succeeded in making it divide around the stadium until he'd done preaching. He used that decent cloud with its delicate grunts and pulses of blue and white to scare the gathered people and curse the world, exactly like you do in your own way, Burger. It's clear you're suffering from an ancient Bulgarian disease: lackanooky. You don't like the world or you'd leave us people alone with it the way we naturally want to be, damn it. I'm a woolly-headed Methodist and resin worshipper—so finally —when the crowd was thinning and the honest rain was at last beginning—I did attack, in pure righteous rage, that pile, that loft and pulpit the doomsters had raised upon a proper football field. And, sir, I would have got more torn loose than a dozen planks of the pulpit if it hadn't been for the substitute evangelists and Jackson's finest. I'm screaming, I'm told, Death to the World Haters!

It was damn near five years back and long before I studied with you, sir, but even then I knew exactly who the Enemy was.

The whole structure (crudely fashioned and utterly unlike the sensitive arches and columns of the Córdoba Mosque, sir) was maybe twenty yards wide and ten feet high, and I could have ripped it down board by board if they had left me alone. How came it, you may ask?

My friend Boykin and I went up there to the great city of Jackson to see our friend Taggart convert for the third time at least, in one week. It's August during early practice and Stream (Taggart) was gone to sing in the Crusade choir every night after very rugged practices: lots of twos on one and bulls in the ring. And Stream is doing well, which is impressive, physically, for evangelical singing and converting is very demanding, both spiritually and bodily, *extremely.* But worst of all is the fact it all flies in the face of his own father. It is against the spirit of our Methodist

Church in Bryan. All that fervid business of giving up the world utterly and washing in the blood of the lamb and in the incredible indelible fountain filled with blood was *against* the generous and nature-loving spirit of his own father. Preacher Taggart hadn't even encouraged his people to go along with the Crusade all that much, and now his own son was vaulting out of the loft every night. Stream's kneeling and crying and carrying on terribly over nothing. What the fuck sins had mealy Stream ever had the courage to commit? If he'd had honey on his finger once, I'd be damned.

We'd heard it from some Baptist girls, the converting he was doing. Stream hadn't mentioned it. Which also pissed us off, it seemed so hypocritical. We went (Royal and I) on Saturday night, to find that all of it was true. AMAZING GRACE HOW SWEET THE SOUND—THAT SAVED A WRETCH LIKE STREAM.

That's why I meant to tear it down.

Burger, they're having it on the football field at the biggest stadium in the state, and Billy G. is telling the peoples nobody in the whole freaking place will be alive in a hundred years, and where *will* they be in a hundred years. In Heaven, Brother? In Hell, Brother, Sister?—waving the floppy red Bible and driving off the rain with his left hand, and, yes, saying Jesus (he says Jesus sweetly, in a Johnny Mathis sort of way—unable to achieve the crashing breath on the glottis, the vulgar but authoritative *Christ-uh* of Preacher Morris, whom you don't know, Burger)—saying Jesus is calling (mildly) while the five-hundred voice choir (including desperate Stream) is humming soulfully and beautifully (and I must admit that the great choir made powerful music—Stream a tenor—especially when, before the sermon, they sang the "Hallelujah Chorus").

That stuff does get in your blood so easily.

And for a moment I'm being captured by the cruel spirit of it— I'm entertaining ideas that maybe this world *is* all loess, and passing. I'm giving over briefly to the logic of Hell—I'm actually desiring the peace that passeth understanding. All those humans in the stadium *were* suffering, and yes, we *would* all eventually rot.

If heaven ain't my home, then Lord what will I do? For I can't feel at home in this world any more ...

I was sinking deep in sin

BUT

the head of ole Son did clear right up, in time, just about halfway through "Almost Persuaded" and when I see Stream coming down the choir stairs to get more salvation. I see Stream, with his wild eyes flowing, and say, "Screw that!" so loud Royal jumps a little beside me—"Jesus, Son," he whispers—but the lady on the other side, she don't hear it, she way down deep in private sorrow, terror, she (a fatty with big flowers over her boobies expansive) is ummmmming in profound resonance, suggesting possibly a talent for administering remarkable hum jobs.

"They ain't serious!" I whisper back to Royal. "Their god-damned logic's screwed. I swear it. If there's a hell, these god-damned people are monsters!" I felt the pure rage rising. "They're a bunch of unimaginative foools. They can't even remember a burnt finger. Foools!" says I, too loud, at the Billy Graham Crusade in Jackson, Mississippi.

Royal shudders.

But the lady beside me understandingly misunderstands beautifully, taking my outcry as maybe the first signs of a gloss-olalia-type seizure.

A very short fatty, she hugs me, banging her vexed small nostrils into my sweating solar plexus—"You coming, brothah, you com-ing?" She's the lonely kind who lives in Bovina and buys in Vicks-burg bananas by the gross. Yes, Lord, Yes.

"I done done it," says I, back. "I've been and gone, dear sister. Many times . . . many times . . ." and then I pick the little fatty off the ground and says, "Death'll never get you, mam. You on the high road, sister," which fills her with joy, it seems, for after I set her down she bobbles out in the aisle and heads up front where the crowd is converting.

"Please, Son," says Royal.

And I did try to gain calm again, as so often I have tried to do with you, Burger.

Burger, Billy G. might allow as how my own sister, Lucy Patricia (God rest her soul), just might be burning in Hell Forever.

Which *is* too much. I'd never read ole Jimmy Joyce back then—but later I learned he knew this too—he *knew*.

The loft! The grim pulpit! Those people unwittingly had built a bad thing, and building wrongly for wrong things is a sin, sir. My daddy's a mill man, a goddamned mechanic, and also a better than fair carpenter, and he never would help to build a pulpit and loft for any half-assed crusade like this. Never would. Daddy knows that a man's lag screws and washers and bolted butt joints ought not serve the haters of the world—he knows toenailing and mitering and mortise and dado ought not build frames against us poor men. Joinery is of this world and so I meant to tear that pulpit down, and damn near did.

If there were hell these people ought to go howling through the streets, they really ought to quit the world—they ought to give the mightiest demonstrations and marches in public places ever seen. Christ, it seems so corny now, in a way, but I was right. Man, you cannot get up and go to work in this world at the world's work if hell is alive with Lucy in it. It's impossible to believe a soul could build cars, sell insurance, teach school, or anything, if hell were possible. Boykin's people died horribly by fire in an auto crash, screaming and melting, you might say, and no man is sane who believes that could go on forever. Even to take time off to brush your teeth with hell around would be dastardly. Fooooools!—and why I went to tear it down, when the first rain began to fall, pitty pat, pitty pat—good rain, sweet rain, giving the lie to hellfire. FUCK HELL, I cried, but by then few were near enough to hear. I'd been seated, head in hands, awhile, a longer time than I'd thought.

Burger, if I believed in hell, loving you the way I do, I'd be on your doorstep crying for you to repent. I'd never leave until you'd taken Christ as your Savior.

I cursed hell loud but with my face to the ground, and I cursed hell in a loud voice just before I arose in the increasing shower. The stadium was emptying, the only large gathering being in the conversion tent behind the north goal post, where my fat lady and Stream were being counseled by ministers and laymen from the Jackson churches.

AAAAAH—UMGAWWA-MATSI-MATSI—we were five

rows back and center and I didn't even go to the aisle for my charge—I crunched five rows over the wooden folding chairs (the kind with seats to pinch your bottom and hardly strong enough to hold me)—crunch and crash, and kicking them aside (also throwing)—I really wanted my hands on that evil wood, those illfitted joints. I was terribly upset. I tore and tore at the toenailing. I tore a dozen verticals and support struts loose and made the entire pulpit sag until the lesser evangelists and police and Royal knocked me to the turf; but these men did not mock my rage; rather, they pleaded —and there was Stream, horror and wonder and awe in his beady eyes, and slack was his mouth above his weak chin.

What a gathering that was. After the scuffle we stood in the rain that was pouring down by then (only the police with raincoats on), and I told them I wanted heaven as much as any man, woman, or child in this stadium on this night—and that the only way for me to get there was for them to let me tear it down: "Gentlemen, if you'll let me tear it down—all of it—I can go to some good true place myself. Gentlemen," and cool rain was making me feel wild again, in a different way, "Gentlemen, it's a hard way to heaven I'm going—and the Lord-uh has-uh said SON-UH YOU MUST TEAR THAT PULPIT DOWN!" My voice was clear and entirely sobless while I chanted my calling and damned if they didn't pay a proper attention to my pleas. They did listen, but it actually didn't seem they were prepared to let me go back to wrecking. And I was disappointed that Mr. Graham and his song leader weren't around, since surely they might consider me a worthy subject for argument and prayer—which was vanity, because I was well attended by my friends, preachers, and lawmen as it was. No doubt about that. The two preachers from the Graham team were sopping and rather peaceful-looking, the small balding one and the athletic-looking Christian. And the dry police seemed little more than confused to find themselves involved in a wrestling match after a big-time sermon. Everybody just stared at me for a brief space.

Then Royal said, "There's been a recent death in his family. His little sister." I was impressed by such relativity in time.

Thrice-saved Stream, shuddering, said: "He's *in*sane . . . a little." Which pissed me. The disloyal bastard—good wingback or no.

"You the *in*sane one, you foooool," said I.

One of Graham's lieutenants, the athlete, in the saturated polo shirt, said, "Let this man be. Let the Lord mend." In a slightly pious baritone—slightly sickening and revolting (for I did consider breaking the ding-a-ling's head) but also mostly decent and understanding, suggesting that said preacher might have made a man had his daddy made his momma take him (the athletic-looking preacher) off whole milk at an earlier age. Coffee and tea, see; slurp it.

"Ain't you gonna plead for my soul?" I asked. "Shit, man, I'm scared of doing even six months on God's own fire farm. My soul quakes, you fool."

"Take it easy," says one lawman, tugging at his visor.

"Son, you know the course of your own salvation. You've said as much," returns Christ's own deep safety, the cunning bastard.

"Right. Right," I said.

"Let's go," said Royal.

"I gotta pay for the boards," offers Son, generously.

"No need for that," says the preacher, mercifully.

"Ain't you Joiner from Bryan?" asked the policeman, a sports fan.

"He's Tod Tag ... and we're from Hamilton," lied Royal.

"Ya'll go on home now," said the preacher, smiling like the young Doak Walker. It was pouring rain by then, a gullywasher, a chunkmover, and at last the fit had passed. I shook in the rain. I shivered, it was so fine, and then I ran. Ah, Teacher Burger, then I ran—great leaps and strides, my arms a-flap—across the field and up the bank toward the parking lot, and I was the Great Speckled Bird, though damp to the bone—a weightless and baptized pachydermatous Paraclete—with Royal chasing after.

PRAISE THE LORD—FOR IT IS LIFTED—I yelled it loudly, flying toward my family's Pontiac.

Burger, you don't understand about growing up down here, in hell. Call me a turd for playing the pure and worldly game of football? You're bad as Billy G. preaching on a football field. Had he understood his religion he'd of had to preach *against* the footballs, that subtle, large, and violent sport, but didn't—no, he simply profaned the field by failing to see it as his enemy. And these Jackson Christians—and let me offer here and now witness that I, too, am a type of Christian, believing as I do in a deity rather like a vaguely intelligent but mostly voracious carrot, squirrel, or *Pectinatella Magnifica* (all men, or Man, a sort of Organic Christ, by virtue of having to die, as it were, which is the very heart of Methodism, and has nothing to do with the clotted sacrificial gore of Baptists, or the tawdry and mercantile abstractions of Presbyterians)—those Jackson Christians (their problem being Jackson more than Christianity) even went farther as profaners—they set a bronze plaque into the turf exactly where the pulpit had stood, just off the east sidelines. Which plaque in bronze has a quotation from Philippians cut in it to celebrate all the souls that got saved in the Crusade—except they spelled the book of the Bible wrong: with two l's: and I did enjoy my revenge the next summer on that very field, and not two months after I'd killed my first man. It was while I was captain of the Southern All-Stars in the Mississippi High School All-Star Game. Our bench was on the east side and I cleaned my cleats every chance I could upon that plaque. I stomped and scrubbed that bronze, because I like Jesus and love the World, like a Southern Methodist should. How's that grab you, Mr. Burger.

36-7: we racked those pussy stars from the Delta up! Behold, behold, I the eternall God, the Lord of Hosts, who am that mighty Leveller, am coming (yea even at the doores) to Levell in good earnest, to Levell to some purpose, to Levell with a witness, to Levell the Hills with the Valleyes, and to lay the Mountaines low. Prepare, Burger, Prepare, for the Revolt of the Rednecks is near a Second Coming—yea, even the Ghost of Vardaman shall rise again. Prepare, Beware, Beware—Be wise now therefore, O ye Rulers, &c. Be instructed, &c. Kiss the Sunne, &c. Yea, kisse Beggars, Prisoners, warm them, feed them, cloathe them, money them (a fine phrase), relieve them, release them, take them into your houses—do not serve them as niggers and necks and dogs, without doore, &c.

Man, Luther would of loved those fancy gentry people we beat hell out of the night I scubbed on chapter and verse. Us Piney Woods Boys beat those Delta Gentlemen. Once more, I say, own

them; they are your self, make them one with you, or else go howling into hell; howle for the miseries that are coming upon you,
howle, Burger. Big Son is coming.

Writing on that letter was some kind of genuine pleasure right
up until the time April started reading it over my shoulder.

"Honey, you in a bad mood?"

"_____"

"You really shouldn't do that to pore Mr. Burger. Son, lemme
give you a haircut. You lookin' real scruffy, a little." It's enough
to anger a serious man who's deep in his rage, except for how her
voice is full of affection, is, in fact, lascivious, which means she's in
a mood of wanting something for *herself*. "Honey, I'm gonna give
you a nekked haircut to ease your mind." Which is something no
Delta woman would ever do.

There's a sound of easy changes and slidings and settlings behind
my back, while I again attempt to concentrate on epistolary invective.

"You O.K.?" I ask.

"Fine. Take off your shirt. You're looking like some kind of
Weatherford." Which I did.

"Yeah? Cut it. Cut some hairs. You nekked?"

But I don't look. I just feel her leaning her titties up against my
back and shoulders.

"Can I cut it without the cloth around your neck?" Smiling in
her voice.

"Woman, you are bad on politics."

"I mean to be . . . I mean to be." She's dragging one of those
razor-loaded comb-type affairs through it to trim it, and then she
begins to clip about with the long pointed scissors. "I'm gonna
have your baybee."

"Right on . . ."

"Polly's in the ground, but me and you are doing fine." No
scintilla of remorse in what she says, as I reach back to touch her
legs. I'd finally put my yellow pencil down, and soon it was the
naked-body problem all over again. Her smooth, hard smile and
easy stance of pressure on one leg fogged me, since I was already

tense. The crispy! "Turn around so I can comb these ducks off. Man, you about to fly."

We had some good times—"Oh my." Royal, me and your wife had some really good times. "Gimme a titty in both ears. Lemme listen to the insides."

"Hush, Son."

Yessir, she used to take me when she wanted, every time. And still that was a great day in the morning. It was real good hairy time that ended banging under the scale-model Jesus—*Honey, there are women who'd be terrified to imagine loving a man your size. You got such a pile-driving ace . . .*

We showered together in the tub, laughing, and I was worrying she'd fall with the baby in her. But she didn't. April didn't fear any more than a loaded pecan tree does. She washed my wide back and never feared a thing. Which should have cured the rage, but didn't.

What I wanted was a little nigger to hug. I'd screwed me a white wife—but really what I wanted was a little nigger friend to hug on. Curious how that came to me while toweling. Crossed my mind to hug a colored. And I knew where. "I'm not waiting. I gonna deliver this letter by hand, on this very day. I'm going to Hattiesburg."

"Be kind, Son. Be kind to your teacher. Be the happy man . . ."

—dreaming gopher turtles and whiptail lizards, conjuring flounder and croppie and siren salamanders, hauling ass in my brand new Impala (more beautiful than statoblast, zooid, or *Monostyla lunaris*), slipping and sliding out that short swamp road, I drove on Cantrell's Second Stand to move my day along. I'm banging at the tonk door in the morning sunshine—and suddenly out of the gloom there is potty Cantrell looking like he expected me— "Hullo, Son. Where you been?" But surely he knows I've been getting in shape for The League.

"Hello, Cant. Man, I need some beers. They gonna put ole Polly in the ground today, yeah."

"I didn' know you was into that." But he did not leer at my grief. Tonk men don't. He let me in.

"She was a friend of mine ... nothing recent."

He said the air conditioning was down inside, but he'd turn it up, and have the bar, and drink more than you pay for. Potty Cantrell brooding (gathering tendrils of brackish eyebrows together over his pulpy nose) with warm breast and ah, bright wings—he's dumber and less inventive with vice than Cothern down at Club Karen on the Louisiana line—he's incapable (because of Sheriff Benton) of stationing whores around his place (no phony fishing cabins out back of the Stand beside the green water)—he don't even encourage the steady singles, quail, to come around his place—and for gambling at the Stand there's no more than pinball machines that don't pay off.

Tolerated syndicated gambling leads to your big-time multiple killings that get covered by the national press—says friend Davis. Which is correct.

The room without its clientele seemed barren and sad, but the little jukebox, potty and dark as Cantrell, was saddest, in the center of the dance floor.

But suddenly my mind had no mercy upon it. *I'll break your heart, ole juke, like you broke Polly's and all the rest. Does Andre grieve? Or does he pluck his reclaimed instruments mindlessly as usual.*

And Ju, the guitar man, was there. He's the man with the broom, the wide push broom, and if I'd hug on him he'd tell it to good-buddy Slater before the day was done. It was Jubal, when my eyes recovered from the light outside, and Cantrell's gone off in his pointy shoes to the distant corner to work on his books beneath a gooseneck lamp. Yessir, there's Jubal pushing cups and butts before his broom, while outside the sun is steaming creation into a quality of wet light the Taborites never imagined.

Strange times when the prince can get it better with blood ...

I sauntered behind the bar and picked a quart to suck down quick. Whoo my! my tummy sang for joy even before I raised it empty up to toot a tune on it. Regal. Then another, but not so fast, to make a superb burp that echoed around the empty room, right when Jubal's skating by the long pine bar, slyly, mischief in his eyes—he know that laaridge ofay going down to something wrong. *And he'll tell Slater.* Which was only part of what I had to know.

"Sunshine, you in the rain," he says, and moves on by. "Whoooeee. It gonna storm someday."

"You right, ole Ju. You so right."

No doubt about it. He's the lovin' colored for me, the one the mind had told my body of. No doubt at all. Slater'd know I had proper respect—he'd know I knew ole Jubal was gone and famous in Memphis and Chicago before John Lee Hooker or Howlin' Wolf—even before Big Joe Turner. I'm no critic of the music, never having played an instrument of any kind, but I knew Ju'd been a famous man one time, on the Bluebirds—he'd been a very famous man a long time back, and even now was on the Folkways label. He's eighty maybe and back home in Bryan sweeping for Cantrell, and sometimes playing and singing on the weekends, but he's not into any kind of deep misery. He slides a bottleneck over his first finger from time to time and makes the treble strings whine. Hug a colored.

I scoffed down another quart and headed for the juke. I'm moving easily now. I'm out my shoes and sliding over the stained floor fluidly, for a hug. Yes. And what I play is "I'm So Excited Now"; a couple more. The goddamn juke gets lit and deals out some lyric misery so calmly you'd think it didn't give a shit. Its bubbles of light start moving up its sides and it cares nothing for all the crying going to accrue to Polly's burst heart, or poor people eating greens and clay. It was a vision Ju could understand—so many greens you start to getting fat in the sunshine—gnawing pregnant at a clay bank—which is the poverty.

Truly I can't actually remember why my soul led me to Cantrell's, and I'm not even positive I knew it was Jubal in his ancient, holy tweed slacks I'd finally hug and raise above me.

But I do know that Slater's laughter out at the Spit—his

laughter (or curse or whatever the hell it was) was on my nervous mind—that, and also Burger's taunt, and then there's the fact I hadn't been drunk for a long time, which Cantrell damn well knew.

And the simple truth is I shouldn't have allowed these bullshit emotions into my pipes—my game should have been the only thing on my mind—San Diego and training camp and making the Bulls should have been the only demons on my mind, but they weren't.

Niggers. What was Eugene Simpson Joiner doing brooding over niggers in a decent tonk—or college professors? I'd been raised to be sympathetic to both, and that should have been sufficient, but wasn't.

In my mind was the line—*unfinished business here.* Like the title of a song. Like words said by some female oracle. Unfinished business here—and Jubal sweeping up the floor was part of it. Sweep, sweep, mother, sweep on!

It was a small thing to do, to hug a colored; but in some way it wasn't so different from Cheryl of the tree house or the fat lady at the Crusade, maybe, and it *was* something to tell Burger about—and it *was* something Slater'd hear about. It was a way to score, obscurely, for decency, and when I grabbed him up the old musician didn't seem to fear a thing.

Whooooooeee—it must of been a sight to see, even for Cantrell staring out of the corner. He'd seen that floor scratched over for hours by dancers whose feet were fingers clawing at proud flesh, but he'd never seen his nigger help picked from that surface and celebrated almost like the popped core of a mean boil. As it were.

Jubal's in this wore-out tweed with knee patches and a smell like ripe olives covered with blue cheese—Christ! the way they dress in the summertime. We get to bopping and sliding and skipping around the box, by that time to something like "Little Momma"—we're all giggles in our fresh beers—and maybe it was a little like some Pore Old Tom and a Good Ole Boy carrying on with all the ancient distances and hatreds still operating, but not much. It wouldn't have seemed a bad jive to anybody who knew us, me and Ju.

I just swung on over to where he's pushing the broom close to the juke and say, "Man, put that broom down—let's have some fine jive in this ole tonk." And Ju said, "Son, you a wild Main." Fine expression. And when we're bopping around, both doing a kind of bop and fucking wing—that's when I picked up my first nigger up above my tall head, that little paunchy and one-time famous spade-type coon—God love him—whirling around and around with him up high.

I need you-uh good lovin'—and to hell with any nigger writers who say the nexus between black and white has got to be flat-out queer. It is more rigorous than that.

Jubal Clifford is way up high above my head, but he (jazzman, coon, and un-Tom) is *not* afraid, lifted as he is by violent and ambiguous love—but Cantrell, with his silky nostrils, is, sirs, now looking at us and the things we do in some amaze, even for a tonk runner.

My thick thumb does intrude on Jubal's bellybutton.

That little jukebox was trying to work everything on out—for it seemed, while it (the box) was yelling all that sound into the room, just like some Disney creature entirely alive and with us in this Very World.

I had Mr. Jubal Clifford, guitarman, near the ceiling of the Stand—so finally I put my nigger down.

Shift and stride, prance and glide, which Cantrell, essentially sedentary and asexual, did continue to notice. He stopped his pencil in midair and stared into the dim, cool light of his room and said, "Ya'll cut that out."

A sad thing to understand.

For here's a human man who understands depravity, is sadly aware of all the Trojan rubbers jammed into the wallets of his room each night—Cantrell knows the fracking animal is sick, and would be whole, if only the preacher's Jesus jelly condoned a good bang or ball. He knows they start to shooting guns at all hours —at lights, beer signs, stop signs, wives who messaround, the brack-ish waters of sloughs that swallow bullets complacently, and their

best friends even, sometimes—because there is no joy in a goddamned tonk.

I picked sweet pudgy Jubal up again, and he was squeaking
like a small child. I did have him high, my thumbs and fingers deep
in nigra fat, and then I put him down again. "No point to cause
the bastard pain," I said to Ju—gesturing toward Mr. Cantrell.

"Uh huh . . . now you go on, Son . . . we both be in it." But still
that guitarman had his grin on.

I went back to the bar and wadded up some dollar bills to leave
for payment. I got back in my shoes and cut out, crying out—
"Thanks, tonk man"—and I was gone to Hattiesburg, to moon
Burger.

I'm headed off down the road when the dead weight of wisdom
sat down on my head like a mortarboard, awkward and ugly, saying the idea to moon was not at all respectful—it said: *Don't moon
the mother at noon:* mooning: to show one's ace. For I had considered it. Literally to shove your ass against a pane to offend the
enemy.

I'd considered creeping across his pine needles, which might
have been a little like across hot coals or a bed of nails. I'd considered easing up to his study window, for inside he surely was
studious and cool. I'd planned, while bombing south on 51 Highway in my football car, to drop my drawers and show my ass at
that un-radical's window.

How shall a man raise himself? At a study window? Climb
upon the air conditioner, for it might just hold! I meant to, but
didn't.

I was too ashamed to, when I finally stepped from my own conditioned car into an atmosphere that was not unlike a Turkish bath.

I'd wanted to and did tell Burger about Polly, mostly, while the
down-home and everlovin' mimosa blossoms fell plumb down into
the true-to-life Caldwellian and Snopsey gullet of a summer noon
in Hattiesburg (all of it proclaiming and publishing how the blues

at an armory dance, or even at the Stand, or fucking on a diamond, blasted my molecules into better configurations than any Bohemian lecture Burger was about to ever give), I did tell him about Polly and other shit, but I never quite mooned him at noon.

I was absolutely pissed, while rolling south in my professional tackle vehicle, but not so much I'd hurt a man who'd done me good.

Hattiesburg is a green, wet town (65 inches a year from now and then a hurricane)—and I found Burger in a narrow, gray house, a narrow house in a wide world, with a yard of brown pine needles, on Twenty-first Avenue, I think.

I'd never been there before. That occurred to me again. I had the address from letters but I'd never been there personally. For that goddamned man had never had me over, while I was his student —and now I was coming as an uninvited guest.

It was so hot in his yard, my nails sweat. It was such a quiet and shrouding green, Burger's air conditioner seemed positively boisterous in the heavy air. It was a window unit sticking out and dripping and buzzing.

Nervous, I went up to his front door and knocked like a little chap delivering flowers, or ready with a singing telegram—since it was a folded letter I had in hand.

"Hullo, Prof." *Good Lord, the man is in his sweats—he's been jogging in front of his air conditioner, or somewhere.*

"Hi, Sonny?" In shrill Midwestern—and he was clearly more confused than I.

So I sought the right sentence: "Have you thought about Billy Rath lately?" Toward the end of that sentence I stepped past Burger into his own living room, which looked like a monk's cell, it was so austere.

"Billy who?" With a slight stutter. Strangely his only one that day.

But I had already begun to dance for him, too, and I was rather pleased with myself for beginning to cavort that way almost immediately, with little rage and less inhibition. I was satisfied that this would finally be more frightening to him than mooning—and surely somehow it was more tasteful. Chanting nearly—"Rath was a great professional FOOTBALL player—long ago I discovered him in a machine—he made me realize ball can make you famous. That gray machine standing in the sawdust gave me a Hero just as you have in your own way printed heroes in my head—though Billy was on a sepia-colored card—he hooked into my mind like Coppe did. BURGER, they will last, while we may rot . . ."

"——" speechless, flooded over with amaze.

"Sepia Sepia Sepia—let's hear it for that nigger tint!"

"Son . . ."

Kicking off my loafers, I began to dance more gracefully, by then on tippytoes lightly, about the bonewhite room wherein I noticed a wall of black bookshelves. I whirled before his astonished eyes, touching easily his low ceiling with my newly razored hair— "Sir, for not knowing who Billy is, I may lay waste to you and to this place—I may indeed become a piney Žižka to your academic papal legions." Though in saying something like that I realized I'd formed an ill comparison, for this place was in no wise popish. "Sir, I meant to moon you."

"Moon?"

"A very large, hot moon—for ole Billy. And Polly." And by then the dooms, conclusions, and despairs were rolling over me— embarrassment—terrible embarrassment for what I was saying and doing—but I went right on. "And you don't know who Jubal Clifford is either, do you?" I was flat a-foot.

"Joiner- er?"

"Let's exercise together," I said, playfully, grabbing hold his hands. And his eyes were wild a moment, and he was rooted in his place on the hooked rug.

"Nooooo."

"Someday I'll kill a man for you. I care so much about the shit you've taught I'll kill for it."

He pulled loose, and eased, by virtue of his will. "I have some I. W. Harper that's smooth as brandy." He was smiling awfully.

"That'll make beer and bourbon before one—but I'm game, today."

. . .

Never one to drink all that much back then, I still drank that one (and he fixed it with three cubes and a splash in a great hurry) like I really needed it. Embarrassment, the both of us. And now I knew the poor bastard *deserved* some explanation, no doubt about it.

—"Burger, what I want to say is something about how I've realized you were probably a track star in college—the goddamned mile, or two mile, or cross-country—something ridiculous like that. Shit, man, what kind of sport is it makes you run all that way and never lets you hit anybody?"

We're seated on a beat-up Danish couch from Ward's, and finally his smile is brave, outright, a little like a Lady from Hell about the time he has got his bagpipe properly stoked. He smiles and wonders why he's the one to catch it from me; among all my teachers, why him? I say, "All the other teachers are camels with only one hump, but you've got two, a bump for knowledge and a bump for will—and Asia is a long way across . . ."

"___"

"Burger, you've *tried* to in-form purely—except for judging how a man should live his life, which was a bad mistake."

"It surely was."

"Mr. Burger, I'm going off to play pro ball in a couple of weeks —and some wise man has got to share my fear."

He shifts and tries to imagine going off to play pro ball. "What frightens you?"

"Leaving things behind." Which made me nervous to say, because it was a lot like running too hard and getting screened. It set him up to say I ought to stay in school and/or do all sorts of social good—rather than go off to The League.

"What's left?"

"Dead bodies."

It was a nice, friendly exchange.

"That does tend to be a problem." And he nearly laughed out loud.

Burger with his spiffy, blue sweats on, and lank hair, was O.K., it seemed. It seemed I was right to seek him out.

"Here, read my letter."

It was absolutely amazing how patient I was while sipping that wonderful bourbon. I'd written it out on every other line of the legal pad in a gothic and jabbing hand, so he had an impressive MS to deal with, though in essence it wasn't all that long. After his heavy glasses were in place, he began to snap each page, as farther he went on, which strangely gave me peace of mind.

Finally he looks up, saying, "I think your analysis of Luther is a little harsh—but the sexual metaphor is . . . interesting . . . and I'm finally aware of things I should have understood before. Especially after the other letters you've sent. But it isn't that I've been an insensitive snob, as you suggest." He spoke in measured phrases in the manner of a leech gatherer. "It's the natural sort of Medieval—or Renaissance—Christianity some of you people have." He's staring bleakly across his own room at Dürer's *Large Passion*—the one where Jesus goes to Limbo, with a foolish devil about to gig him with a rough stick; it's the one whereon a goatish female devil, with sickening odd dugs, does blow a nasty horn. "I thought I'd have to be a Protestant to get to you people."

Choke. "To *get* to us?"

"Yeah. I wanted you guys to like history . . ."

"*Like* history?"

"Yeah . . . enjoy studying history . . ."

"Mr. Burger, me and my friends come to it naturally. What amazed us was that *you* liked it—that and how you seemed to abide killing so easily. Which did—does—seem contradictory of your feelings about football." I was trying my very best to be calm in spite of the superficial shit he put on me. Lord, I did feel my head was light, and I did feel that every tendon was severed, every artery —I felt my marrow chill and feared I'd become incontinent.

He got up slowly and got us both a bigger drink. Oh he was very melancholy, sipping, but also, at last, strangely strong. "This is all so . . . mustering, Sonny—you and that beautiful wife out in that classroom—all you crazy people—and I should have understood from studying in Nashville—but it's not the same . . ." He trailed off, drinking too much at once.

"Tell me who you are, Mr. Burger."

He pooched out a thin lower lip, and squinted, while also curling his long toes. "I'm the man who shouldn't be here."

"They buried Polly today."

"I'm sorry."

"She was easy in her body, but still it broke her heart. She wasn't the tightest pussy I ever had, but she could shudder best. And now she'll have a hard time keeping it all together until Judgment Day. She's a loose and drifting woman."

"They tend to be."

"Jesus!"

"Right!" he said. He did say it.

"I need to see my daddy and my momma, one more time."

"You should . . . and then go play your game."

"Sir, do you *believe* in Žižka?"

"More often than not. Every now and then. It's wonderful that you and April will have a child. That's real good." He says it calmly, then gets up to find his cigarettes on top of his unit. Lights up. "April is a good girl, and she's as smart as you. Don't hit me." He's smiling like a brother. He is relaxed, drunk.

"She'll live forever."

"No she won't. That would make it all too easy. If the great ones did."

"Sheeeiit! You *do* know. I know ezakly who you are." His gracious, austere living room seemed to recoil when I said that, it seemed to flex its shelves of paperbacks and bookclub hardbacks, and the air conditioner seemed to skip a beat. "If I presume."

"Don't." In his skinny sweats he was a mystery. He was a natural man, but Daddy was on my mind.

"You're a good man, Dennis—you really are, and, in spite of faking it, you're a great teacher."

"I appreciate that as much as you know I do. Go see your people now."

"Yessir."

.   .   .

Which was my single close encounter with Mr. Dennis Burger.

I took a leak in Collins, then headed north toward Memphis, toward White Haven. I drank black coffee in Canton and in Batesville. I wanted to be sober when I got there.

9

WAY DOWN YONDER in New Orleans a fellow can take stock of his puritanical sorrows—he can clean his pipes, as Davis would say. At the Napoleon or Acropolis a Joiner can bleed off the bile, bad blood, melancholy, and general wrath—then, having suffered this excessive but nevertheless austere cure (say thirty Dixie beers through an evening of napkin dancing with an extraordinary Greek woman name of Toula), he will surely return to Bryan or Jackson or Yazoo City (wherever)—he will, certainly, then return to his wife and baby, by the air conditioner's might. Fracking-A. And why not? It's been going on for centuries.

It's not at all like visiting the Joiners in Memphis.

April never asked Henry a thing about Maria, and when I got back from New Orleans—this is not long after I'm out of The League because of the broken arm (the cast's still on the forearm) —she never asked more than a commonplace about the trip. How's Daddy? Perfunctorily. You better, Son?

Maria paints his face. She's been painting it off and on for twenty years, and she says it's the best she ever had, both because it shows the most character and also because it does in fact sell best (Henry's face) on the streets of New Orleans at her red shed with wheels. She rolls it from place to place in the Quarter, crying, "Spiritual Portraits for sale." She says they're getting better as the scars grow older. Maria says he's been dying of something fine for a long time—and the older scars and also losing weight are making it clearer and clearer, whatever; the cancer.

"She's proud to paint me," he says, as we're driving toward N.O. "She really enjoys to do it."

I'm going south with him because, while hunting dove with Henry (he pumps off three shots from one knee and drops the outside two), I decide that I could use a stadium fix, whether I like it or not. And he's not so sighted as he once was.

April has been telling me it's unnatural I can't stand to watch The League games on T.V., however much my disappointment at getting hurt. She says, Son, go to the Sugar Bowl, it'll do you good —so I get tickets from Coach Topp and try to do myself good by going, hitching onto Henry who's headed that direction, but to no football game, and H. is high on conversation about Maria and Maylene, and also I notice, horribly, that probably he seems to have a hard-on in the pickup, an actual old man's stand under his loose khakis. He *will* tell me about his life now, and I never made that bowl game. I can't even remember who was playing.

I've noted that every man has got a time and place to shoot his mouth off, and Henry's is the Louisiana line. Hell, he opened up about the time we bombed past the Club Karen, which was, of course, for me, redolent of memories of Polly; so immediately I was the perfect audience for Henry all the way down to the Crescent City. It was the pain that passeth understanding—and not at all like Memphis, where *my* daddy is recently successful and semi-rich from inventing the Joiner Guard, an electric eye device that keeps even the dumbest man from being able to brad, nail, or tack his hand to the box he's working on. The Joiner Guard shuts the whole thing down. Going to New Orleans was another thing entirely. I never saw that goddamned football game, not a single play.

Henry says I ought to stick with him and forget that *foolishness;* which shouldn't have surprised me. He lets that G.M.C. on out, while exposing his left knobby elbow to the wind. He has got on, in December, for it is a warm day, a loose-flowing gook shirt, one of them terrible silky mothers like you always see in Panama City, Fla. He's warm enough, he's lecherous as an old sparrow, and he *will* tell me how to keep things from going wrong. "Get yourself

a line of work, then fuck around on the sides." He grins and spits
out the window. "Don't matter what it is so much as you like it.
Understand. Open one of them Jax."

You put an expectant grin on that already taut face and you've
got something pretty goddamned terrifying. Even sipping beer in a
green morning on wheels won't help it much.

I never made the Sugar Bowl. I flung my ticket out the window
five, ten miles outside Bogalu. Burger, that, sir, was another fucked-
up radical moral act, though not so close to the bone as when I
threw my wedding ring into the Sabine, four, five months later.

Henry says, "I'm gonna show you a real good woman and some
good food if you'll forget the *foolishness*."

"Right, man. I'm with you." I shuddered, slouched, and sucked
at my beer, rolling through the vegetable and labyrinthine caverns
of Louisiana. I wanted Henry to stop and let me eat live oak leaves,
but I didn't mention it. A tunnel of ravenous green, while headed
south toward Lake Pontchartrain.

Some species that live in streams build nets in which they capture food upon the drifting water. But most of the caddis fly's life
is spent as a larva, the pupal stage lasting about two weeks—the
adult living about a month—*Rhyacophilia fenestra, Neureclipsis,
Molanna uniophila, Limn-ephilus combinatus* (animal *and* plant
debris), *oecetis cinerasceus* (twigs)—*Leptocella albida*—and *Tri-
aenodes tarda* (leaf fragments!). Onward!

Would that the old and dying man had hung me over the hood,
down over the bumper, like a strangely arranged trophy deer, so I
could lick up the white line on the highway (Louisiana 41), so I
could lap up the fucking miles. Let's hear it for Slidell. Shit yes, in a
G.M.C. pickup truck, on the hard road down to New Orleans.

Just before this trip I've lost my game—at least for a while—
and I'm suspecting I never want to go back to it—and my wife is
making a great production of the new baby (it's like the nursery,
which is our bedroom, is a basilica, with everything in order: nave,

apse, and high altar)—and the rational President of these United States is a month dead—and now, upon a pilgrimage meant to heal, I've got to hear mad talk about dusty Maylene and viscid Maria. Zupp goes Jax. I'm an intruder on the life of Henry! Live spelled backwards *is* evil.

Son, a long time I worried my wife was dead because of me . . . even though Roy's driving when we hit the bridge . . . She's dead a long time before the crash—but still I thought her death was my own fault. I loved ole Roy and Merle . . . and I did love sweet Maylene—Son, that girl was perfect for a while. First time I ever saw her she was swimming in the Steele and she had the most beautiful little body you ever saw . . . But she's crazy, like Roy was.

Helen's ugly . . . God damn that woman is good and ugly. I'd married her otherwise, and missed the pleasures of my life. I swear. Maria is the best.

I come down here the first times right after May died. I come down here to get away from trouble, but I ended up by havin' fun. Which is what I always wanted. He's pondering and sincere. He's mixing up thirty years of personal history.

And not even good food and drink could cloud the ugliness I finally saw in that huge room at Maria's. Maria sat in some kind of velvety and padded rocking chair (huge brass upholstery tacks beginning to break free) and fired her brain waves into Henry's head. She nodded and rocked and was in complete control of everything he said to me while we were there. She seemed a priestess directing a tyro—she was a priestess who had the god she worshipped under complete control. A slight and brutalized deity he was, but he was hers and he was right there with that tall glass of straight bourbon gripped in the scarred fist.

Christ! He rambled and for a second I thought the man was profoundly drunk (after three belts of Maria's booze and the beers we'd had coming down), but drunkenness would have been too good to be true, and a superficial understanding of what was happening—for the truth was that he was becoming hysterical—he was transcending drunkenness and years of pain and the cancer that was in him, and I was positive that his continuing narrative would finally move toward some definite conclusion and realization, a basted denouement of sorts, and I feared the getting there. I was lost in a dark wood and only these two ogres could free me, if they were so disposed.

"Like my face and Sam Chalmers . . ." Henry's glittering eyes were gay. "Like my face and how it worried ole Sam, and I like Sam pretty well—I've worked for him thirty years, but I had my fun when he comes up to me on the mill yard and says, 'Henry, I saw a picture for sale on the sidewalk in New Orleans and damn if it didn't look just like you.' He looks at me steady for an answer. 'You do go down there sometimes, don't you?' And he was so sure he was telling it, not just asking. I told Sam he's right—I do go sometimes, like everybody else—but it was like I wasn't paying any attention to him. Then he's proud enough to ask me again if I ever get my picture painted while I'm down, and he starts to get a grin on, which was the best part, because I looked on him like he was suffering from the sun out there in the hot mill yard.

"One thing about having a face like mine is nobody can read it very easy and Sam felt like a fool for asking—

" 'Henry, it sure looked *something* like you . . .' He's hurting, he's afraid he might of hurt my feelings. Ole Sam was feeling bad he'd ever got involved about my pictures.

"The one he'd seen was the most realistic. Me as a mill worker— the only thing unusual being the face of Franklin Delano Roosevelt mixed in with the pink of the clouds in the background above the mill roof, you know.

"I told him the kiln's got to be worked over this fall, and I said it just like I'd never heard anything at all about my pictures, and Sam said for me to do whatever to the kiln that's needed, and it's then I really laid it on him. I said, Sam, you better go back in the office where it's nice and cool. He didn't know what to do then, with me talking to him that way and showing I thought he's crazy. I took pleasures in that meanness," says Henry, smiling a smile so broad everything gets a stretched white around his sliverish mouth, like he's eating glazed doughnuts. "But Maria don't think it was mean at all, or anyway she thinks it was just the right thing to be doing, because Sam Chalmers won't ever forget that picture as long as he lives, and that's what we want—ain't it, Honey?"

Maria smiles a gaudy moist smile of agreement and dismisses long rods and folds of Murad smoke through her vasty nostrils.

"It's Maria," Henry goes on more slowly, "it's what me and Maria wants . . . my picture put in all kinds of rooms and hands and stared at time to time by everybody . . ."

Maria breaks in: "I want the people to see Henry's *goodness.* I want the people to see the pure face of his mortality." She's a concentrated person.

She's tall and almost fat and gives off a sweet and sour odor up close, but still she is terrible concentrated. I believed she was evil, but still she had the same kind of concentrated energy you find in really productive people, you might say. Like St. Claire Granville or Morningside Robbins.

We park down the street from her place deep in the Quarter, then go up two, three dim flights, to meet her coming down to greet us energetically, O Lord, in a heavy brocade smelling of cheap wine and probably peculiar spices and herbs, coming down, and she is groaning, "Hunoree, Hunoree." Yessir, in the humid dim light of the landing, she strikes my fancy as kin to poor Julia—though Maria is surely brighter, being Italian, Spanish, or dark French. Maria Santillo ushers us into a wide, long room, does, in fact, lift and carry Henry, by way of a massive rising hug, over the threshold—"Hunoree, O, Hunoree"—into a very large loftlike room with great windows that reach from ceiling to floor. They open onto a narrow porch. It's a heavy room full of small *objets* and big paintings (mostly of Henry), though the first thing I noticed was a pot full of feathers, somitch at least six feet high, and no slick production line article at all; in fact, I guess it has been recently thrown; if such a thing can be thrown—and these peacock feathers are not so much *in* it as stuck in*to* knobs of clay all over the sides, carbuncles of clay on a blue pot big enough to hide one of the forty thieves.

"This here's my son-in-law," says Henry, glowing in the particolored room. "He's a good boy an' come to meet you." He hugs her again, with his feet on a Persian rug, avian in design for the most part.

"Ah!" she says, "Ah!" about three times in such a way my tinklepotty draws up into my body. "Ah, I see." And I believe she did.

"Refreshment?" she asks.

"Shore," answers Henry.

"Fine with me," say I, dropping into some kind of massive throne chair.

Those pictures of Henry have about them, at their best, something of the quality of American primitive painting. They're a little like the kind of grim things you can see in some old houses in the South to this day, and in the North, too. In these crude but inspired old paintings you'll sometimes get a picture of a child holding a pet or a playpretty of some sort, but the awful thing is that the face doesn't look like a child's face at all, and the body is often ill-proportioned. A four-year-old will have a fully mature head, or even maybe an aged visage—and one in particular I've seen (one where the old face is on the chubby body of a little girl who seems a tad dwarfish) shows the child holding a rabbit—a little girl cradling a pink bunny in her arms, but when you look closely you can see that she has got a fierce grip around the bunny's throat. The child's eyes are slits and old and the bunny's eyes are bugged out fearfully, and the little girl's hand itself shows the white tension and pressure of the grip and the wrinkles of age. The grip means to cut the life breath out of that creature. I saw it at Mary Montague Barber's place in So So.

Maria's are similar to the above, but also opposite. Maria composes with the same awkward anatomy, and there's always something ambiguous about Henry's age, even in the ones before he was burned. The difference is twofold: 1) The bunny picture has an insignificant background, nothing more than a conventional meadow and wood and river, while the pictures of Henry always have a *significant* background—if Henry's a fireman, there's a fire

station—if Henry's a millman, there's a mill building and some
ricks—if Henry's a shlumberger operator, there's a shlumberger
in the background. 2) In the older primitives there is that age and
evil in the face (the very image of Original Sin), but Henry's faces,
even the scarred ones, always suggest the soul of an innocent and
defiant youth—Henry's faces represent, it seems to me, the Per-
fectability of Man.

Ugly, ugly, ugly . . .

Henry explained to me that before he began to retire recently
he didn't go out into the streets of New Orleans much. He just came
up here to the apartment and took his ease with food, drink, and
loving—but now he's part of the scene. He said, "Now I'm part of
the *scene* . . ." He must have picked the phrase up on the street
from some Beats or something, because Maria never uses cute
phrases. He said he goes about the town nowadays and admits that
he is the subject of the "Spiritual Portraits" of Maria Myle Santillo,
and there was even a reporter from the *Times Picayune* who came
around thinking to do a feature on the two of them. Maria allowed
as how the offer of the article was tempting because it would increase their sales, but she refused—she and Henry decided that
fame might violate their relationship.

Jesus. "Time enough for fame," is what she said.

She said that years from now the art historians might want to
snoop around and write them up, and that would be fine, in time.

They had many stories to tell me, but mostly it was all about
Kinch Jolly. It was Kinch Jolly who was on the vexed and packed
mantel (it's busy with eighteenth-century-type figures—shepherds
and shepherdesses—and also little African objects of more or less
the same intent, though not so detailed)—Kinch's the only other
face in the entire room except for Henry's and a couple of Maria's
self-portraits—a photograph in a gilded wooden frame of a smiling
World War II soldier with his hat on. I passed it while I strode to
gather breath after Maria's drink. I paused before that shy expression, supposing it was some kin of Maria's who was probably killed

in action on Iwo Jima or on the French coastline. Which Henry
noticed and was pleased by, for obviously this person was important in their lives.

I wished to hell I was back in The League with a whole body. I
wished to hell I was back in Bryan with my wife and baby. I'd even
of been relieved to be back at the Stand, Foots riding hell out of the
niggers. Or out at Slater's shack eating greasy ham and eggs and
listening to him talk about Justice and Reason.

Henry says, "He's this soldier she's painting before she meets
me. He's this pore fellow who's Maria's friend before I come to
town, and it was early in the war and he couldn't understand that
when I was down from Bryan he was *out*. He never understood
how he couldn't come up here when I'm in town.

"Fact is he was out entirely, unless he just wanted to come and
sit and just get painted. Because she's getting patient enough to
wait for the times when I came down from home." And Henry,
who's standing behind Maria's rocker, smiles down on the thick
black hairs of his lover. He smiles in praise of her ability not to
require a military dork *every* night in the 1940's. He's pleased with
her for learning to be faithful. He's pleased with Maria.

She claps her long green nails over the intricate designs of
brocade, those mauve and bloodly whorls, that cover her bosoms,
and nearly swoons at the tenderness of the compliment paid her.

How many days has she worn that heavy dress?

Henry: "She went on painting other people when I didn't come,
but Kinch he wanted more than painted—he hollers and screams
outside the door there the first time he knows I'm staying the night
here with Maria. Brings his guitar up the stairs and sings 'All
Around the Water Tank' to us at the door. Sings to *her*."

She lets out a breath that withers me over with the objects of
the mantel, where I'm growing increasingly desperate. I'm staring
hard into the face of this shallow soldier.

Henry: "Kinch's a terrible racket and pitiful to hear, singing hymns and love songs, then pounding at the door, and the neighbors yelling. Maria says, 'Now go on, Kinch—go on, honey. You can't come in here at night no more!' "

Old Henry was standing there speaking for Maria, and she's right there under him puffing away again on her pseudo-Mediterranean cigarette and sloshing her noon rum around in a deep glass, and goddamn she looked like a huge toad with a Roman nose. But the trouble was it was obvious to me that he was telling it all the way Maria'd made it up for him. Not that it didn't happen—but it was her that made him believe it amounted to something like the Second Day of Creation. It was her (and, by the by, his) own little sordid personal myth, and she'd made him the hero of it, and it was clear as the fried chin on his face that he liked the hell out of what she'd done for him.

She rises from her wracked chair and puts a record on the very modern stereo that sits beside the potted peacock feathers—

Exsurge, quare obdormis Domine?

exsurge, et ne repellas in finem . . .

The one about how your belly is in the dust. And I thought to myself—*well, hell, really, it ain't no stranger than pro ball. Try to enjoy it.*

Goddamn Gregorian chants for New Year's Eve Day—

Kinch—

He came back the next night and this time he goes out the hall window onto the long porch that runs the whole face of the building outside each floor. He came back the next night and this time he had a pistol to go along with his guitar, and this was the part that Henry and Maria loved the best. It's then that Henry's voice becomes most sonorous and wonderful to hear. "We're lying up here in that bed over there in the dark, with the window open onto the porch, and we hear his strummin' and strummin'." It's a four-poster of metal, and gilded, covered with a counterpane also of avian design. "She says, 'Kinch, you get out of here . . . Kinch, that you out there?' and she says it just loud enough for him to hear it. 'Kinch, you know that balcony is rotten—now go on honey—an' be careful.'

"And I could just make out his face and I could see him squatted down out there across the room. He's doing chords on his guitar. He's not really singing this time. He's saying off and on, 'Got damn you, Maria.' But he was, I guess, kind of singing it, like he's about to make himself up a song, but mostly talking. He hits chords and swears at her like about three minutes, and then he starts to shooting—no more than some kind of target pistol—and shoots over the bed and into the wall just over our heads. It got me up. It, by God, got me out of bed." He points at the weary yellow plaster of the wall directly behind the bed, and I notice that it's only a yard square maybe that hasn't been covered over with some kind of cloth of intricate design. The bed's at the far end of the room away from the window (twenty, thirty feet or more)—and Maria has painted a big red circle around each little hole.

Poor Kinch Jolly, for the love of God, because when he sees the dark shape of Henry rising from that bed of scented love, he's frightened, the soldier is upset scared, he rises from the sorrowful crouch where he's been strumming and starts running along the porch toward the hall window he came through—and one foot goes clear through the porch floor. You can't trust those long balconies in New Orleans. Kinch yanks himself loose but then breaks on through again at the next step. He's trying to keep a hand on the pistol and one arm around his guitar. He's off-balance and tangled and falls against the iron balustrade, which comes apart from that rotten floor, and down into Burgundy Street goes a big section of the balustrade and all of Kinch Jolly, too.

Who'd have expected it—a soldier, one gun, and an old guitar from Alabama falling down into the narrow street, three stories. It created one helluva scene, with Maria howling from the bed, and people running out of the building when they hear the scream and the clattering, and then, of course, the police. And then the police *and* M.P.'s, because they're never far away in the Quarter.

But Henry had it under control in no time—he was competent as hell when the chips were down, and he had it all cleared up in half an hour (Henry accounting wonderfully for the detritus of midnight mischief)—everything was thoroughly explained by the time young Kinch was settled in the base morgue. He explained to the police and the M.P.'s that this pore fellow was drunk and bothering a lady upstairs and that the fellow even took a shot or two at the lady, and they could come up and see, which they did, with Maria still shrieking at odd moments as she stalked in a white robe and tore at her hair now and then. The civil and military law both understood, and the waiter across the hall substantiated Henry's story, as did others in the building, and also one Negro who'd watched it all from the street.

Henry says, "That nigger was really excited. He told the law he *knew* that man was trouble."

It was just one of these things that happen on Saturday nights during wars, World War II, 1943.

Kinch Jolly—and Henry was continuing on, but now in an angry tone, and Maria has got her face set in an operatic scowl. I could tell they had something more to perform. *Head-on tackling is easier.* Henry's teeth are clinched for his strangest role. "He's a fine young man but things like that happen. When she's settled down she comes out and says we should of invited him in to talk and then there wouldn't of been any trouble and he'd still be walking on the earth. *She* says we could of all had us a little talk—we could of sat there on the sweat-through sheets and had us a good heart to heart—*she* thinks we could of sung songs with Kinch picking. Yessir, she says it might of been the Christian thing to do." He has left her chair. He has stationed himself near the fateful window. He's making a speech—"*She* says I could of told Kinch about poor May and he'd of understood and gone away. He'd understand he needed a younger woman . . ." And he managed to cry, actual tears that were stripes from his eyes down to his jaws. "Nothing should of happened!"

"Don't seem probable it wouldn't," say I, trying to do my part. Siding with my father-in-law.

"She gave me love and sent me away six months—because of that goddamned Keeeinch."

"Ah! Because we had to celebrate what it was that killed him." *Celebrate!*

Henry—"You tell me I'm wrong for grieving over May like I did and then you run me out this house because some fool goddamned boy from Alabama falls off the porch."

"He died that we might live—and I sent you away because I

had to come to terms with my passion for you and the vision of my
Art. I had to conceive a vision worthy of you and Kinch."

"Kinch, shit. You painted his picture six months and sold ever
last one."

"It was a tribute . . ."

"You never painted no pictures of Maylene."

"I was jealous of Maylene. I was jealous of her weakness and
all the things she shared with you. I can't paint a person I don't
love . . ."

"You should of."

Then they sulked awhile, which was a relief to me. It seemed
for a moment that this whole play was after all no more than a
family argument, and not a particularly serious one at that. I'm
sitting about ten feet from her and for a moment she seems as comfortable and banal as any lady in the Wednesday Literary Fellowship back in Bryan. She's proud, straight, and fulsome in her
rocker, and she isn't really gross at all. Her heavy hair has fallen
on both sides of her shoulders, and for a moment, while she has her
eyes closed almost peacefully, she seems quite lovely, and Henry's
love for her is entirely understandable. In fact, she really isn't banal
at all. In fact, she's a large, intelligent, and sensual woman I'd like to
fuck.

But then Henry rushed across the room and fell before her on
his knees, undoing my youthful reverie.

"It's Kinch's porch, ain't it?"

"Yes, my dear, Kinch's porch . . ."

"It's Kinch's porch even though it's been fixed up . . ."

"Poor Kinch . . ."

"Pore Kinch."

"We meant no harm."

"We sure didn't."

It is remarkable how quickly one's moods can turn around, for
suddenly again I was scared shitless and figured the next thing was
to bring that feathered pot over and start boiling pore ole S.J. in a
witch's bath.

But actually they didn't do me any *bodily* harm. In fact, it seemed they had forgotten I was in the room at all. Henry pulled up a straightback in front of Maria's rocker (right after he'd removed Kinch's picture from the mantel)—and with that picture between them they both sat chattering knee to knee.

Judgment failed to hold me in my magisterial seat, though it carefully tried to. At that moment it finally let my feelings go their way, both hatred and friendship, even the friendship I bear myself, without being changed and corrupted by them. If it cannot reform the other parts according to itself, at least it does not let itself be deformed to match them; it plays its game apart. A batch of Montaigne crossed my mind about the time I rose and retreated to the kitchen area to assault Maria's rum. I swallowed, then turned back into the vault and noticed that they also had a box of letters between them. I listened carefully and discerned to my horror that they were a correspondence of several years that Maria had kept up with Kinch's mother.

She'd told Mrs. Jolly that she was in the habit, being a widow, of feeding servicemen from time to time and that her son was clearly the finest young man she had ever had into her home. She'd explained that his death had been a horrible accident and the result of the pressures of war, because he certainly wouldn't have been drunk otherwise. (?)

Which made it clear to me that the service authorities had been rather cryptic in their report to the Jollys, but Maria hadn't. *What story had Maria made up to fill in the interstices?*

Henry and Maria mooned and carried on over those letters and handed the picture of Kinch back and forth for a good ten minutes. *Pass blocking is relatively simple compared to this.*

It seems that Kinch had been the son of a smalltown druggist and that his father had planned great things for him, including a college education at Alabama Polytechnical Institute when his tour of duty was over. And Mrs. Jolly had reported that Kinch was a regular whiz at mathematics and physics and that their principal had said Kinch was the best salutatorian they ever graduated from Renfroe High School.

Kinch this and Kinch that—then suddenly they realized I was still there. It was Maria this time who turned and spoke for them—
"So you see, Son, why it is that we have such a bond. Now you understand why I have dedicated myself to showing the great soul of Henry Smith." Henry rose and replaced Kinch's boyish face on the mantel, then he returned the letters to a small rolltop desk. "Now you understand why I have worked so hard to share my vision with the world and why Henry is so cooperative." It's like listening to Miss Prockwhistle back at Bryan High recite "Crossing the Bar." "Son, my talents may seem slight to you, but for Kinch and Henry I have given my all in all—I have done my best and I *am* confident that my work shall endure through all the ages of man—for I have sought to communicate the *ages* of man to *men!*"

Henry's face was utterly expressionless. He was positively ghoulish but he was affirming what she was saying. His living face and all the painted faces of him, however modified, were all affirming her witness; then his real face offered a wan appreciative smile and all the "Spiritual Portraits" smiled confidently, too. My stomach was wild and my gorge was rising, as Maria went on—having risen and walked across the rug to prop her overwhelming behind upon her little desk. Her plump ringed hands described great parabolas before each breast as she spoke—firing each word it seemed like a bolt directly at me, or a stone—

"The sickness is in him now," she declared. "The sickness—but we shall overcome the sickness. We have a plan." She stepped, as she spoke, into a shaft and pool of noon sunlight, a very glory, on New Year's Eve Day. "He will stay with me until he dies, and when that comes he will be cremated"—spoke with complete authority—"and I will keep his ashes in the pot . . .

"And I will mix some of these ashes in a final painting—unless I choose to begin a series of childhood portraits—I will finally compleat the ages and vocations of Man, and I will sell it like the others, and in some ob-scure home it will hang, with Art and Life united in one matter!"

Art and Life, for the love of God!

She pirouettes and shows her garter clasps. "Life and Art united in the Mystery that brings Life out of Death, in a vision that will always transcend the Material. In *my* final painting he will be

seen in his true Spiritual Self—his earthly husk will have been shed
and only the Spiritual Body and Vocation will remain. I will call it
'The Apotheosis of Henry Smith.' I will write *his* name on the
canvas for the first and last time, and I will sell it to the highest
bidder."

She will auction Henry?

But when I turned again to the man himself he was radiant—he
was radiant and full of joy.

"I have taken impressions of his head in plaster . . . I may turn
to sculpting . . ." as she trailed off.

Yes, Henry finally became radiant and in no way related to the
strong man who had cared for the kilns and saws in Bryan all those
years. He was not the man who had lived in a rugless clapboard
house for fifty years, but it was a great face, however slightly disgusted I was.

"Boy, I know what you're thinking. Don't you believe I don't,
because I do . . ."

"Henry, you got to go home to your own daughter," I said.
"You got to go . . ."

"Boy, I'm disappointed with you. I thought you understand.
April she lets me stay down here but she don't understand what it's
been . . . I got a pain in both my head and belly and my bones are
rotten as Kinch's porch was." He looked at me hard and decided
to start to quit. "Son, you look puke pale." With something of a
gentleness.

And I guess I did. Merciful heavens, I was drunk and sick and
everything and they let me go in a little while. They both ended by
being kind to me. It was as if they grasped how hard it had all been
on me. I said I'd best get on, and no I didn't want lunch. I'd catch a
Trailways back.

"Son, you oughta stay for her food."

"Maria, I'm sure it's great, but I'd best be moving on. God love
you both."

I went over to the Acropolis bar and fondled a Greek woman
until the evening. I caught the bus back to Bryan at about 7:00 p.m.

and it took me all of New Year's Day to sober up, back in Bryan, with April and Aubrey and Helen.

They are everywhere. We all know the peculiar people all over the place. Knock on any door, as the saying goes. And my feelings about all strange people are probably related to having grown up in the home of sane people.

There has got to be some sense of order and proportion in this world. You quit wearing a tie and the next thing you know people are running naked in the streets. Get all the women in the world in pants and a fair number will end up dykes. It's a sorry state of affairs. And there's that fine old gentleman from Bryan County who'll die in the apartment with no other solace than a neurotic mistress. But probably there are worse things. I damn well know there are.

II

Mary Ann's not consistently easy in her body the way April was. Mary dances well enough and April doesn't, but April is easier (though maybe not so specialized) at almost every other move— which is a pity for me and Mary. Mary Ann can move around the rooms here in Fort Worth and seem graceful as can be in the midst of her dancer's exercises—stretch and stride, prance and glide—and also those frantic windmill motions of the arms—and that strange bending, while sitting naked on our rug, of torso down until the head's between her legs, hands behind the thrusting head—but, still, more often than not she articulates herself in an awkward, taut way. I'm considering now how she is out of bed.

Sometimes she does look comfortable flopped down in her loud chair—but, sadly, most days find the muscles across her moley back knotted—and when she's even doing something domestic like picking up a frying pan you notice how her long arm muscles stand out like a straining runner's, and her bowels are always loose at such times, and she spends hours in the shower ruining critical paperbacks she can't keep dry even with the clear plastic raincoat she throws over her wretched body, which isn't simply because of her drunk, promiscuous father and relatively staid mother, and it's not even her Catholic education did it, because Latin doesn't necessarily strap the flesh and screw up the tendons.

Her people came in here a couple of weeks ago, and she did great, as I did, for a while. It was, in fact, an almost charming encounter, for a time—initially shocking but finally charming, even graceful. Though maybe our good form resulted from long training in getting caught.

It's after supper while M. is reading in *American Renaissance* and I'm ass-deep in *Fresh-Water Biology*, John Wiley, New York, 1959—because teaching Life Science this fall at the U.P.S. has really tested me—even though I agree in theory with the idea that everybody on our faculty should have what they call mobility in the disciplines.

Anyway, we're settled in for study (I at my cypress desk, she in her Duchamp chair), both of us fully clothed in pj's, already, like a couple of Russians on a forced vacation, with the dishes done, when there comes a knock at the door.

People visit us from time to time, but I'm damned if Mary doesn't recognize her father's knock. She hopped up without her big blue book, she's on her bare feet and pressing both hands into her sides at the waist, like a woman trying to deny her pones, though of course, as a slim thing, she has no pones at all. She glances at me furtively, like possibly an *Anax junius*, the common harmless dragonfly, has appeared in our living room. She's excited—batting her dark authentic lashes—but she isn't deeply frightened.

Another knock (in fact, two quick knocks of vague authority) —and she's across our fabulous rug to let her family in.

It passed over my mind that I was glad I'd been working out recently and wasn't entirely a doughy heap. When I saw those people in our door I was relieved my fat was less, and delighted with the simple unsplit blue of my pj's, and I was glad, yea, glad, to have on my boxer trunks beneath. Rising to meet them I was just a little proud to face what might be called a semisophisticated crisis.

.   .   .

Damselflies and dragonflies mate in flight . . . there was a young man from Kent . . .

"Well, hello there." She didn't yell—MOMMY! DADDY! Though I almost wish she had. "Come in . . . come in and meet Sonny."

hot damn

———

"Sonny, these are my parents."

I say, "Hi there," nervously, while gathering up to a tall slump.

"Are we . . . ?" offers the slightly botched ex-military father.

"No, no—come on." And my dear Mary, in her slickish pink nightclothes, was positively radiant when they did come on in.

During those first desperate tender moments (to phrase it in a juicy but accurate fashion), I did gather them lovingly all together and see a family, nuclear and defeated, from the modern world, a kind I'd rarely known. But I did recognize them, and Mary was clearer in my body when I did.

Mrs. Porter was a younger and less crimped version of Helen, with the big difference being a long, vexed cigarette in her mouth, and eyes that, however mean the slits tried to get, said, "Don't cast us out. Let us in," they said. And Colonel Porter was a boozer like so many others, but, also, he was saying, with his pink eyes somewhat muffled below his coarse orange hair, to me—"My God, man, let me know who Mary is with you."

Clearly, all they had left was their girl, their one child, and whatever she'd become—which sounds pat or worse for being so pitifully true. Their daughter and I (for clearly they'd suspected she was living with somebody) were what they felt they had to get at, to gain reason; so they stepped in, filming the scene like documentary movie artists entering a room where some weighty and probably awful historical event had occurred, or was occurring, or soon would. They seemed to believe that everything would be all right if only they could, with passionate disinterest, record the scene of the conspiracy.

Thank God the place was unusually tidy and clean, even domestic. Thank God we'd taken down the blown-up fuck pictures she'd ordered from a tract published in L.A., replacing them with our standard Modiglianis and Turners and Hoppers. We'd corrected our pictures three days before, after Mary had decided, with some reservations, that I was correct in saying that the sex act couldn't be caught in static visual art.

"Momma, Sonny is my husband, even though we're not married." I wish she hadn't said that! In fact, I felt a moment of rage at her being so goddamned predictable. She has been very, very sweet for about a month—she has delivered an incredibly reticent raunchiness all over the house—and she has been attentive to little things like my needs for coffee and cookies (which I'm using instead of ben and peanut butter these days)—indeed, all of her cooking (especially the sweet and sour porky) has been extraordinary lately—and so, of course, it follows that marriage is in her mind. Some form of it. What else?

"He's big," says the Colonel, glaring, without accusation, as one might glare at a member of the Peaceable Kingdom, out of jealousy.

I say, "Ya'll come on in an' sit rite down now an' I'll fix us all toddies an' everything's gonna be just fine"—affecting fancy but nevertheless down-home Southern the way I sometimes do: Son a mixture of gentry and good ole boy: but, fuck it, it worked. They suffered to grin like tourists who find weird pictures on the walls of tombs.

The Porters settled down, the old man in my lover's chair, and Momma in the straightback at my big cypress table by the front window.

I didn't even rattle the cubes as I prepared their drinks, while listening from the kitchen to some petty shit about how we simply wanted to know how school is treating you—the degree, the Ph.D., of course—and anyway we've never seen Six Flags Over Texas before. I listened and watered the bourbons and didn't even shudder. God bless those people, I thought.

I went back in, passed the drinks around, and sat down in our Sears edition of a Danish Modern chair, fearing the mother would collapse, fearing I'd get lockjaw from the nail I'd repaired it with. I settled in and listened as they talked the talk of the tiny ruined modern family of today (friends of days past in Spokane and Formosa and El Paso)—but it was clear that the Colonel wanted words with me. He cast his puffy eyes against me like I was some obese jay who'd robbed his nest—but, for all latent hostility, he did seem to be aware he wasn't so grand himself, being as he was a type of ex-military cowbird.

"Let's shoot the bull in the kitchen," says I, casually, yet in a manner that suggests affectionate comprehension of the intricacies of the immediate situation, "while the women talk."

He's tall and thin with a little belly of sour dough—he's mostly a long, semi-erect slice of raw French fry—but finally he does muster the least suggestion of a manly shiteating grin at the cracked corners of his mouth. He says, "Yessir." Gets up and follows me around the corner to the counter by the stove and refrigerator.

Colonel Porter held his glass in his left hand, though obviously, by way of watching him open a package of Raleighs, he was essentially right-handed. I realized I had to raise that man above himself.

God bless the child!

"Cheers."

"You live with Mary Ann?"

"Of course." Which seemed exactly the right thing to say. "I'm divorced and responsible," which was a falling-off from the first response, once sounded. "I love your daughter and intend to marry her."

Fuck it!

"You must realize . . ." But he never got it said because he didn't know what it was. He looked gloomily down at his ice cream pants as if to check for raspberry stains.

"Listen, Colonel, I realize all kinds of stuff. I know that me and Mary are a shock—but if it wasn't me, some little fruity prick from school'd be here—or some animal who's a helluva lot worse than I am."

"You played with the Bulls!" A major glory afflicts his face. He's remembering I'm the football man Mary mentioned dating, in a letter.

"Correct."

"You got hurt. The arm!" With feeling.

"Right."

"Are you . . . going back?"

"Maybe."

"——" and his silence indicated a return to the sexual plight of his daughter.

"Colonel, we're really doing fine. So don't mess up a decent thing."

"Decent, huh?" He clicks his ice, but it's not a fervid clicking.

"Right. Right." Presenting the full unmodified clownish disarming smile—just as the women step up to the kitchen door.

I'm almost inclined to say I wished to bolt at this fresh sight of Mary and her mother, so stern and passive they were, standing together, inspecting, to be inspected.

Yes, they were quite a pair—Mary with her long black locks over one shoulder, and that ax face and nose I've come to love— and Mary's mother's gray hair (mostly a pepper and salt) piled up loosely on her head above a face that spoke of how she'd never got her life and faith together in the flesh (a three-pack-a-day face), a shot-down skin that lay back on the skull and said that after all the skull is where it's at and all there is, which isn't so; and it's especially sad to see a Catholic who, in spite of every effort, still doesn't have the Hope of Resurrection in the Body.

Hack around with overt rituals too much and you'll miss the point.

My goddamned Mary and her mother—and Mary *is* decent, for all the sociological and psychological bullshit she may have come on with at first. Mary had her arm around her ruined mother. She was, as usual, trying to be loving.

. . .

Lord-uh . . .

that first night I met Mary I was groping up Sandage Street outside toward my station wagon, drunk as a lord on beer, and I saw this slight creature in the light of the street lamp talking to an older woman who seemed to be some kind of Arab, at the older woman's car outside this house (it is a narrow house though sometimes I think of it as an apartment), and I say, "My dear, you're a pretty thing." And she says, "Come in and have some coffee. You need it." And I'm immediately wondering whether this broad's a common slut—except I can't go with that reading because even in a dim light I notice a face of sensitive beauty.

"Indeed I need some coffee," says I, while she gracefully dismisses whoever the woman was that brought her home from the restaurant where they're both working. I come in and drink twelve ounces of cute espresso coffee out of a tin cup I demanded instead of the fucking demitasse she offered. It's this room, although it wasn't the same then, before I moved in, bringing the cypress table and my own tastes in other things.

I come into this dark-haired woman's house, where almost at once I'm engaged in psycho-socio-economico talk about how it is that such a fine specimen is wandering the streets of Fort Worth drunk, and I tell her to cut that shit, getting tough because this crazy woman really doesn't want a man to let her go on so. I ask her to tell *me* how come *she* asks in strangers off the street—and then I tell her not to—because I'm not interested in analysis—I tell her what I want is sympathy!

I tell her I'm divorced for all intents—and run off from home and son and vocation, whatever in hell it ever was, for nothing more than thoughtless cruel murder—and how come does she ask in a double killer from off the streets? I tell her don't give me no *empathy*—lay on the *sympathy* is what I say—which does perk her off the academic line quick, though I can tell she isn't frightened, having some natural instincts after all.

Friend, that first scene in this room with Mary Ann had got to me. Friend, I never needed a nice lady more. Even near the end with April wasn't the worst because I never thought the shit would happen, and even when it did it didn't hurt much because I was so numb. That first night with Mary Ann was early in November— I'd been damn near bumming five months—N.O., Orange, Silsbee, Houston, then heading north—and I hadn't even had the courage to visit my teammates in Dallas (not even Side and Pauline), and I was very tired and lonely, and horny as a nine-balled wildcat, and here's what seems to be a clean girl, and sleek, who's obviously intelligent, in spite of all her abstract lather, and what I did want by then was sympathy and some loving to remember. So I cried.

I felt it coming so I let it happen, like when you know it's better to puke than suffer the whirleybeds all night. I did blubber some. I made almost a litany out of the AFFIDAVIT CHARGING CRIME OF MANSLAUGHTER.

Manslaughter: now there's a word to reckon with.

. . . did then and there feloniously and unlawfully while in the heat of passion, by the use of a dangerous weapon, without author-ity of law and not in necessary self-defense [it was, in fact, self-defense] *kill and slay one Raymond Magee in violation of Section 2226 of the Mississippi Code Annotated (1942 Recompiled)—all this being against the peace and dignity of the State of Mississippi.*

Which motherfucking affidavit wasn't ever even processed be-cause goddamned Davis in cahoots with Royal (I think), and both in cahoots with the D.A., decide not to—they decide it would be a far, far better thing to exile my ass, Davis saying this *freedom* we offer you does not *necessarily* mean you're beyond the reach of the law, because he (Davis) or the District Attorney, at any time here-after, or any other citizen, or anyone else for that matter (meaning probably April), may bring up the matter of said dead Foots Magee before the Grand Jury and try for an indictment, which will most surely take place if they ever see me around Byran again.

Mary really liked my story at first. At first she thought of it as exciting rather than grotesque. I rang it out as loudly as a damp bell, and I got my way with her. Or she got her way with me. At any rate, I must say it was a seminal evening for me, for I'd never known a woman to go at it so thoroughly, you might say. Mercy. It's an old story to the jaded, but it was strange news at the time to me, and disturbing.

And I don't cry often. I cried over the affidavit that never got written, and I cried over the exile that was in fact in force. And Mary's carrying on about how troubled the harsh world is instead of wordlessly pumping out that puréed breath we all admire so much. Then finally I get her into her bed and begin what seems to me a tender and competent S.O.P. screw. I'm washing along in the warm tide—I'm holding on and lying back a little to keep the loving up a while longer—and I'm especially enjoying the smells of the sheets and this girl's room in general—all that—then suddenly—she slips loose and starts a rapidfire series of questions: would I like her to do so and so and such and such? And don't forget the fracking buck lateral thingamabob. It really hurt my feelings. I felt sorry for Mary and whatever the hell in her life had made her think she had to ask.

"Sure," says I, sympathetically, "if you want to." And then I went back to crying.

She's awkward except for in the bed, and there it's all too often studied. It's an old problem in the recent world.

Enough! Enough!

I went outside and backed the station wagon down to her house. I hauled in the cypress table and my suitcases and a couple of boxes of books. She's holding the screen door open and she's saying, "This is great. This is really great!"

"We'll see," I'm saying. "We'll see."

I wanted to tell the Porters I'd been trying to do right by their daughter.

"Sonny, Mother wants to know exactly who you are." Mary speaking softly in Standard American and with no apparent fear. "Mother..."

"I'm a grammar school teacher." Which caused Colonel Porter to spew out the swallow he was taking. But I went on unruffled for the moment: "I teach at the Unitarian Progressive School, and I do a damn good job of it, sir."

"That's very nice," says Mrs. Porter, who's looking about as

comfortable as a prune in a martini. "That's your vocation then?"
In the way only a bitter but convinced Catholic woman can say it
—in a voice that's sly with every egg that will break out with the
worst shapes of malice, finally.

"For the time being."

"_____"

"He'll go back to pro ball," pronounces the Colonel.

"Don't count on it," says Mary, who's on my side, who's *at* my
side. "He's doing fine. He's got a reputation as a teacher."

We're all standing in a cramped space. We're all damn near stiff
in bestial unmotion.

"He could be a starter when Robbins retires," blurts the Colonel,
who reads the *Morning News*.

"Listen—Got damn it—my vocation is my business—and that's
not what's on your mind anyway. What's naturally on your mind
is me and Mary living here, and I don't blame you."

"You're right," says the Colonel.

"You're damn right I'm right, and you might as well play like
we *are* married—you might as well play like I'm family." I'd finally
stepped into the living room and was hawking good sense as best I
could, while knowing something was disgustingly slick about the
presentation, however true and fair it was. "Look at this place!"
says I. "Look at these goddamned rooms. Are they dirty, or ugly,
or really vicious? Hell no! Look at all these books and nice shit
we've collected together. Notice that table made by my own
father."

"It is lovely."

"Go look in the bathroom, because that's clean, too. Me and
Mary are nice people. And we'd like to love you." I quaked in my
soul—but it worked. My God did it work. For Mrs. Porter walked
over and embraced me, and I her. We hugged, as recollections of
middle women back in Nancy's Cafe in Bryan swam into my mind
like devils moving over the surface of a Dürer print. Mrs. Porter
really wanted peace of mind. She held on to me for dear life it
seemed. Then I picked her up and kissed her on a sour cheek, which
stopped her niggardly tears and made a squeezed giggle bleep out.
Then I shook the Colonel's hand. Then I volunteered to mix another
drink for everyone.

Everyone wanted a stiff drink—for we had passed the reef or bar or some barricade or another, it seemed.

"You're married then," states her father. "You're married. Jesus! Good luck!"

And things got better awhile after that. Mary and I sat together on our ersatz Persian rug and babbled repairing sentences about our lives—how we were struggling together to maintain old values of art and life, and family, within the difficult context of the modern world—which pleased the increasingly drunken Porters. I even entertained the Colonel with a few football stories, and he especially liked the one where I admitted how nervous I was in that first game with San Diego during exhibition season—nervous and frustrated—because goddamned Robbins wouldn't even show for early practice, him considering it demeaning at his age to fool around with a bunch of kid players almost young enough to be his sons—me busting ass and scoring very high on my game grade, but knowing that when Robbins showed up in two weeks my job was his, because on a football field that old coon has more moves than I ever dreamed. Morningside Robbins, my good buddy, and I hadn't even seen him for a whole year, though he and Pauline are only thirty minutes away in Dallas on this very weekend.

Shit, me and Pauline Robbins, who is a Negress from Waterloo, Iowa, had more sex by way of glances and kneerubs and tiny finger touchings than most dully lustful people will have in an entire lifetime!

I haven't even gone to a game all season. I haven't even watched one on T.V.

All while Mary is going on about how probably both of us will finally take degrees and teach at some college together, beating whatever nepotism clauses might be in force. She's saying such foolishness as that while, after a third hard hit from the Dant, I'm confessing to the Colonel that, yes, maybe next season I might re-up a contract and play again.

And Mrs. Porter got relaxed enough to speak of the wonderful historical imaginations that created Six Flags Over Texas. She and Daddy loved the boat ride.

And her father was telling a story about his admiration for
Chiang Kai-shek and how Formosa was an Asian haven for our way
of life, and how the Orient wasn't respectful of life the way we are,
which might have driven me to fruitless argument had it not been
for my sudden bewildering passion for Mary. And thank God the
Colonel was bagged—thank God the Colonel's lady herself was
tight enough to accept my foolishness as fun and something like a
crazy antic at an officer's club. Thank God Mary read the scene as
nothing more than something close to praise for her parents.

I rose to my haunches and began to hop. At the very instant I
saw the Colonel first fall drunkenly against his bride on our ratty
couch, I rose to a hunker, then, squeaking shrilly and wiggling my
nose rapidly (and speedily puckering and unpuckering my mouth),
began to hop about this miserable room. I hopped and stomped my
feet as rabbits do during their ritual dances beneath the full moon,
which cracked up all my newly acquired kin, the Colonel laughing
drunkenly so hard he drooled a little, which hurt me to see; so I
hopped over to where he was slouched, and picked him up—and
thank the Lord for the high ceilings in this old house—I picked that
surrogate daddy of mine up above my head and stomped flatfooted
at full height about the room. Hell, I even began to clog a little (in
the fashion of the noble yeomen of Tennessee) when he waved his
worried arms and tried to laugh some more. I felt his sputum fall
onto my hair, but the women didn't seem to notice; they didn't
notice or, from some terrible reason, they didn't care. All Momma
Porter did was blow out a catarrhous, coarse laugh that seemed to
relieve some minor province of her misery.

Then I put the Colonel down. Then all together we had our last
laughs of the evening.

"Wonderful. Wonderful," was hacking Mrs. Porter. "Wonderful . . . but, O.R., we've got to get back to the motel and leave these
young people to themselves."

She's thinking honeymoon.

"Yeah, hang in there, Son"—and Colonel and Mrs. Porter were
heading out the door exactly like it was 1945 and all the world's safe
for decent Western lovers to build their lives in.

"Call us tomorrow . . . the phone's in Sonny's name as of this
week. Eugene Joiner."

"Eu-gene! Thas a name," warbles the Colonel.

"We will, sweetheart," says fairly steady Mrs. Porter.

And they were gone and out the door to the front porch, leaving me and Mary finally grotesquely wed.

"Hullo, wife."

"Hullo, Dad."

We giggled and fell to loving on the floral rug.

III

It's been a type of relapse since that night with her parents—nothing but food and dull loving, mostly food, because it's what I seem to have on my mind most of the time out here in Fort Worth, even though Mary is trying to make me concentrate on loving. I can't stop eating.

I eat peanut butter. I eat it on crackers and with milk sometimes by the hours at all times of the night. Great gooey loops and curls of it on the saltines; then sloshing the sweet milk over it to get it down so it won't stick to the roof of my mouth. I put peanut butter on Wheaties for breakfast, and I eat it on hamburgers and hot dogs for lunch and dinner. I'm rejecting all of Mary's Chinese food. It's a nasty thing, worse, I think, than beating your meat, which I don't do. Jar after jar after jar of good ole Jiffy. I wish to hell sometimes I'd gotten myself a proper mistress like Henry's Maria—a real freak —instead of this normal American I'm in hell with now.

It's irresponsible. Patently irresponsible, as Mary says; and I never did this sort of thing before failing with the pros and screwing up my marriage. It's a cruel and subjective thing. It's worse than drinking and ben. But peanut butter, Christ, the way it smells and feels—that sensation in the throat. And I always stand up while doing it, which is perverse, I think.

Who keeps this house clean? I do.

Mary Ann's face is prettier than April's but otherwise she's physically shot to hell, and it's me who has had to make her bathe regularly—got her on the soap again. She's a whiz at the bed games. She says, "Would you like sixteen for a change?" Jesus! Sixteen! They'll try anything. It's fine to be intelligent and get a Ph.D. but it never hurts to sweeten the ole snatch, by God. Spends half the day in this tiny metal shower we've got, but she used to forget to soap up—the goddamned thing being just big enough for me to stand in, and then the spigot usually shoots scalding water down low into my chest hair and nipples.

Mary lets herself go down to soft, pale skin (for all her exercises, which she doesn't do regularly) and then talks to me constantly about how what this country needs is a new breed of Puritans. She says we need to shuck off our decadence and our inability to face the outside world. We need to come to grips with reality and have at it head-on. Mary Ann says we ought to return to the rigorous health of our fathers, and that, Christ, agreeing with April, I ought not to feel silly for making honorable mention on the Council of Christian Players' team—because, she says, in spite of the decline of metaphysics, there is still the bright essence of the clean vital life and the purely fleshed-out spirit to be found in some of that tradition. And it's not easy to tell her what she is.

Having been soaked in Western Civilization, everything from cave paintings in France to the Platonic Faggot Genet, she *believes* that there is what she calls a *necessary* order in history. She does not realize that mostly her teachers have avoided the temptation to get their asses into action, and therefore create a Reason to protect them from all the milk they never spilt, the piss ants, including A.B.D. Burger.

Lord God, she's ridiculous, and the worst part is that with all her education she still doesn't know how to read or write history. She worries about what she calls *tendencies* and *movements*.

Good God, I'd rather be a sheriff in a creed outworn.

Damn fool once spent an entire night of good grass smoking arguing with me about whether or not Luther was a reactionary, and trying to convince me (which she damn near did) that Martin was to blame for five hundred years of bad sex and anti-Semitism. She kept shouting, while she's slicing up a newspaper with one of my grammar school blunt scissors to make a goddamned Chinese flower, that Martin was *medieval* and that though the church was corrupt he was a worse corrupter. No, what she said was that Martin was *stupid*. She's still an Irish Catholic.

Bull he was, and he had himself a blunt face—look at the portrait by Lucas Cranach the Elder—but his mouth was sensitive, and often his mind was clean.

Martin wanted salvation and thought he'd got it there in the Greek word *metanoia:* change of heart. He had faith that he had experienced a true change of heart, and he had to have such confidence as that, and when he came back from his exile in Wartburg with his full head of hair and his beard, he did have that faith. So what the fuck if he didn't understand the humanist intellectuals, what if he really didn't, for a long time, understand church politics. His name be praised (I agree now with you, Burger)—Martin just knew that his faith must clean the Church of all its lies and foolishness. Mary should love him.

God love the Abstractionists, but they must learn that history can't be written backwards from Bergen-Belsen.

You got to love Martin when he says—*After I had pondered the problem for days and nights, God took pity on me and I saw the inner connection between the two phrases, "The justice of God is revealed in the Gospel" and "The just shall live by faith"*—saw the connection, saw the connection. Let the Reformed Church be damned. Let the Catholic Church be damned. Give me Martin and St. Thomas, The Great Ox himself.

Luther entering Worms in a Saxon cart, goddamn it, was just like Vardaman (don't quote me) entering Kosciusko, Mississippi, in his ox-drawn wagon, the White Chief himself. Both great men—and I'm no racist like Vardaman got to be, and finally I'm no killer-German like Luther, but I do know they were neither of them actually looking frontwards or backwards when they did what they did. They were being themselves, right now, and that's all a man can do.

．　．　．

But God damn him, Luther *did* turn on Müntzer's total revolution—he did finally stand with the nobles as Mary will in time. And he did write these pitiful words that I recite: *Thus it may be that one who is killed fighting on the ruler's side may be a true martyr in the eyes of God, if he fights with such a conscience as I have just described, for he is in God's word and is obedient to Him. On the other hand, one who perishes on the peasants' side is an eternal brand of hell, for he bears the sword against God's word and is disobedient to Him.* And the clincher is the beauty I've mentioned above: *Strange times, these, when a prince can win heaven with bloodshed, better than other men with prayer!*

See Müntzer and his squat, stinking peasants behind their wagons at Frankenhausen. Poor blind fuckers—blind as Brueghel's blind men tripping and falling down the path into the slough. No more hard-ons in the codpieces, and no more turns of the kermess—no more drunks, and then once dead they're off like a shot to flaming hell. I wouldn't have that for either Billy or Foots. And it do seem strange that Luther'd send Foots Magee to Paradise, while consigning Dolman and Jubal and Rosey to eternal fire.

Whooeee—here come Foots Magee through the gates of fucking Heaven— *Hey, man, where's my cheese sandwich?*

Strange times.

I'll write April and Royal and Davis and my people one more time before I die of peanut butter. I'll bless them all, for they need my love.

But Mary does manage to get up and go teach her classes, and take her classes, and she does get all her papers written on time, which is rare enough among graduate students (with me doing a lot of the reading for her, making sure she gets in the details with the theory shit): she's doing a paper on "The Image of Eucharist in Medieval European Literature," and she is brilliant, writes a hundred pages in three days and knocks out the prof's eyes, but even in such a fine effort she forgot to mention the Bohemian Taborites and the great statement by the loveliest Martin of all (not Luther, for I am now speaking of the chiliast), Martin the Chiliast's beautiful vision of heaven. Dante being a morbid slug compared to Martin the happy Chiliast—*these elect still living will be brought back to the state of innocence of Adam in Paradise, like Enoch and Elizah, and they will be without any hunger or thirst, or any other spiritual or physical pain* [notice the following sturdy prose]—*and in holy marriage and with immaculate marriage bed they will carnally generate sons and grandchildren here on earth and on the mountains, without pain or trouble, and without any original sin.* On the mountains and near unto the bayous and creeks, on diamonds and beneath goal posts. *Then there will be no need of baptism with water because they will be baptised in the Holy Spirit, nor will there be the tangible sacrament of the holy Eucharist, because they will be fed in a new angelic mode—not in memory of Christ's passion, but of his victory.*

She left that out. She's a nice girl but she doesn't understand that Martin Hüska is more important than Luther, *or* Martin of Tours. She thinks she's far out but still she reads *official* history. And notice how my Martin has a proper respect for food.

Dear April, Royal, Stream, Bobo, Davis, Miss Gresham, Polly, Coaches Morgan and Topp, and Foots and Billy, and Slater and Ju and runty Cantrell—etc.—may the grace of the almighty Father, or heavenly God, be granted to you, that it may be faithfully received by you, as befits saints. Let us be very vigilant, for we do not know what hour the third angel will blow his trumpet—

And at once the sun will blaze, the clouds will disappear, the darkness will vanish, blood will flow from wood, and he will reign who is not expected by those living on earth. Therefore let us be ready for the Lord's coming, that we may go with him to the wedding. And who is ready? Only he who remains in Christ and Christ in him. And he is in Christ who eats him. But to eat Christ's body is livingly to believe in him [livingly, the man said], *and to drink his blood is to shed it with him for his Father. And he takes Christ's body who disseminates his gifts, and he eats his body who livingly listens to his word. And in this way we shall all be Christ's body.*

And through this eating the just will shine like sun in the kingdom of their Father, when he comes in clouds with his glory and great power, and send as representatives his glorious angels to sweep out all scandals from his inheritance.

"Son, that's not *imaginative* literature. It's not what this paper's about."

"What the hell's your definition of *imaginative?*"

"Those people never produced a great *artist.*"

"The Bohemians never produced an artist? You, baby, have a goddamned puny definition of art. God damn, an anthology of tracts makes better reading than 80 percent of your belles-fucking-letters. The whole goddamned education process ought to be over-hauled."

"Do it, Son, do it!" And what she suggests isn't offered in sarcasm either. She sits across the room here in the big wicker rocker I bought the other day and looks at me with hate and hope and admiration—she desires for me to rise—she dreams of a time when I'll be slim and able to create syndicalist grammar schools of my own. She sits in her jeans and blue work shirt, and dreams of when I'll head H.E.W., and she doesn't know the difference between syndicalist grammar schools and H.E.W.

She can't understand how I can start a revolution in Bryan and yet desire her to be dressed in black wool and delicate lace. The poor benighted girl doesn't believe that syndicalism is consistent with lace and black wool.

I told her she sure as hell must have more than those five cotton dresses she teaches and goes to school in, huh? Shapeless mothers that make her look half knocked-up. She's making tuna and peanut butter sandwiches out of a can, having learned my worst habits, and she looks at me like I just said a very nasty thing.

"Goddamn, Mary, I know that any girl from El Paso and Formosa has got herself some pretty clothes somewheres. I BE-LIEVE that in your trunk there, where I have never pried, is secret garb not yet set on by my eyes. It's wool and black and it's tight at the waist and gathered a little beneath the bust—it's got a high collar and has got yards in the full skirt, yards and yards—and beneath that fine dress lies a lace bib, very high collared and with delicate fluting for your pretty neck—and also hidden I'll find subtle attachable cuffs for your tiny wrists—lace that will leap from the black collar and sleeves—black dominant but set against stark, austere, bone white." I told her I knew it was there, and the fact I'd guessed right visibly moved her.

She's a tall very thin lady with dark hair, a hipless woman she is, with moley dark skin the least bit papery, but still pretty unless she parches it in the wind or boils it in water.

She put down the fish, washed her hands under the tap (no soap), and walked to the ancient trunk where there was in fact exactly what I had described, except that the bib and cuffs were on top the dress—and she had silk underthings, which I suspected but failed to mention in my prophecy. She opened the hump-backed trunk and dug down to where it all was, and she did seem to smile with pleasure to have me find her out.

"Son, how'd you know?"

"Because your daddy's a soldier and your mother's from Roanoke, originally." I was a peafowl, male, in ardor. "I want to dress you in these things."

She says that's fine. Do what you can. But there's a shrill glint in the corner of her right eye.

"If you'll let me dress you in those beautiful clothes I'll get back at it and lose down to a trim 235 pounds. And I'll get a Ph.D. and I'll seize power for both of us."

It was an inspired moment, to say the least.

I admonish you in the name of God, to make this letter known to the whole community.

· · ·

She is a pretty thing, with a face so strict you could slice butter on her nose, and a large mouth that does not overwhelm her strong chin, which mouth is mean at the edges and ripe in the middle. She's half Jew and half Celt, Momma putting the sensual edge on, Daddy the rage for order, the combination creating the afflictions of abstractions and the dim skin that tends to dry quickly. But the night of which I speak was rare—she'd inadvertently used my Palmolive soap (for at source I'm a conservative) that morning, so when I peeled her from said jeans she was, yes, glossy as the fracking Mother of God, her pale flanks smooth as piano keys. Her legs tend to break out in a rash when she's nervous, but mostly this had not been a nervous day at all. She was unblemished, relatively speaking.

I bathed her again allover with the Palmolive, and she was lax throughout, a sullen lovely girl, but I did feel as if I might be condescending a little.

Consider the towel, consider the Great American Cannon Towel, a fresh one, fluffy almost as a poodle bitch. I dried her lovingly with such a towel, and then returned to the trunk. I dug down in the locker and found the perfect slip, that would show lace, to complete her costume—and when she stood there with the perfect panties and bib and slip on, I began to pull black wool over all of it, and I was amazed at the transformation.

"You're a fool," she said. But I let that pass, I was so happy.

"Let me brush your hair a hundred times."

Please, you can trust a man who begs, and for a time I really thought I was gone from April as I gently scrubbed and tugged at her long skeins, with the brush of simulated pearl I've recently bought for her.

And when she went clear to the bottom of the trunk, bending, showing also the lace slip I'd lately hung on her, she found the black heels that made it all indeed sublime.

No stockings. Jesus! No stockings, no clasps. "Screw that," she said. "I'll be uncomfortable enough as it is."

She was a goddamned grown and elegant lady that I could love while struggling at any barricade. She was shut of plain clothes and the silly, makeshift culture of workers' clothes on a middle-class girl.

"I feel a little guilty in these."

"That's *dumb*," I said, admiring her as I would have a picture I had painted, or a riot I had started.

"And what now? Now that you've made me a debutante again. Now that you've taken my mind away." She shivered in her clothes to settle them. She sprayed herself with deodorant to take the smell of mothballs off.

Mary Ann is a kind and generous woman, and she makes me feel protective, but when you get right down to it, we're like two dogs, an old hound and a wormy bitch. It's Fort Worth, a dry city with scrawny trees, and she'll get her Ph.D., and I've got a fairly good job now teaching my children that—*Leroy, the whale ain't no fish, boy!* It's not enough to make a life of.

Fort Worth, whatever the distance in miles to Dallas, is still a long way from The NFL, and also from the quiet breakfasts in Bryan, at Helen's. It's not the crisp sheets and the little baby crying in the evening. Mary Ann, rightfully, says it's wrong for me to go on thinking this way—but sometimes I'd give a hand or a whole arm just to find one of Aubrey's diapers in the toilet.

Mary Ann says that most of my past was an indulgence in childishness and that both of us must have faith in the capacity of the human organism to mature and redeem itself. She says she knows she's not much better than I am, and she wants us both to fight our way back. And that's a nice idea maybe, but the truest thing is that Mary Ann and I met in a *street*, not at the World Champion Tobacco Spit, which Spit ain't ezakly the Garden of Eden, but it was considerably better than the misery and drunkenness I met Mary Ann in. And she's stupid about football—she doesn't even suspect how grand it can be—like my first game against the Giants, when, in fact, I did feel that maybe I *was* part of some lean new breed of American men, which, after training and exhibition season, took some extreme imagining. For a few minutes I thought I was quick enough. With Clarkson out from a groin injury, and with Marabonito temporarily stunned, I went in on defense and blocked a field goal: a field goal *attempt*.

And that's rare as hens' teeth in The League, or any league for that matter. I'm lined up at left defensive end and the blue shirts across from me are a goddamned blur. I'm lucky as hell because when I jam across I catch a good handful of jersey and some shoulder pads—I yank to the outside and without breaking stride I'm in the lane. I drove into the lane and jumped high. I got way up there, like a goddamned Dodo bird that hadn't learned humility or good sense or even the elemental rules of flight, but I deflected the ball. It was better than the time I busted that smart D'Lo quarterback for Royal Carle—and they got a picture of it that was picked up by the wire services and printed in hundreds of newspapers. Lord, what a picture it is. There's four of us Bulls going high in the air for the ball, all of us rising out of a pile of Giants, and me the one out front, the highest Bull, and the ball is shown just as it touches the tips of the fingers of my outstretched hand—with me turned just enough so you can make out my number.

It was nominated for Sports Picture of the Year—all of us suspended up in the air in the bright haze of the stadium lights. It's a kind of halo effect, and somebody said it looked a lot like the Marines in that famous picture of the flag-raising on Iwo Jima. I've still got it framed and up in our bedroom here in Fort Worth, but Mary Ann, who lacks insight, has taped this little card about the size of a postage stamp onto the bottom of the frame. In almost unreadable script it says: *Hail to thee, blithe spirit!/Bird thou never wert.*

My favorite by Mr. Shelley is his "Hate-song":

> *A Hater he came and sat by a ditch,*
> *And he took an old cracked lute;*
> *And he sang a song that was more than a screech*
> *Gainst a woman that was a brute.*

.   .   .

Trouble was I wasn't a *defensive* tackle; I was an *offensive* tackle, and they had no plans to change my position, blocked kick or no, since blocking kicks is most often a fluke, and anyway being on the offensive team is more prestigious than being on the defensive team. It was a confused and awkward event in spite of the praise that came my way. It was nice to have Clarkson and Robbins praising me in the locker room. It was great to have those big spades dancing around me and flapping their arms in imitation of a condor's flight, and I also enjoyed the free beers. And the *News* said: *Joiner's performance is an auspicious arrival:* which is pretty fancy stuff for a rookie.

Trouble is there aren't any great pictures showing me driving over somebody on a quickie block, and there aren't any pictures that show me leading interference for Sam Campion as he cuts up-field on one of his famous runs. I did O.K. on offense, but when all the ballots are in, I'm just another tackle who got hurt and didn't last out a whole year in The NFL.

There's just one picture of me barely staving off the herculean charge of St. Claire Granville, who has damn near pushed me on top of our passer; and for some reason I don't remember I've got this peculiar smile on my face in that picture. It's an ambiguous look one might get on finding one's twelve-year-old making out in the bushes with the widow next door. The other Bulls saw it in the paper and were so amused by it that they put it up on the bulletin board in the locker room. They were so tickled they drew a red circle, and put a caption toward the bottom of the picture in bold print: WHAT'S JOINER SMILING ABOUT?

I was an easy mark because I'm large and because I was so goddamned painfully quiet at training camp—but mostly because I was neither greatly bad or terribly good—I was a competent football player. Here lies S. Joiner. He was a competent tackle all his life. I came in second or third among the linemen on the forty-yard sprints, but on the agility drills I didn't shine—I was strong enough, but I didn't react perfectly to defensive variations such as the rare angles the ends crashing might use.

IV

I couldn't even enjoy April when things got insufficient in The League, and I knew she couldn't really be enjoying it completely either. I couldn't take much pleasure in her cooking and I couldn't take much pleasure in her body, even though there is that special wonder in humping a pregnant woman—the knees and elbows trick, and how finally you start working at greater and greater clockwise angles, moving from twelve o'clock to damn near five, as time goes by and the baby grows. No real pleasure though I tried to be as appreciative as possible.

Pro ball. I saw the folly and the glory of the cripples and the gods—angels and demons and workmen, like on the buttresses of the Cathedral of St. John's at Hertogenbosch, in Flanders, which creatures may be the most wonderful and sad works of art in all the world, or at least they were to me, that partial season with the Bulls. At Hertogenbosch those damn near lifesize fuckers sit astraddle their benches which are flying buttresses, great stone arches that rise to support the skin of that lovely pile—a sorrowful beast who's obviously reading a dirty book stares away toward the roof and the sky—a bland but certainly competent stone mason with a winsome smile continues to hammer forever—then juxtaposed to the gentle workman is another demon whose paws seem more vegetable than animal (they seem, in the picture, like rotted stone cabbages)—and finally there is a carpenter who contemplates a nail and some kind of medieval measuring rod, while dedicating all his work to the Majesty and Power of the One Holy and Terrible God. All of them carved long ago, then left in line astraddle their buttresses, to be seen from afar, high on those slopes, and they were probably never meant to be looked at closely by anyone save God.

And a beautifully postured angel with flowing stone garments on stares levelly away from the corner of the roof.

. . .

It may be corny, but in Dallas, once we're toward the end of exhibition season and can stay with our wives again, I'd spend many hours in the tub soaking my bruises and looking at the art books I'd borrowed from Momma. I'd doze in the warm water— and in those days I never thought of *Procambarus blanderingi* or *Procambarus clarki*—I'd doze and listen to the sounds of April pottering around and fixing up our new apartment, doze and dream of me and Robbins and Mojack and Clarkson and Coley Sellers and Bill Wallick as Breughel's blind men staggering toward the slough —or I'd see us all with lopped unnatural limbs and toothless moron faces, dragging around on homemade crutches, like in *The Cripples*. But they weren't nightmare dreams—they were mostly ambiguous and somewhat proud dreams that suggested endurance and simple dignity. Skittering and blubbering and crawling around in the sparse grass and dirt, we were all finally in this dream transformed into the several hounds that follow Breughel's hunters down the snowy hillside home. Which is a relatively serious fancy for a meathead in a tub in Dallas, Texas.

But one dream was bad, no doubt about it, and it damn near frightened April as much as me. It happened about the second Sunday we're in Dallas, and after I've had a pretty fair game in exhibition against Cleveland (which we lost), Side praising me for good moves on my pass blocks, on Saturday night—but on Sunday I drank some booze and even popped a little white mother I hadn't used for the game, and things got not so fine, quickly. I even shit a little blood before getting in the tub.

Zonked a little and bone sore and drinking—I'd set the tumbler on the tub ledge—I came on something grim. It was that incredible *Isenheim Altarpiece* by ole Nit Grünewald. I'd played over it be- fore. I'd studied that wonderfully dead Jesus, that greenish clab- bered somitch with his arms pulled out of the sockets (probably a just reward for too many arm tackles), before. And I'd always thought St. Anthony's devils in the left-hand panel were pretty great, though not finally up to Bosch or Dürer. Nit's O.K.—a true feast of action and detail work and extraordinary color—but he'd never bothered me before.

And the one part of that altarpiece that had never even appealed to me was the Resurrection picture, which was probably because the Risen Jesus is just a little bit too ostentatious and mannered and zany. He's jumped up out of the tomb with perfectly articulated winding sheets strung out below and behind, and the halo he's flying in looks like the apotheosis of Magee's Good Gulf sign, and his face is wholesome and smug as an eighteen-year-old Dutch center's, and he's holding up his arms and hands like a faggot official proclaiming the ultimate Platonic Touchdown: or Takeoff. I know my Redeemer liveth, but I hope to heaven he don't look like *that*.

Also, the soldier in the foreground at the bottom is too self-conscious about his anatomy—and the second foreground soldier looks like he's hunkered down to take a dump.

None of it did much for me until that afternoon when I fixed on the third soldier in the picture, the one who's toward the rear of the Resurrection picture. In the print of the whole panel (and it covers most of a page), he too, seems nothing but mannered—though that big-assed rock that hangs in the air over him does make his position precarious—he looks positively uninteresting until you turn the page and look at the big *detail* that features only him—the background soldier—in Momma's book.

Nit's probably just fucking around with perspective and fore-shortening or something—he probably never thought much about that figure—but what it did to me was terrible. The clothing and the armor, and especially the elbow and knee guards, are done with wonderful strength and fluidity, like he lined it out and stroked it off in a precise hurry. The light on the almost quilted cloth of the humped back is stark against the black background, but the soldier's left arm is too relaxed and the hand is too graceful—there's almost something confectionary about them—especially the left hand holding a black sword too casually between thumb and first finger.

It's the heavy head and light legs that wrecked me in that dream, when I began to doze and sink, out of confusion.

That soldier lunging forward at the Resurrection seems at first the emblem of a perfect drive block—for we are told that the correct way is to drive your head into the soft part, as if to impale the bastard, then pick him up, ideally, like a baby piked and waved in triumph.

The light on the helmet is perfect. It's bright enough to call attention to the head, to make it look like a Valkyrie's titty, and also there's this luminous and vaguely disturbing disc that sticks off the backside of the helmet, which I don't discern the function of. It's the helmet plus the legs that bring on the horrors, because, my friend, those legs have lost control: or never had it: they're almost muscleless, and they *are* boneless. And, sweet Christ, the delicate slippers of the soldier hardly touch the ground at all. All the weight is up front in the head and shoulders of that *detail*—that poor cocksucker is just about to crash down clatterandbang on his unseen terrified face, and when he tries to get up he won't have any legs to stand on. They'll be flabby as balloons or gone entirely. They'll have been wiped away like something insubstantial as cotton candy. He'll damn near be a basket case. His pretty slippers are not touching the ground, are not dug in, and in my bickering, sore, and chemical sleep I screamed—cried out—howled and rose like a drenched weeping whale—THIS IS HELL—then slipped down onto my ass, damn near splitting my tailbone in the fall, while April was rushing in to comfort me. I wallowed and floundered in that big tub, but the worst thing I finally saw that day was fear and disgust in my wife's eyes. So I fished Nit out of the murky water, climbed out, and tried to make myself useful around the house.

April did enjoy the other players' wives. She did love to sit with that fine group of women at the home games in Dallas. She's not exactly what you'd call a stick-out in every group of women, and especially not when they're seated, but coming down the aisle to take her place in a box at the Cotton Bowl, moving like a pregnant giraffe, she's the one you'd focus on.

She can go a long time with minor troubles so long as she's busy and has nice friends to talk to.

Our apartment in Dallas was pretty classy, and she did enjoy the other couples who lived around us. Especially the niggers. It was one of those stockade jobbies with the swimming pool down in the middle of the drill yard. Tuscany Plaza is what you might call a banal and energetic community of tentatively successful young marrieds, for the most part, because there are very few lascivious fornicating singles in the compound. And Pauline and Morningside Robbins were right next door to lend the place some genuine maturity.

Fucking Coley Sellers had once been the greatest junior college guard ever, at Kilgore (which is also famous for its Rangerettes), where he starred in the Little Rose Bowl two years in a row—and at Texas A&M he'd been consensus All-America both years—and he'd been All-NFL four times (every goddamned sports coat he ever put on had his All-NFL pin in the lapel)—but by the time I saw him coming into the dressing room in San Diego he was a tooth hanger on an expansion club, and he could hardly walk: him being surely the source of my terrors, later, over Nit's picture, though often as not that kind of reduction is futile.

Coley Sellers was (is) a cripple. He still had a powerful build in the arms and upper body, but he actually had to walk on the outside edges of his feet, and the sides of both knees were zippered with scars. *He can't possibly still play this game.*

But Robbins, the great spade tackle I was understudy to, when he finally condescended to show for practice in San Diego, shed his garters and *Esquire*-type stockings, and predicted that Coley would make this ball club one more time, because we weren't exactly the Green Bay Packers or the Chicago Bears.

That poor bastard is a cripple.

Robbins loosed his $11.50 "Kipper" tie, placed his flashy black hustler's 6–8 flats compulsively next to each other in his locker, then pondered my question about Coley. He whispered that Coley couldn't walk so good since all the operations but that he could still run pretty well—he said Coley still was quick and had damn good lateral movements. He ain't so good as Mojack, who's also old, over across the room with his Catholic medal around his neck, but he'll make the team. He won't get cut unless he's hurt bad again. Sellers is no longer the best at rushing a passer, but you don't run over him, and he needs the money—"Sonny, maybe you better worry about yourself the next coupla weeks. Coley be all right. Coley's a good football player." Which chilled my blood. *He can't walk so good but he can still run.* I'd heard that's possible, but until I watched Coley Sellers on a football field I never believed it. He waddles bowlegged around the locker room and in the dining hall, at San Diego State, in his Bermudas, and he makes me get up on the trestle table and sing "Dixie" at the top of my lungs (Side bellowing with glee), but on the field, on defense, at end or tackle, Coley can still embarrass you. He can actually outsmart the best there is, namely Morningside Robbins, by yelling in his face.

Under the dry California sun it's a fairly short scrimmage, and Coley goes BLAAAH in Side's face, and waves his hands frantically before the great Negro tackle's muddy eyes. BLAAAH-YIP-YIP— two times he does it (two different plays in a scrimmage Side probably didn't have to be in to get a job), maybe five, and before the afternoon's over, Coley's made a gathering of rather impressive personal tackles, having discombobulated Mr. Robbins, to the amusement of all attending, including me. Which is enough to satisfy the management that old Sellers is still a valuable cog and factor and necessary to the Bulls' inevitable unsuccess. Coley on all fronts was proving himself to be indispensable—*Make Yourself Indispensable*—which is the motto of some Italian family or another —and, sirs, indispensability is goddamned well a prime virtue in any line of work at any period of history. Coley's come to be a vile man—but his union of wit and residual physical talent must be respected. He knows how to keep a job.

Coley's a thickening, weathered mother pushing forty, an actual cripple when he's sorely walking to the pisser late at night. In fact, when he thinks he's unwatched, he lets his ankles turn in, and his feet go scooting along the tiles like sad pontoons of skin. But on the field he'd make himself forget his tortured ankles and knees—he'd rise up upon the balls of his feet—his ankles and knees braced and taped—and sprint almost like a boy. He was very fucking fast on the forty-yard dashes. And he did have great power in his arms and hands. Shit, he'd jam your head off if the officials got lazy and quit watching the action carefully.

Coach Poteet, while watching Coley run plays in sweats one

day, said—*Coley's remembered everything he ever learned about this game.* Coach Poteet is concerned overall with the defensive unit and is recognized as the most brilliant writer (scholar actually) in The League, because he's best at watching other teams on film and prepares the best *book*—Fucking-A—Poteet is a potty high-I.Q.-type, with a rare, complex sensibility, who never tires of watching football flicks. I've stood in the dorm hall and watched him take notes from the game movies of our opponents, Poteet working that plunger up and down, running the plays back and forth, and I swear to God that after two observations of a play he can tell you what all twenty-two players are doing. God damn! Poteet could have been a full professor of calculus at anybody's university. *He is a great student of the game*—which is to me the highest praise I can pay any man about anything. He was middling-good linebacker with Georgia Tech in the late forties, and he was by God Bill Wallick's coach when Wallick was with the Rams, which was an intersection of mind and body the like of which probably won't come again in our time. Poteet: *Look at him!* [speaking of Coley] *He's doing drill—but he's thinking how it'll be in the game. Sonny, he's good. He's a good football player.*

Nobody knows how to look at anything any more.

SING DIXIE YOU BIG SONOFABITCH—AN' DANCE SOME. Me on the table and making a fool—*up in the morning and out on the job*—in San Diego at training camp. MISS-SIPPI WAAT—WHAT'S THAT SCHOOL YOU GO TO, BOY? Coley ain't no nigger, but he's after making me one for condescending to him, he thinks. He'd noticed how I looked with pity on him —an' what you're *supposed* to do is smile broadly *always* when Mr. Coley he come around—you spose to make a big joke with Mr. Coley—tell a pussy story or tease a trainer—'cause everybody knows or else *should* know that Mr. Coley is old and tough, and cripple, and mean, an' he was great once, too.

Fuckin' Coley loved to set off cherry bombs right outside the dorm windows late at night—and often as not beneath some nigger rookies' room—and everybody thought that shit was cute. Even dapper Robbins tolerated that goddamned Texas peasant, Coley.

It's a kind of ritual to make some rookies (the secure ones) perform on the night of the first cutdown, or maybe it was the next night, and I didn't mind giving that silly Ole Miss yell, "Hoddy Toddy"—hell, he might of made me "Call the Hogs" the way they do in Arkansas—but what I did mind was Coley's attitude. He treated rookie nigger flankers better than he treated me, making them sing no more than a couple of blues songs, which they enjoyed.

Coach Poteet and Coach Sepoy, who's in charge of the offensive line, they knew I'd been doing a piece of work on Coley—they knew that's why he abused me. And he wasn't done with me yet.

He made me eat ground beef raw one night, with nothing but pepper and salt on it, which was abuse. I got lightheaded with pure rage in my body, and I looked on Coley with eyes to kill him. I hate that rat-raping, whore-hopping, motherfucking, shit-eating sunnavabitch, in spite of him being, around the camp, the harlequin of the front four. He's a depraved, worthless, four-times-married redneck football bum, and I hope he ends his days jabbing at dead rubbers with a litter stick, in Gary, Indiana.

It got very quiet at the table that night in San Diego, very quiet indeed, when Coley Sellers shoved that plate of raw meat across the table and said eat it. "Put a little pepper an' salt on it, an' eat it." Pig eyes, pig mouth talking.

Don't pray over it too long, Son—that's nigger buddy Side talking. He's sitting directly to my left in the refectory, and he knows this shit is purest abuse. *Do what Coley says.* So I did, slowly, playing like I relished that raw ground round.

"You a mean dude," says Coley, grinning from across the trestle table. "You such a mean dude I shoulda got T-bone." There were some titters up and down the table, but not many. The others knew damn well this was unusual treatment. They could tell that Side (who actually had a lot more power with that crowd than Coley) wasn't entirely pleased with such treatment of his understudy. And good Coach Poteet—he didn't dig it too much either—because I saw him wink at me from across the room. It's a hang-in-there wink. I chewed and chewed and tried to remain calm about it.

"Thank you, Mr. Coley." I ate it, making the rest of the meal a problem for everybody else to concentrate on, and I went to our meeting that night and sat through the Ram movies studiously, taking copious notes on my legal pad that's attached to my old clipboard. I didn't puke until late in the night, after I'd slipped out of our room and gone down to the head for the old finger trick. Then when I'm up and washing my mouth out under the tap, I hear a shuffling coming through the door. Yeah, Coley, who has got a bad bladder so much sometimes you suspect his leg sweat while working out or playing really isn't sweat at all.

"Hey, Coley, I just puked your goddamned hamburger."

"Yeah . . ." But he wasn't concentrating one iota. He's shivering as he hustled to the trough. "Les you an' me go inta town an' give some woman a dose . . ."

"We got to hit tomorrow," says I.

"Fuck hit." He's shaking his dick almost angrily. "Common. Les go givem a dose." His ruined almost Charles Laughton-type face is squinching and unsquinching like a muscle in a spasm. "The girl in the cafeteria she wants our ass."

"Goddamn, Coley, it's too late at night."

"Fuck late." And I was putting the old man down without meaning to. But I couldn't figure anything else. I had a pregnant wife at home who I'd done enough bad to, already. I couldn't do right by Coley. There was no way. "Les go sneak inta the park an' ride some rides! Yeah!" He's getting animated as hell. He's up on his toes and swinging his huge arms around. "The Tilt-A-Whirl! I done it before. Won't do no fucking harm to sneak in an' ride." *Coley wants to take a midnight ride beside the pounding surf— which would be a proper dose.* "Son, I snuck in once in Chicago an' rode the Ferris wheel a long time—and they came out and took pictures. That was fun. I really had a good time." He's back down flat on his feet and he's definitely looking pissed-off. "No fun at all?" and he looked at me like maybe I'll have to eat some more ground round before I get some sense. *And what's wrong with the bumper cars or maybe even the roller coaster and people come to take pictures of it—maybe a fine but probably not:* I was afraid to. I suffered a failure of the imagination. And then he slides away and out the door, leaving me primed to hurt him. I still tasted blood and bile in my mouth.

Back in the room I notice how Side is sleeping, his *Changing Times*, that Kiplinger magazine, fallen out of his hand, and how his reading light is still on, and I realize this nigger's as old as Sellers but still in his prime, because he's moderate and has a good wife.

Coley got his dose the next day. I chose to be offsides. On the call of *down* I fired out at Coley's head and neck before he was completely ready—exploded in his sorry face and jammed the great Coley Sellers backwards until he collapsed, and then I churned over his body, driving hard with the cleats, and made the funnyman bleed. Which makes the funnyman want to fight.

YOU HAD IT COMIN' COLEY—says Side—who'd rushed onto the field to stanch the troubles. Me and Coley, after exchanging a few obscenities, shook hands, but we were never friends. Morningside Robbins.

V

You can't trust these educated women. *What was April?* Contrary to obtuse opinions, they are easily attracted to a regular fellow who sells State Farm out of Hernando (which is close enough to Memphis for culture) but votes National Democratic and takes them to the Coast a lot, buying pink champagne and mellow, mellow wine to get them loose and carnal, and praising them for selfless devotion to their own children and in various charitable causes for the old, the blind, the deaf, the halt, the maimed—of all colors, races, and creeds—and for niggers and necks in general. Also, and contrary to what you might believe, they do love to capture a semi-educated meathead whose overall body they profoundly crave but can't find the spirit to put out for with thoroughgoing gusto until it's too late

—meaning not until the fleshy bastard has gone to pones, a soft dick, and a bad heart before he's forty.

String it out, raise a little hell along the way, or, worst, really proliferate the mental images, and they go flap crazy.

I did bathe her again (which, curiously, seemed to please the girl—especially the lathering of the teats, the belly button, and snatch)—but I did brush her hair and dress her up. I even took the car down and had it washed and vacuumed (which she couldn't have cared less about) before the party. Just because I get carried away a little with her academic friends she runs off again, leaves, and maybe for good this time, though her stuff's still here. I spanked her once, but she had it coming.

Pretty, pretty, pretty. Hit, hit, hit! It's December, early, a perfect chill in the dry night air, and she was lovely to look at as we rode over to her teacher's house. But she didn't like it: being lovely. She kept hitching around on our car seat to show how uncomfortable she was in her old garments. She never answered once when I'd compliment her at almost every traffic light.

You're a beauty, Mary.

So we both had something of an edge on when we got to the Roses'. He's a Jewish medievalist and is having with his wife a gathering for a fairly select group of students, but I refuse to describe the tasteful rooms it went on in.

It's one of those deals with Manhattans and lots of Scotch, the whole thing swiftly breaking into something like five groups of about three each, and all these good students are hot to dump on ole Lyndon as soon as possible—to get the evening going on a guaranteed common and agreeable theme—which activity is human and predictable enough—them being youthful intellectuals mostly from Texas, Arkansas, and New Mexico (the disloyal shits)— though a couple did say the President's Civil Rights legislation is

O.K.—this insight, however fleeting, showing some evidence of complexity and variety and tolerance in their considerations.

Mary shambles and slouches in, for she absolutely refuses to carry herself correctly. I've told her it don't look good to stoop so, allowing the breasts to come together, to join almost like they're Siamese twins or bugged and crossed eyeballs—but still, because she has such sweet garb on, she receives high praise from everyone including the Roses. Which praise for her appearance she dismisses with a modest curse or two, and a mildly sarcastic curtsy.

She'd promised not to curse too much, agreeing that *damns* and *hells* would be sufficient punctuation, and that *piss* at the outside would be the extreme. Momma says P-us when she gets a color off completely, or when R.S. moves while modeling; it's slightly like Maria and Henry (I'm quite aware), but not much. Momma's mostly rough Constable or Church, while Maria's very crude Gauguin.

Mary Ann's not overdressed for one of these occasions. In fact, it's plain she has probably been underdressed for most of these occasions before. The women were all turned out very nicely and in no way was I out of place to have on a sullen tie with the Harris Tweed I'd ordered from Sears. It's clear to me she's always been too plain with these people.

Elliptio crassidens—Anondonta grandis—Pisidium dubium.

Rose is a slightly tight-assed, trim guy with a Vandyke-type beard and what appears to be a wen high on his pale pate, but his wife is a beauty out of mind whose titties are bunched up under some kind of Long Empire dress that shows damn near everything topside. She's the one who settled in with me on the couch after the first few drinks and the introductions that convince me Mary has talked behind my back and set me up as some kind of Trotsky of the interior line. These bleak unsatisfied students are interested in my *opinions*. But screw that!—because all I wanted to do was get a buzz on and watch my girlfriend being happy and graceful and confident. I had every intention of *not* talking—easing off to the built-in couch with Mrs. Rose who sits gracefully upright but lets me slump in peace—and by God she is genuinely pleased I work for the U.P.S., and she don't ask if I'm going back to pro ball. Her silvered hair's in long spools of curls that look something like a sherpherdess's, and her exquisite hooked nose adds a certain stability to her visage throughout her animated talk. She turns up her closed-pored and deeply creased palms and wants to know more about our techniques at the U.P.S., which excites me because I'm satisfied we do it right more often than not, and she's absolutely delighted, rattling her rings, when I explain how Paco and Billy Dwayne and L.C. go from Latin to shop to biology during the course of a single afternoon. It's a sort of remedial conversation that seems to make her clit swing like a clapper. *Muffled gong sounds from between her silky legs. Nay! Rather, the thuds of a velvet mallet against the oily parchment drumheads of her labia.* Something like that. But she is a nice person.

Yes. Mrs. Rose *will* hear about how we teach them Latin by the names of Fairy Shrimps (*Anostraca*) and Tadpole Shrimps (*Notostraca*) and Water Fleas (*Cladocera*). She's delighted and laughs and jiggles her wonderfully liberal boobies. She says she hopes that we'll stay *funded*—and then she asks how I got into this work—she acquires that dour but passionate and affectionate expression Semite women use just before they check you out for dingleberries. Leaning downwards, she exposes cleavage, and drops also the point of her nose, suggesting clemency and also a certain probability of cleistogamy in the nostrils (those most secret nose hairs), for, bursting as she is from her Empire raiment, she does seem the finest flower of tolerant and mildly aroused interest.

I got in trouble with the Movement. I got in trouble *with* it—not *in* it.

Yes, it's terribly difficult.

I'm a fugitive from odd justice.

Mary has mentioned something about that.

Those people at school gave me a job and I've tried to do my best.

She's a wonderful girl.
She's O.K.

Hazel Rose is O.K., Leo Rose is O.K., Mary Ann Porter is O.K.
—but this dude has been getting fat and raw and high again and it
broke out because there's no use fooling myself about the techniques of the U.P.S., for all their virtues. Those goddamned people
over there have been more than decent—and especially Mr. Chapel
the headmaster who hardly ever misses an opportunity to encourage me (he's the one who got the educationist from the University of Texas interested in doing a thesis on my work)—but it's
no use because I ought to be spending time out of school with those
kids, but I don't.

*—Bow before these poore, nasty, lousie, ragged wretches, say
to them, your humble servants, Sirs, (without complement) we
let you go free, and serve you, &c.*

*Do this or (as I live saith the Lord) thine eyes (at least) shall be
boared out, and thou carried captive into a strange land.*

When I'm at school I'm drifting and almost making the third
thing, in a trance, like in a good game, or at good loving, but not
quite. At home here I study, which is clear and lucid and incredibly
pleasant most of the time (dear Christ how I love the peace of
study on booze and peanut butter and ben), what with the $96.72
stereo I bought for Mary last spring and the new rug and the
various pictures upon the wall—*Rangia cuneata, Proptera alata,
Elliptio crassidens, Lampsilis ovata*—having at the etymologies, the
whole wonderful business—but over at the U.P.S. it's a hot, mechanical high (though not without sentiments). The practical work
of instruction gets done well enough and the names and faces
register, but when the little orange buses come to take them home, I
forget.

I've tried but I can't get interested in their extracurricular en-
vironments—and above all it's a sin and a crime I haven't taken
those chaps over to Dallas to a ball game. It's really wretched I
haven't done that—especially since they've asked so many times:

me saying, Yeah, and, Some time we'll do that: but I don't and probably won't, and I didn't want to speak of those errors to Mrs. Rose, who is so enthusiastic about all good things.

*Procyon lotor—Lutra canadensis—Mustela vison—Ondatra zibethica—Myocastor coypus—Sylvilagus palustris—*Ha!—*Oryzomys cooperi—Sorex palustris—Condylura cristala* (the fucking star-nosed mole!)—*Myotis lucifugus—*yessir— *Loose the bands of Wickednesse, undo the heavy burdens, let the oppressed go free—and break every yoake.*

I bust my ass teaching those peckerwoods and coons a load of crap they surely ought to learn—if anything of value's to be saved —but most of which will be useless to most of them. I pound away at Maxilla and mandible and thoracic legs, but I don't do for those boys the one thing they'd never forget me for.

Let's hear it again for the FLYING ROLL, for once-swift Billy's mother who *did* a FLYING ROLL into that casket.

Ancistrodon piscivorus! Cottonmouth. *Olor Columbianu!* Whistling swan. It's all the same.

—*Deale thy breade to the hungry, and bring the poor that are cast out (both of houses and Synagogues) to thy house.* Yessir! On Judgment Day the Lord God will forgive me Foots and Billy but He'll never forgive I never took my charges to an NFL game— *Cover the naked: Hide not thyself from thine owne flesh, from a creeple* [from a freaking creep-le], *a rogue, a begger, he's thine owne flesh, and his theft, and his whoredome is flesh of thy flesh also, thine owne flesh.*

—I'll spend ten thousand years in Purgatory watching game movies and especially all the plays I fucked up on—backwards and forwards—Christ! JOINER, DON'T YOU LIKE SPORTS?

—*Thou maist have ten times more of each within thee, then he that acts outwardly in either—Remember, turn not thine eyes away from thine OWN FLESH.*

I only spanked her once.

AT THE PARTY—yes, mam, our educational system fails to properly respect Hygeia and Telesphorus. Yes, we must consider the daughters of Asclepius—who are Iaso, Panacea, Aegle, and, above all, Hygeia, who was, of course, closely associated with her father as the goddess of health. And most certainly we must pay mind and body to the guardian spirit of convalescence, Telesphorus, who is represented wearing a hooded cape, the costume of those who have lately recovered from serious illness.

At the outset on the couch—and even after I'd been stricken with guilt about my thoughtlessness to my students—the conversation with Mrs. Rose was still mostly jesting and japing—as I pointed out that we must not underrate the goddamned hooded cape of Telesphorus in our curriculum.

For example, the sweatshirt and the hood of the training and convalescing athlete should not be demeaned, as it participates in this ancient and palpable myth of Hygeia and Telesphorus.

All are joggers, yes, and many take singing lessons, that their hearts may not be broken nor the aural sense diminish, and many is the gym class! And that's the trouble: body from mind being cut off so often, in this modern world of today.

Here, finish this. She wants me to get plowed and make a fool.

Yessum, let's hear it for the Guardian Spirit of Recovery! Gimme a T . . .

Hazel, my dear, the usual idea—and it's a sound one—is that physical culture should be *included* in education—but *included* is not enough. Strong in mind *and* body, to be sure—all that good stuff the late, great Jack Kennedy wanted—and no wonder!— what with his back and bad eyes and those hormones always making his face puffy—him being physically probably worse off than any President this century—which century includes F.D.R. who *was* a creeple. Check the facts. I have it on the best authority, which is a brilliantly documented and gracefully written little-known work by George T. Gart, entitled *Official History: Bosh!* J.F.K. was a physical wreck long before L.H.O. and Co. cut him down. And, Hazel Rose, if you don't know the work of George T. Gart then you can't possibly know what's going on.

Oh? She keeps a composed face but rocks on her knees.

I read it the other night. Listen. Why *not* have an updated picture of Cardinal Bessarion—the Great Renaissance Humanist—
doing bench presses—doing remarkable and godlike bench presses
on his back in his remarkable and godlike study. Or commission an
entirely new picture of the Cardinal doing laps while reading
Cicero! It would be a difficult but not impossible task—and I
should write to Mother and/or Maria about it. WHAT, MAM,
WE MUST GAIN IS THE SAME RESPECT FOR TELES-
PHORUS WE HAVE FOR JESUS...UH?

What Mary paid no attention to was the fact I never raised
my voice throughout the body of the first exchange. Not once—
though I did smile at Mrs. Rose at peculiar moments, to be sure,
dropping my nether lip, and I did break into a rank sweat at one
point from the single I'd popped back at the house before I washed
her (Mary Ann): it's a cool flat high—except for the sweating—
but never at first did I raise my voice, and she (incredibly clean
and beautiful Hazel Rose) never winced once. She could tell this
dude was nervous in some grief and she went along with it with just
the least narrowing of the luxurious skin over her eyeballs—for
she is a Jewess with epicanthic folds, like a Delta woman.

*You'd actually raise Hygeia and this Telesphorus person above
all the greater gods and goddesses?*
But of course—for none *are* higher. What *could* be higher than
Health and Convalescence? What? Mam, Hygeia and Telesphorus
understand the Mystery of Secular Resurrections and finally fore-
shadow the metaphysical one: the supraphysical one, to be more
exact. Dante should have let those two Greeks into Purgatory at
least—for convalescence *is* the mortal type of conversion and resurrection even though our education does not place Recovery at the
center of its theory—and that, mam, is a damn shame and a good
way to miss the point. We believe in *progress*, but not deeply in
re-creation. We assume that our educations will push us up a stable
and irrefrangible inclined plane, but they won't.
Telesphorus, huh?

Right! And I'm not talking about what's called Remedial Education or Continuing Education or Adult Education or even Education for the Culturally Depraved. What I'm concerned with is a radically new approach to educational theory and practice—the results of which might well suggest rituals to cure Fuckupedness!

Fuckupedness, huh? Hazel Rose has dropped her slippers and is sitting on her legs upon the long white couch. She's showing knees that have soft furls pulled over and under them. She's playing along like it's some witty game. *Like Yoga. Maybe Yoga would cure it. Or lessons from the "Kama Sutra."*

Not quite. It's not that simple. Everybody should practice some yoga—breathe deeply—pull a string through the nose—and swim some each day—but that's merely *maintenance.* It's not TELESPHORATION. Now. What I call Telesphoration is a habit of bind and mody that accepts decline, backsliding, defeat, and misprision as the basic facts of life, while resisting them, and also while looking forward to the STRANGE RESURRECTION.

Strange Resurrection, huh? Aren't you talking about Original Sin and other Orthodox Ideas? She's now bent far forward, her elbow on her knee, her stark chin in her olive palm.

Not at all! Except in the sense of not letting your left hand know what your right hand is doing—which left hand–right hand business comes down to us by way of parable—and parables are in no way orthodox, are they?—being so caught up as they are in the practical detail work.

Go on.

The gist is the matter of the *mortal* left hand and the *immortal* right hand. Yes, one *must* be of two minds about lying and diving...

True.

... for Telesphorus teaches us to read good books and to see good movies, and to be loving, scientific, and generous in His name. We are, in fact, admoni-shed to bruit the cry openly in the streets—TELESPHORUS LOVES YOU—TELESPHORUS LOVES YOU—ALSO LADY HYGEIA. HAIL HYGEIA, FULL OF GRACE. For this we know is necessary to give the people confidence in their mortal modies while they're lying, and also in their binds that dive. And surely you must see that Jesus *is* strange, and that he should be kept out of the big picture as much as possible.

Hazel, my dear, whatever other sumptuous ideas we may entertain, and confusing, we simply must transvaluate the old practices of Christian Witness. See. We must mostly witness for Telesphorus, not Jesus—because Telesphorus is really with us in this world and doesn't promise much at all except we'll get back in shape from time to time, and also finally find antibodies for all the dread diseases that plague the human race. God damn it, Pope John is so much admired, but he's an anachronism. Dr. Salk is the hero of this age. Why, when we were kids we couldn't even go out much in the summertime because of *polio epidemics*—whole summers wasted—afternoons reading comic books in front of the fan, and drawing airplane pictures in a dim light—swimming pools closed! —football practice postponed!—NO EXERCISE.

Yes. Telesphoration does have the advantage of being entirely Scientific (even Geriatric) in that He (Telesphorus) encourages us to stay strong and get well as soon as possible and study hard while preparing to fail to do as well as we'd hoped. Certainly! And He Who Disciplines AND LOVES this creation teaches us that those of us who do pass must be conditioned scientifically year after year after year to immediately make our physical *and* mental knowledges available to the failures, as it were, immediately after having savored our successes—because never should we diminish or denigrate true success, or winning. Thus does Telesphorus teach.

That's healthy. It's a generous liberal attitude.

Yes, mam, Telesphoration is a kind of mortal bearing of one's fellows' burdens. And it never, never includes the least suggestion of immortality. To the contrary, it points up again and again that— BUDDY, YOU AIN'T GOT YOUR MEAT BUT ONCE— SO PRESERVE IT—HORMONES—TRANSPLANTS—LET'S HEAR IT FOR BODY FREEZING—LET'S HEAR IT FOR TELESPHORUS.

What about Jesus?

Glad you ask . . . now listen carefully and don't mention it to anybody. Not a soul. Promise?

I promise.

O.K. This Jesus is strange—and the whole deal is now-a-days you got to be a *secret* Christian. Jesus is im-portant because of only one thing—which is he'll let you have your body back—he'll show you how to remake it and use it better than ever . . . forever. You . . . have . . . got . . . to . . . be . . . a . . . secret . . . Christian. Hell, it's actually depraved both physically, politically, *and* morally to be a practicing and overt Christian: because now we can see how it's a license to fuck off. Let's face it—Christianity in this modern world of today *encourages* Sloth and Murder and probably even the more vicious forms of Capitalism—though the latter is a thorny issue I won't attempt to brook or parse in depth at this time: it being a trivial social occasion.

———

Honey, this Resurrection stuff is critical—it can blow us all skyhigh if it's not kept a secret.

Your old man with his pussy beard on finds me banging your mortal bod as I'd love to and he can almost with impunity maim me unto death if he believes that God Judges and that I have a chance of after-life . . .

Fat chance.

. . . he can kill my ass and feel like I'm grooving on some palpable Angel in Heaven if he takes this Resurrection shit too seriously. Dear heart, too much confidence in the Resurrection—or the Resurrection in the wrong hands—can and does encourage all the most excessive forms of Fuckupedness.

Fat chance he would—she being diverted toward inscrutable thoughts concerning her husband.

Listen, dammit. Too much Hope is dangerous but no Hope at all is just as bad if it gets carried too far, producing, as it does, Hypochondria: Melancholy in the Belly: the Miseries—and objectified, as it were, into so-called sociology it (Hopelessness) can create fertile soil for Fascism and/or Communism. But Hypochondria is the root of all evil. It is the root cause. A man or woman with no Hope at all *will* brood over his skin too much, every fucking runkle and bump, every cigarette and Gibson—and I'm not suggesting that one should *use* Gibsons and cigarettes and peanut butter—for Telesphorus would break us of our bad habits, and can, but what, without Hope, then?—so we clean ourselves of vice and still have no Hope?—why, the natural man will say, *Fuck "that"!* *Gimme a Camel.* Right? *And a shot of neat Jack! And a red zoomer!* It's really simple.

What we must do is creep or hop up to the dude and say, clearly, though with the merest suggestion of doubt: FRIEND, HE IS PROBABLY RISEN.

O my dear, O my dear, for that's the only thing can finally save the hardest workers and rollers from despair—and surely it is a sad thing that we can only share it with those who have lived as if it wasn't so, those who have forced themselves to accept the terrible responsibilities of their mortal bodies, those who have avoided the pitfalls of Church and Godless Atheistical Communism and Freudianism—here's some dude who has paid his taxes and worked hard and suffered to love his wife and family (mostly) and friends—he's been *for* pornography and *for* Stevenson—he's bought Easter Seals (while smiling wanly)—he has even got the flag of the United Nations in his living room—and yet he has no Hope in the Flesh.

My dear, what you should do is sit down next to him and tell him not to fret. If you think the poor man has been graceful most of the time, tell him he can't die. Say to him, "Christ is risen." He'll appreciate it. Hell, he'll damn near believe it.

I've never done well at parties (except maybe for the one with Dianne Harvey and the pigs)—and I certainly didn't do well at the Roses'. That got clear in a hurry. I didn't mean to be bad, but Mary, who was in a mood over her clothes, among other things, thought I was awful to Hazel. Mary'd been passing back and forth in front of the couch every now and then—she'd been patrolling the area with her sweet ears open, and finally she pulled up short in front of that couch in a goddamned semi-rage.

It was her I-hate-you-when-you're-giddy rage, one of the worst kinds—it's the fury of a mother (or father) when her kid doesn't offer a firm handshake to adult guests, or when he does start jabbering about schoolplay in the midst of company.

Mary, hands on hips, and bent forward stiffly in her handsome black dress, says, "Oh, shut up, Son."

"Oh, leave him alone," says Mrs. Rose, but she doesn't mean it, She has wearied. Correct. She pats my knee, but it's clear she's ready to tend to the others.

"Yes, mam," says I. Rather heavily, stricken by this quick reversal. "I'll go. By God, I'll go." I excused myself from Mrs. Rose, and from Mary, and headed toward the door, passing through the gathered students who didn't seem to notice, they were so caught up in their own bullshit.

Mary caught me at the door.

"It wasn't my blather with that lady that bothered you—it's the goddamn clothes. You're pissed because I want you pretty sometimes," says I.

"Like I don't like *you* to be fat."

"___"

"Son, you're a foolish witness for both Christ and Health. You weren't *helping*."

"That's bad." And I felt it *was* bad.

"It's awful."

"You're drunk?"

"Yes," says ole Mary.

I told her she was drunk and unkind and that I was leaving.

So I checked out from the door and I swear I never expected Mary to follow—I figured she'd stay and that already, because of the clothes I'd made her wear, she'd split the sheet with me—sobeit —but just about the time I gunned the car to warm it up, she climbed in, pertly, and immediately began an attack the likes of which I'd not expected, speaking in a low, cautious voice, while methodically taking off all her clothes—tossing each piece out the window one at a time, beginning with her right shoe in the Roses' drive, as I drove away.

She's saying—*I didn't survive the nuns and the military shit for THIS—I don't deserve to be EMBARRASSED* . . . *after all I've done for you—you will leave me you will leave me you will leave me you never meant to do otherwise—because you're a*—and on and on in an almost casual incantation about how she'd got me the

U.P.S. job (which was true) and how she'd taught me so much (which was true) and *GOD DAMN YOU SONNY I MADE A HOME FOR YOU*—which was surely true—*you'll leave me leave me leave me* ...

Well, I turned off the main streets and got lost a couple of times while trying to avoid well-lit intersections, wondering what people would think about those dainty things they'd find near the curb in the morning—but she never managed to embarrass me— and seeing in the rearvision mirror a slip flutter and coil and fall behind ain't at all like the burst of a cigarette that's been cast out! It crossed my mind that in this frame of mind she might throw herself out of the car—which did worry me—but I never was embarrassed because I had it coming—and I planned an honest answer for her before we got home. It was going to be the wrong one, to be sure, but what set up to say came freshly into mind and it was reasonable.

Beautiful! She's butt nekked and shivering there on the front seat by the open window—she looking like a goddamned plucked broiler—but she waits for me to come around and open the door for her! And I held her naked wrist in a strong grip as I walked her to the door—all, all of her lady-clothes shed! And she never spoke another word until she's settled in her chair and I've fixed a drink for both of us—and there wasn't any light on except the glow out of the kitchen. YOU NEVER MEANT TO STAY WITH ME—I COULD TELL IT BY THE CRAZY TALK— YOU FUCKING NIGGER. She finally did yell it, rather than hiss.

"Incorrect."

"No it isn't."

"Yes it is."

"I've got a plan ... for *us*."

"_____"

"We'll get married."

"_____"

"We'll get married and go home to Bryan. I'll write the Sheriff tonight and ask permission to come home to be a Deputy. And he'll

let me. I'm going into law work . . . I'll get us a nice little place on
the edge of town and build bookshelves for you. Hell, you and
Bessie'll get to be friends . . ." I'd gone on pleasantly even farther
than that before I realized she was on top of me and howling—
Lord, screaming!—and kneeing the living daylights out of my belly
and chest. She's gone entirely insane for the moment. So, by God,
what I did was turn her bare ass over my lap and spank her hard
once or twice. Then I shoved her off onto the rug.

She gets up slowly, breathing heavy, but obviously calmed
some. "I'm tempted"—in a voice that's full of bitterest self-con-
demnation. "You're serious! You crazy bastard, you're serious!"
"Damn right."
"You *will* marry me . . ."
"Yep."
"If I'll go home with you?" She's looking down at her crimping
toes.
"Ezakly."
"But you're positive I won't."
"____"
"Which is correct, Son." She said it flatly. "I won't do it." She
gets into her jeans and one of my Southern Athletic Dept. T-shirts,
stuffs a few dull things in her rucksack, and calls a cab.
"Where you going?"
"Back to the Roses'."
"Have a good life."
"Same to you."

We sat in the immoderate gloom in silence until the cab came.
We just sat there and stared at each other until she left, and I didn't
walk her to the door.

She's been gone two weeks. No calls. Nothing. Nor have I. For
which I guess we're both proud.
She can't stay gone much more than two weeks—

VI

Two pictures by Goya have been on my mind the last cold and lonely days: *Esto es lo verdadero* (This is the truth) and a lovely brush drawing called *Mirth*. In *Truth* a fulsome bare-chested farm-wife welcomes home a shot-down bearded farmer who's holding a hoe in his right hand—they're both pictured in a glory or halo, with a sheep standing by—and it's probably some kind of allegory about how Spain will rise again. Actually, the lady is a little conceited-looking—suggesting, with her fat but wholesome face, that the farmer is some kind of dumb prodigal, and why the hell did you stay gone so long? And the sheep needs to be sheared.

Mirth has got these two old, old people dancing joyously in utter space (no background or horizon at all)—a vision of geriatric ecstasy flying in negative gravity—a bald and toothless old man and an old woman whose face suggests acromegaly. God damn I've pondered *Mirth*. What a blessing to whirl in raucous good spirits near the end, or maybe forever. Jesus, they've hung in there all those years together through all the natural misery, and now they celebrate the wonder of their endurance. Beneath their long heavy clothes, that dress and robe, their arms and legs are flung wide, and they're grinning. They're cavorting deliriously. They're having a freaking ball. Which is how it ought to be.

And maybe that's what Momma and Daddy are doing in White Haven. It's something they've had for a long time that I never got the hang of. I got there that time a week or so before I went to San Diego—and after the misery with Polly and Burger—and I wanted to get the hang of it in the worst way, but couldn't. They were great to me but it wasn't exactly instructive. They're sitting out on the steps of their wide, new suburban home, in the dusk, and both of them *run* to greet me when I turn in. They're at sixty and still they run to hug me, both Daddy and Momma—and where's April? —but they don't really care she didn't come—because it's their own creature they want to be with. They are my parents—the painter who lately won an Honorable Mention at the Mid-South Fair (a handsome watercolor of a swamp), and the inventor who perfected the Joiner Guard to improve safety conditions in box factories. Their other houses, including the one I grew up in, were set on their lots in a different way—the front of those houses was the narrow end, but the new one ostentatiously lies on its side. But what the hell, so long as it pleases them?—and, dear reader, it does, as it should. They are wonders hugging me, in Tennessee. Which is a better state, in spite of Memphis being too cleaned up and lacking sporting life, and pro ball. What we did is like it was so often in the past. Momma takes my left hand and Daddy takes my right. We walk around together in the yard because I'm at their home. We walk up and down in front of the house and we talk about how good the flowers and grass are—and the three of us will drink a beer on the front stoop together. Momma goes in to get them. Grass that's thick and neat as a crew cut on a good head of hair, and rose bushes, on a clean street. It ain't no bad street and they're great, reasonable people. Hell, gardening and painting and safety inventions are right up to date—my people are what the world with luck is coming to. No bread and goddamned circuses for R.S. and Maisie! No narcotic T.V. is necessary for them. They've got a little one in the kitchen for news, but that's all. Momma studies art books, and Daddy reads magazines, wondering. They go to the Methodist Church, enjoy a square dance club (remarkable for R.S.), and admire Senator Gore. They hated the deaths of Kennedy, Evers, and the three young men in Neshoba County (about which they wrote me in a letter), and they worry about their son.

"Congratulations on the invention."

"Thanks." He purses his heavy mouth and squints pridefully.

"I didn't know you knew anything about electricity."

"I got it down, at night school in town."

"It actually shuts the machine off with an electric eye?"

"Sure does."

"Well, I'm goddamned proud of you."

"So am I," and he gets up off the stoop and walks out to the street, just when Momma's back with the beer.

"What the hell's wrong with R.S.?" I ask, when she is settled down and has got her arm around me.

"He's worried about you . . . he's worried you'll get in trouble for no reason."

"Oh, for God's sake, Momma," and I was almost angry.

"Well he is, and so am I . . ."

"Why?"

"All that traveling you'll have to do."

"Traveling?"

"To play the games . . ."

"Right. Well, it's safe and I'll be careful."

"R.S. wishes you'd make a teacher." About the time R.S. is coming back up the walk.

"_____"

"So do I."

"Daddy, I'll do it right before long—after I get a little nest egg and retirement benefits playing ball." Which was as close as I'd ever come to making sense out of football to R.S.

"Makes sense . . . makes sense." He eases down on the other side of me and sips his beer. They both put their arms around me again, while also touching each other, as we watch the sun begin to settle into Arkansas, tenderly.

O my God—O my God—O my God—I wrote them after I got run off and ended here in Fort Worth, but they didn't answer. How the hell could they?

10

DALLAS AND THE LEAGUE was better than Bryan for a while—it was a hard and glossy life there in Tuscany Plaza that we enjoyed more than I ever expected, in some ways. The bad times with Coley in San Diego (and the feeling I'd jumped ship on Slater), and the afternoons with the likes of Nit in the tub, and late in the night the time I beat on the cypress table until my hands were swollen—these were sometimes the exceptions—Side saying it was all just part of a first pro season—the *freshman year*, as he was pleased to say.

It's worse than being hot for a woman. It's the bitterest kind of hunger, collecting pictures of Connor and Groza and Pihos and Luckman and Van Buren—and dreaming of playing with the god-damned Browns, and the goddamned Packers, and the goddamned Steelers, and the goddamned Giants, and the goddamned Eagles. For a long time I wanted to be a Philadelphia Eagle.

Man, I used to hitchhike the fifty miles from Bryan to Jackson to the State Fair just to get into that tent arcade where the pictures were. The average kid goes to that sort of thing to see the lady with her little brother growing out of her side, or to see a slut pick up a silver dollar with her pussy (which I did see once and must allow is amazing), or maybe the once-extraordinary Sally Rand—or they go for the thrill rides and the motorcycle stunt drivers—or maybe because they want to show the cow they've raised—but not me. Because I had me a unique experience that first time I slipped off with Bobo and Royal and hitched up there in Myron Crofton's pickup truck.

And the first time I went I thought I knew where I was going, the way we all do, while seeking the mysterious—and like every-body I did get that infusion of tentative ecstasy, a kind of Thomas Wolfe-type joy, when we came running around the corner of the Health Department Building and saw not just the glow of the fair's lights on the horizon—not merely the pearly haze that's over the swamp as you drive into the city—but the actual things themselves: the huge tents and towers and strands and strands of light bulbs, and the pavilions. That's fine and that's the S.O.P. American experience —like being the kid in Little Rock who gets up at four in the morning to wait at the baseball stadium in the chill and the dew because that's how you get to be the bat boy for the exhibition game—by being the first one there—it's how you get to hand Ted Williams his bat. And all that shit is fine, but it isn't what I got the first time I went to the fair, in Jackson.

The wonderful thing I hitched through the pine-scented dusk for was waiting in the tent arcade. It was between the machine that lets you try to pick up the trashy little toys and stuff with the magnet and the machine that shows the girlie dancing—A Penny for a Sports Picture—it was the little gray sports picture machine, mostly baseball, that also contained a few college and pro football stars—Paul Christman and the likes of Baugh—none of whom ex-cited me when I saw them advertised along with Musial and Slaugh-ter and Luke Easter on top of that machine. But what I got was Billy Rath, Billy Rath, Billy Rath. I was compelled to put a penny in—click goes the copper, crank goes the crank, and with my twelve-year-old right hand I pluck Billy fracking Rath out of the machine.

At first I didn't understand.

I didn't have any idea what a Billy Rath was. It could have been an image from some obscure mythology—Vodyanoi or Polevik. My sports picture card had a face and a name on it I'd never heard of. It was a football player without a doubt, for he was squared away like a linebacker without his helmet on—a lean sepia face— and it claimed to be a famous one. Then ole Billy let me have the word right there in the tent on the sawdust, with the clatter and stink and whirr of the arcade all around me—Billy told me how proud he was to be in that machine at a fair so far distant from the

Pennsylvania coal town where he comes from—he said, *Boy, you didn't think they took pro football serious enough for this type of honor.*

And I've got to admit I can't remember what exactly was on the back of that card—and there wasn't much of a Rath legend still around when I got to The League years later—except something about how Billy had had great character and had taught the great Alan Ameche the tricks of pro ball, and how he'd then just faded away to tend bar in White Plains, New York, I think. It seems he simply disappeared from practice after Ameche got his job. He wasn't cut—no goddamned waivers—he was simply gone and un- heard of for several years.

But still and all, whatever he historically was or wasn't, it *was* Billy who taught me the beauty and value of going to heaven in a penny arcade sports picture machine. And I was not and have not been deceived—for after that night I knew something cool and se- cure about success in this great country of ours—more than Bo or Royal'd got out of having their palms read and from looking at Sally Rand's old titties, after they'd paid the Mexican a dollar to sneak under the tent at an early age.

I went back to that arcade several years in a row. I'd always put the pennies in until I got the pro football player, discarding every batter and pitcher. I got a Tom Fears and one time even the young Jim Ringo, which made me want to be a center—I was never dis- appointed. Somewhere in my drawers at Momma's house in Mem- phis is Billy's photo. I ought to write home for it.

I really did enjoy flying from city to city—something Royal is terrified of—and running out into the stadiums was a thrill— especially since I knew ole April was safe with Pauline back in Dallas and watching me and Side on the T.V. Trotting onto the great fields of the nation was a great satisfaction.

Cities like New York and Washington and Philadelphia were a treat to the dude, the Eastern being the conference with the best cities in it. I went to the museums in New York City and then wrote Momma that her Vermeer prints were better to look at than the so-called originals in the Met, damned glass and bad light not helping said so-called originals. Walk across a big-assed room in what's supposed to be one of the great museums of the world and what you find is one of Jan's ladies botched by glass and bad lighting—I'd expected better. Momma, we might as well just concentrate on the copies.

I stood in front of the *Guernica* half an hour, discovering to my sorrow that in some basic way it's silly as hell—*affected* would be Momma's word—but still I looked on it, at the Museum of Modern Art, in N.Y.C. It's a big, fancy, and impressive picture—but that's not at all how it was in Guernica when it got bombed. Shit, an intricate medical painting of a severed head would do as well.

Side and I slipped away from the team on a Saturday morning in New York City. We drank beers at a delicatessen and went to look at pictures—especially the *Guernica*—and all those smallish little sensitive men and women with their babies on their backs (in metal and canvas papoose-holders), they knew we were probably professional athletes, but they never bothered us. Side—he's stooped while staring at it—says, "Uh!" To the big picture. "That's some kind of hurt bull!" But nobody in that crowded little white room responded. It was one helluva ninety days in The League. And also he really dug the Monet flowers.

I wrote letters by the dozens to my people and Royal, and one or two to Burger, all of them intended to illustrate how broadening and exciting this new life was—and how demanding and even scientific the game was, what with the play book twice as long as in college, and because of all the film we looked at. I even wrote Benton about how cool the police in New York City were, with their horses. *Proud blue figures on horses, in that cavernous city*—something like that. Informing how I'd work for him if he'd let me ride around the county on a horse. He never answered.

I wrote Burger he shouldn't worry so much about the modern world of today because there seems to be natural order and terrible sanity to the Urban Good Life. All that Bohemian mythology was no more than quaint. Yessir, the secular world is on us and it's pretty good. In fact, the world is probably saner and friendlier than ever before: *Mr. Burger, Marx realized that Rome didn't go socialist even when by all calculations it should have. Think about "that," Dennis.*

Yes, heady it was to be on a jet plane from N.Y.C. to Dallas, Texas, after we'd beaten the Giants 28–21—Side telling me how we might win seven games if Roper'll get serious about reading defenses. I'm sipping some kind of airline broth and dreaming of being downfield like a cat after the safety man, blocking for Sam Campion. They're doing it because an offensive tackle has completed a good piece of work, like they did for Wallick once. All those hardassed Bear fans yelling for the offensive right tackle of the *other* team—because they knew he was the greatest there is, at his position—because all he'd done was play a perfect game, his position being worth three yards on every play. The Bears kept doubling up on his position, stacking on linebackers, but Big Bill just swept the whole purple crowd out as he drove forward. The Rams gained where Wallick was—and where he wasn't was even easier than where he was, *because* they'd weakened their other positions to compensate for Wallick. The sweet rumor raced through that bittercold stadium—that if you watched the offensive right tackle of the Rams you'd see an amazing thing—and even the least informed fans (the women, and the weaker men who never watch anything but backs), they caught on to it.

Then the finest of gestures: the Ram coach (and probably it was suggested by Poteet), sensing a curiosity, called Wallick out of the game in the fourth quarter so he could come off by himself and get his rightful cheers. That was when the people of Chicago did rise to their feet and give that man the greatest hand a lineman ever got for merely doing his job right. When Bill Wallick pulled his helmet off his head that Sunday afternoon he'd lived a proper life. Somitch probably had a six-colored Möbius dancing in his brain that day—at the very moment he was back on the bench—with the pains attacking his chest again.

What the hell, Burger—to be aloft with a Negro friend beside you next to the window of a big jet plane—us talking about the City and a winning game—that, sir, can rub out many past bad times.

Daddy, I wrote, *the life you've made is a good one, and I'm proud of you. You can hardly imagine how proud I am of you I love you so much. But more is needed than medicine and good roads! Much, much more. Good doctors and good houses and good schools—you made that very clear—and I appreciate the fact we finally got drunk together—and I loved it how Momma hitched up her skirts and smiled no matter how hard we yelled. But there's more to it than that. It's J.F.K. now, not F.D.R. and F.D.R. wasn't all you thought he was. And Bilbo as you know became an evil person who hated colored people. And you like Huey Long too much. It's a big wide wonderful world we live in—and your brand of Populism don't cut it.* All of which I mailed to my father.

Flying in a jet plane will warp a fellow. It's a prime vanity to skim over cities and states and towns, and it can also be very unnerving: you think you're above them all, but then you realize how down below the clouds they're practicing and practicing and practicing, and studying how to bring you down. As Side says: *SAVE MONEY! WORK FOR THE BILLS WILL COME!*

And Momma, don't worry! Coach Sepoy and Poteet are good men and won't let anything bad happen. Momma, study the Hudson River School. You can do as well in a Southern way.

Robbins liked to lecture me.

II

I talked at Side plenty but I never lectured him. I confessed and questioned. Side lectured. Rightly. I told him about the wildcat at the Spit and how raunchy Polly was falling apart in her grave back in Bryan—and how Julia's brocade still hangs heavy in my mind—and of long-toed sister Lucy waiting for the Resurrection at Rawles Springs—Billy's head bones broken—and ornery grainy Slater who's after my ass to start some shit to rectify the evil done black men the world over: I told Side how the only nigger I really knew at all back home thinks I'm worthless for playing more ball.

He ain't no Chief Nigger, he's an injun—Side grinning vilely against good Slater, whom he has only heard about but never seen.

You might say it all came out too passionately, so much it upset April, in Dallas sometimes. *Hush, Son.* She thought I was playing second fiddle too enthusiastically with the Bulls. One time, pulling the pillow over my face, I told her in bed I was backing up two other guys—Maribonito and Clarkson—and never did talk to them too much. That Negro man's our friend and neighbor. He's the class in The League and I'm proud to be . . . *Still, it's only because Side's colored.* Partly—but fuck theyut—because there's far more to the quilt and weave of him than being colored. *He'd like you better without the begging*—April also lecturing, early on a Monday morning, nude and huge in the belly with Aubrey—which big belly with its pooched-out bellybutton was an immense and pale third eye to that woman. She was some kind of human-mocking creature like the adventurers of long ago in the Age of Exploration fancied they'd find in distant lands—so I rose up from that bed and shoved her bare ass against the wall and threatened to kill her if she strikes at me again that way with words. Go to hell. Which wasn't a nice thing to say to a lady with a baby. Mine.

They were always there—the three-time Parchman losers and low-I.Q.-types out at Chalmers' Mill, working on the green chain—

muscling and groaning and even chanting over the green lumber before it gets to the kiln, because it's all that kind of natural man can do. I've seen those dusky mothers day after day bent simian over that big mill table, sizing the rough-cut boards for Henry's saws—and at noon they're eating goddamned sardines and goddamned peanut butter (in Nabs) and Moon Pies, and washing it all down with Dr. Tichner's Antiseptic—and maids in white gowns are walking their rounds, also, in Bryan—some of them the women and wives of those poor bastards chained to the green and in hock to Chalmers for five years at least, by way of the old man's evil no-interest loans. They're the kind of niggers who, if they ever run off again, are not about to go back to Parchman Farm, again, conjugal visits or not—the boys on the green chain hold court in the streets when they run off to trouble the last time.

Groans. Groans and chants that you'd expect from beautiful wooden primitive statues made in Zambia, over the roar and miserable whine of that mill, where Daddy lost his fingers. And one day (I'd been pushing the bobtail International with Slater, delivering a load of finished lumber to a Laurel yard)—and just when we pulled back into our home lot, there's a big green—blackgreen and vicious with nipples of wind darting down from time to time—somitch of a cloud, a whole freaking front, folding in over Bryan from the southwest, with sticky lightning (*cosmic electricity* the law calls it, if it knocks a man dead) jabbing down bolts as it comes, and suddenly our place is struck. Shit, it's struck several times and ways—with an orange fireball that rolls like a fast fluorescent pumpkin along the power lines into the plant, and also with a shot onto the main steel roof beam. That whole big silver building glowed, was luminous in the deep air, the very second before me and Slater ducked in the cab—then when we were sure we were alive and for some stupid reason had run inside that colosseum-sized building (where everything is shut down in a radical silence for a moment and there's that shrill smell of small electrical fires), we find Roy Boykin and Daddy and Henry and Warren Ray more or less bunched in one place in the middle of the cement floor—they're stooped a little (Roy hunkered) with vague eyes—until Henry begins to yell—*GET OFF YOUR KNEES, GET OFF*

YOUR GODDAMNED KNEES—to all the coloreds in the Mill.
Slater and I were side by side at the main door and Slater says, "Mr.
Henry better see to where *his* knees are." To my wonder, as the
storm passed.

I'd just never got it in my head they all had it that bad, because,
without saying it in so many words, Daddy and Momma'd given me
the impression that colored people had gained a special dignity by
way of their times in slavery and bad luck. Being black to my family, and corny as it may sound in the present day and time, was
both mysterious and awful—and Ollen, when I was twelve, the
sunlight violent on the sink and a box of Duz, rubbing her red
panties back and forth on my exposed white tummy, her raspy
though wet bush breaking forth both through and around said
panties, was indeed strange to me. White people had to work at getting strange, while niggers were born to it it seemed.

And R.S. did say that people like Foots and Dalton Fletcher
were *jealous*—but Daddy never winked or leered—he never in-
tentionally conjured images of miraculous niggerfucking. He just
said the word jealous and left it ominous and dignified.

Daddy never went out of his way for colored people all that
much that I know of—except for wanting unions and good wages
for every man. When he'd speak to a nigger on the street, it was
like he's talking to a crone or a witch or a shaman (somebody
straight from the coven) or some kind of sacred animal out of a
Biblical text, he was so respectful—and it really didn't make any
difference to him what their age and sex was, because they were all
versions of the third thing to Daddy. The only white persons I ever
heard him speak of in a similar fashion were Henry and Polly and
Momma and Roy and Helen and Merle and Dalton and Davis—all
of whom are prime strange.

Guernica and a picture of Henry as a weird planter, by Maria,
and that picture of Jackie climbing onto the wounded body of
dead Jack, were the three that caused Side to say *Uh!*—hauling it
up from his heels—that blatant vocable—sounding it like he's com-

ing forth with a long and stringy fiery wad that's delivered from the small of his huge black back, which is similar to when you get it like all the marrow of your legbones is in it.

It's a joy but also just a little scary. Yessir.

What an evening and a night that was, with Moaningsad Robbins and his inky—goddamned Yankee bluegum—wife, Pauline (they mix it less in the High Midwest than they do in Port Gibson, or So So), who's from Wat-er-looooo, as they say it in Iowa, where she is from, the daughter of an electrician-preacher who wisely got the hell out of Chicago; Moaningsad being Side's original name given to him by his mammy—*He's a fine small chile but Moaningsad*—in a shack, with hounds circling, out from Epps, Louisiana— his momma persisting in calling him by that difficult polysyllabic name from the cold night he's born on until she died of weariness, in Monroe.

But most people just called him Sad—both black and white— *Sad Robbins makes Little All-America*—which ain't no kind of good luck or optimal conditioning to make up a healthy child by any standards. It fit, however, and still does, even after Pauline changed it—the wonder being that both names work just fine, and neither. Right now his name should be Jerome.

Now that you've got "me" and are All-Pro again you shouldn't be called Sad . . . or anything of Moaningsad. You a mountain—and I live on the Morningside. You ain't no shady side of no hill, Big Daddy. Your name now is Morningside. And Morningside loved to mention how she renamed him in Chicago, three, four years ago, when they'd just met, and right after he'd made All-Pro the fifth time. It's a story that got picked up in all the newspapers—this wedding of a pro and a scholarship girl at U.C. being news on all fronts in Chicago: CLEAN JIGS TO LEGALLY WED. Hell, even *Time* noted it—how the great tackle's name had been changed by his young wife, how he had legally changed it on his checks and everything. The gentlemen of the press speculated on how it might affect his game. His new name. Which it didn't.

Side made All-Pro his first year in The League and continued on.

. . .

"That's easy—EASY—for you to say."

"An' it's easier for you, Jerner. You got ways to go."

"Meaning?"

"What I *mean* is *I* went to school where this game's what you learn an' all of it. Willy College don't produce no Rhodes Scholarships. I learn a game."

"Which you care about . . ."

"I care about *me* . . . and Leen . . . an' you an' April, sometimes." He pushes down hard on the meat with the spatula. He damn near bends the flexible part off it. He likes cash money and a nice place to live integrated, and he likes being friends to me and April (though he quietly shit on me when I finally quit)—and he likes to get asked how it is in Big D, after so many years in Chicago, on the radio and the Teevee—"I say I *luv* Big D. I say I loves this expansion club—an', Jerner, you an' me up on this ledge is Good— an' this Turkey whiskey is GOOD." He jives in his sneakers in front of our portable grill—then peers, like he's conning for enemy masts, off across the drill yard and the pool to the far building of Tuscany Plaza, where a fattish salesman-type in a crew sweater is staring at us. "That fuckah over *there*, he wants to be over *here*. He's *dying* to make the journey to where *we're* at." Side smiles broadly, revealing his false front teeth.

"Let's invite that bastard over for a drink," says I.

"Jerner, you . . . are . . . sooo . . . dumb. Man, that boy is enjoyin' wantin' more than havin'. He come over here an' he'll brag a whole year at the office how we booze an' cook our own meat an' are not so great *up close* . . . *in person*, ya know?" Side's patting on our supper and confident he's making everything clear. "Jerner, you got to be *strict*, dig—you make *them* come to *you*—on our terms, ya know? Because that fuckah over there is *nothin'* an' we make him nothin' nothin' by askin' him over—so he can hurt us." Another smile out of the old sorrow. "That . . . is . . . it!"

"What's it?"

"It . . . it . . . man, you are *dumb*. *It's* it. We're it an' he ain't." Aiming the spatula at me, damn near daubing grease on my T-shirt. "It . . . It . . . It. They done." Pointing to the steaks. Side—he has beat his way out of the ruts and mires of Louisiana—Side's had the triple miseries, but now he is a famous man, and accepted, by way of football—and he has got a strange attitude toward the game, which forced me to grin that afternoon in chilly early November in Dallas, while staring at a sky that stretched westward the color of gunmetal, to say the least. He slipped the done steaks on a paper plate and we went inside to the women—who'd set a smart table for us.

The picture came framed in a plastic coughsyrup green, and wrapped professionally—*Here it is, sweetheart, and don't worry about paying. Let's call it a gift.* Very chummy and scented and out of the blue, Maria's note was on a purple paper with a scroll of tiny red flowers across the top. It was an especially curious execution of Henry, with brows and eyelashes added. But the rest of the burns were carefully done in livid pink and pitiless white. He's sitting in a tux—no, hell, it's some kind of pin-stripe, tails and spats (Manet whites—something dead in a bullring), and he's sitting austerely in a wingchair, black, on a berm: that's the foreground. In back of him across a ditch is a prospect of cotton fields, and in the distance are snow-capped mountains.

Side, when he came into the room and saw it that evening, was struck dumb—then, bending massively forward for a better look (and drawing his soul, instinct, his capacity for grace into a tumor behind the bridge of his wide nose), asked: "What's that? I never saw no mountains in no cotton fields no matter how many pills I took."

At which point April turned from the just-fired stove, apparently unconcerned by Side's rebuke of our most gratuitous and serious attempt to make a room a home, and answered, "Why, that's mah daddy, painted by his lovah, Mr. Side."

"Uh!" says Side, throwing his hips into it, and also swinging his scarred black arms loosely in the warm, thin air of our Dallas apartment—his arms covered by silky, full sleeves that make him look like a gargantuan candy man.

"Fraid I agree," says Pauline, speaking into the refrigerator.

.   .   .

April and I laugh, tentatively embarrassed, and explain how the old man is maimed and a little touched and probably dying of cancer, and how it's no great matter to us that the thing ain't exactly perfect, or realistic—we say it'll be a comfort to us here in Dallas—which makes our colored friends try to smile benevolently.

After we get back inside and put the meat on the cypress table, we stretch seated on the couch, and I *know* Side's not done with pointing up my ignorances. He has undone his silk sport shirt, exposing kinks of already gray chesthair, and it's clear enough he's throwing off sparks inside his bonebox.

"Jerner, you want this thing to be something it ain't. It ain't no religion, it's a job. It ain't nothin' but hard work to please a bunch of jock-sniffers."

"For good pay."

"Son's just not satisfied," croons Pauline—lovely black Pauline —and her skin is no ideology or metaphor—This Way to the Negress—none of your colored woman, none of your nigger gal, hell no. She's thin and gallant-looking, with a small round head atop a long jade neck (she so black she greenish)—she's got a flat and open face, with determined big eyes of brown. In fact, she's much like the one who lived across from where we'd sometimes load lumber onto the train in Bryan. On the spur at the back lot of the Mill. This Negro woman would walk down from a rickety second-story porch (she's a tall mare like Pauline) to willfully hang out her washing, ah God—and Stream says: *Gawd, look at that Negress*—which woman padding around her hardyard in loose garments barefooted with a helmet of puredee Negress hair on was what all that sex and race shit was all about in those days—all the novels me and Stream and Royal read—like *Mandingo*. Uh! We read and discussed it closely. Black almost as pitch and easily as graceful in the stride as Polly. With eyes bulged a little—and a way of looking coyly down toward her button nose without the least suggestion of getting them crossed. "It's Sonny's nature not to want just work." She walks out from behind the counter and across the room so she can ease down on my lap. "Son's one of those boys lookin' for heaven, like you were once," hugging my neck. Which kind of talk is doing more harm than where she's plopped in her rayon-silk and proportioned pants. The talk's harder on him than where her smooth arm is.

Side crunched down damn near on his back and made a long noise—"EeeeeahhOooo Dayuuummmmm—" but he's not mad, not in a rage, yet.

"He's tellin' us he's suffered," says Pauline, offering it generally in a description of anybody, then getting off me and prancing back over to where the salad needs tossing, and where April's not exactly satisfied herself she grasps what the hell's going on in Tuscany Plaza.

"Bip bip beeup big Booooomm," goes Side, "women don' want nothin' but preachers with foot-long dongs who hurt people when they have to. Preachers and mean bastards who make lots and lots of cash money."

I told Pauline and Side I thought they were a couple of self-centered darkies—because originally this conversation was about me—and now they presume to ring in a family tiff.

"Tiff!" He's up stretching, pulling back his shoulders until you can hear his spine pop. "Tiff, hell, it's a race war. I'm too light for her," and then he chuckles the way a grown Negro man is able to —something like a five-hundred-gallon oil drum being pushed over in an otherwise empty warehouse. (Remember the one about the Aggie who spent the night in the warehouse because he couldn't spell?) "Man, we been at this thing a long time, an' it's not about to go away. Tiff tiff tiff tiff tiff—" he skips over to the table. "Let's sit our bright asses down an' eat some food an' drink some wine an' try to realize we are the best people there is."

Before I can say Jack Robinson he has seated both our ladies and has begun to lead us in the most comfortable of all possible conversations about the State of the Union and other players and coaches and their wives—but most especially how Coley Sellers had better marry the widow from Longview he's seeing, because otherwise he *will* burn out before the season's over and be back in Waco coaching a junior high, or maybe just suffer a total state of physical collapse and die. He handled his silver carefully and correctly as a

surgeon—he was acting out a monolithic and articulate gracious-
ness for the ladies—but I could tell his soul was still as mean and
distant as any mongoose or suricate.

Whatever, it was one of the few times I ever saw April integrated.

I'd stand behind him at early practice in line to hit the blocking
sled—and he was always swinging his head from right to left and
squinting up his chocolate eyes even on the cloudiest days like he
was looking off far, checking each vista that ended at last in the
Pacific Ocean, and also those close around in the pink California
dust, determining that nobody or thing was creeping up on us—
then when he was once again down in front of that machine, he'd
groan an oildrum groan like he was asking himself how it could be
he was actually going to hit it ONE MORE TIME—the goddamned soiled pads of the dummy and the coiled springs to absorb
the shock. It always seemed to me he ought to be the president of
an emergent African nation instead of a pro lineman who must still
take suggestions from white coaches.

I could outrun him every time at forty yards, and I was larger
and heavier and stronger. He meant to prove it to me that I was, for
what it's worth, which after what happened showed to be little
indeed.

He proved it again right after that nice meal in which we'd all
talked Democrat and football politics and gossip—Coley all too
easy go soft while the President of the United States he a sick dude
but mostly a hard Irishman evergoddamnedchance he get, yup,
with whomever—after I'd been forced to agree (women of all
colors grinning) that Mr. Kennedy was pretty cool and probably,
for all his blind and wretched Catholic and Eastern provincialism,
not a bad, entirely, influence on the economy and taste of the nation
—though even then, after the buttered peels, I still remained mostly
Johnsonian, considering all Northern money probably illgained off

the sweat of Southern necks and niggers, like me and Side; but none of that was to any avail because our guests didn't trust Texans under any circumstances—and they sure did get some terrible reinforcement within the week. Uh!

I could see he couldn't sustain his good manners indefinitely—I could see he was worrying an issue not to be solved with glib table talk, so I wasn't entirely surprised when he shouted, after the peach ice cream, "Let's have some contests!"

He demanded on a full stomach that I arm- and leg-wrestle him, and then that we have pushup contests—two-arm, then one-arm. He busted a gut trying to beat me, but couldn't.

LET'S HAVE SOME CONTESTS—flaring after the cream, off the wall, breaking out from behind his squinched and seamed brown face. Said we'd fight on the floor and then the table—*CLEA THIS DAMN TABLE*—which the women did in haste. Recollect the usual picture of the fellow accused of rape in the Jackson papers and you will not be far from Side's expression at that moment, when in him it all sprung loose.

Turkey and Rhine wine say it's O.K. to me, so we do fall flatout from our chairs at table and start to it—me winning on the deep shaggy pile of the carpet with both arms and one leg (losing the right), knocking over the long couch and destroying one of Helen's Choctaw pots that had sat awhile on an end table. Fun! Fun! Fun!—my gorge rising—rolling on the floor with the great nigger, silk to flannel (I'd put a proper shirt on for supper), and noting from time to time how the black and white women are amazed and angered at what their nice fare has brought on.

Side's up on his feet and scubbing both hands back and forth across his shaved head—he's breathing miserably and he is ashen, the way they get—*CLEA THE TABLE . . . ONE MORE TIME, JERNER.*

Yessir. *This somitch is out of his mind.*

Lord God, I loved it, finally, at the table, right arm to right arm, eyeball to eyeball—both of us sick at the stomach and sick to our hearts because of these necessary spontaneous contests. Christ, how we did struggle there—and I swear I didn't think nigger once while deltoid, pectoralis major, triceps brachii, biceps brachii, and brachioradialis strained. It was fun right up until I felt that rare

steak climbing into my tender throat just about the time I flattened
the back of Side's hand on the table.

*Serious. What is serious? The average man would give a finger
to know what he does is serious, right ordering of crops etc. A man
dies and what has he lived for? Fucking? Fighting? Maybe we remember that much even after we're gone.* When I cut down on
Foots' face in the rain with my .25/.20 I knew what I'd lived for—
but it wasn't something I'd had when I put Side down.

I ran out on the porch and threw up over the railing. I barfed
meat and potatoes and wine and booze and what had once been a
lovely cool salad down onto the sour grass of the apartment yard.

Then there's Side at the door when I wheel around—he's vexing
his mustaches—"You win, Jerner, you win at that . . . but there
ain't no pleasure in the game . . . no pleasure at all." He's both
filling up the door frame and holding onto it while leaning out—
am I that large—"We in a crib, man. Nothin' but a crib!" He came
over by me at the railing and starts to yelling. *HEY . . . HEY . . .
EVERY FUCKAH IN THIS PLACE LIVE . . . IN . . . A . . .
CRIB.* Haroop and he chucks his. God, he's so sick I thought he was
dying of it. Morningside Robbins. Several neighbors did appear,
opening their doors, including our friend from across the way,
which Side notices while lifting his fouled mouth: *HEY, OLE
BUDDY, COMON OVAH . . . WE KILL YOU IN THE CRIB
. . . FOOTBALL FOOTBALL FOOTBALL FOOTBALL—IT
SPELL OUR NAME—OH, SON, I . . . AM . . . SO . . . TIRED . . .
Verry tired, verry tired.*

"Sad, get your tail back in-to this house," Pauline, insecurely.

"It ain't no house—it ain't no house . . . nothin' but a fuckin'
crib, Pauline." And he is the best there is.

I can damn near weep to think of them. No way in the world
for those nice girls, both with clean hair and sleek pants on, to get
into the type of hardrolling Hemingway bullshit me and Side were
suffering right then. No way no way Pauline unhappy her old
man too perfunctory about his game, the way he's always talking

how he'll run the first Negro Chevy place in Monroe, or a sporting goods store in Shreveport. Lotsa luck. Pauline wants to *enjoy* being a star's wife. She feels she *deserves* it. And April wants me to cool it, generally—she wants me to think more about Aubrey in her belly and to be generally satisfied and to quit making things so serious.

THIS A ROOM—IT AIN'T NO HOME

What they both wanted was for their men to be more relaxed and generally steady—lovingly confident—casually dedicated to their vocations—they wanted us to laugh a lot, happily, with a specific gravity—we were to be witty, charming, and brutal, when facing any threat to the castle, from over the moat. We must be tender in the bed at the outset, but turbulent and irrationally extruded at the bit.

Goddamn women.

Mary, when she come back, I break her face.

They dawdle around all day, thinking it's some kind of goddamned privilege for us to come home to a narrow room, and sour cream and chives. What a man wants is the, er, *NAKED MAJA*, both fair and brown.

Let *them* get graded on their performances, in slow motion, week after week after week. See how they like it. It's terrible. Me and Side live in a steamy world of chattel men and wounds and newspaper reporters, constant scrutiny of every move we make, and then when we come home we are supposed to easily unwind—a coupla beers and a downer and we're supposed to take sublime delight in a merely pretty table. What I wanted was to pour all the Turkey and all the Rhine allover Pauline, then lick it all off before I banged her black bod—Mr. Robbins wanting the same with my bride—and that's exactly the reason why after all this misery and truculence me and Side told them to shut up and fix us a triple—after we'd gargled with Lavoris—so we could enjoy watching *High Noon* on the T.V. Which made him cry more.

It could of been *Viva Zapata*, *On the Waterfront*, or *From Here to Eternity*, but it wasn't. Jesus, that was a bad two weeks, damn near too cruel and predictable for belief. What we did get was *High Noon*, and while ole Coop and Miss Kelly get going in that great movie, Robbins stretches forth his legs and begins to sob.

The women shut up good when he told them to get the drinks, but when he started crying, they doubly got quiet, actually retreating into the kitchen again behind the counter.

"What the hell, man?" I glance over at him furtively.

"What the hell, what the hell, you pearly ass"—he blubbers. I never knew that man well enough.

"It's just a movie..."

"It's *it*. He *got* to do it." He's got his head in his hands and he is sad, profoundly sad. God damn. "Fightin' an' fuckin', me an' you, Jerner, is all we do. Because we *got* to. We believe it! Ole Coop believe it. Everbody believe it."

"Shit, man..."

"You soooo Dumb." He started choking again and I figured he's sick again. "He's *got* to face the man who hates him. DUMB ... I'm gonna sell Cadillac cars and smoke big seegars." He starts to giggle. "She gonna help him. She gonna help her main. Here come the fire—but she *will* help him. She got to. Whoooeee, she got to do it for her man." He finally fell back peaceful when the crossfire on T.V. started up, but, after all, which was a lot, he never let me understand. He's all pinched up back behind the eyes and nobody knows that man, nobody, not even Pauline. "Go *home*, Jerner. Go home an' quit worryin' and takin' pills. Shit. Get some de-grees an' make money some other way ... cause you never make it right this way," and he's waving his arms and hands again throughout the interior air. "You gonna hang aroun' this league ten years an' get nothin'—nothin' but crazy ... an' you crazy enough already." Looking at me when he's done preaching, he looks old—he looks so old he could of been a slave for Lee himself, but still painfully alive.

"How come you keep on doin' it?"

"Cause I don't have to anymore. Ha! Thas why. Cause I been at it so long ever thing I do look good. Older you get it look better an' better," sipping and grinning. He's suddenly the happy man.

.   .   .

"Both you men are *fools*," Pauline affecting a niggerish pout in her voice.

"No we ain't," says Side.

"Are!" says Pauline, both round eyes vivid with decent affection, at last, for both of us.

"We ain't no bigger fools than Coop and he gonna get ole Grace. BANG BANG—clippidy clob clippidy clob. Uh!" Thrust out both arms, blessing the set we got pulled in front of us at the couch. Then he sits up carefully to stare at the women. "Listen—we are sorry we mess up the good fooood. We sorry, ain't we, Son?"

"Right."

"You *sorry* foools!" And you have to go far to see a more beautiful and uncomplicated and relieved smile than the one all over Pauline at that minute. She does a kind of shoulder shake behind the counter, while continuing the happy smile, all of which brief female action fills me with pity—which pity in this case was not undignified or a signification of no character—it was in fact the purest straightout emotion I ever felt for four people in one place at one time in my whole life, including myself. I notice how even April has got her wholesome smile on again. And we finally did have us a good time once the goddamned movie was over.

Time was when I couldn't recollect them so fondly, and with some good reason; but now I think I understand why he has never looked me up over here in Fort Worth, or even called me. And I know it's Side who has made sure nobody on the Bulls has paid me much attention, even after the write-up of my teaching got into the Dallas papers: except for Coach Sepoy, who did drop a note, from Dallas to Fort Worth, saying they'd be interested in me whenever I was ready again. It bothered the hell out of me to be cut off so completely, but after all it is consistent with everything he tried to teach by precept, if not example.

They are very curious people, but they are a good couple, which is rare as hens' teeth these days. We never knew them long or well—but in spite of their troubles, whatever, there never

seemed any doubt they were *married*. Married. Jesus. Momma and
Daddy are married. Davis and Bessie are married—though I hardly
know Bessie at all, even after all the years in the same town. Maylene
and Henry weren't. Nor Henry and Maria, though it's close—and
maybe that's just a kind of marriage I don't understand, like something sanctioned in the Balearic Islands. And maybe April and
Royal finally will be, along some Scots plan. Maybe Mary Ann and
I will be. She'll have to settle on more conservative ways before
we'll ever make a good couple, but surely it isn't out of the question.
Dance dance, they did dance together after the movie, and even
April seemed to get caught up in it. The four of us playing like we
could calypso and waltz and bop and slowdance, in that room that
finally became luminous and warm, wherein we did move together,
exchanging partners decently, in affection. April and Pauline put
down a pail of whiskey sours between them it seemed and the two
of them were lovely together, giggling—Pauline lifting April's
blouse to show Side the elastic part in the front of her slacks, where
the baby rode. They got quickly drunk together and one time even
whirled around together, holding hands with arms extended,
cavorting like little girls in a schoolyard. Which ought to be some
kind of profound lesson in race relations, but isn't. Maybe it's something about married people—but I'm not even sure of that—for the
lesson would be pretty depressing: a stupid argument and a meal
ruined so people can get comfortably drunk together. Uh! The
neighbors offended by our obscenities on the porch. Pretty hard to
recommend as a moral program. We'd put ourselves through some
rigorous changes to get into our pleasures and probably we all
looked pretty depraved when as a body we fell asleep together on
the couch while a science fiction movie ticked along on the late,
late show.

O, Mary, it was a passing game all the way against Pittsburgh the
week before they shot the President and a couple of days after the
party with Pauline and Side, and I was by God earning my pay
against Pittsburgh, keeping the lane open and feeling good. It was
all so crisp and easy a little high and with the least Turkey in my
belly to level it. I felt I had on small tight springs instead of cleats,

all on a Sunday afternoon. Rack! Rack! Rack! I'm a ballet dancer
and Whirlaway on a high blue wire at the Fair, all alone and weightless in the light. For three quarters I experienced a perfect solitude
of immaculate achievement superior to killing, and Side, who I'm
in for because he has a pulled groin muscle, was proud of me. He
pulled it the very day after we'd had our contests.

"You're a good football player today." Side sat by me on the
bench in dapper street clothes and he was terribly proud of me:
"Verry good, man, very good." And once when the offense was on
the bench, Sepoy also came over and said I was doing it *right*.

It's the difference between being an offensive tackle and a defensive tackle. Great defensive play calls attention to itself, the P.A.
calling out, "Tackle made by Granville." I've always felt that
somehow the psychology of defense was slightly crude, slightly
negative, while offense, especially during a game dominated by
almost flawless passing, is an unobtrusive and almost delicate violence, by comparison, something akin to the craft of the potter, the
weaver, the man bent over his lathe. Crack, but not like breaking a
dry twig—more like bending a sapling shoot until it gives. My
right arm almost at the wrist. It's a compound fracture of the ulna
and there's a crack in the radius. At the hospital I raised hell and
wailed to April about how it was rotten luck. But I was lying! God!
When I realized that it was over, or at least that some of it was over,
at least until next season, and that I had a way out—out on the field
when I felt it giving and breaking under Delaney's cleats and when
I saw the bone sticking through the skin, when I was positive it
was broken—I've never been happier. Poteet he walked me over to
the bench and as I passed by, also with Morningside's arm over my
shoulder, I yelled out loud, "Give 'em hell! Give 'em hell for Big
D!" It was corny but the guys loved it for show and the papers
printed it. In the locker room with my jersey being cut away from
my arm, I told the gentlemen of the press I wanted to thank them
and everybody in Dallas for all they'd done for me. And I could
hardly keep from grinning. How 'bout that, sports fans?

11

SHE SHOWED UP back here at the house last night. Rose let her off out front and left, fearing conversion, I guess. She comes tripping through the door with one pillowcase full of books and one of clothes, and she is happy and calm. "Can I come back?"

"Sure . . . it's your house."

"It's your phone," smiling beautifully.

She was in some kind of pretty new wool suit—she was perfect, having no stockings on.

"Sonny, let's try again," in a chipper fashion.

"That ain't no good line, but it sounds like a fine idea."

"Oh, Sonny!" which ain't no bad line, especially since she's throwing her arms around me.

Yessir, I'm glad she's back.

It got clearer and clearer while she was gone: we are paired. Also, if we don't go on a way together, I haven't learned a thing all the summer and fall in the midst of stories. It is the decent thing to do, and that's important. The decent thing to do is to take my new lady to White Haven—I *must* introduce her to my people. I'll take her like a new fiancée, though maybe girl or woman is better than fiancée. April has never been anybody's fiancée; nor mine, nor R.C.'s. Moon Pie never had no fiancée. All he ever got was the leavings of a good wife. Mary is my good woman now. She does want to go on talking and loving with me. Good things. So we'll go off in a couple of days for Christmas with my good parents, a decent thing, and then we'll swing on down to Bryan for a visit with Davis and Bessie. We'll pass through Jackson on the way but won't stop there this time: only later when things are naturally more sophisticated will we stop to see that crowd. Jesus! Decent. Decent. Decent.

Mary understands how long to stay away. Right up until neither one of us can tolerate it.

She has been brooding and unhappy over at the Roses'. But she has kept her own mind, not letting them talk her out of me. She's back in her own good time and it quickly came to loving allover these Fort Worth rooms, and crying, and something of a serious statement from her, while everything is going on. Sitting naked on our bed, she requires that I take her home with me—she's smiling wanly and demands to go with me. She's sitting smoking and she's satisfied—says, "I'll show my love. I'll go to Mississippi." Fine. Fine. We finish off the reconciliation cigarettes than start back at love again, and then we sleep together in a hug, which is a very good thing to do.

II

April and I were packing up to leave Dallas when they shot the immaculate President of the United States—she's wrapping Henry's picture in a blanket and I'm taking the legs off the cypress table when the shit hits the fan over on the west side. My arm's in the cast and sore but I'm so happy to be leaving nothing is bothering me until the T.V. goes crazy with news of the shooting—*Kennedy was gunned down by an assassin apparently standing on the overpass above the freeway*. Sic.

Yarborough: *DASTARDLY . . .*

But Pauline rushing in was the beginning of the worst part, she's rushing and grabbing at and hugging first one of us and then the other—she's kissing and biting and hugging wildly—*THEY KEEEEEL THUH PRESIDENT*—she keens and yells such a thing even before anybody is sure ole Jack is dead. All she has got on is shortshorts, a U.C. T-shirt, and gin vapors, which gin she has clearly been into since Side left in the morning, and long before anybody got shot. She's heavy on the sauce and obviously more miserable in general than either of us had suspected.

"He'll be O.K.," says I, holding her racked body close to mine. "He'll survive this thing. I know he will," peering over her, who is in my arms, beneath my head, bawling. I'm trying to pray for good news. I'm trying to forget the pain that's under my arm cast.

Johnson is the President.

DALLAS, Nov 22—President John F. Kennedy is dead. . . .

Kennedy was gunned down by an assassin, apparently standing on the overpass above the freeway. Sic.

Gov. John Connaly also was shot and critically wounded. He was riding in the same car with the President.

A call for B-positive blood was reported to be circulating [curious prose] *at the hospital. It is assumed that this is for Connally, who is in the operating room.*

Connally was undergoing an operation for a gunshot wound in the chest at 1:30 p.m.

Prseident Kennedy, it is reported, did not have B-positive blood. That's how the story started in heavy print in the evening paper, including the misspelling.

Gunned down, mother, gunned down is how the Texas paper said it on that day. And I promise that's the last quotation.

That was certainly a bad day for the Nation, no doubt about it, but I think the worst of it was how the assassination thing ruined the relationship between us and Side and Pauline, or damaged it for a long time horribly.

Pauline went flap crazy it seemed, and then Side.

Right after the killing she continued to drink and roll and moan on the couch in front of the T.V. She kept saying, "Don't make me go"—and I didn't understand how to react to her. At first I thought it must be some kind of colored hysteria I didn't know about—but finally I canceled that idea out because she's from Waterloo and educated at the University of Chicago and not especially fond of blues music.

She'd flop on her back and pull her shirt up over her haid, exposing some kind of simple bra that wasn't much more than two napkins on a soft strap—she'd kick her legs like a child in a tantrum, with the result that both April and I felt guilty about our own lack of expressive emotion and sufficient grief.

And in retrospect—after having known Mary—I suspect it was probably Pauline's good education and good sense in general that probably made her act that way when they shot the President. Mary says she acted exactly the same way—even to the point of tearing her hair out in big gouts and batches.

It was the patriotic and decently pious thing for that woman to do on such an occasion. Yessir, no matter who the fellow is in private, a shot-down President of a great nation should be grieved excessively. It was insane to us, while we tried to continue packing as the news reports kept coming in. "Stop, stop, stop," Pauline would yell. "You can't leave here. You got to stay."

To hell with that, I was thinking, because I'd had about enough of the great world and the struggles of contemporary history. *I'm gettin' out of this town* is what was in my mind, amid a riot of disjunctive emotions.

April's boxing pots and pans behind the counter but still she's thoughtful enough to say I better go get some booze because it's likely to be a long night, the way *ya'll* are drinking.

"We got plenty," says Pauline, moaning from fetal position on the couch. So I went next door to get Side's half gallon of Crow. God, that girl could drink. She'd flop and sweat, snapping that round ball of a head back and forth on her long limber swan's neck —she'd groan and cry out as Cronkite carried on, and then she'd coil up dead silent. She'd seem right on the verge of passing out, but she never did. Just when she'd seem at peace, the fog would clear and she'd start talking as clearly as any political science professor, for a few minutes—"These people should be destroyed. There is simply no excuse for this. These people have got to pay. All of them. They're all guilty." For a moment she's bolt upright on the couch and talking like an intelligent woman at one of Roses' cocktail parties. "This couldn't happen in Iowa City or even Chicago, not to a President. At least they should have to pay an Assassination Tax." Then she goes back to howling.

Assassination Tax? Jesus, I never knew her well enough. That girl and I could have gotten along beautifully together in a better world. I'm sure of it. She's incredibly smooth and black and really bright, with a version of absolutely calm but energetic sensuality radiating from her most of the time. And when she's sober she smells faintly of citric acid and cloves. The way she'd look at me was passionate to the extent I knew we had some needs in common. Me and Pauline are the kind who should of run off to L.A. together, and there we should have got on hard stuff together, C and H, and in a secure water bead we would have swum forever, feeling like we'd both had a fine bowel movement, before we died.

When Side came in from work at about 3:00 p.m., it didn't get a helluva lot better, because that man was the opposite of his wife, but just as bad.

He's deep into himself, burned because some people on the team seemed pleased when they heard it, and he don't give a rip about what's on anybody else's mind around the apartment. He couldn't care less his pretty lady is sour with grief smells and booze (Lord, the way drunks smell), because they are probably going to make him play on Sunday. He suspects it, and he was correct. "Fuckin' Commissioner won't take one day off for the President, not one damn day." He says it, sits down, paying no attention to anybody, stares at the set without a word for an hour at least, looking like a priest overseeing a rite, judging. More than an hour, because the next thing he finally does is get his large ass up and go for chicken in a box for supper.

One more thing about that afternoon: Pauline at one point grows lucid and says that maybe April will go into labor tonight so we can call it J.F.K. Joiner. Uh!

April says, "No, I wouldn't have the baby here. Not on your

life." She's packing some toilet articles and hardly raises her voice from the bathroom, but it carries.

"You ought to! You ought to!" Pauline goes on.

"No she shouldn't," says Side and then goes after the chicken.

We'd gotten to be pretty good friends with those people and it is a damn shame it didn't last, for it was pretty progressive for a white guy to room with a black guy on the road and also to be good friends socially the way we were—which did exclude us from lots of prejudiced couples on the team. And it was all Side's fault. I ought to call him and tell him so right now. I ought to call him and tell him he's a selfish and exclusively interior man who doesn't pay enough attention to the people who come and go in his life on this bank and shoal of time. Bastard went home about 7:30 and locked himself in his room for more than two days. He stared at that picture of Jackie climbing onto the wounded body of dead Jack, said "Uh! I ain't playin'," got up and left for good. Which was the last I ever saw of him—his back going out the door—and almost the last I ever heard him say. Right. That was it, period, and he kept us in that goddamned city for another whole day and a half. He wouldn't even let his goddamn wife come in the bedroom with him.

She's yelling and pounding on the door—"Don't kill yourself, baby, don't hurt yourself!"

"Go on now, go away," gruffly from behind the door. "I ain't *about* to hurt myself . . . but I won't play Sunday. You tell that to Poteet, Jerner. You tell those fuckahs I'm gone till Monday afternoon."

He uses me. He simply uses me for a day and a half. We have to take care of Pauline Friday night and all of Saturday and part of Sunday. Two days! Which wasn't easy, the apartment being in a mess. Her wearing April's clothes and being thoroughly drunk the whole time, and finally requiring nothing but vodka in everything from orange juice to Cokes—and then there's Poteet on the phone wondering where the hell his All-Pro tackle is, for the meeting Saturday afternoon. I tell him the great man is so ill he cannot rise from his bed of pain; which Poteet didn't believe. But at last he said,

"Tell him to get his tail well in a hurry." And—"I wish you weren't hurt, Son."

I lied and said that I, too, wished to hell I wasn't. I said Coley'd do O.K. on offense for a change, what the hell?

Man, I'll tell you what—it's a problem to have a beautiful drunk colored woman around the house for two days when your wife is pregnant, heavy pregnant; but April took it well.

She finished packing and even helped me to load the small U-Haul on Saturday morning—a hard thing to do with one arm—(which trailer we hardly needed since we'd put so few things in the furnished apartment—our own bed and the table being the most of what was ours), and then she dedicated the rest of her energies to caring for Pauline. We packed all but the bed and a few utensils and the toaster and some plates and clothes and the T.V., and then we settled down to watch the results of the great event and mind Pauline, while her self-indulgent husband sulked next door in privacy.

What I wanted was traveling music on the radio and to be heading East in my own car alone with my own wife who's carrying my own baby—traveling music on the car radio and gloaming settling around the Vicksburg Bridge. But what I got was blather and comment about Oswald, and speculation about his porcine momma, a very Sea of Bad News that spilled out into that poor senseless, deprived, semistripped apartment. I kept on telling myself that all this carrying on was as it should be (including Pauline's unmitigated excess—seizure after seizure all day Saturday until I was positive she'd been carrying on some fantasy affairs with the dead man), but I never quite convinced myself.

"Goddamn, Pauline, it's not the first king to get killed. He's a nice person to us, but he's a pain in the ass to lots of people—in 491 Zeno was buried alive—Maurice was decapitated in 602—Constans II was bludgeoned to death in his bath in 668—and Alexius V was blinded and maimed in 1204—to name a few. It comes with the job."

"OOOooo"

Piss on her. It was a crying shame, but the Republic *would* survive, and no matter what the fools say, Johnson will be recorded as a better than average President. I believe I actually could have done right by Mr. Kennedy if it hadn't been for Mr. and Mrs. Robbins. Flop and thrash, flop and thrash, lecture, lecture, brood, brood.

She calmed down after they shot ole Lee on Sunday. She relaxed and said for us to go. Just when I expect to get some fine sentences from her on vengeance she quits squealing and boozing and simply gets calm. "Ya'll go on now. I'm O.K. Side'll come out in the morning."

"I think we should," says April. "Helen's expecting us."

Those women hardly even reacted to the most exciting thing the whole weekend, which was Ruby doing *his* murder on prime time in front of God and everybody. "SON OF A BITCH"—I screamed when Lee's face squinched up and he clutched his sweater at the belly. And I could also hear a dim commotion from next door where Side's obviously listening to the clock radio.

I ran next door to ask if he'd heard it. I told him to come out and watch it on T.V., but he wasn't having any.

"You got to be hungry," I yelled.

"Go away," and his radio is blasting out the dirty deed.

So we did. We went away and I didn't even go back to tell him goodbye after I'd put the bed on top of the table in the U-Haul. Why bother? We gave Pauline the key to give the manager on Monday morning and left her standing in one of April's sacks up on the porch. She looked like an African princess meditating on her warrior's fate in the hands of the Portuguese. She waved limply but didn't quite look at either of us. "Keep in touch." I think she said that as we were going by the swimming pool of Tuscany Plaza a last time. "Write."

I was a one-armed man commanding a submarine with a small caboose, heading East, slowly slipping beneath the waves. Yes, certainly that is it. Certainly whatever the West is it seems to be out of water and maybe that's the difference and why it is so vulnerable— Dallas under the big sky hasn't been under an ocean for a long time (but don't check my geology too closely) and so it cries out and is afraid. O tall and Vulnerable City, you are no place for whales. The ancient inland sea begins in the pines—the needles of the beach and the combers of ground fog. The salty memories begin to lap at your wheels somewhere near Longview—and you are well beneath the raunchy depths by the time you get to Bossier City Buzz buzz. Whatever. I'm sure I could see a tide that evening on the road heading home with my lady and her baby.

"Sonny, it's over," she said mysteriously.

"Yeah." Yeah—but I didn't want her to go farther into it—and I absolutely didn't want her to tell me how glad I was to be gone. That was my secret and none of hers, and had she not stolen it we might still be married.

"Aubrey'll be born in Bryan."

"Yeah." I turned up the traveling music about the time we reached Tallulah, about the time we passed the Green Frog Recreation Center, which has a facade of pea green with a huge frog of medicinal green painted on it. Beneath the weird light of the mercury vapor lamps that frog was a demon to me, worse than any Vodyanoi. Buzz buzz.

She rode beside me as we crossed the Vicksburg Bridge, she sat correctly straight up with her hands folded over her belly as barge lights twinkled upriver in the heavy atmosphere—and right then and there, about the state line, I should have realized the evils I fled were no worse than the evils I returned to.

III

The bad time came in the spring and it was Stream and it got to be a fight, a Friday night fight at the Second Stand. He gets beered up because even though he's a good book salesman for Mantis-Thrall Inc.—since he was cut off from graduate study in Nashville because of Incompletes—he thinks he is a failure. Since he started selling in February, he's been checking in at Bryan about once a week to see me, on his way to Southern or some junior college to hustle texts. Checking in to plague me, when he can, with doubts. I'd been doing fine the whole of January, and most of February and March I held out against his onslaught—if it was him after all that I was holding out against. Somebody.

He sees us fallen together at the same time, twin devils in a fall that's far from fortunate. I didn't want to be hard, at first, on a suffering man, but finally I did have to point out the fact that my broken arm bones weren't exactly the same as his flunking out. I wasn't in line for Rookie of the Year—but I had got a job and I'd done well enough with the Bulls, and next year (or the next) I'd start, no doubt about it. We'd be shooting the shit at the icehouse late at night, or at my new place, or at the Stand, and I never convinced him we didn't share a common fate. He managed to help drive me crazy, but none of it was because I'm like him. *Both of us died a little over in Dallas*—he'd say that so soulfully, too often.

We've both got our guts up against Cantrell's long pine bar— says "Sonny, look at you—you're a fatass—you'll end up a bum like Foots. We're both worthless." He's casual in his voice while speaking across the bar into the mirror where both our drunken faces hang. Goes on about how athlete's heart will get me. Then he starts on how Royal Carle Boykin is the only one in our class who has got any sense at all. (He won't even grant that Bobo had at least some cunning to marry that terrible pale Delta woman to get the land he always wanted.) "Look at Roil," says Stream. "He's up there in Nashville preparing to be a swell young lawyer. He's swingin' on to glory." (Actually Royal was at that minute up in *Jackson* doing research for a paper on Negro rights—the history of them in Mississippi—during his spring vacation. And clearly the real trouble was that when he and Royal were in Nashville together last semester, Royal was too *busy* for him. Second year law school. Hot stuff.)

And it really pissed me off to hear Stream talk that way about himself, and me. I'd been moving at my own personal viscosity and velocity, making private discoveries while handling lumber out at the Mill; I'd been staying home as much as I could stand it, playing with the baby, getting used to loose pussy; and Stream had absolutely no rights in the matter. He's the worst kind: tells you what your subject matter and style should be, swears by *Esquire*. Anyway. He says Boykin wouldn't cross the street to have coffee with either of us. "Sonny, there's something brutal and un-liberal . . . and . . . *dated* . . . about you and . . ."

Before I realized in my mind how mad I was I'd picked him off his stool and tossed him into the middle of the dance floor, bowling over some of the couples in the process—then we're rolling around under the tables with everybody yelling at us to stop or go to it. He'd finally conjured demons with his talk. He'd got at the horror going on.

Like how I'd been sitting cautiously on our bed's edge just the night before, trying to think how things might soon be good again, and how sometimes I surely did enjoy the baby, and how I was going to get back in shape again not so much to play ball but just so I could live longer and watch my boy grow up, scratching my feet abstractly, sitting there on the edge of our bed in a tiny robin's egg blue room (April having suffered an acute attack of bad taste just about the time the baby came—she'd been stricken by a desire for *happy* colors, suggesting that probably her racial origins were Russian, a type from the bitter steppes). I was winding the alarm clock and daydreaming, feeling comfortable after a long day of physical labor, so I wound until I twisted the crank right off the back, ruining the spring. Stream's talk brought the violent sadness of the previous night back into my body. God, to break sweet April's clock made me feel so guilty, and also terrified, for no good reason. I rushed up to the living room and went to work upon that clock. I tore at the damn face of it, trying to get inside so I could fix it, all the while making these sort of clobbery groaning sounds over the clock. I realized I had to undo some little nuts from the back, which I did in a hurry with my fingernails—then tore again at the face and pulled it apart from the back, making my fingers start to bleeding. But once inside I could see it wasn't any use. There were

all these pretty clean toothed wheels and gears, but that one big
spring goes pooching out over the side. It was broken and there
wasn't one goddamned thing I could do about it. Busted at the
connection. April comes up the hall, bounding almost, carrying inside her all the splendid recreational and recuperative powers of
young motherhood, from the bathroom, where she has been washing and scenting her body, and she wants to know what's the
matter. I tell her to have a gander at her Westclox—look at the ruin
of it—all its handsome little gears and shining wheels and the
delicately strong mainspring that used to make it tick—all of it a
waste because ole big-fisted Son who's daydreaming had gone and
fucked it up. I had the pains then, the bad flat pains from asshole to
teeth—but they didn't keep me from throwing the big parts
straight through the picture window of her orange room. She
wanted to call Dr. Saucier but settled for getting me a big glass of
whiskey. She was being understanding once again, so I tried to
appreciate her attitude.

Now you take the average woman who has been hit real good
by her husband twice in one week, and has a little baby asleep in
its Pepto-Bismol pink crib down the narrow hall, and you, friend,
won't usually find a woman who's willing to sit on her peach couch
to mind her husband—but *she* did. That goddamned woman was
hanging on. We're sitting there with pieces of glass spread about
the floor (she'd immediately dumped them from the couch pillows,
so we could sit), the rain starting to pelt in on us, and she says,
"Daddy'll fix the window tomorrow [which he did] . . . don't
worry . . . I'm sorry I've said the wrong things"—we're in our pj's
and nighty, getting wet—but she is hanging at my side and trying
to make sense.

I didn't know how to handle her anymore, didn't want to. I
finished the drink, tacked a poncho over the window, and went to
bed, which was my next mistake—because by then she's decided
loving was the answer.

Yessir, it's the garish simple life of love and family for ole April
—loving, eros, fucking, sex, affection, creature comforts out the
gazoo, and bright colors. (Christ, after I left, she made ole Henry

move into that house, so she could watch his health—no wonder he went madder than usual—and, Lord, he must be glad to be back in his own strict, fierce place now she's re-married and up in Jackson; if he isn't dead already and spread around in Maria's paints somewhere, in another alien room.)

I'd gained to nearly 315 pounds in the time since Dallas, though you cannot be sure because house scales won't weigh it—and I wasn't about to subject myself to the ignominy of the commercial scales at the Mill, everybody inspecting the big needle like cash money was involved in every pound. It was doing other things, like eating and stacking and thinking, that conflicted with loving. I'd of lost it eventually if she hadn't leaned on me—though there wasn't much else she could do but lean on me in bed the way I bore down on my side, raising hers. She wanted me to lose for my health, but for some reason the fat didn't discourage her desires. It seemed, in fact, that she had some idea to screw it off me.

She did the usual lovely tricks with hands and mouth to no avail —and then she started on the flattery: how I could do *anything* in the world I wanted to, when *I* decided to, and how, after all, she thought my working at the Mill was wonderfully . . . *eccentric.* Lying up beside me like a suckerfish against a shark. An obese shark?

She's trying to make up for Monday night when she looks over her 10:00 p.m. coffee and says, "Son, you're *glad* to be out of Dallas. Why not admit it?" It's casually offhand and not the least aggressive, but still it was my own damn secret—she'd stolen the secret I'd wanted to *tell her,* in my own good time. "Son, I think you're too gentle for it . . ." AAAAH! And the look upon her face was intended to be sexy—like said gentleness was the raunchiest thing she could think of. "You're plenty good, but most of them are ob-sessed." Which did it.

"God damn it, *I'm* obsessed. You think I'm not obsessed?" unconsciously swinging a backhand across the table that banged her shoulder hard enough to knock her to the floor and also spill hot coffee all over her. I hustled to bathe her in cold water from the sink. "Jesus! I'm sorry"—but I couldn't think of anything to do, after I had her cooled and had stopped her tears, but go drink beer at the Stand.

.   .   .

She was trying to tell me I *could* play more ball, if I wanted to. "You can do *anything* you want to," in a lascivious voice that suggested gratification of sexual desire and also any vocational plans I might have. She's slap up beside me with nothing on now, and the baby is groaning in his pink tent nearby—because she wasn't about to move into the other room for a month or two more—and anyway I think it turned her on to fuck with the baby in the room. "Sonny, Sonny, let's make love. We'll both feel better."

Bosh. We'd done it night before last and even with her on top I got to pumping so hard (leaping up at her with the hips) I broke the bed down, to spite the extra slats we'd put in. No more of that for a while.

I got out and went into the dark living room and curled up on the damp couch, while a gentle rain was settling in outside. A nice rain so close to the ear is a notable pleasure, not to be denied, with sex or without. "Western Wind" ain't the only way to enjoy it.

Correct. One of the worst things that can happen is when a soul in misery begins to notice the symbols around the house, or actions symbolical, like with that silly clock. There's many a man has busted a clock, said "damn," and let it go at that.

But a fat dude, just outside of town, suffering tachycardia and/ or the first stages of angina, won't be so obtuse: he'll see the signs of everything.

Like the house I got her when we came home. It seemed just like the others that millpeople lived in stretched out along the highway to both the southwest and northeast of town (like Henry's or Helen's—like the one I'd grown up in, and also like the one that for a long time was the Boykins')—narrow two- or three-bedroom jobbies set on a couple of acres (small houses on big lots), set deep away from the highway in a strange isolation from the town. It should of been just like the others, but it wasn't. At Daddy's house I could come home at dawn after carrying on with ole April in some motel, and I'd say—"House, I been at it again! The bag busted an' surely she's knocked, betcha!" Daddy's house would shrug its simple roof and say I ought to stay in my own bed more: "Simple as that, boy; sleep in your own bed." But my new house never did learn to talk back to me.

Henry's was made of oak mostly, and the siding boards outside were vertical and stained, not painted or shingled, and was reputed to have cypress floors—Helen's was old soft pine that finally got covered with asbestos shingles, and had gutters to make it different, goddamned copper gutters she paid a mint for—and the thing that made Daddy's house so unusual was the thick carpet grass we'd sprigged in over the years, two acres of carpet grass—Lord God— for that's a helluva lot of sweating and sprigging, and pine trees all around, and flowers, and a terrific birdbath he worked a whole summer on (a small fountain in the center of the pan was triggered when the bird lit on the rim), and Momma who sat in the yard like a queen to paint her pictures (her stool'd go down three inches in the mat); even the chickens in our pen out back had carpet grass to lime; Daddy planted the loblollies when it wasn't anything but bare ground, right after Lucy died.

Yessir, the white people at the Mill were different. Helen still owned the stump of the buzzard tree.

It was pitiably romantic of me to rent a place out there when I came back—and I guess it was pitiably romantic to take a job at the Mill.

Yes. If you live southwest or northeast of town, where the white millpeople do, you don't have the same experiences as townspeople. It's a strange class. Because in town if you're a doctor, a coroner, or a coach, or a preacher in some standard church, or a druggist, on some streets, you're likely to have Negroes as backdoor neighbors. They're right there to observe, day in and day out, coming and going, and sometimes on the weekends you can hear them raising hell at night across the alley, or the tracks. This is called demography, and is important, I'm told.

Even being downcast or outcast or poor in town, like a Foots or a Weatherford or a Terrell, is different—because then you live away from the niggers in a little house on a *small* lot (in town)—having these small lots and not keeping things neat and being sullen is what defines necks, tonk people, low Baptists (Free-Will-type), and Holiness people—which is different from my people! You live in town on a *small* lot and in a *small* house and you're both depraved and deprived. You pay city taxes for the privilege of knowing you eat shit.

Sam Chalmers has always known his people would be well off on large lots outside of town—out there in a little house you're substantial working people, goddamned good yeoman stock come halfway into modern technology—out there you are relieved of the decayed habits of both necks *and* owners: professionals. People on the edges and out from town are *amateurs.* Yessir. And colored people don't work on your mind much if you're an outfrom.

Some preacher like Taggart can try to get you exercised about colored people, but probably it won't take.

I come home from The League and The Assassination and from living with Pauline and Side, and there's a boycott going on, and Slater wants the school unified, integrated. He comes right into the shitty little living room of the shitty little house I'm living in—he's greeted by April who's about to deliver any day—he's well received (affectionately on my part, I must say)—but the business about the boycott and school confuses me. "I'm for that," I say, handing him a beer. Which seemed enough.

"Talk to the businessmen—tell the school board."

"Who's on it?" Embarrassing. Here's this intense Negro friend, and here I am back from the wars expected to do good—but I don't even know who's on the school board. Dexter Betner and Sam Chalmers and Dr. Saucier, certainly?

"____"

"I'll do what I can."

"Meaning what?"

"I'll talk it up . . . at Nancy's."

"____"

It's curious—because it was clear as the pits in his black face he'd really just dropped by socially to bother me, and to get a beer.

"I'll talk it up."

"Great." The Indian Negro has got his mouth put over the opening in the beer cans like a flautist.

Then I told him all about Side and Pauline and the great world of The League, lying about how progress is inevitable in great business and athletic ventures like pro ball, getting giddy as the worst sort of phony liberal you can imagine.

Even April comes into her freshly painted orange room and tries to act graceful to our local Negro acquaintance—by telling Slater how she'll be so glad when he gets married so she can get to know his wife.

Then I told him what I didn't know until I said it. I said I wasn't about to do more than talk good up—because I had *discoveries* to make. "Slater, I got discoveries to make. Quiet ones. I'm going to work at the Mill and make discoveries." April, gross with child, stiffened a little because she hadn't heard the Mill idea—and didn't care for it.

"Gonna listen to the animals?"—Slater tooting dull notes on his nearly empty can.

"Take your goddamned sunglasses off when you're in the house, will you?"

Though it was bright enough to blind a man in that room.

It was a terrible town and a terrible house to live in, but I couldn't show it, with the baby coming.

Only Davis and Coach Topp (the one time I saw him) were upset about the President's death. All the rest seemed delighted— they *were* delighted—said so again and again at Nancy's—Foots and Saucier and crewcut Preacher Morris, and Henry—everybody seemed to think I was blessed to be in Dallas on the great day when they shot the little bastard J.F.K.: not that Johnson was any better, much better—though it was clear they could tolerate apostates better than gentiles, including me. *That wall-eyed mother—he screwed ever nigger secretary in Washington—an' then let Mawtin King do it to his wife, before his own eyes!*

.   .   .

Terrible people. I'd fork around in my eggs and then cast a weary eye down at the flamingos still dipping their beaks in gray water on the wall. I'd get me a piece of jerky to go with my coffee, and then I would talk. *No no no no no no no—he was making a good President—and we got to integrate and hire colored people in this town if any progress is to come—because the way it is is un-just—it'll be an adjustment but the future lies in recognizing that there have been great black civilizations in Africa—there's nothing so supple and lovely in the history of art as the Saharan rock paint-ings, a combination of abstract and representational, done when the desert was a fertile plain, before 2000 B.C., when the airborne moisture went away—Oxen spotted—utterly graceful and peaceful elephants—to say nothing of the deliriously treading hot giraffes they did—and figures ceremonial—my Christ there is a picture in the desert over in Africa of a herd of cattle painted in 1500 B.C. so active they move before your very eyes even now—Bornu's warriors were the greatest—fracking CAPARISONED HORSES —and what say of struggling with the TSETSE FLY? and the Majestic Kingdom of Benin —the incredible churches cut out of sheer rock in Ethiopia (AFRICAN NIGGER CHRISTIANS, with some white blood in them just like all of ours)—think of the ruins at Kilwa, comparable to the mosque at Cordoba, Spain—and listen, you somitches, I've lived with a colored tackle who, when he's in business, will beat you all at a bad game.*

I spoke softly but firmly, *too* softly, however firm, and they hardly responded—they seemed to think I'd contracted a curious Texas disease—a virus of New York City—a plague in Cleveland—a psychological rash of the soul—but it would pass, they trusted.

Davis sitting in the morning down at the end of the counter tapping his spoon against his thick white coffee cup: "You're crazy, Son." Double talk for the ruck, from the Sheriff. Two meanings at least—agreement and *Son, that won't do no good. Yet.*

I'm satisfied the only thing I ever got through to them was

some kind of football talk about how good Clarkson and Robbins were—and how I had roomed with a good nigger.

Foots said he never roomed with a nigger, but allowed as how it was different in The League those days. "They strong sometimes, but they still niggahs. Dumb. Never make a center or a quarterback."

"Will too do it," I'd say.

I gave up on Nancy's after a couple of mornings. I started concentrating on house and home and family, which wasn't much better.

EUPHORIA—April was suffering a colorful euphoria—bright pinks and blues and oranges. Cheap red and yellow curtains, plans for flowers in the spring, and why not put out winter grass right now! We had our good bed and the cypress table, but the rest of the stuff she got was blond shit bought on time. She called it stopgap furniture—since we were being frugal—until I decided what . . . to . . . do. The wretched couch was lime green. Even Helen was concerned, having a taste for darker colors, tints like the flesh of an old plaster Jesus on a black cross. But I did what I was told. I painted and fixed up that goddamned house until the baby came.

April bought me a book soon after we got home, the *Handyman's Book*. With a picture on the front.

There's this cool Doak Walker-type Husband, with a pipe in his mouth, and he's drilling a hole in some kind of board or another with his bit and his hairy arms. But this is not the best thing about this particular dust jacket. Nossir. It's the wife that I loved best. In the background, where the older and more naive painters would have put cedars and ruined castles and ships about to go under the horizon, there is, sir, The Wife, in an attitude of praise and adoration. She's standing beside the jigsaw of the "Handyman," and she, my friend, is about to have a double reverse convoluted orgasm because he is so *competent*. Had the same man made All-Pro at squatting guard she couldn't have looked so pleased. Had he just finished the standard work on Fritz Steinberg she wouldn't have had that look of horny passion and security-ridden carnality upon her uninspired face. Think of it! This man knows all there is to know about the clean-out plug at the bottom of the U-trap under the sink. He, sir, is the master of the drain auger.

I can affirm with confidence that if your problem is just that of moisture showing under the basement walls (not that there's a basement outside the Holiness Church anywhere in Bryan), you can often cut down interior humidity seriously by painting the inside walls with concrete—or plastic-base paints.

April had a baby on December 15.

We lived on the southwest side, where the weather comes from, farther out than Henry's or Helen's (which themselves were far enough out to be in Stone Creek District for years). I myself had grown up nearer in on the northeast side.

We (April and I) lived four miles out and far enough I had to drive like hell, I thought, she and Helen trying to ease me from the back seat, to get her to the Clinic, where I waited from 10:30 p.m. to 6:30 a.m., when Aubrey was born.

Dr. Saucier, that semicompetent old fart, was of course in charge, and Helen was generally ministering, administrating, looking like a sexually aroused chicken hawk.

They brought him out before he's even cleaned off (a ritual the Zande would have never imagined). He's covered with blood and hot from the snatch, and has the most horrible sloped skull you can conceive, his brow rising at a very slight angle back toward the point of his slimy head (he's been born under the caul—which he'll need as Royal's son). It's like a bloody football (the plastic-toy kind you get at service stations) with obscure but essentially human features at one end.

"Beautiful," cries Helen, like she has spotted a litter of field mice from three hundred up.

Dr. Saucier—who's the jaunty, semiskilled, silverhaired, helpful, local G.P. to the hilt—smiles above his gory gown and says, in a voice more cajoling than comforting, "Son, the boy is . . . fine . . . and blessed." While fingering the dab of caul that's about where the laces should be.

"The head!" I cry, too loud for a late night in the Clinic, even when you're hysterical.

"Shush," says Helen, bunned, almost fondly.

"The child's head is perfectly . . . fine . . . Son—it'll take a few days for it to . . . shape up."

"They'll mold it," says Helen, suggesting a rite that boggled my mind.

The floor tiles in the Clinic were the color of a smoker's teeth, but the light seemed violent on the poor babe's face, so I asked to hold it, so I could shade him—Lord, the love you feel with your own new baby in your arms—which pleased the assembled company. "Aubrey Smith Joiner, by God," I said, proudly, trying to offer a normal father-type statement. "April's O.K.?"

"She's a strong girl—a *strong* girl."

"Right."

What else? I went over to Southern to see Jakes and get recs, avoiding Burger.

I went to N.O. with Henry on New Year's. Henry who was strangely unimpressed by the birth of his grandson. "Might as well thank the trees for leaves," he said once.

I went to work at the Mill the Monday of the second week in January. Showed up. There were coaching and teaching jobs available at Mendenhall, Pinola, Columbia, and Jackson Provine, and he could substitute teach in Bryan—if he'd give up talking like a Communist at Nancy's—if he'd give up the Stand and start drinking at home, like Morgan and Topp did—if he's quit having niggers into his house (the locals had noticed). He could go down to Southern for graduate courses under Burger second semester, if he wanted to. The dude could do a lot of things he didn't.

. . .

Slater was lovely, just lovely. I enjoyed the hell out of him, until Stream came home and made it grave. Slater finally created himself as a real person for me a couple of times while we sat out on the front stoop, smoked cigarettes, and drank Jax.

One night during Christmas me and Slater and Davis sat out there on a chill night and shot the shit. The porch light was out and April's gaudy curtains were pulled in front of the extinguished tree.

Slater, three years at Tougaloo behind him several years ago, and now in the pay of the NAACP and other groups, sat there and said he knew the boycott was a hard thing. Davis says, "Tough . . . but necessary. Don't quote me." Grinning in the dark.

It was a genuinely exciting thing to be doing—except I might as well of had my head in a burlap sack. Here's a local nigger and the Sheriff on my steps talking the great issues of the day, but it don't penetrate. Seemed natural as could be—but none of the business of how long to hold out and for what, and the trouble of hauling groceries and stuff from Jackson—still, none of it seemed so profound as the Sheriff and the agent of progress wanted it to be.

It was a warm sensation, and brotherly, but even their recollections of Buster Doleman's wet corpse and the continuing threat of Magee's Raiders never penetrated until later. The dude lived in something worse than a tree.

I'd say things like, "We're in it. It's happening." Or: "Everything will happen," as the stars went on about their starry business and an occasional car or truck passed by upon the road. I was trying to be accepting of the life process.

They tolerated. They waited.

The second week of January I showed up for work at the Mill. I wasn't hired, I just showed up, on a crisp clear winter morning, with Henry. I picked him up myself, honked him up at 6:45—he came out and got in without the least surprise, and he never questioned exactly what I meant to do.

Sam Chalmers questioned me. Sam comes over to where I'm straightening some sticks in a bin. He's a slim, stooped fellow, round-shouldered in an expensive white shirt above his starched khakis and shoes with wing tips. He's the richest man around but it don't show, too much.

"Hey, Son, you gonna do some fixing up at the place?" He thinks I've come to buy.

"Naw, Sam, what I'm gonna do is be your stacker and loader. I'm gonna stack and load and stay in shape." I'm arranging some long 2 x 12's and Sam seems to get the picture.

"Fine . . . you still got the football money?"

"Right. No-cut. What you pay's fine."

"That'll do it. That'll keep you strong if you put some runnin' with it," Sam's voice dissolves, and he goes back into the house trailer that is his operations office: Chalmers' Industries. No more questions. Very little comment—except finally from Henry, that first afternoon, at the pisser trough, in the little shack behind the kiln. He sidles up beside me and unself-consciously lets go a stream, while chortling resonantly inside his grilled head—chortles, then tugs on my sleeve so I pee down my leg a little.

"Whatcha doin', Son . . . Hey, you like it out on the yard—all that . . . good . . . clean . . . work, huh?"

"Yeah."

"Well, you just as crazy as the rest these people." He folds his thang back in and goes off.

I was offered an opportunity to operate a fork lift, a Hyster; to cruise timber in West Feliciana Parish, La.; to drive truck; to prepare to take Henry's foreman job when he's retired; to learn to be a saw mechanic like my father. *Son, you could do it real good as a salesman. Those retail boys would eat you up.* Lord God, a salesman.

I loaded trucks and stacked in the bins, flipped sticks off the dry chain a couple of days, pulled down hard on many a Lebus binder, securing loads on the bobtails, and that was all, while making discoveries.

.   .   .

And then one night—this is the Wednesday before the Thursday clock, the Wednesday before the Friday fight and the Saturday revolution, and the Sunday exile—one night, as I had so often done, I was in my pj's out on the berm talking at my house. This had been going on from time to time since the first night Coldstream came through on his new job. *Depression . . . Regression . . . Irresponsibility*—he had all the words—*Paranoia*—he had me figured—and just when my days at the Mill were beginning to get ritualized —just when I was gaining the proper muscle memory so I wouldn't try to strain the big boards. I was just at the point where once again I could grab a 24-inch board at the end, lift a little, give a flick, sending a shiver down the length, to raise it up a level, or over, or into the truck's bed.

Wood is good work. It's like a drug. I was like a moron stacking blocks.

"You're like a moron stacking blocks," said Stream one night, down at his uncle's icehouse.

It was an average clear March night, but the house wouldn't talk back. It sat there, born with asbestos on, gutterless, silent, like a piece of marble cake beneath a lover's moon, like frozen Brylcream, wordless, containing wife and child and mother-in-law (for all intents)—because the baby had the croup and because April knew that Helen liked to be of aid.

"House, we've been through this before."

"_____"

"What you've got in you won't last."

"_____"

"All fall down. Even Helen . . . and Henry, dear God."

I flung the quart bottle high to the moon and damned if it didn't sail in an arch and crash in a burst against my false chimney, more than forty yards, a distant tinkle in the chilly air, that must have reached my people in their beds—the baby coughing, April turning and vaguely reaching for me (amazed preconsciously to find herself level on the mattress, fat man out), Helen drawing her sour flesh into a knot on the rollaway in the guest room. As the bottle rose the moon shone through it at its apogee. I've seen few prettier things.

Unless it was the mist down on Steele's just a little later. The mist on that slow water a little beyond false dawn was about the most gentle and almost oriental thing I ever saw. Yessir, it was some kind of night and dawn for lovely things. I desired them—something attractive and seemly, formal even, suggestive of durability. Maybe I'd put me a Jap rock garden out back, strewn pebbles in a flowing conservative design. I wished I was in Samurai costume, so I could take it all off and go for a swim, removing the shoulder guards, the torso sheath, the cased sleeves (metal of intricate design), the horseback thigh guards, the leather shinguards, my pantaloons, kimono, and breechclout. Maybe if I'd got down to the breechclout I'd of left it on to swim in, after having arranged all the rest of my garments there on the grassy bank. For that breechclout is an interesting, one-piece thing with a string collar affair you put your head through. Then it hangs down your front like a combination bib and diaper with strings on the bottom corners. You pull it between your legs, then tie it all securely, belting with those strings. I fancied that would be a nice thing to swim Steele's in. I'd be standing rare in my cottons. I'd be looking down at the neatly folded exquisite brocade of the robe meant to cover my armor.

I'd snuck back into the house to get another quart and my keys, on tippytoes lightly; I'd skulked out quietly to take my ride, at dawn: near it. Ending at Steele's bridge. It was an easy experience, imagining the kind of clothes I should be in, but finally it was the swim that was on my mind. Nothing but the swim, and the idea to sweat under water.

It seemed exactly the right time and place to sweat beneath shallow waters. You feel both waters when you do it, but it requires hard work to get there.

Took off the pj's once down to bankside in the pale green of the spring grass near dawn, and then I waded in, out to the middle, where it was waist-deep, deep enough to swim, and then I moved slowly *away* from the bridge, following the bayou back into the dense overhang of woods. Sloshing away from the tender light around the cement bridge. I headed upstream nearly fifty yards to where the first bend was. God damn it was chilly. God damn I got goosey and even started wondering about snakes and frogs and such, to say nothing of the possible chunks of dead bodies locked on a log I'd shove loose. God damn that mushy bottom was strange on my feet, and the water itself was opaque silver, and brown and black beneath the fog I parted as I walked along. I closed my eyes and headed toward where the bend was. When I got there I went up on the bend's bank and looked back toward the bridge. Beautiful! Like looking up the aisle of a wet church, and the bridge was like a small silver altar to swim under. I'd swim all the way down as fast as I could—passing under Steele's—and then go right on another thirty yards on the other side. I jogged hard on the soggy bank, I jogged in the dim light of that swamp, almost to the point of sweat, and then plunged in.

Panic, rage, ecstasy—Who in hell knows? but Christ I did swim hard and rather elegantly at that, fluttering just right with the feet and legs, doing a massive sweating crawl in Steele's bayou—I felt saline solution letting out and swaddling my skin as I strove along, passed beneath the bridge, and continued on. God, it was tiring, God, I swallowed bayou water and nearly drowned about the time I got to the other side. Somitch—it was exhausting finally—but that no doubt was exactly what I'd wanted. Going down to my knees on the messy bottom, staring up into the swamp on the downstream side. I wondered what I was doing there, even though the sweating had been strange and good. I turned around and could still see where I'd cut my wake in the water and the fog. Stood up to full height (naked in that growing morning) and saw these persons up on the bridge. Oof. Wretched embarrassment to be sure. I ducked back in, submerged, in fact, and thought about trying to swim underwater up to where my clothes were. Sunk in that water again was a truly miserable embarrassment. Then the fortunate thought came—about the time I mean to break water again— *Shit, it's not people at all: it's ghosts.* Ghosts don't care how naked you are. Ghosts couldn't care less about what a man does with his early mornings. It was entirely comforting to gain this confidence. It's a man and a woman and a little girl up there on that gray old bridge, they're walking over it and have merely turned their heads to notice what's going on below. They do not have their elbows and arms propped up on the railing, mocking. They'd have a look, and then step on, and then another look. I'm running through the water— "Hey, y'all, where you going—where the hell you going, ole ghosts?"

Man, I could hear it so clearly, it seemed. Billy says, "We're O.K., Son, we going to Louisiana . . ."

"You catch a death of cold," scolds Polly.

But Lucy never in her vague shape said a thing, which hurt my feelings a little. They all were spiffy, in a kind of gray garb like maybe a machinist would wear. Billy in some comfortable uniform, the woman and the child in simple ghostly dresses.

I yelled at them but didn't stop driving through the water, and when I came out the other side where my pj's were, they were gone.

As I'd sloshed up to the abutment, they were down at the south end, and they did seem interested—but when I'd got my pants on (hoping, I suppose, for a proper visit up on the road), there wasn't anything. Up the bank I ran, peering down through the clearing mist toward the southwest, but there wasn't a thing there—the moist black surface of the road and the lights of a truck coming on, but that was all.

Back home was a helluva lot worse than ghosts. The women are up and walking the baby in the living room. I've patted myself off the best I can, but still it's plenty moist in those pj's.

Trooped right on in: "Howdy, ladies. Y'all look mighty pretty in them robes."

"Where you been?" Helen who hasn't got her hanging moss gathered off her shoulders yet.

"Swimmin'. Freshens a feller up. Oughta try it some time, Helen."

"Shush, Son." That's April—so I go over to her and thump her as hard as I can right in the middle of her forehead with my first finger. Thonk. She starts so much she damn near drops the baby.

"Don't shush me, ever again . . . Helen, tell Sam I'm sick." Before I go off down the hall to bed.

It had the making of a bad week.

I was evermore after doing it right that night—no little table or alarm clock could satisfy—in fact, all those tables and chairs and peoples and bottles wasn't going to be enough to satisfy. All those skinny-necked, long-haired women (though a few were bouffant and spray-netted) and their boys with the bad postures, they got off the dance floor in a hurry, skittering on their spike heels and slick soles like scared cats on Formica, like rats on in-clined plate glass. I could see them scatter while I bent down over quivering Stream in the middle of that floor, while I was scooping him up, so to speak, getting a good grip on thigh and neck so to, in a twinkling, jerk him up over my head. In spite of his thrashing and yelling out in pure terror—"Sonny, Christ, Son, please don't hurt me"—in spite of the animated burden I'd raised, I still took time to look around that room. *Davis ain't here. Nowhere to be seen . . .* Foots—yeah God—Foots was up on his feet in a far corner, he's cheering and slinging beer around in sheer delight—Foots and some younger Weatherfords—a rancid cousin or two out of Lurch's family—and Cantrell appalled behind the bar. Vicious company, the perfect bad company for a *miserable situation,* and the emo-tional lice allover my body under my shirt and pants wasn't in the least like how it was with ghosts. *These people have never read the* New Republic, *Burger.*

I flung him real good this time, real good, right into a booth where some kids from the junior college were cowering—he landed on the table and slid into the pine wall and the juke feeder that's in the booths, gathering them all together in a tangle of screams and arms and legs. I watched them all collapse together for a moment, fearing just a little somebody might get cut by the broken glass—and then I sauntered back to the bar where a few hardrollers hadn't moved—had held their places as calm aficionados of tonk fights—and beautiful creatures they were, so calm in their Penney's slacks, so positive I'd recognize their peculiar status in

all this—goddamned lizards with tight pants on, with pistols probably stuck down in their boots. *You might get shot:* I thought that.
Which bothered me. Because I didn't want anybody to get hurt.
Not hurt to the point of dead. Later I think I actually meant to kill,
later and later, but not right then.

When I got to the boys at the bar, it was a cool fury by way of
beer and exercise, and also I'd noticed the beer ads all around the
room. As I stepped back to the bar amid the subdued but nevertheless ravishing chatter of the room, they caught my eyes—the
brilliant snow scene that shifts by way of mechanical devices slowly
into a spring scene, all green; shifting then into the seaside-in-the-
summer scene; finally the golden fall; each with the same beer can
in the foreground. Many signs all around the room caught my eyes.
Glistening cascades of beer, glasses filling, refilling, in the signs.
Baubles and multicolored wheels, rotating. Fountains of light. Jax,
Regal, Miller, Bud and Schlitz—all with their terrible machinery
filling the senses with a most ex-treme beauty. Oh my! Glass tubes
with bubbles of colored water circled signs of girls in bathing
suits who drank their beer lasciviously—their veins alive with ichor
of beer—luminous, brutal, tasteless slaves to serve illusion. It flashed
into my head that I should smash each one in turn. But what I
wanted was more than any fracking sign. I wanted some epitome
of ugliness and banality and pain.

I turned to the boys at the bar (suddenly diverted from my rage
against metal and plastic and electricity). They stared bravely at
me (at least two did) as I panted: smiling, in fact, they looked like
their faces had been drawn by a bright two-year-old on damp
cardboard, obscurely.

They seemed about to speak at the very moment I charged—
put my recently healed right arm down on the pine bar and then
ran the length of it, sweeping off all the bottles and glasses, and
damn near running over the two closest hombres. But they escaped
to corners like the rest, never pulling gun nor knife.

I was Mars and the Colossus of Rhodes, and they tell the great
story of that night (and the next night) until this day. They re-
count those deeds around the town, the whole county—in schools,

houses, homes, and tonks. Fat men who suck the last drags of their cigarettes on the front steps of Protestant churches before the preaching, *they* tell it. An occasional nun and priest does too, no doubt about it. And Slater knew, Slater knew while it was going on, I'm sure. I have supplanted the reputations of all previous tonk fighters, drunks, losers, and noaccounts, which is an entirely worthless thing to have accomplished.

The jukebox was my triumph. Not quite the epitome of banality, not quite. For one must realize—even as I did that night— one must realize that the music is O.K., even positively beautiful, if, for instance, it is Hank or Johnny Ace or Chuck Berry, or even Elvis—sometimes—or the very best of Jerry Lee Lewis! Yes, the music itself does sometimes approach a certain simple formal elegance, and it does embody something of the essential passional nature of many Americans. From great places like Bina's Bar in Brockett, N.D., to Marvin's in Slidell, the same aesthetic and cultural forces obtain.

Give Cantrell credit, for all the greats were on the juke I killed.

What was it then, you ask, what element, aura, essence of absolute juke was it that drove me to such wrath? Ha! I say to you, Ha! and close now one, now the other epicanthus over my light-blasted eyes—motor power places gigantic forces (faces?) at his disposal, which, like his muscles, he can employ in any direction— these things that, by his science and technology, man has brought about on this earth, on which he first appeared as a feeble animal organism and on which each individual of his species must once more make its entry (oh nich of nature!) as a helpless suckling— these things do not only sound like a fairy tale, they are an actual fulfillment of every—or of almost every—fairy-tale wish. All these assets he may claim to as his cultural acquisition.

Indeed, indeed, BUT, this juke, this newfangled organ of pleasure was ug-ly. Fat, fat, fat. Squat creature with its bubbles of light a-blinking, it sat moveless and courageous throughout my assault on the room—O stupid, fat, mechanical creature, less beautiful even than beer signs. (Stream likes to quote the poet who says he wants to be a golden bird upon a golden bough when he dies. Well, I figured that with my luck they'd make me come back as a small fat jukebox like the one in the Second Stand. Ah, God!—the irony, the irony—for I would not mind being the vehicle for the songs of Johnny and Hank and Chuck and Elvis, if I could be a trim machine, a lean machine, something a Scandinavian might design. But to be fat and squat, a blinking thing of chartreuse and fuchsia and mauve: No, no, no, no, no—that, sir, cannot be tolerated.)

That machine at the very center of the dance floor of the Second Stand Club in Bryan, Mississippi, was the ENEMY.

Now. I shouted at that room and all therein. In fact, I lied a huge, loud lie: I said if they were not all quiet this instant, QUIET, I would draw the two small pistols from my boots and shoot at random. Nobody who knew me would ever believe I'd ever carry a gun, but the strangers in the room were less secure.

I walked very forthrightly and gracefully toward the center of the room, the room now almost hushed, the box itself asleep, nickelless, unsuspecting. Gracefully, I say, for my ancient powers had returned: I was an agile 265 again, I was moving at a brisk walk, as a pro does, toward the line of scrimmage.

On my knees I unplugged it from the floor (it hadn't been playing for a few minutes but its bubbles and lights were still on as I approached)—

At a half kneebend I embraced it, clamped my arms and hands on both sides (peaveys of bone and muscle to help my work)—then I lifted it up before me in almost priestly fashion—my juke a vast, dark now (NO LIGHTS), monstrance—in hushed adoration I carried the jukebox before me toward the door. There were oooohs and ahhhs from the room. There was the bleak voice of Cantrell crying—"For Chrissake, Sonny, please . . ."—another voice (female)—"Quiet, damnit, let's see what he does." *Where's Stream?*

All rose at once to follow me toward the door, where the fit was very tight for both the juke and me—I teetered on the wooden stairs, then cautiously stepped down onto the gravel of the lot, where again I slowed, stumbling on the goddamned cord. But still they whispered and followed after. As I walked up the short dirt road toward the highway.

O Fortuna
velut Luna
stater variabilis,
semper crescis
aut decrescis;
vita detestabilis
nunc obdurat
et tunc curat
ludo mentis aciem,
egestatem,
potestatem
dissolvit ut glaciem—as the wretched tonk people marched behind, they should have chanted like Orff's drunks—they should have done that, but they didn't. They giggled and laughed nervously as they stumbled after, because it wasn't any ritual to them. *They* ain't got no sense of ritual.

She would come soon, no doubt about it.

Out on the highway, where there wasn't any light except the small sign that advertised the Stand with red letters on a black background (the light from three small bulbs that were goosenecked over), I halted. The people lined up to my right and left along the road. They chattered lowly, while my arms ached.

Cantrell's voice close up behind me: "Put it down. Sonny, goddammit, put it down or I'll call the Sheriff."

"Call him."

Finally I saw her coming. In the distance I saw her lights, lights wide apart, a huge, flat-faced Kenworth. A problem, for I must hit the bumper and grill, not the windows. I must not kill the driver. She would pass us at about fifty miles per hour, so my one toss must be perfect. I gripped harder with my hands, set my elbows like a man making ready for a short set shot, or a free throw. *What does the driver see now that he's caught us in his lights?* And many jumped back into the ditch when a nearby fellow yelled—
"He's gonna throw it."

Which I did. I flicked it in front of the truck to watch it blasted literally into a thousand pieces.

It all happened on several levels and in many domains of my imagination, but I remember them all with clarity—especially the strange frequency of The Dream, The Lights, The Song. True, I was under tremendous physical strain, true. My arms clamped, my hands damn near crippled because of the force of the grip against the plastic and metal sides—the awful effort it took to keep that graceful balance as I walked out, and yet, and yet, my very arms and hands did glow—Moby-Dick-type corposants—ah, my sweet one, the true Saint Elmo's fire streamed along my wretched flesh and set the plugless machine to playing. It was then they had begun to follow me, my people, my fellow sufferers of the tonk. And the song it played as I bore it along was no single, simple tune—it was funky blues and a hymn and a chant, *chansons de mal mariés*—something for the moon and the sun and the slow dark waters of every bad bayou, river, and creek. Fuck it. It seemed pretty.

The late March night was thick with pine scent, and the road was moist from an early evening shower, and a strong breeze (almost a wind) tried to sweep the litter from the parking lot. It made beer cups and the foils from rubbers and napkins skitter and run along the rocks as we strode along.

But best of all was the slow explosion of the juke against the truck—each bit and piece of metal and plastic was on fire, each fragment of record was luminous and sang the part of song it owned—they wheeled in the air amid an awful cry of words—guitars, harmonicas, and drums (all the instruments)—then settled on the shining highway like the critical dust of a nebula. Something like that.

No one was hurt, not even the driver who did pull over about a hundred yards down the road, they tell me.

After the thing was done, thrown, and in the fraction of a second between the explosion and the great cheer that was sent up all around me (and, Lord, those people loved it, except for Cantrell

—they did let go a splendid risible scream of sound a lot like joy), I realized that Stream had gotten away. He must have fled about the time I whipped up on the boys at the bar—*to the icehouse*—for late on Friday nights, when he's in town, he minds the icehouse for his uncle. He's sitting up on the dock and reading *Grit*. He's confident the dude has proved he's worthless. He's confident the law has got the dude in tow by now.

Stream never believed I was serious about the Greeks at Marathon and at the Hot Gates, even though it was I who'd told him the story of Thermopylae, of how the Lacedaemonians held out three days until Xerxes got to them by way of a traitor named Ephialtes. Stream didn't have the details on all those things. He liked to make fun of me because I liked to wear my Bulls' jacket all around town. I didn't talk football with Stream either. I talked the subjects he chose and often beat him at them, up on the icehouse dock, at night on weekends, when he came to town. But still he had the gall to call me immature. I'd been out there on that loading dock with that little fart many a night, talking about Cromwell and Pope John and Queen Elizabeth's underwear—but still he condescends to me.

In the confusion after the explosion I sprinted back to my car and was on the highway headed back to town before those people knew it. Cantrell saw me go, and he did call Benton, but most of that trash was so drunk and silly they hardly noticed when I nosed the station wagon through them, getting away, honking to beat the devil, screaming "Wild Side of Life" through the open window. I felt somewhere between Vandamme and the dumbest shit in creation.

Stream was sitting on the dock at the icehouse when I skidded around the corner, sitting, in his uncle's rocking chair, talking to Slater, telling Slater of the troubles. Slater's sitting on the dock itself, hanging his skinny legs down. So I drove the car into the dock exactly where they were. I banged it hard enough to ruin my fender and grill. It knocked a big chunk out of the dock front and then a part of the tin roof shuddered loose and fell down on my hood. God, what a noise! I slipped from behind the wheel and held the dash with my aching arms at the moment of impact. With the doors popped wide, with the motor smoking a little, I appeared fully armed in huge splendor, ready once again to stalk my prey.

"Now whad ya do *that* for . . ." blurts Stream. So I yelled up to say I never gave him permission to pity my ass. "You're crazy drunk, Sonny, you're in bad trouble . . ." And I answered I was cold sober and just about to commit coldblooded murder.

Slater, he's standing back up against the wall by the ice tongs and the Coke machine, and he is obviously not quite sure of himself when the argument starts. Takes him a minute to cut down on me, just about a minute. "You don't do no good, Son."

"Shut up . . . nigger."

Stream's whining—"Sonny, they killed another one . . . they burned a church and they blew an old man up. Rosey Jefferson, who's been helpin' Slater—" sob, sob—"This evening . . . while we were at the Stand."

"Then why are you here?" I say it—slowed a little.

"Because I'm scared. The Sheriff . . ." Slater said.

"Davis said for him to stay here. Davis . . . is going to put him up for the night. He'll pick him up in a little while," Stream explains.

It's curious—because for a moment they had me—they had me shamed but good—they'd almost calmly brought me to my senses with serious bad news. I knew it was bad about Jefferson, whom I didn't know. Slick Fletcher, and Preacher Morris, and Winston Roberts, and Foots. I wondered whether Foots had burned and killed before he showed up at the Stand. Davis being one helluva good man. Jesus, what a good man! If Stream had taken it easy for a couple of minutes more, everything would have been just fine, but he didn't. He noticed I was slowed and weakened a little, probably even the shivers that were on me. He went to pieces in his sentiment, beating at his skinny thighs and his belly and chest with little fists.

.   .   .

Me and him will go to hell because we don't do more—he's got a whole catalogue of what's gone wrong with me and him. Blubbering and clabbering his words, a goddamned maddened sermon right there on the dock. People are dying and we don't do nothing! Our Negro citizens being murdered! We're the young leaders of the community and are guilty. *The young leaders of the community:* only Stream could talk like that in a fit. Slater has been patient, too long, too long, too long, O God, O God, Sonny, we are so utterly, utterly worthless. Slater forgive us, forgive us our sins. Sonny ask . . . ask . . . Slater to forgive . . .

He'd blown it. Man, I couldn't listen to that shit from Stream. I simply couldn't stand the way he picked his words and formed and uttered them. I might have to settle up with Slater and everybody, but I wasn't about to be worthless Stream's way, in any way that chinless, blubbering, motherfucker had to offer. Maybe if Stream were dead—excised from The Community—maybe if the likes of puling Stream were not around to make all virtue stink—maybe I'd get some good done then. I'd kill him with the Cascade Baling Rope—I'd kill him in the cold room. Right. Right.

"Yeah, man, yeah," I said to Stream. "You got something there, but take it easy. All of us have fallen short . . ." I beckoned him toward me and the locker door, suggesting an intimate word not for the black man's ear. I opened the door as he stepped over, and then I shoved him into the cold room. "Stay there, or I'll get you with a . . . pick"—to Slater, before I went inside with the Preacher's Kid.

The Cold Room. This will be about the Cold Room at Taggart's Icehouse. Its beauty came to me for the first time. When the big latch had clacked shut behind me, and with Stream standing like a scared doe in the far corner, I stopped. Often before I'd thought of the cold room as *strange* or *interesting,* but only then, with the wrecked dock and car and juke and tonk behind me, did it seem such a beautiful and fitting place—such a fitting place to kill this turd tapper. He could stay right here forever, no rot, no stink, but finally that didn't seem right, for Stream. And coldblooded murder in a cold room struck me as funny. Poetic caves of ice—or polar floes—caves or floes at either pole—for Stream. I should have put him in the machine that sliced ice out on the dock, but its horrible ripping and cleaving sound was unpleasant to consider. It was cool and still except for our breathing and the puffs of our breath, and the sound of the compressor pump beyond the walls. I thought I heard the sound of animals but put that out of mind awhile by cursing Stream.

Ole Stream, he wasn't a hoplite now. He'd got himself behind one of those five-hundred-pound blocks of ice and he was begging me to explain. If it's because of the teasing, he never meant it.

He was very scared and started circling around the walls—he's got his back to the frosted water pipes. Frail bastard, circling, imploring, and slipping on the cold, wet, slats. "Son, baby, you're sick..."

"I may be sick, but I'm not disloyal like a certain pansy bastard who's about to get his ass killed." And he did believe me.

He was pushing those wonderfully strict blocks in my way as he circled—and when I saw what his game was, I started sliding them back at him. I'd smush him a little. I was laughing because here in this absolutely lovely room (except for the low ceilings that made me stoop) I was finally going to bloody up and butcher him—was going to tear bone from socket and meat from bone. I was going to get the butcher man before he got me. Kill death. Kill death. And then I'd sit quietly at my proper trial, my fair trial: I'd sit quietly like you read about, and it would be hard for all the people to understand how such a peaceful soul could be accused of murder.

It got to be a little dance between us, and I guess that almost unconsciously we were trying to stay warm. I could see how both of us had goosey arms. Push, shove, push, shove, and once again I began to hear the sounds of animals—something maybe like the push and shove of blood in a bull's heart, but maybe not—maybe more like the breathing of a vast herd of buffaloes in a winter Wyoming night three hundred years ago. I let up on Stream—not pushing so hard—and he settled his face like he thought we were getting better—while really I was merely easing in for the kill, like the Indian on the ridge, hearing the slow breathing below, and patient as he moves down among them to secure his meat and hides. And of course I could still hear the sound of the compressor motor ticking away beyond the wall.

Without the terrific cold of the place I think I would have fainted from exhaustion—I'd been a busy lad that night—and the knowledge of how tired I was even made me angrier, and brought to mind all the times I'd pressed on anyway . . . I started smelling sweat, blinking my eyes that were stinging with it. I knew my T-shirt was crusted with salt and weighted down and covered by my saturated pads and jersey. Which, of course, was a confusion in time: the shirt being only crusted the second day, when it has dried overnight . . . crusted before practice. The soaked jersey and pads was a during-practice sensation. I remembered the tiredness of the last windsprints—when your knees go inward, buckle—knock-kneed—can't for the life of you run right, and yet you do run, toward the shapes in the trees at the end of the field—you run —they jiggle before your eyes as you thud along a last time toward the locker room that's in the trees. Finally you're inside—out of the drenched equipment and the cold shower water is rolling down you. You lie down on the shower floor, on the tiles, on your back— you slide slowly back and forth beneath the spray. That's good. The bunched muscles go sweet and loose. It's peace of mind for a job well done.

I got the tongs in my hand as I danced past them on the wall. They were on a big nail and a pick was stuck in a beam beneath them. But I never thought of using the pick to puncture Stream. I only wanted the tongs to brandish at him, just playing the game of slide and catch with the mammoth ice cubes, and wind coming shorter and shorter, and the pain. Pushing the ice at him with one hand and waving the tongs with the other in that dreamy place, with the sounds of animals. A new sound of sobbing starts out of Stream—and I'm drifting while the pushing became merely automatic. I put aside the petty thoughts of my past and began to consider the fate of the mastodon (or mammoth?)—the Great Woolly Mastodon who was perfectly preserved in permafrost, with one leg raised in the arrested movement of a step, and with a perfectly preserved piece of grass still in his mouth, and it was all because the crust of the earth had shifted suddenly and caught, in a few seconds, all the animals in an instant freezing.

IF THE HOAR FROST GRIP THY TENT
THOU WILL GIVE THANKS WHEN NIGHT IS SPENT—

Before my very eyes I saw the burial of the Great Woolly Mastodon—so I shouted those lines to Stream in the cold room—lines he'd said he'd loved; but at this crucial moment he'd forgot them. He just kept on blubbering about "how we had more important things to do in the human community"—as they were stopped dead in their tracks, while eating, stock-still and dead, an entire continent as stiff as a photograph. The dust that rose from the shifting crust settled and buried it all. The mastodon, when they dug him up, was fresh enough to eat.

"GODDAMN IT, TAGGART, AIN'T NOTHING MORE IMPORTANT THAN MASTODONS AND ANIMAL SOUNDS"—I lunged with the tongs a last time, jamming the block against Stream so hard it knocked him down. Poor bastard, he just pulled his legs up close to his body and stuck his head between his knees as far as it would go. Had himself balled up just like he was about to be born—and it was then that Benton came busting through the door—while Stream is sweetly praying, "Jesus, Jesus, O, sweet Jesus"—even maybe a few bars of "Jesus Lover of My Soul" were heard, a hymn I especially dislike.

Slater had minded me, trusting (foolishly) that the law would arrive in time.

Davis: "Stop in the name of the law!" Clearly it was a bad day for him, too. And he actually pulled his gun on me.

"Man, we're just . . . playing."

It was quite a gathering out on the dock. There's Slater and Davis and Henry and a couple of niggers I'd never seen before, and Cantrell (Cantrell's in his Buick, he's sitting in his Buick, and he looks mortally pissed, an extreme brown study, you might say), and April. Oh my! She's pale and dull-eyed, standing by her father.

But her father ain't dull-eyed—he's bright-eyed and bushy-tailed as a flayed old man can get. He's got his perfectly horrible grin on. Fun Fun Fun—it's written all over him.

Davis: "I'm binding you over to Henry." He speaks like he's the town crier in London. Binding? Henry? "You'll have to pay for everything . . . the jukebox . . . the truck . . . the dock here." I notice that Stream's runtly uncle was over in the office looking mistreated about his dock and roof. "The juke . . . the truck . . . the dock . . ." He makes his list of properties again.

"I got the money," says I. "Gimme a check."

"We'll tend to all that at dawn." Goddamned Davis was spaced worse than any of us.

All those people were staid-looking, but you could tell they'd had a good time, even Cantrell, even Taggart. Everybody but April and Davis. Even Slater—who's about to be the first black man to spend a night in the home of a Bryan County sheriff—Slater has obviously had a pleasant thought or two, because the thing he did was wink at me. He's stuck up close to Davis and trying to dig the serious issues of tonk fights and icehouses, but just before I go off, bound to Henry, he casts a knowing wink at me out of his narrow black head. This thing ain't done, is what that mean wink said. Davis was crazy, but also he was confident, about something.

She'd had herself a bad week but except for the way her face looked you couldn't tell it. She's on the dock in a simple print, a wide-collared thing with a low bustline (buttons down the front) —she's showing a lot of smooth chest skin over her ribs, and all I could think about, wonder, was did she have her panties on on this particular night. Surely. But I'd never know.

Whatever, she was showing signs of being fierce, the honey hair thoroughly brushed and pulled back into a ponytail (the next thing would be a bun), and I couldn't blame her. I knew I shouldn't blame her.

The dude's bound over to Henry. Sobeit. "I'll drive her home, but I'll stay with you."

"You got to," says Henry.

• • •

I was amazed the car would run. I beat the hood closed, got in, and cranked her up. The grill's messed but the radiator's holding—the bumper's gone but the frame's not jumped too much—and the doors didn't have to be slammed but twice. Good car. One light worked.

"Hey, Stream. I get you later." I said that to him before my wife and I left. At the time I didn't mean it. All I meant to do was scare him more.

"We'll get together tomorrow," says Davis. Like it was an invitation to ten o'clock coffee. *What the hell's he up to?* Presentiment. Presentiment. Presentiment.

I headed onto Woodrow Wilson and out the highway to the two-mile stretch where we all lived.

"I took the baby to Helen."

"Good idee."

"Son, I'm scared." It's chilly but she has got the window rolled down and her elbow out in the wind. She's far off across the seat the way you hate it in high school.

"So am I."

But that was all, except for the goodnight without a kiss, just before I backed out and went to Henry's. A thoughtless thing, because I didn't go far into the drive. I made her walk thirty yards alone up to the door, where cassowary Helen waited for her. April slammed the car door twice (without comment), then she walked unself-consciously toward that mean house, her light dress whipping in the breeze, exposing the backs of her thighs. Walking away from me, with her belly muscles still a little soft. It got me in my Jesus. Jesus, like in the worst tonk songs, I wanted to run after her. It occurred to me I ought to ask her for advice. I ought to sit down and ask her to explain me to me. But that's not a thing women like April understand, or appreciate. A fucked-up man they will not tolerate. I didn't fully know it right then, but when Helen's door closed, we were done for.

• • •

The hiatus, the eye of the storm (though the natural storm had not appeared yet), the way station on the mountain road, the port of last peaceful recall was there at Henry's in that night—Henry's curious old rooms were an irrelevant but recreational domain for me to rest in before they all came after me.

What a wonderful fellow. What a fine place. And the curious fact is that I hadn't ever been in there before, never through the door itself. I'd been on the porch a bunch of times; I'd knocked, I guess, to bring him out sometimes; maybe I'd even peered in; but I had not been inside, which suggests a thoughtlessness and a lack of curiosity. Probably I feared it would still be nasty the way it had been in Maylene's time. Roaches and spiders; dust balls floating like tumbleweeds over a man-made, futile prairie of floor; cruddy dishes in a foul sink; a stool and tub green and alive as any petri dish; antediluvian ashtrays chocked with butts of Home Run cigarettes (or Wings). Foolishly. No reason at all to think such things, for Henry wasn't that sort of creature—and anyway there is the crucial fact that Helen, every day, when he is gone to work or to New Orleans, comes over and cleans his house. Every fucking day she could, the old bitch! I'd seen her start out across that field so many times I didn't believe it. She'd visit there between 7:00 and 7:30, before she had to leave for work, and after Henry was gone, but in my thoughtlessness I never let it register until that night. She does that—and then the both of them spend all day at the Mill—she keeping books in the trailer office, he outside in the mill building proper, hardly ever seeing each other, except on Fridays, when he came into the trailer to get his check, from her. Shit! Her desk sits by a low divider in that small trailer room, and for years that crone has handed over to Henry his check.

"Thankee"—I hope to God he said a thing like that to her each week—to Helen who by that night was the one who wished me gone—who probably had already dreamed up Royal Carle for her daughter-niece.

It was the cleanest place I ever saw. Barest, cleanest, most utterly reactionary, most masculine, most strictly illuminated in its planes and objects by old brass floor lamps, except in the kitchen and bath, dudes with shades like dried human skin, and there must have been four in the living room—a living room, one bedroom, a kitchen, and a little bath—barest goddamned lived-in space I ever saw, but still a type of beautiful. A cheap, black tufted couch in the living room (the thing I'd sleep on), but nothing else, except for the lamps. A room that's freshly papered in a tiny gray floral design, with only one piece of furniture in it. No drapes, no curtains, no pictures (the subject of Maria's "Spiritual Portraits" didn't have a single painting in his house)—nothing but old blinds like parchment pulled down (with small lacunae in them) to keep out the world's eyes. A bare waxed floor (cypress, by God, put down by the man himself to please his bride), wide cypress boards waxed tastelessly by Helen. One space heater (L.P. gas) whose clay was the color of ivory. *Helen has papered this place.*

The old man himself was standing in his living room. He was staring over across his couch toward the blinds. Henry was standing in his underwear when I came through the door, and he was altogether stranger than a ghost to see. But what a wonderful sight. His whole head and face and a portion of his chest was all scars, as I knew, also his hands, and his arms up to the elbows, but the rest wasn't. The rest of him was the whitest skin and the best preserved I'd ever laid my eyes on. *Good god, he's in perfect condition.* He's sixty and muscled like a miler. His hood and gloves of scars accentuated the rest of him, his perfect old build.

"Son, it's a shame to see a young man run to fat. Lose his health." Vainly. Turning on me when I step in. "But you're fightin' it. You're fightin' it. That's good." A voice like mercury blown across a steel plate. "You havin' fun now. That's the important. It's good what you done to Cantrell."

Fucker don't even wear boxer shorts! Wears athletic-type undies, like a boy does, except they hold bull balls and a class-A prick. Christ, what a cod.

"Son, it ain't the niggers . . . I hate niggers . . . but it *ain't* the

niggers." A-rabs! A-rabs! Henry is an A-rab. He's archaic as anything you'd realize on hash. I was in some kind of austere A-rab's
room. Or some old Jew's.

"Yessir."

"It ain't the niggers more than ole Helen . . . the Sheriff is all to
the best . . . to take that nigger home. Son, you got to hate niggers
. . . but this shit of killin' niggers is worthless . . . only a white man
is worth killin'—like Communists and atheists. You take Raymond
Magee—he feels *obliged* to hate niggers. He's after killin' niggers
because he thinks it's what you do." *You shot Sammy Davis—a
great talent.* Henry has thought this out so he can tell me all about
it, since I've been bound over to him. He's been standing in the
middle of his room preparing. He puffs a Camel like a fried martyr
and goes on. "What Henry says [What Henry says!] is hate
niggers, but do not kill them. They bad and got it bad. They . . .
disturb . . . our lives . . so I hate niggers. Always have. But Foots is
worthless. He's *obliged*. Nobody has got to do a thing . . . unless it's
from the Lord. Maybe for a good woman? Obliged is . . ."

"Have you got something to drink?"

"Have it. We got wine—wine, wine, wine." Spoody Oody.

"That'll do." Fine. Right. They got me, Momma.

"You ought to take my job at the Mill. Wood's good work.
Take my job . . . stay with my daughter . . . and fuck around on
the side. That's what Henry says." As I follow him into his pristine
kitchen to get a fresh bottle of Rhine out of the cupboard. Goddamned Virgin Mary Milk.

"Right. Right."

"But that'll never happen. No more than me and May. April's a
lot like May, though it don't look like it."

"May was . . . O.K. . . . wasn't she?" Between great gulps straight
from the bottle.

"She's in-sane."

"Oh?"

"But there's worst things."

"Like what?"

"Ugly's worst. For a goddamned fact it is." He peers out his
kitchen window to see if anybody's watching from the woods half
a mile away. "Gimme some of that."

.　　.　　.

Then he chose to show me around, like any householder, padding on his horny feet into his bedroom. A heavy iron bed with stiff sheets and a comfort on it, a large oak linen chest, a deal chest of drawers, a deal chest-on-chest, framed pictures of Maylene and April atop the chest-on-chest. "Just alike," he said, waving a burned hand at two of his women. "I've slept here most of thirty years, and mostly by myself. It's a good thing. I go to New Orleans to sleep with women." He looked at me like I didn't understand the virtues of his system.

"You never brought Maria here?"

"No . . . it's May's bed. I'm loyal that way. You got to be loyal. To things."

Hardly any mirrors at all. One. A small one in the bathroom, a piece of a mirror he used to shave with was on the sill. And there's a framed photograph of Roy and Merle Boykin standing in front of what looks like a '41 Ford, on the sill by the mirror.

"They were good people," I said.

"The best . . . Merle's a little fat, but she was the best."

"And Roy?"

"He's the greatest one with a story I ever saw. In-sane and lazy as hell, but a great talker. Royal's not theirs. He's a bastard we got at The Home."

Back in the kitchen—"you old sonofabitch, you've made yourself a life. Haven't you?" He's a very scary person to be following around, but I didn't feel in any immediate danger.

"You could say that"—winking from his slick face—winking from a browless and lashless pale, blue eye. "I go crazy sometimes myself, an' hate people in this worthless town—but nothing's all that bad. Finish the wine, Son. So you can go to sleep."

He gets me a counterpane out of the linen box that has his initials cut into a block that's nailed to the front of it. Bending without the least effort, his belly unrumpled. "Maybe I'll stay around for tomorrow. Maybe I'll hold off on Maria. Do her good." Winking again. "I'll be at the Mill when you get up. But there's eggs and bread in the box." Speaking affectionately but not exactly to me. "Roll up in this. It's one that May's momma made." Which I did, and after a while slept the sleep of the blessed. Wine does that for you—then bags you in the morning. It's an old patch quilt, and it smelled good. "There's soap in the bath, Son. Take a bath to freshen up. You smell terrible. There's extra towels under the lavatory."

"Yessir."

Which I did. Scrubbed off in the little tub with legs—bathed with Lava soap and felt I'd never been so clean. It was close to morning by then, so I shaved, too. With Henry's golden, toothed Gillette safety razor (for still he had some fine tough scar hairs at the point of his chin), with some kind of fancy brush and scented soap Maria must have got for him. Staring down at the mirror on the sill. I took a fairly healthy dump in his old commode and then went off to the couch like a natural man. I knew those people were after me (including Henry?)—but on that weary couch, and wrapped in May's sweet counterpane, I didn't care. Hell, I'd even washed my shirt and shorts in his lavatory, so I'd be ready for the coming day. I wrapped up naked on that couch and tried to fathom all the horror going on around me. Dead Negroes complicating my life—a football team in Dallas still complicating my life. Stacking lumber and playing with the baby had been just fine, and moral. Fuck 'em all. Out on the yard, breathing God's sweet air, I was moral! If they'd only let me alone six months, everything would have been just fine. I knew my own velocity. I'd of done good. Moral/Good? Then I got to thinking about Davis. One juke burst in my brain and I could hear a lowing sound in that dark room, the grate burning about ten feet away, but mostly I tried to think of Davis, my good friend, who wanted to *use* me.

Thinking about Davis made me rotate on the couch and tangle my covers between my legs. I'd done right not to go home with April. Davis had taken Slater home to Bessie with him, making him the first sheriff to take a nigger home to his wife. I tried to imagine how that would be: *Bessie, this here is Mr. Slater Jackson, one of our Colored Citizens, whose life is in danger because of Slick Fletcher and Morris and Winston Roberts and Raymond Magee— mostly Magee, because he is an ex-football player—because of the boycott they want this nigger dead. Bessie, four-hooker, this black man has got to sleep upon our couch this night because that LAW- LESS BAD CROWD is up-set* [Boycott the boyars—damn right]

—Bessie, this skinny Indian nigger (good-looking, ain't he?) don˙
want nothing but the right to vote and a good school to send his
children to, when he gets married, and the right to sell rubbers at
Betner's Drugs, if he is qualified. Which we both know he has got
the right to . . . Bessie?

Mostly it amused me, at the time. What the hell? My wife and
baby were asleep across the field. They were safe, and I was safe,
for the time being. What would Side think? He'd be thinking about
his investments on the stock market, his cash money and his plan
for a G.M. agency. I pulled the covers over my head, exposed my
bare ass, and went to sleep.

The morning of the second day meant to be clear enough, but
actually was ominous, when my eyes cracked open—it was like
popping open two seals of the realm. The silence of a falling star
lights up a yellow morning, alone at Henry's, I thought. Sat straight
up like I'd heard rimfire. Nothing. A bare room in Mississippi. Except for Helen standing at the door with a dust rag and what looked
to be a note in her hand.
"Cover yourself!"
"Yessum."
"Here—you son-of-a-bitch," handing me the note.

Until you pull yourself together, I'd rather we were separated.
Love, April—through an embarrassed wine hangover, but gaining
some courage in frustration.
"Helen, did she write this?"
"She did. She wrote it and asked me about it. She was crying; I
said it was fine; the thing to do. I said I'd bring it to you." Helen
was aware of the hatred my eyes showed. She knew I was just about
to jump her. Because that was it! That was plenty, and I was just
hurt enough to jump up naked and run at her. Which I did. She was
gone fast. She was off that porch and checking out across the field,
though I didn't go farther than the porch: "BUZZARD,

BUZZARD, BUZZARD—I HOPE A BUZZARD EATS YOUR
ROTTEN CHERRY."

Don't be unkind was the thought that came to me then. Do not
be un-kind. *That woman dusted while I slept and then she slammed
the door on purpose.*

I washed and shaved again.

Somewhere above I have described the death of Jubal Clifford,
famous guitarman, in front of Betner's Drugs—the hangover from
the wine, the terrible shotgun blasts, the injured Beatniks, the
destroyed head itself of Ju (his ruined face), the brains and skull
mixed with the suntan lotion on the sidewalk. Davis in a rage: "In
broad daylight. In broad daylight! It's happened in broad daylight!"
Maybe I never mentioned how I threw up right then and there.
Collops of dead Jubal. Wails of Yankee sycophants. The wounded
girl would have been pretty if she'd brushed her hair. She was a
little wan from improper diet, but pretty nonetheless, in her terror
and grief, with splatterings of blood all over her denim shirt. "Son,
let's get together," says Davis. "This is terrible." He was weeping. It
was a lovely day except for a green cast off to the southwest, as
pretty a day as one could imagine on a heavy spring Saturday,
brains and blood and guts in rank profusion, while all around the
countryside the jonquils bloomed. "Son! Where you going?"

"To watch a basketball game." Dry heaving, I got that out.

Before I left I reached into the busted window display and got
a bottle of Listerine to wash my mouth with. I gargled and swished,
then stepped around the mess into the car.

"You gotta testify! You gotta testify!" Davis, squatted among
the dead and wounded, after rubbing his bloody hands down over
his mustaches: I saw that through the car window, while backing
away.

Though I passed Helen's, where April and the baby were, it
wasn't them who were entirely on my mind all afternoon. My

emotions got moral and generalized (even classical) while drinking beer at the house, and after popping a zoomer or three that Dexter'd given me for my belly—my mind could not concentrate on the T.V. set shots—in fact, it was probably exhibition baseball, March being an odd month for sports, unless you have spring football during it—yes—I was positive that I'd been mad in the first place to come back to Bryan, wood or no wood, because even a beautiful landscape redolent of pines (and harboring ghosts) cannot compensate for a society that tolerates the death of a lovely black guitarman I'd danced with.

Listen, Burger, it's easier to accept dead Presidents than Jubal, or Doleman, or Rosey, or those three fine young men they killed and buried in Neshoba County, or the greatest of them all: Medgar Evers. Absolutely. Famous Political People, Nationwide-types, is one thing, but killing these persons trying to do good in a decent local way is quite another.

Generally speaking, I got myself into a flat high stupor that afternoon (puking three, four times into the john when the images of Ju's slaughtered and gouged body rose into my mind again)—I got high and decided this wasn't any place for me (others beginning to agree)—I had become, let us say, too sensitive a plant, and sophisticated, to tolerate this shit.

Wasn't anybody coming after me either—which did piss me off. I peeked out the new picture window on several occasions, but nobody (none of the State Police or the local law) was even driving slowly by the place, conning me, nobody, and checking out the back window from the kitchen led to the same conclusion.

There was some fine new weather creeping up from Louisiana, but that was all. There was soon to be Shook from the tangled boughs of Heaven and Ocean/Angels of rain and lightning . . . / Like the bright hair uplifted from the head/of some fierce Maenad —Mr. Shelley ran through my mind.

I'd been bound over to Henry, but not even my good friend Henry came after me—nor April, nor rancid Stream, nor Davis (who'd promised I'd get to testify), nor Slater—not even Helen. At least I figured Cantrell and the truck man from Bogalou would come by for their compensations, but they didn't. I signed onto a blank check made out to Davis—put it on the blond end-table, left a little note to April by it: *Honey, give this to Davis to pay the debts with. Sorry, honey. I love you and that baby whatever*. Because I did.

I piddled around while taking the legs off the cypress table, while getting it out into the bay of the station wagon. Had to take the table or she wouldn't have considered my going serious. No way. I'd pack a little, juke around (shuddering blubber) a little to Jerry Lee or John R. Cash or somebody on the olive rug in the living room (in front of the picture window so they could catch me if they wanted to), retch a little in the pot, take the trestle legs off that perfectly unvarnished gray table—waiting.

Then I went out front and sat on the stoop for a long time, watching the sun go down, watching the sun go down behind a bank of running clouds. "Hey, ole wind, you're comin' on!" Rumble, rumble, it answered: "Comin' for you"—rumble.

You got to grant to them Romantic poets some good sense in trying to communicate with The Weather. It's what's wrong with San Francisco, and other places out there. No weather.

"Hey Storm!—when you get here, blast the shit out of this house. Make sure nobody's in it tonight, then blow it to fucking kindling. Nobody has actually kindled in it—but you, Storm, can have it for kindling." Which did finally make the house shrug and shudder a little behind me. Whooee—finally I'd get a rise out of that cheap house with its bawdy interior.

Many cars and trucks came and went along the road rapidly—and the night came in with wind and small rain at first, and lightning off in the distance, promising more. I was a lost tonk wrecker with salty pussy on my mind, a juggler, an ole hop frog about to leap, a snake about to slither down a branch, a generous storm about to break. Frogs, birds, foxes on the sneak, bursting droplets at my feet and on the roof of my battered car, and mercenary soldiers, and football players—these were where I was naturally at. It may be a kind of unsocial attitude, but with the loving drench about to fall it was the one honestly in my body.

Got into my car and drove away.

I was going to New Orleans, was going to get my soul beneath the chandeliers of the Roosevelt Hotel (something tasteful)—drink beer in that famous, dim bar and watch the ruffles (white and starched) that spring from under the tiny skirts of the girls who serve. Concentrate on bought ass in the Quarter, find a Greek woman—maybe even go over and get some loving from Maria. For she would give it me, especially since she's keyed up expecting Henry who didn't show.

It was getting easy on the way out toward Steele's—I was slouched down and hauling ass through the increasing rainfall, with hardrolling traveling music hitting at me from the radio—something like "Crazy Arms" by Jerry Lee—and I blame the final undoing on that telephone booth that stood in the rain that night. A.T. & T. as goat again. It's about a mile northeast of Steele's and I'd pitied it on many nights before—standing as it does like a lit bum waiting for a handout, or a priest's booth with no sinners in it—I'd passed it most times with hardly more than a metaphor for a thought.

But on the night I meant to quit my town it seemed to gesture as I drove toward its circle of wet light—it beckoned in the rain—which by now was a true chunkmover, a deluge—and surely what I ought to do is call my wife to say goodbye—maybe to call Side and say that eventually I'd come to his woman's way again. So I did park and jump inside. So I did hit the brakes too hard, spinning twice in the road at least, and coming to rest with the back bumper whacked against and bounced off that booth. I got out and climbed inside, feeling vulnerable in the only heavy light around, climbed inside and fished in my khakis for a dime. Hey, buddy? Fished, then realized that fucking box had caught me.

Claustrophobia! Oh dear Christ—the metaphysics of claustrophobia may finally be the sum of what a large man's book is all about. I'm 6 feet 7 inches, bunched in a bright box by the wayside, with a terrible storm coming down, to say nothing of the b and b inside my veins, and the result was a howling panic. The brutal light was all around me and somebody had scratched "Maureen Terrell fucks" on the black phone itself.

There was thunder and awful lightning as I began to shake that place from the inside—convinced I couldn't ever turn around to get my ass out. Its concrete foundation was loose and soft and sinking in the ground (also, the whole construction had been given a lick by my car)—Lord, it even occurred to me I might be electrocuted myself, if the thing capsized, by the power lines (which it did), leaving a large pile of moist ash as my remains. I rocked and rocked, holding the sides of my casket, then jamming left shoulder against the black phone, and finally it did capsize, with what seemed to be flashes of blue fire all around my captured body. It crashed down a little of the slope, my chin taking a terrible lick on the coin slot. And then there seemed a quiet covered me. The rain had not abated, had if anything increased and was dripping into the booth, but somehow I felt a little more at peace once fallen. I was satisfied I'd drown there. Yessir, they'd find me drowned like a small whale in one of those glass tanks they haul them around in from supermarket to supermarket, to amuse children.

I'm doomed, sure enough, until I notice other lights, and hear the folding door rattling behind my soaked back.

That incredible Pauline has got her this line of darker color that runs from between her breasts down to the navel, where it dips into that shallow pond and rises on the other side. It goes on down below the yellow elastic toward the nitty gritty. Make the strictest of men a muff diver, a Watusi muff diver. A true lover had better learn to tang the lady's Rwanda and Burundi or she's fair game for any bright Bryan boy. Funny things turn around in the mind when the chest has got a hard pay phone under it. I was pleased. I never made that call. She still is most precious to me because of things we hardly ever did.

There were loud words in the rain behind me and pullings on both shoulders and my belt. "Get up, Son. Get up from there." It's a nervous colored voice. Slater's. I rose, did rise, dear hearts, from that dark room, and found myself standing drenched before good ole Slater Jackson, head nigger of a bad storm. Someone had come.

Tonto Slater, he was standing in the blowing rain and he was, it seemed, not surprised to find me there at this peculiar trail's end. God did he look good to me in his wet denims—"Son of a bitch—Slaterbuddy—Slaterbuddy, I seen the root of it all." I clap down both hands on his narrow shoulders. "Slater, the ax Must be laid-uh to the root of the tree—by the E-ternall God-uh, thyself, saith the Lord. Slater, Brother, I'll, by God, at last, howl them down for you —and as I live, I will plague their Honour, Pompe, Greatnesse, Superfluity. Sheeiiit, Slate, I will NOW confound them into parity. Parity . . . Parity . . . Parity." It was fine to find good words again. I could feel the amps burning in my head. "Slate, strange buddy— you and me are going to get us some E-quality an' Community— we're gonna put the heel on the neck of horrid pride, murder, malice, and tyranny. We gonna chop it all off at one blow. THE CAUSE IS UNIVERSALL LOVE—UNIVERSALL PEACE—PERFECT FREEDOME!"

Mercy, it *did* feel good to be standing and preaching while standing in that box. My arms stretched wide, mouth open to swallow the rain. Glory glory glory glory

"Let's get out of the rain," says Mr. Jackson.

We got up in his old Dodge pickup, where he slipped to me a pint of rum to mix with another little ben I'd just dug out of my windbreaker. He joined me in both rum and ben and I loved him for it. He was using me and liking it, driving. Driving! Toward trouble! Fuck me over, anybody—I was ready. Yes. I'd served the lyric griefs of Polly and April and Pauline and Stream—I'd tried for the grand theme in The NFL and certainly (fault me not) I'd been the good, junior scholar. Husband, cocksman, tackle—Joiner'd strung it out, and here with Slater I meant to be a radical Bryan redneck at a Southern Missolonghi.

. . .

Bound to bound to bound to—bound to go with the man that night. I locked my wagon right then and there beside the felled booth (a small sadness overlaying at the thought of how my car might get stolen with clothes and gray table in it) and got in with Slater.

We were both pretty high, but still it was a serious drive, and obfuscating, through the diminishing storm. He slicked his hands a lot on the wheel but was in no great hurry—and more than at any other time during our mere acquaintance, he seemed concerned that I understand him. He'd spent the night on the couch in the Bentons' living room and couldn't say enough for the Sheriff's hospitality, or for fulsome Bessie, who'd sat up in the kitchen and talked justice with them. He kept slicking his black hands up and down on the steering wheel in a way that suggested a terrible nervousness, though he rode easy, though his voice was mellow and controlled as he spoke of his affection for the Bentons—and for Dexter Betner (yes, Lord, and of course I'd never suspected), who had agreed to hire him (Slater) as a part-time cashier, to show good faith.

Which raised a disturbing conjecture. Maybe the Raiders—and it *was* Foots, for Slater'd seen him pulling the stocking off his face as they bumped around the corner down the street from Betner's, Slater having arrived at the scene of the crime just as I left—maybe the Raiders had only meant to shoot out Dexter's windows at first —maybe it had only been bad shooting because of the stockings (with no eyeholes?) that got Jubal, or maybe they just happened to include him in on the spur of the moment, as it were. Maybe they'd seen me there, too, and had meant to get me, too. God knows.

And Slater, after taking a sip from his pint (using that curious puckered embouchure of his), says that at the moment Davis has a bunch of them down at the courthouse—Foots and stump-legged Slick Fletcher and Preacher Morris and Winston Roberts, at least. Davis and Dexter (who is the J.P. to boot) and poor old sotted Mayor Jernigan, and maybe even Sam Chalmers, they're carrying on down there with the Raiders and trying to foster incriminating comments by way of whiskey. Whatever, Davis plans to charge Foots before the night's over—but it is a damn shame the boycott had so reduced the number of possible witnesses on Woodrow Wilson. Which swam in my highly structured mind as we drove along at the end of a wonderfully secure rain.

Slater's been to see an old woman that evening in the storm. That's why he's on the road and finds me inevitably. Some type of old aunt he goes to in pain, a crone of sorts and parts, who lives out from Stone Creek, name of Momma Lucy (who I'd never heard of), which fascinated me. Old Negro women being obviously kinder and wiser than old white women, I guessed—and I must admit that hearing he'd been to see a woman sent out lewd thoughts in my mind—because he'd simply said, "I been to see a woman." Hot damn. Because I'd wondered what his sex was. "An *ole* woman, Jerner, a very *ole* woman. I got *young* women other places." You do? Right. Right. He's got to be an Indian. He's secret like an Indian. I concentrate as best I could on how this old woman must be—a face like a side of old bacon, rheumy old eyes, the stump pipe, mice running in and out under her foul old dress, her nether parts scaled and withered. Which old woman told him there wasn't much sense to it—but go on—go on and take the job at the drugstore— go on and try to get good done. Speaking, I imagined, while gumming salted batwings and sipping moondark from a Mason jar. And trust a white man now and then.

"You got *young* women, huh?" thinking to tell him about Pauline, thinking it must be a *very* young woman he's talking about, a child, a kinky pickaninny. *He molests children?* No no no no no

"I don' love up no wildcats." And he's not married because of dangers attached to his work.

"You didn't actually come looking for me?"

"We thought you run. Me an' the Sheriff."

"Shit! You never even come to the house."

"Never thought you'd be *there*."

"Because of my wife?"

"Yup." Gossip! All they do is gossip. Get them proper responsibilities and they might give up gossip.

"I see ..."

"Obviously," pronouncing every syllable. "Obviously, all us men are . . . fools. Fools!" says Slater Jackson, driving, but slowing.

It's down to a real small rain and both of us are bewildered by the time I find out where we're going. Where we're going? Just as we headed off into the ruts of the church's drive, just as we sillion up more of the grounds in front of the burned church. A sight to behold. It was a whole bunch of weary-looking colored people.

It's a wide clearing fronting an old stand and St. John's Creek, a clearing that had had Negro churches on it for better than a hundred years. Years ago I'd sometimes go by there on Wednesdays, Saturdays, and Sundays and see them there in their fancy clothes. Sometimes we'd hear the Holy Spirit working itself loose inside the building—great preaching and singing—and sometimes in the sunshine and long afternoon heat they'd be moving around the cars and sitting in chairs out on the grounds, lots of laughing and jacking around, because there was new whiskey, I was told. The churches wore out once or twice, or burned from bad wires, or lightning, in the old days—but recently they had burned down twice from the Raiders, no doubt about it. Once rebuilt by a group of young Christians from the North, none of whom I ever knew, it was burned again.

"Rosey was the actin' preacher. They blew his truck up. They threw a stick at him I'd guess, an' got him. Then burned it down again." A wrecked truck (a truck with a wrecked cab) was sitting about fifteen yards ahead of us in the mud and weeds.

"Sure did. Sure did." We're sitting in his truck and the rain was almost done. Looking out the window, I started to cry a little. I knew a dozen of those people by sight—D.R., my stacker buddy at the Mill—an ole ex-Parchman boy named Ray, who worked the green chain. But to make much of my emotions would be wrong, because the emotions weren't in the best objective sense political, or social, or even what you'd call humane. No way. They had coats and raincoats on and lots of curious headgear and they were preparing to leave their little service for Rosey and Ju, and for their church. It was a cold sensation all down my chest, under the windbreaker. A cool-type pity for everything. Hell, I even felt a cold pity for that pile of blackened timbers, like they'd been the palpable limbs of some obscure creature. All soiled by rain.

"They've had the service an' I should of been here," said Slater. "The funerals are tomorrow but they done had a special meetin' out here."

"All this shit just keeps on going on. Goes on, has been . . ."

Toots on his empty rum pint, then: "Ob-vi-ous-ly . . ."

It's mostly the old people still milling, and some white Civil-Rights-types, who I couldn't concentrate on. "I got a few words to say to this congregation," I said.

He looked at me peacefully, then got out his side. "Do it."

I got out and clumped over into the wretched boards of the little church. I stood there feeling absolutely foolish, and I tried to pray that the spirit of the Lord or Žižka or somebody would move me. I managed to climb up on the communion table that was still there in the midst of the collapsed building, and God damn my eyes if I didn't think my routine was the corniest ever. I was worse than Billy G . Was sorry I'd climbed.

Then I saw that nobody seemed to think I was all that curious, teetering up there. They weren't even going to gather around until Slater said to: "Listen to this boy. Go on an' listen. He's all drunk an' messed up, but listen." So the remainder of them did come over. It was pretty dark even with some truck lights on, which helped my embarrassment, which finally gave me a little energy to talk with in a confused but sincere way to these fine people. Yessir, I made a little speech before I left. I told them that a Council without a Balance is *Not* a Commonwealth, but an Oligarchy. I said the Gods of Justice were with Them and Loved Them. I cried Havoc and the Blood of Christ—I asked Forgiveness for my Race—and all the time I was reaching for them I was also reaching for April— Filthy blind Sodomites call Angels men, they seeing no farther than the formes of men. There are angels (now) come downe from Heaven, in the shapes and formes of men, who are full of the vengeance of the Lord—and are to poure out the plagues of God upon the Earth, and to torment the Inhabitants thereof. Some of these angels I have been acquainted withall.

Stood, tottered, raising arms, brandishing, with a bitter chill that kept rushing allover portions of my body underneath my clothes.

"That must be embarrassing to remember," says Mary.
"It is. It is." I agree. Mary is a wise woman. I will believe she is wise.

And when I was done I walked among them, speaking of the good future we'd all share, embracing some soaked old women I thought might be the widows of Jubal and Rosey—then I went off at a distance to speak of the little raid I'd recently realized in my mind. And I keep trying to get clear about what I actually said to them, because I know I meant to suggest no more than scaring hell out of Magee and his crowd. Clearly, I was a man thinking I was on the super-rational autopilot (ole Iron George) while all the time I was handflying. When I was slipping the first cartridge into the chamber I was wishing I was down at the Karen, juking with Polly. Scared to death I'd hurt Davis, but then ole Foots he come.

Mary—Royal—it wasn't a revolution at all, in any objective sense. It was just another killing, a killing like so many others, and probably a worthless killing, because I do wish ole Foots was still alive, with all the others. Probably I should call it a personal revolution, a turning around inside of me. I could call it that, except it didn't happen exactly that way. I should have known something on that night, or the next day, but I didn't, exactly. I knew they were all running through me, or maybe I was running through them (just another case of being the blundering oaf I am)—I knew that much, but the big picture never got printed up inside my mind. I've never had a proper course in psychology, economics, and sociology, so all I had was smells of Negro women in black rubber raincoats, and curious looks put on me from these people, confident looks of fear —casual looks of rage from my fellow conspirators—men I never got to know.

But I'm not embarrassed to tell it now. I've been slowly growing out of shame these months with Mary. I don't even care if they filmed the whole thing, hidden cameras and sound devices everywhere, color and stereo. I hardly care now. Let the devils run it all in slow motion backwards and forwards forever. I'll hardly care.

Straight out, Mary.

After the embarrassing talk I offered to the grieving black people, I climbed down and went over to Slater, who's still next to his truck. I said I was sorry. He said that was true enough but O.K. I said let's go into town and shoot it out at the courthouse, where they're having that foolish meeting.

"It's not foolish," he said, scowling, contradicting himself, his eyes glistening.

O.K., but all I want to do is drive in, shoot out the lights and some dark windows, raise a little hell, and then get out. I'll prepare a note and leave it on the steps—something about how the black community will never again tolerate in Bryan County the wanton murder of black peoples. Dig?

People are leaving the churchyard. They've been tolerant but have had about enough for one day, including too much rain.

Slater looks at me high and casually, rubs a long finger under his Indian nose.

His expression against me was calm and ecstatic, with what seemed to be something of a resolution expressed by his clenched pointy teeth. "We are *Fools.*" Says that and walks away from me to a small group of men still standing over near the wreckage of Rosey's truck (I conjecture that they might be checking for small parts of human flesh). Three black men middle-aged maybe (who turn out to be from St. Louis, co-workers with Slater—because he's not about to get his locals in on this madness) and one male white Civil-Rights-type, name of Rawlston it turns out. And it was a lively conversation I was at first excluded from. Groans, laughs, smearings of hands across faces. Lots of Uhs. Finally, they call me over for brief introductions. They'll do it. But it's clear they don't consider it exactly the Concord Green, and they don't even look at me friendly. They comment on my size is about all. They'll go get some guns. And off they went.

Slater and I stood there on the deserted grounds in the dark and hardly said another word until the lights of the other truck showed up again out on the road. I pulled our lights on and wrote the note on the cardboard of a six-pack I found in the bed of the truck. It was plenty damp but I wrote on it with a lipstick he gave me from his glove compartment: *NO MORE KILLING OR BURNING IN BRYAN AND WE MEAN IT.*

"How's that, ole buddy?"

"That's just O.K."

Up on the road again we stopped so he could get our guns from the men who'd follow us into town.

"Tell them to shoot for about half a minute. Tell them to shoot at dark windows and street lamps and the lights on the courthouse —after I've left the note at the door." I said that sort of thing just before he went for our guns, which turned out to be a .22 for him and a .25-.20 for me. "Then get the hell out."

Slater: "The Sheriff is gonna be pissed if this goes bad. He's doing what he can." Looking high but dour.

It was a dead-assed Saturday night if there ever was one, the Sheriff having shut down the movie for the nonce. (*The Egyptian* had been scheduled, a rerun)—it was a still wet nighttime we drove into under the lights of our town.

"Will they get out of their truck?"

"Probly."

"You shoot from behind the front tires. Me from the back."

And all that happened was brief. Brief and cruel. The old Federal-ugly was sleek from the lights in the yard (three round mothers to a stand, like at a pawnbroker's), when I snuck up the walk and stuck the cardboard between the big front door and its loose jamb. Then I tiptoed back. Nobody to see at all except our fellows. Nobody. Though the lights on the second story were on, where the Sheriff and everybody were. I could hear their raucous voices. I stepped to the back of the truck and dropped my arm as a signal for our fellows to commence firing—just before I dropped myself down by the wheel to shoot at the lights over the front door. Blam blam and the little crackings of the .22's as it started getting darker. My own fine carbine .25-.20 shuddering, jumping forward in my grip, as the lights around the tall door exploded and extinguished. Jam the lever down then squeeze it off as comfortably as you please. Except for the lights of the second story, where surely the meeting was getting agitated, and where we didn't shoot, it got dark quickly, including the street lights up and down Wilson and an ad in Nancy's front window.

Slater was standing and pumping .22's with remarkable accuracy, impassively. "Do it, Slate," I yell, just about the time we get fired back at.

Whooeee—it did break down quickly. Foots, from the darkened front door in what was a yellow-looking jump suit by mostly moonlight (like cool service station attendants had started affecting), did appear—and he looked like the mythical El Dorado, a character who's sprinkled in gold dust—he's pumping, also, shotgun fire at us—rather, he's shooting at will indiscriminately. He's a proud fat sight on the porch, but when he loads again from his wide pockets (and it seems all us revolters paused to watch him reload) slipping them rapidly in, and then starts down the steps toward our truck, it got to be an altogether different type of event. The first blast he pumped off from his hip tore through Slater's window— and that's when the group I came with united together and shot and killed Raymond Magee. Punched holes in his golden ruined uniform. I myself, I think, released a round he swallowed (his head turned slightly, his jowls a-waggle)—which round tore his remaining back teeth out and ruined the side of his sanguine face, motherfucker. Bad times. Sweet Christ! Please save my Soul! I'm sorry we killed that wretched man. He hauled himself almost in slowmotion up to an erect posture, seemed almost to dance a little on the toes of his brogans in the awkward dim lights from the second story window—he'd been ruptured more than once, including, I think, one by Slater that burst his buckle and eased those pants that were riding in his asshole. He swaggered toward us down the walk, one hand over his mouth, one over his bleeding bellybutton, then collapsed on the cement and started crawling toward me. He lifted his horrible neck and face like a turtle crushed in rubble, a blind mouth, a bleeding mouth, his pig eyes popped wide: "A grill cheese. Gimme a grill cheese," is what he guttered, just before he died.

Slater was down beside me and said there wasn't anything to do. I said GO—take your people and run—leave this place. Which he did without further hesitation, drove the hell away. He and his semi-anonymous buddies drove off in a hurry, leaving me to pick up dead Foots and start carrying him toward the door, where Davis in a rage it seemed at first was standing scouring his mustaches with a forearm.

ME AND THIS POOR DEAD SOMITCH ARE AT YOUR SERVICE, LAWMAN—EUGENE JOINER AND RAYMOND MAGEE ARE HERE AT THE SERVICE OF THE SOVEREIGN STATE OF MISS-SIPPAH. I lifted him up to my face and kissed his head. I carried that worthless large man in my arms toward the Sheriff. I kissed the sour hair of an ex-All-Pro center. Then I dropped him at the feet of my friend, the Sheriff. Crying. Which was not embarrassing. That was not at all embarrassing. Looking through my tears, I was, however, amazed to see a calm look come over the face of Davis.

Before he did anything else, before he moved the body or talked to the gathered people, he led me to a jail cell in the back of the building and up a flight. He told me to wait at the door. He got Lysol and scrubbed it down with a mop and a brush and a rag. With his own hands. Then: "Five hundred dollars is what you're worth for bail," said Davis, leaving his janitorial articles.

Came to me on a sudden that I was in a jail cell, about morning this came to me, not knowing whether I'd slept or not, but at least the sun was coming in from outside. The next thing I'm sure about is Davis once again in front of me on the other side of the bars— he's speaking in an agitated fashion and waving a check at me.

"April give me the money. Got it right here. Follow me," says Davis, who needs sleep in the worst way.

"Yessir."

"Come on."

"Open the gate."

Downstairs there is a little ceremony, a preliminary hearing, only roughly recollected—though it was sometime Sunday morning. The gathering includes the Sheriff, of course, and curly Dexter (in his role of J.P.) and April (whose face is rigid) and Henry (who has the grin) and Royal Carle Boykin (who was called down from Jackson by Stream) and Stream himself, all in the Sheriff's austere office.

Davis is saying he doesn't think there is probable cause to bind Joiner over to the Grand Jury. Davis tells Dexter that binding or not binding is in his (Dexter's) discretion.

Dexter says he'll have to hear testimony before he can find no probable cause.

But, says the serious and increasingly contented Sheriff, even if Dexter finds no probable cause, the defendant, whoever he may be, is *not* beyond the *reach* of the law. Clearly, the District Attorney (who lives in Mendenhall and has gone along with Davis), at any time hereafter, or any citizen, or anyone else for that matter, may bring this thing up before the Grand Jury and successfully try for an indictment. *And*, says the Sheriff, going on cheerfully, in his own offices, on Sunday, which ain't exactly a good day for legal work (with my wife and friends standing around), if they do get an indictment, then the person arrested will be bound over for trial before the Circuit Court and sent to Parchman. If he ever comes around this county again.

Dexter tells me I am charged with manslaughter. He jabs a semi-liberal finger at me and asks, "Do you plead guilty?"

"Er . . . Hell no. I plead *not* guilty." I could tell I was supposed to say that.

"Riiiiight . . . Get on with it," says Davis to Dexter.

Dexter swears the Sheriff in and the Sheriff swears he isn't sure that Joiner's shots caused Magee to die. He's only sure that Magee shot at somebody and somebody must have shot back in self-defense most likely, whomever.

Dexter with great dignity, after only a short concentration, for a liberal druggist, says, "I find no reason to bind this man over to the Grand Jury."

And that was that, slick as a whistle, except for some brief goodbyes.

Man, I'd been exiled and didn't want any more of those people, unless it was for us to all start hugging and kissing, wiping away and wringing out this error, death and misery. Son goes joyously back to the Mill as top stacker. Royal is celebrated for remarkable efforts in the cause of Negro legal rights. Stream grows satisfied with being an effete bookseller. Henry to scented Maria. While Davis is elected Lawman of the Year. No way.

Royal hasn't said a thing through all this legal hash—he's obviously moot out of confusion and something bordering on brotherly sorrow (with no dream that the sleek woman at his side is *his*, Jesus, because she *was* his)—he's strapped in his suit and smelling grief in the bleak air, but what he states, at last lets out of his mouth, is stupid, small, the image of his meager soul: "This is for the best, Son." Piously. "We've spent the whole night working it out, with people."

I told the little nutria I knew he'd done his very best. Thankee, Royal.

April was stock-still and never said a word. She stood there like a dead body that has been frozen for melting at a better, later date.

"Goodbye, girl." That's what I said.

And then Henry hustles over and tugs my arm, smiling like his portrait has just been selected for the National Gallery in Washington, D.C. "You crazy, Son. But you the best crazy I ever saw. Sneak back to see me."

"Thanks, Henry ... and, Stream, I'm gonna get yours ..."

. . .

As Davis drove me out of town I felt caught, tired, resigned, and freed. Mostly tired. God damn I was tired.

But Davis was, shall we say, soulfully chipper, saying there's enough money in my account to pay for everything I've broken, and: "This thing has turned out fine. Just fine. Considering. Foots *is* gone." He casts a cool eye on some colored children rolling a slick tire along the highway on the other side. "God rest him . . . and everybody else is covered. You and ole Slater are *covered*— covered and covered and covered, by God. Slater can go on with his good work. With me. And this place will have some peace for a while." He's really enjoying himself. He feels his work is reasonable. "We won't even tell it was you that ruined the phone booth. Hell, the telephone people should of been out to fix it by now."

I told him he was a good sheriff and a good friend. I even hugged his neck before we parted on that road. And he hugged back, before I went to New Orleans, then west to Houston, then north to Fort Worth. He liked me then, and I'm satisfied he'll even like me better when I show up in town again, in a week or so, with my new woman.

A Note on the Type

This book was set on the Linotype in Janson, a recutting made direct from type cast from matrices long thought to have been made by the Dutchman Anton Janson, who was a practicing type founder in Leipzig during the years 1668–87. However, it has been conclusively demonstrated that these types are actually the work of Nicholas Kis (1650–1702), a Hungarian, who most probably learned his trade from the master Dutch type founder Dirk Voskens. The type is an excellent example of the influential and sturdy Dutch types that prevailed in England up to the time William Caslon developed his own incomparable designs from them.

The book was composed, printed, and bound by The Book Press, Brattleboro, Vermont. Typography and binding design by Constance Doyle.